HAMMERSTONE 1149 A.D.

Til Death Us Do Part

(the 3rd book in the Hammerstone Series)

Mark Anthony Parks

Cover: Bill Slavin
Set Up: Marlo Hemming

Order this book online at www.trafford.com
or email orders@trafford.com

Most Trafford titles are also available at major online book retailers.

Print information available on the last page.

ISBN: 978-1-6987-0254-4 (sc)
ISBN: 978-1-6987-0252-0 (hc)
ISBN: 978-1-6987-0253-7 (e)

Library of Congress Control Number: 2020913500

Trafford rev. 07/29/2020

Trafford
PUBLISHING® **www.trafford.com**
North America & international
toll-free: 1 888 232 4444 (USA & Canada)
fax: 812 355 4082

ACKNOWLEDGEMENTS:

Hammerstone 1149 – you have all been very patient since Hammerstone 1148 - To Have and To Hold was published, not far behind Hammerstone 1147 – The Birthright. You know what they say about life's best-laid plans....well, 20 years slipped by and life had some plans for us that made finalizing 1149 (spoiler: and soon to be published 1150 A.D.) take a back-seat. I appreciate your forgiveness (and enthusiasm) while you waited.

My cover set up specialist, Marlo, is still pulling it all together to present to you. My very good friend, Bill Slavin, has shared his talents and expertise with this cover (please see more about Bill Slavin next below). And my wife, Patty, is right beside me these 36 years, still cheering and supporting my dreams and ambitions. Our children have both graduated post-secondary and both gotten engaged this past spring. We have much to look forward to and can't wait to see what the future holds for all of us.

Mark Anthony Parks
Cavan, Ontario
July 2020

Cover Art Work for "Until Death Do Us Part" is by illustrator **Bill Slavin**. Bill has illustrated over 100 books for children including the award winning Stanley series, Transformed, and the _Elephants Never Forget_ graphic novel series (which he also authored). He is currently working on a graphic novel trilogy for an older audience. You can see more of his work at www. billslavin.

Until Death Do Us Part

Dedicated to:

My mother,
Lorraine Parks-Ymker

#1

Maken wept. She wept for Robert, for herself, for the baby growing in her womb. Long hard bitter tears, the kind that knots the stomach into a tight ball of pain and leaves eyes red with despair.

An hour ago, Neil Cleeves had returned from the abbey and the news that he brought was incredible. If not for the ready confirmation of all that rode with the new captain, she would have not believed his tale.

Cleeves had led his men to the monastery, riding hard all the way. The Mother Superior herself had shown Neil to the cell where, to the astonishment of all, they found Sir Robert's cot empty and the room deserted.

In the heavy silence that followed Maken tried to gather her wits about her. She noticed that Cam Fontennell, the Earl's favourite, was not present.

"Why is Fontennell not here?" she demanded.

"I left him behind on the chance that his lordship is found." A hint of condescension crept into his voice, "and besides we were in need of a horse."

"Why? What of Robert's charger?"

"Far be it from me to lend out his lordship's best horse without his express command."

Maken tapped her fingers impatiently against the arm of her chair.

"And pray tell us Neil, who then needed a horse?" she hissed.

"Upon hearing of her brother's unfortunate wounding, the Lady Katoryna had renounced her intention of taking her vows and has returned, in her word m'lady, to help her mother run the castle."

A collective gasp rolled through the solar. Evidently Katoryna's Norman pride had not suffered during her months in seclusion.

Maken paled and, fighting back tears, wrapped an arm protectively around the curve of her belly. Wearied, she ordered the solar emptied and only when the last servant had left did she allow her thin veneer of control to shatter and, alone, she wallowed in misery.

When she was spent, and her tears had dried and her belly ached from her heaving sobs, she squared her shoulders. Burying her youth, she steeled herself for the long days ahead. She promised herself that her child, yet unborn, would live to rule Hammerstone. Harder now, older, she was a mother scared for her child.

Maken called for the serving maids to draw her bath and as they laboured to keep the water hot, she lay back and planned how she would save herself and the baby. The water soothed her. How wise was Robert, she thought, to insist on nice hot baths. It helped her think more clearly.

As she dressed, Maken called for the steward and for Fulke, Robert's famous body guard. Taking a chair in the centre of the room, Maken's servant girl combed out her auburn tresses.

For a moment, Barclay was taken aback at the sight of Maken sitting like a queen, a rich robe about her shoulders, the maid carefully working her hair to a rich gloss. Maken wasted little time.

"Cleeves, he knew nothing of the Earl's arrangement?"

"No, nothing."

"We can do nothing to send her back?"

"No," he answered, stealing a glance at the servant girl quietly combing her lady's hair.

Maken saw his gaze and said, "Fear her not, she knows full well, if she repeats but one word of our conversation, I will marry her off to old Marley, the swine-herder and she can spend the next twenty years caring for him, his pigs and his six wee ones."

The girl brushed with renewed vigor.

"Still, we must be very, very careful. As news of Robert's troubles spread, the danger to all of us shall be greatly increased."

Maken stood and waved the girl away. The frightened maid ran to the end of the solar and sat as still as a statue on a low bench along the wall.

As she paced, Maken spoke. If she was to be depossessed of her husband's wealth it would not be without a fight. After all, she was legally wed in the eyes of the church, and the next Earl was growing in her belly.

As for Katoryna, the terror of her lessened. What was she but a husbandless spinster? Her main source of power, Sir Reginald, was long dead and her confederate, Roger, long gone. Soon she too would be gone. God willing.

"Barclay, our first priority, ever and always, is to find Robert and bring him home safe and sound. I was with him last and I know his wounds were not mortal. All of Hammerstone must not doubt this. Especially Sir Robert's liege-men. They must remain loyal!"

Barclay nodded; all of this he agreed with.

She continued, "The harvest must be completed and stored, and the castle repaired. The village must be rebuilt and quickly. I would that we soon find Katoryna a husband. No doubt she will look to usurp my rightful place and deny the son that grows in me. I'll wager ten pounds she beds Neil Cleeves within a week. I shall keep gathered about me all who are loyal. Now we must not waiver but stand firm!"

Barclay looked at Maken in a new light. Like a fox cornered she was all teeth and sharp claws. "I agree fully m'lady," he said.

There was a rap on the solar door and the maid jumped to answer it.

"Fulke awaits your pleasure m'lady," she said looking back at Maken.

"Send him in."

The giant wrestler entered and came to Maken. He bowed. He had taken Robert's disappearance hard. The life had seemed to drain out of him. He knew not what would become of him; Hammerstone was the first real home he had ever known and he would be sad to leave it.

Fulke was not a man given to idle chatter, nor open displays of emotion. None knew him well. He was a listener, not a talker, so Maken could guess not what the huge Belgian was thinking.

"Fulke, thou knows our good master is in peril but for now we cannot help him. Although I believe him to live we must be ever ready to protect his birthright. If by some mischance of fate God has laid claim to him, then the new lord of Hammerstone grows here."

She patted her belly. "I would rest easier if I knew ye were standing firm with us."

"Be ye assured then m'lady. I will guard thee even until my last breath." A hot tear ran down his ruddy cheek. "Never let it be said that Fulke forgets a kindness shown nor a friendship given."

Maken hugged the Belgian, wrapping her small arms about his massive frame. She stepped back and cleared her throat, "Come then you two, let us see how goes the cleansing of Hammerstone."

Coming out of the Keep, Maken could feel the stares of many eyes upon her. Each soldier, servant and serf strained to glimpse the lady's face to see for themselves signs of the great strain Maken must surely be feeling. Would she wilt in the face of headstrong Katoryna?

Around the tower, the bloody and grisly task of removing the dead was underway. Carts pulled by mules were drawn into the inner bailey. Bodies and body parts were dragged clear of the ruined stable and barracks. Slain invaders had been thrown over the outer wall in the heat of battle, into the black waters of the Ouse. Still more, many more, remained to be cleared from the bloody parapet wall.

The Earl of Crewe had been found, his lifeless body torn and battered, with no less than five of his wounds deemed mortal. Maken found this fascination with death to be bizarre. She was at a loss to understand. What did it matter how one died? And yet, the men stood in a great circle about the Earl's carcass, many bending low near the body, that they might count for themselves the gouges and holes. The Earl's body was naked, only his signet ring had been recovered and delivered to Barclay. The rest of his lordship's personal effects were long gone.

Maken felt no remorse at seeing the Earl in such mean estate. He had been the author of his own misfortune. The wounding of Robert rested squarely on his shoulders. Maken spit on the corpse and bid the men to burn it with the rest.

Her father, Myles, and Garfield, the captain of the Earl's archers, met her in the centre of the cobblestone courtyard. Both Saxons were wearing the green of the troop. By the look of their eyes, Maken guessed that the two had not slept since the night before the castle had first been attacked.

Garfield bowed low to Maken and promptly the whole yard followed suit. Even Myles, who had little patience with such Norman pretensions, nodded his hairy head and studied his young daughter, for it was curious to see her in such a foreign light. Not for the first time in her life, Maken surprised her father.

She did not redden nor shy away from the salutations of the throng, but rather, she boldly climbed up upon one of the hay carts that she might better address the people and be more easily seen.

"My friends," she began, "We have won a great victory! But at heavy cost. Many are wounded and some will never be the strong men they were yesterday. We weep for our fallen comrades. We have lost our captain, Ewart. A heavy blow!"

She had their attention and continued, "Even so, fear not, we are unbeaten, we are still secure, the castle is scarred but not weakened. When his lordship returns, **and he shall return**, his great faith in you will be justified and confirmed. Much of the village was burned, but fear not, as soon as the castle is repaired and the harvest fully reaped, we shall build new cottages for each one lost."

At that bit of news tongues began wagging and soon the word would spread over the countryside that the Earl's lady had guaranteed the rebuilding of the village. This was no small thing, for many a rich baron would happily have let his serfs freeze rather than help them rebuild. Only castles were deemed important enough to keep in good repair.

When the chatter had died down Maken made her last point.

"But most important of all," she said, "will be the safe return of Sir Robert. Ye have all heard rumors and lies, whispers in the dark, that our lord is mortally wounded, but I was with him when he sustained his wounds and I can tell thee truly, Sir Robert's wounds are not serious. Only his loss of blood prevented him from coming straight home."

As Garfield helped Maken down from her makeshift podium, Neil Cleeves came striding out of the gate tower. Huge he was, broad shouldered and a head taller than most. His physical presence alone gave him an air of authority. Whether or not Neil would be a leader of men remained to be seen. He was a loner, as apt to go off by himself as join with the other men-at-arms at the Boar's Tooth Inn. Maken eyed her new captain warily. She knew she would have to dominate Cleeves or risk losing the respect of the guard.

She waited until he stood near and then asked sweetly, "How goes the sealing of the secret passage?"

"Well. It goes well. We shall be finished on the morrow... Maken."

"Well done, Cleeves, and you may call me *'m'lady'.*"

She smiled up at the large man and continued on before he had time to retort. "Now Neil, gather about you a half-score of trusty men and return to the Abbey. Bid Fontennell return at once and then have your men search the country thereabouts. Perhaps some clue as to Robert's disappearance will turn up even though you are a day late doing so."

Neil Cleeves nodded, too surprised to speak. The Saxon girl-child had put him in his place easily. He collected ten men and departed.

Garfield followed Maken and Barclay over to the half burned out barrack. The Belgian, Fulke, beside him, never allowed Maken to get more than a half-dozen steps ahead. The archer realized he had underestimated Myles' daughter, but wondered why she had risked Neil Cleeves wrath, sending him away when he could be better used here. He listened as Barclay and Maken surveyed the ruined barracks.

"Well, Barclay, what says you? Is this the worst of the damage?"

"Yes, thanks be to the Holy Mother Mary! And that timely evening rain," added the steward.

"If it were up to me-" Barclay began.

"It is," Maken interrupted.

"Well then, what say we forget about the second floor barracks for now and erect a new roof on the stable. The troops can live in the lower keep, just like in the old days and that way the castle repairs will be done in less than a fortnight."

"'Tis a worthy plan Barclay."

The four walked gingerly around the busy men clearing the courtyard, weaving past the carts loaded with their gruesome cargoes and the debris knocked off the walls during the battle. They paused by the drawbridge to watch workmen lever great round boulders into place below the thick timbers of the drawbridge. Barclay could still hardly believe that such an opening had ever been there. It was obviously an escape route in case the castle was overrun.

Barclay was the least surprised at Maken's firm resolution in the face of Robert's disappearance.

Robert inspired confidence, and no one knew this better than Barclay. A short year ago the steward was a lowly butler and now he oversaw the castle and ran it well. If he could do it, then so could Maken. As for her little speech, it did not overly distress him. She had, after all, acknowledged that the castle's security came first. Looking for the Earl, repairing the walls and roofs of Hammerstone...these things he was anxious to see completed also, and he wanted to hire at least a full score of armed knights for the winter. Robert had never seen the need for more horsemen and this had been a sore spot between the Earl and his steward. Maken had heard the two argue over this more than once.

"I would rest easier if we had another 20 horsemen," said Barclay, avoiding Maken's eye.

"And I also," she replied. Barclay hardly trusted his own ears. He waited a moment and, recovering himself, added, "I shall undertake to find some stout men."

"That would be fine," she said and then walked on.

In the village common they stood and looked about the ruined cottages and the damaged inn. Some people were sifting through the ashes of their homes, looking to recover anything that might have survived the flames. Others were rounding up the livestock that had been scattered the night before. Everyone bent to his or her labours, many in shock, feeling for the first time the direct sting of war. In all the terrible years of the civil war and strife that marked Stephen of Blois' reign, the mighty arm of Sir Reginald de Courtelaine had protected the lands about the Ouse. Not only did his Saxon underlings walk warily in his presence but his Norman peers did likewise. Hammerstone was a rose whose thorns rendered her untouchable.

Maken counted the blackened foundations. Ten. They would have to build ten new cottages and repair the inn. She tried to remember what Robert had said once about re-planning the village, something about the outer gate being too weak, the village too scattered. It hadn't seemed very important at the time.

#2

The afternoon was spent talking with the Lady Camille and Father Hubert, forming a plan of what they should do next. Once again they were in the solar, away from prying eyes and ears. Through the open shutters the odd snap of wind would send the sweet sickly scent of blood into the room.

If Maken hoped her mother-in-law could control the fiery Katoryna, she soon learned otherwise.

"My daughter was ever her father's special pet and he let her behave however she liked. She cares not a wit for my opinion," Camille shrugged. "I am sorry Maken, but I would be deceiving you if I said differently."

"And what canst thou say, good Father? Can we not send Katoryna back whence she came?"

"Nay, Maken, your sister-in-law, for whatever reason, never actually took her vow. The church has no claim to her."

Maken drummed her fingers on the small round table before her. How could this be, she wondered, that Katoryna could live as a nun and yet not become one.

Father Hubert continued, "She was yet in training. The Abbey at St. Hild's is known for its rigorous testing of their adherents before they are allowed to take their vows. She was not able to complete her training until they felt she was truly penitent and pure."

Maken slowly smiled and spoke, "Well, if Katoryna will not join the church, then we shall just have to find someone for her to marry. Some one old and rich and a long way away!" Maken drew quiet and said in a whisper, "But how?"

#3

Once again, Cam Fontennell found himself on horseback, travelling the long winding road along the Ouse River. He was weary, but glad for the empty miles. The past few hours had been terrible, the castle attacked, and Sir Robert wounded.

Ewart, their much loved captain, was dead and, to Cam's utter dismay, Neil Cleeves, his hated enemy, was the new captain. Cam cursed his luck; it was a bitter ale indeed that he had been forced to swallow. If only he had told his lordship of his suspicions. And now what should he do? He dare not mention his fears to anyone least one think him jealous of Cleeves. And what of his own place among the men? He was still an archer, but without Sir Robert to attend to, would he still be welcome to live within Hammerstone's walls? Barclay alone had guessed his infatuation with the lady. Would the steward allow him to be near Maken now? So much had changed.

In a curve in the road where the hill cut close and trees grew thick two men armed with oaken staves and sharp knives watched the young man trot almost under their noses. After the horseman had disappeared around the next corner, the one bandit turned to the other, "Ye are feeling charitable, to let him pass without paying a toll?"

"Aye, lad, that one we'll let go, perhaps he may have a better use one day," said Bung.

Bung's companion and trusted lieutenant nodded, although he could not begin to guess why his leader would suppose the young rider would ever be of use to them. More likely, thought the bandit, it was the hundred pounds that Bung had gained earlier that day, carefully hidden in a stout leather bag. No doubt the weight of all that money had left him feeling rather slothful.

As for the Bandit King, the one hundred pounds never entered his mind. Bung knew of Cam Fontennell, knew of his murdered family and knew of his unusual ability with the longbow. Of great interest to Bung was that Cam, a poor orphan, became overnight the Earl's favourite. A butler in a fine suit. The Earl had disappeared and now, wondered Bung, what would become of the favourite? And if Cam fell from grace who could profit from such a thing?

A fine white lather covered his mount by the time Cam rode across the heavy planks of the drawbridge of Hammerstone Castle. He dismounted and gazed about in wonder. Already the inner courtyard was bare of rubble and the stable was shorn of its second story. Teams of men swarmed over the now roofless building laying newly cut wooden beams across the expanse between the walls.

Inside the keep the Great Hall was abuzz with servants setting up the long trestle tables and lighting lamps. In the kitchen the great cook-fires roared and snapped. Huge iron pots boiled and steamed with thick broths of vegetables and beef. At another two boys, bare to the waist, stood at either ends of a long spit, turning a large boar. Loaf after loaf of round bread lay on wooden serving trays, still hot from the oven.

Cam smiled at a couple of serving girls as he made his way through the crowded kitchen. Among the younger maids he was a marked man, with several of the girls vowing to take him to the altar, not only for his comely looks but his growing fame as an archer.

The sweet aroma of roast pork and fresh bread engulfed Cam, knotting his empty belly in sudden hunger. Yet he pressed on, ignoring his need for victuals. At the top of the stairs in the hall leading to the solar, he met Katoryna. He has not seen her before but knew at once that this must be the Earl's infamous sister. Her proud Norman bearing declared her station.

Cam bowed, saying nothing. Katoryna pursed her thin lips and cast an appraising eye over the young man before her. Cam thought the lady looked terribly thin - she likely left the church for want of a good meal.

Katoryna's glance wandered over Cam the way she might look over a horse to purchase.

"Well, well, what have we here?" she said fingering his collar, "And what manner of livery is this? Surely not the hire of the house of de Courtelaine?"

"I am one of the Earl's archers, m'lady!"

Katoryna slowly walked around Cam, even lifting the hem of his jerkin to admire his hose.

"And what, pray tell, are *The Earl's Archers*?" — some brigade of boys pretending to be soldiers?" she laughed.

"Nay m'lady!" answered Cam, the color rising in his cheeks. "We archers are in the employ of Sir Robert to protect all that is his."

"Come now, such tales ye youngsters tell," she teased, mocking him.

He fought to keep his temper. "I can tell thee, m'lady and any soul within these walls will equally attest that we archers have twice been called to take up the bow in defense of the Earl's interest and twice we have carried the day!"

"And what of you, youngster, dids't thou earn thy wage?"

"Aye m'lady and then some!" he said, angered at her tone.

"Temper, temper, I like that in a man," she said, taking her leave.

Halfway down the stairs she turned to see where he was headed. The solar.

The look of him awakened in her old familiar urges, ones that she had not felt for a long time. Too long a time. Of course she knew all about the archery troop, the two attacks on Hammerstone, about Barclay and Garfield, and Cam Fontennell. As soon as Katoryna had arrived home, she called for her favourite maid and disappeared to relax, eat and hear all the gossip.

To Cam Fontennell, Maken had changed before his very eyes. Older, sadder and stern. The bubbly girl was gone. She had donned a tight-fitting hat in the proper Norman fashion, her flowing locks hidden away. A crease seemed to have etched itself into her forehead and, when she looked upon the archer, it appeared to him that her eyes had lost their sparkle. Still, she smiled at the sight of him and bid him sit by her for a while.

Cam bowed and joined Barclay at Maken's table. Father Hubert stood a few feet away lest the servants find it unseemly that their priest should sit too near a lady in her bedroom.

Maken nodded to a serving girl stationed against the far wall and instantly the girl hurried to the table with a platter bearing a goblet and a flask of beer.

"Drink Fontennell, drink for ye must be dry after your quick return," said Maken. Cam drained the goblet gratefully and when he was done Maken spoke again.

"Now Cam, tell us – and I pray ye omit nothing - tell us everything ye can of Sir Robert's disappearance."

Cam spoke, "After the rest had gone and I was alone, I went straightaway to the Mother Superior and begged her to give me leave to re-examine his lordship's cell. This she allowed. Now as it happened, Sir Robert's cell was at the very end of a long hall and quite secluded. Next I paced the hall up and down and found two bloodstains. Nay, fear not m'lady they were but small spots and one was very near a door leading to the inner courtyard. Then I walked outside the abbey around the walls and sure enough there was a great sweeping elm that rested its mighty limbs across the abbey wall. I climbed the elm and found rope burns on one of these limbs. From these signs, I guess that Sir Robert left the abbey by this route. Later, after I had searched the surrounding countryside, I returned to the abbey and spoke to a certain Sister Hildegard who had ministered to our master's wounds. On the Holy Word she vowed that his wounds were not mortal and if not for his loss of blood he would surely have been able to ride within a fortnight. Of this she was sure."

"Thank you Cam, ye have lessened my fears somewhat although we still are no closer to finding out what has befallen my husband," said Maken.

"Kidnapped m'lady, maybe by some Scots. Of that I have no doubt," said Father Hubert.

Maken turned to the priest, "How do you think so Father?"

"Of course, there is no other way."

"If it is so," said Barclay, "then it follows that we should soon be seeing a demand of ransom."

"Do we just wait then?" asked Maken of Father Hubert. He seemed to know of intrigues of this nature. He was Norman born and had often witnessed treachery of this specie.

The priest shrugged, "Well certainly we must wait but we should continue our search for the Earl. A reward for news of Sir Robert might be helpful, especially if the reward were a generous one."

The idea was met with unanimous acceptance and Maken left it to Barclay to set the amount.

Father Hubert rose saying that the day grew late and he had to commit the dead to the ground. Before he reached the door Maken stopped him, holding his arm and in a small voice asked, "Why do such a thing?"

He thought for a moment, "Money perhaps – I can only guess."

He gently pulled from her, "I must be away Maken."

Maken called for her robe and in answer to Father Hubert's questioning glance she said, "I, too, should come."

When their footsteps had died away Barclay sat down heavily and poured himself a good measure of ale. Cam watched the steward sip his drink. They had not spoken since the younger man had told Barclay his fears regarding Neil Cleeves.

It was well that Cam Fontennell had the wit to hold his tongue for right now the castle needed Neil Cleeves and right or wrong he was the only man among the Earl's household that could hold the men together and lead them. Whether or not he in turn could be reliable was another thing. Barclay would have to worry about that another day for now he had other more pressing matters. It was time to put Fontennell to the test. Many things now Barclay would have to do and he would need someone trustworthy and intelligent to help. And someone with courage. Fontennell fit the bill, but he was young, maybe too young.

Barclay drained his cup and spoke, "What do ye think of the priest's guess?"

Cam scoffed, "About the Scots? Nay it was not them. How would they know Sir Robert lay within the walls of the abbey?"

"What of Giles and his friends?"

Cam shook his head, "Nay, they fully intended to take the castle and met Sir Robert only by chance. No doubt they planned to take Hammerstone and with their prize secure they could return at their leisure to deal with the Earl."

Barclay nodded his head in agreement.

Cam continued, "Now we cannot know who spirited his lordship away but I would wager the one called the Forest Ghost is not as far to the south as we all thought. The boldness of the act and the quiet way it was accomplished, were hallmarks of the Bandit King. And doeth ye not recall how last winter when Sir Robert hunted this same bandit, it seemed the hunted always knew our whereabouts. Only the Forest Ghost would have known so quickly of Sir Robert's wounding and his stay at St. Hild's."

"I fear ye are right." Barclay paused for a moment and said in a low voice, "I also fear ye are right about Neil Cleeves."

"Well then, why didn't thou speak of it?"

"Silence, Fontennell! Silence!" Barclay hissed. "Danger is everywhere, especially for the lady. Danger she cannot imagine! Just as I feel ye were right about Cleeves so am I right about you. You admire the lady Maken, 'tis as plain as day."

Before Fontennell could protest Barclay silenced him, "Now take no fear, nor offence, at my words. I speak only out of need. Again I say to you, danger is all around us! Will ye stay and help Maken or are ye of a mind to go?"

Cam Fontennell stared at the steward, "Go? Go where? I have taken an oath to the Earl and the Earl's heirs. I shall not go!"

Barclay leaned close to the young archer, "Listen then of how ye can best protect Maken. The Earl's liegemen, knights all, shall sup here tonight. They will be of a mind to test Maken. We must show a united front and support her. For that we need Neil Cleeves. For a time at least."

"Secondly the Lady Katoryna is against Maken and would dearly love to see her cast out. And for that, she will try to recruit allies among the men. I would like you to try to win her favour. Learn of her plans and keep me informed, for I fear that she will try to fetch home her brother, Roger, and together they could likely force us out. Do ye understand?"

"Aye, but what makes ye think she will take an interest in me?"

"Because my young friend, I know her well. Art thou a virgin?"

"A what?"

"Have ye been with a woman?"

Cam grew red in the face, "I don't know what that would matter!" he said, embarrassed to be speaking of such things.

"Ah, well, Katoryna likes virgins. I do not know why, but no matter."

"Why, what manner of lady is she? Did she not just spend the last few months in an abbey?"

Barclay chuckled, "Aye, that she did and it must have nearly put her out of her mind." He smiled, "Look, lad, don't worry. Just befriend her and become her confidant and if possible learn how she plans to find her brother, Roger. Let the rest take care of itself. You never know, you might even enjoy yourself."

#4

Fulke sat in his usual corner in the huge kitchen. He was a popular guest among the servants and whenever he had a free hour he could be found on his stool near the bake oven across from the cellarer's door. From his perch, Fulke would keep the kitchen maids spell-bound with tales of far off places and in stitches with many a jest. His stool was at such an angle as to easily watch the staircase leading to the Earl's quarters so that if his master should decide to go forth, Fulke would be ready.

It was a different woman that descended the stairs with Father Hubert. Her free-flowing locks were modestly hidden under her tight fitting cap. She walked slowly, neither stopping to gossip nor looking left or right. The kitchen sensed her mood and all fell silent until she had passed.

Fulke followed the two out of Hammerstone Castle and into the remains of the village. Along the creek that marked the west side of the village the mourning crowd waited patiently for their priest. At the sight of him a row of women stood apart and began a low murmur of mourning. Father Hubert stood quietly, letting the keening be fully heard.

As the women chanted, Maken looked upon the neat row of the fallen, each wrapped in a shroud of white, hidden save for their faces. Maken wept, seeing the faces of men dear to her. Deep within her the baby moved, or so she thought. She paled and wavered and an arm slipped around her giving her strength. Looking up she saw it was the Lady Camille, who had come to honor the dead.

The grieving women stopped, and all were silent. Father Hubert began: 'Dominus Vobiscum ...'

The Lady Camille studied the villagers as they intoned their responses to the priest's words. She had never been to a Saxon burial, as her late husband had forbidden it. She had followed the priest and Maken, curious and anxious to be of any help. Camille born in Genoa to a family of shop keeping merchants, had none of the Norman prejudices that so coloured the age.

Father Hubert knelt by the first body. The deceased's family slipped forward. The grieving widow produced a penny to give the priest. This was the soul-scot, the benefit paid to the church on behalf of the dead man's soul.

Before the money could change hands the Lady Camille whispered to the priest, "Thy scot is paid by the castle, good Father." And she slipped a shiny coin into his hand. This she repeated along the row of weeping families one and all.

Now there were some with a mind to refuse the lady's overture, to scoff at her Norman name. Perhaps, the yoke of Norman rule they had found too hard a burden to ever forgive. Others felt the need to lash out at someone, anyone, in their agony and grief.

But these folk, whoever they were, when they came face to face with Camille and saw the tears of sorrow on her cheek and perceived that she too, though rich and mighty, wore the same heavy mantel of pain as they, were moved to accept her offering.

Maken stayed among her friends even after the dead were carried to their gravesite and buried.

Time and time again, throughout bitter hardships and unrest, the local Saxon population turned to Myles for guidance and strength. Through years of harsh Norman rule and bare cupboards, it was the woodcutter who found food, who poached the Earl's deer and lay nightlines in the Ouse for forbidden trout, so the wee ones might have meat in winter. Even now with abundant food and the Earl's dungeon empty, the villagers still gathered at Myles' doorstep. As luck would have it Myles' cottage lay north of the village and as such did not receive any damage. His loft was soon full of homeless neighbours.

The two mistresses of the castle accompanied the priest to Myles' already crowded home and two chairs were quickly surrendered for the ladies. For many it was their first good look at Sir Reginald's widow for while her husband lived she was a prisoner of Hammerstone, its grey walls the extent of her world, and still she rarely walked among the village folk.

Camille noticed Edwina, Garfield's wife sitting close to Maken's mother, her wounded leg hid under her wool dress. Camille made her way to Edwina and asked of her pains. As the two spoke a cluster of wives kept eyes toward them, their curiosity regarding the seldom seen widow, heightened by her presence. Her soft voice had never been heard and odd it sounded, seeming to be neither Saxon nor Norman.

Garfield, who stood leaning against the fireplace mantel asked, "M'lady, thy voice has a curious ring to the ear. Ye hardly sound Norman at all."

Lady Camille laughed, the absurdity of her life coming, it seemed, full circle. How many times through the long years of her marriage had her husband belittled her for her odd accent and Mediterranean blood?

"Mé salliance!" *(a bad match)* implying he had married below his station, he would scream in French at her whenever he felt she was not worthy. All those years she was not Norman enough and now through Garfield's question, realized that the local Saxon population had no idea about her life.

"But Garfield," she explained, "I am not Norman." She looked around at the curious faces staring at her. "Where do you think I come from?" she asked Edwina.

Edwina was taken aback, she really wasn't sure of where Camille hailed from, only that the Earl had found her someplace south. She shrugged her shoulders and another of her neighbours fairly burst with the answer, "In foreign parts m'lady, away south in London-town!"

Garfield gave the women a look of pity, "Hilda, love, London Town is not foreign — it is in England, just as we are." Hilda was saved from her embarrassment by Camille who volunteered that London Town might as well be foreign, so different it was. Garfield's curiosity was up and he pressed Camille to tell where she came from.

"I was born and raised in a City called Genoa which is a port on a beautiful warm sea. It never gets very cold, even in winter it never snows. The houses are whitewashed so that on a sunny day ye can hardly stand to look upon them, they shine so in the sunlight. The streets are all paved so that ye never need to get muddy." And Camille, speaking aloud of her homeland, suddenly felt a deep raw surge of emotion, and she was homesick for the smell of the sea and her mother's sweet smile and her happy childhood. She could speak no more.

Maken had slipped outside for as much as she took joy in sitting among old friends and hearing the local gossip, she had greater things to consider and many hard decisions ahead. Trading stories would not make them any easier to make. Now she could better understand Robert's love of a good long ride. It was the quiet.

Myles followed his daughter out of the cottage and down along the creek. When she sat on a log and starred at the gently flowing water, he joined her, his knees creaking as he sat. He said nothing but his presence, the very nearness of him, calmed her.

"Father Hubert is certain that Robert has been kidnapped and that we shall hear soon from his captors," she said, not taking her eyes off the sparkling water.

"Aye, lass, 'tis a common sport among the Norman folk."

"He lives, father, of that I am sure."

"Of course."

She stared moodily ahead, "Surely father, they would not dare to kill him?"

"I know not of these things, Maken." It was ever his experience that a Norman would kill nearly anything, but he did not mention this opinion to his daughter.

Life roared on so fast. Where had the little girl gone that once cheered his heart and home? Was she to be a widow before she was a mother? Things for a time had seemed so hopeful and fine. Even he, Myles, the most pessimistic of men, had taken a brighter view. And now this. How long would her Norman neighbours leave her be? Would the wee one in her belly ever grow to be a man? His hard life had made Myles a realist and he knew better than to waste time with 'what if's' and 'maybes'. It was better to take it day by day, one coil at a time.

And this he told to Maken, urging her to not lose hope but rather fight hard for her sake and the sake of the child growing within her. He knew that she would need the will to fight.

Maken knew it too, but she knew it was only half the battle. She was desperate to keep their enemies at bay, make the right decisions, to do what Robert would have done so that when on that happy day he would be restored to her, he would be contented with her. Wearily she stood.

"Shall ye come and sup with me tonight, father?"
"Aye."

****

Just as Barclay had predicted, the Earl's principal vassals, those knights who held large land grants in Sir Robert's name, all arrived at Hammerstone castle accompanied by their own heavily-armed liege-men.

Long before curfew bell the great hall was filled with men, the strength of earldom jammed together in one large sweating, chattering, and boasting mass. The serving girls had to fight their way through a loud gantlet of groping men in order to get their tables ready for the supper platters. A serving girl, having finally pushed her way back to the safety of the kitchen, said breathlessly to one of her fellow maids, "Have a care in the hall, lass. If I had a half-penny for every pinch I've taken tonight, my backside alone would buy me a tinker's cart!"

The Earl of Malton had, in sworn service to him, many knights that held lands. Of these vassals the richest owed a tithe of many knights service to Robert and the least owed five. All together Sir Robert could call on what amounted to nearly one hundred mounted knights, all sworn to defend the Earl and do battle in his name.

Forty days a year did each knight owe his lord and the feudal year ran not January to January, but Michaelmass to Michaelmass, the feast before All Hallow's Eve and even though the feast was not yet come, Barclay had decided to close the books on the year now, while Robert's vassals were already assembled and before they had a chance to let doubts about Robert's future grow in their minds. Barclay knew full well that the longer Robert was missing the more his vassals would call for a successor. The King, too, would soon hear of Robert's misfortune and God help Maken then. No doubt the cash strapped King would marry Maken off to the highest bidder after emptying Hammerstone's coffers first. Barclay pushed himself away from his table. The roar from the crowded hall was getting louder, carrying even over the din of the kitchen. The steward looked down at the busy scene below and noted that the feast was all but ready. He closed his books and locked them away in his strongbox. He shooed away young Colin Fontennell, his clerk-in-training, and the boy happily headed to the hall.

At the solar the steward met Fulke who, as his custom was, sat in his chair against the solar door so that none might enter except past him. Fulke was not asleep though he sat very still. Seeing Barclay, he rapped hard on the heavy door. "The steward awaits m'lady," he announced.

"Bid him enter."

Fulke opened the door and as Barclay stepped past Fulke whispered, "The lady has no idea of the nightmare ahead." Barclay stared into his friend's eyes and was startled to see the beginnings of tears.

"Aye, Fulke, we must pray for Sir Robert's speedy return."

Barclay eased his way into the lord's solar, his mind taken completely with Fulke's show of emotion. How out of character for the normally unflappable Belgian. But, thought the steward grimly, he knew of what he spoke. Maken walked unknowingly on the brink of an abyss.

She stood surrounded by her maids, as her mother-in-law tugged on Maken's under-dress. When they stepped away, Barclay noticed that Maken's belly had magically grown from the morning. She had a definite round bulge now.

The maids pulled Maken's dress over her head and helped her push her arms through their holes.

"What do ye think, Barclay? Can ye tell that I am well along?"

The steward smiled, "Aye m'lady - clever! — The evening meal awaits your pleasure," he added.

After straightening her cap, Maken pronounced herself ready and, closely followed by Camille and the maids, the party made their way to the Great Hall.

"The Lady Maken!" shouted Fulke as Maken entered the crowded feast hall. All talking ceased and all attention turned to the dais. Maken walked through the stillness taking her place besides Robert's chair and bidding the Lady Camille to take the next chair to her left.

To the right of Robert's place sat the steward and beside him the first of the Earl's vassals, Sir Guy Northands. His was the place of honour nearest his lordship's since he held the largest tract of land and the best manor. Sir John Thornton of Fosse was allowed the dais also for although he mounted twenty horsemen, his was not the estate that Sir Guy held, but lay to the east along the Ouse and included the Earl's grist mill, a happy circumstance which paid Fosse a share of the tithe for every bushel of grain harvested.

The last of the Earl's principal vassals to sit on the dais was also the oldest, Mortimer House - a knight well into his fifties and the only man among them that had actually rode with Sir Reginald's father, Raymond. Happy was old Mortimer to find himself to be supper mates with the Lady Camille. He had liked her from the moment Reginald rode into Hammerstone with her in tow.

As Mortimer sat down he spread his sparse white thatch of hair evenly across his bald crown, "Ah, Lady Camille, 'tis good to see you."

Camille smiled at him, "You flatter an old widow." The veteran knight turned red with pleasure. Mortimer was now past his days of glory and the last of his years lay before him, but in his time, he was a fierce man of war, happy to be ever in the thick of the Earl's nearly constant campaigns. Trusted by the older knights and lionized by the younger, Mortimer's support would be a great help to Maken's hold on the castle. Slyly did Camille play to Mortimer's vanity. "Reassured am I," she whispered into the old hairy ear, "that my son's wife has ye to help her in these trying days."

Mortimer House nodded, happy to agree with her.

"My son too shall be glad to hear of it when he is released, for he was ever saying that ye were his father's best saddle-mate."

Mortimer was by no means political nor was he usually quick-witted. Not stupid by any means, his decisions were logical. The process however was a ponderous one and, given two facts to consider simultaneously, Mortimer's mind could attend to neither. Naturally he chose to focus on the more pleasant of the two, namely, Camille's high opinion of him. Riding to the castle earlier, he had been ready to cast Maken aside in favour of Katoryna de Courtelaine.

Keep the line Norman and all that, but by the time he later left Hammerstone he had agreed to maintain neutrality - at least for a time.

Sir Guy Northands was not of a mind to speak openly of his lordship's troubles. Long years of experience had taught him the value of tight lips. He would wait and watch. The young bride's rumoured pregnancy was more than a rumor. She was well along by the look of her. The last year had been hard on Sir Guy. Hard and unsettling. First Sir Reginald's unexpected death and the curious habits of his heir. Sir Guy, for one, was dead against arming the Saxon population. They were hard enough to control without encouraging them. He might well have forced the issue with the new Earl but for Sir Robert's amazing military success. Although he himself had not fought at the battle of the ford, several of his men had and they had nothing but high praise for the Earl's abilities. Every bit his father's son they said. And the Saxon bowmen left a bloody field of what once was a proud showing of Norman strength. Sir Guy had been at the great banquet when Sir Robert had destroyed the huge Belgian. He still could not frankly believe it, seeing the Duke lose a fortune. No doubt Sir Robert was to be feared and it was this fear that had kept Sir Guy from opposing his liege lord's strange ideas. But Robert was gone and things were different now.

****

Cam Fontennell was late for dinner. After he and Barclay were done talking, he had agreed to do whatever he could to encourage Katoryna's friendship. Not that he expected the lady to give him much opportunity. On that point he was sure Barclay would be proven wrong.

The words of the steward proved to be prophetic, however, for no sooner had Cam left the solar then he was stopped in the hallway by Katoryna's servant girl. "Fontennell," she hissed, "Stay a moment". He stopped, "Why, my day is too busy to be trading gossip with ye."

She did not reply but instead stepped back and swung open Katoryna's door. She gestured that he should enter. For a moment Cam stood still, not sure if he should enter the lady's apartment alone. Remembering his promise to Barclay, Cam laid aside his doubts and walked past the maid and into the room.

Cam heard the heavy door swing shut behind him. He was alone with the Lady. Katoryna sat in a high-backed chair near the apartment's only window. The shutters were open and Katoryna sat in the sunlight. She beckoned to Cam to come forward. This he did, bowing before her.

"M'lady."

"So you are the great archer?"

"I can hold my own."

"What else can ye do?"

"Pardon m'lady?"

"What are your duties and how is it that ye stand so high in my brother's eyes?"

"I am his lordship's squire and on the strength of Sir Robert's good graces am I in such an office."

"My, such modesty!"

A gentle rap on the door interrupted them and the servant girl entered bearing a flask of wine and two goblets. These she placed on a small round table which she in turn picked up and placed in front of the lady.

Katoryna bid Cam to retrieve a chair from the side wall and join her in a taste of wine.

As a matador measures the bull, so did the Norman lady consider the young archer, her dark eyes watching him over the rim of her goblet. Cam Fontennell took his ease, sipping the red liquid, the cup in one hand, the other hand carelessly draped across the arm of his chair. He found Katoryna an interesting study, her bold manner unsettling but her black eyes compelling. He decided that the lady was pretty and found himself happy to have agreed to Barclay's suggestion. But of all this, his features gave no hint, his eyes gazed impassively at the lady as he waited for her to state why he found himself in her rooms.

"Ye say little," she noted.

"Aye, m'lady, I have many faults but a loose tongue is not one of them."

"Well then Fontennell, what are your faults?"

He smiled at her and leaned forward, "It is said that blessed are the peacemakers, in which case I am doomed, for I love battle."

"Really? What is it about war that ye like? The honor? The glory?"

"Oh, no m'lady, I care nothing of those things. No, it is the fight itself that I like. To see my enemy laid low, his blood pouring out and his eyes wild with terror." Cam laughed, "Aye, m'lady, that is my great weakness."

Katoryna's eyes shone just as Barclay had said, she loved bloodshed and sure enough she begged Cam to tell her of the battle at the ford.

This he did but in the most general of terms. Katoryna stood and gave her servant girl a nod. The girl slipped out of the chamber. Katoryna refilled their cups and pulled her chair nearer to Cam's. They drank the red wine and she whispered, "Have ye killed many men, Fontennell?"

"A few."

She leaned in closer so that he could feel her warm breath on his cheek, "What is it like Fontennell? To kill a man?"

"Every time it is different, sometimes ye never even see their face, nor hear them cry out. One, I watched die a slow death of wounds I inflicted and I can tell thee truly, I gloried in his agonies for he died badly."

"Oh," she breathed. "Did you know him?"

"Only by reputation for he was well known hereabouts. His name was Sir Jean de la Mere."

Katoryna gasped. Surely this youngster was mistaken. Sir Jean had not been the leader of his Free Companions because of his kind nature. One of the best knights in all of England was he named. He had won many a tournament, taught her brother, Roger, many of his tricks and unknown to anyone else, had been Katoryna's first lover. Could this lean young man, Cam, so innocent looking, have possibly taken the life of a Norman so renowned? And if it was true, what a curious turn of events, for her to be seducing the very man who took the life of the one whom first seduced her. She nearly laughed just thinking about it, for it suited her nature to see humour in such things.

"You knew the man?" asked Cam.

"In passing. Sir Jean was a paid soldier in the employ of my father. Now tell me how ye could slay a man such as he."

Cam proceeded to tell the lady the whole lay of the battle at the ford. From the first news of the attackers approach, to Sir Robert's ambush, to the dreadful rain of death the archers inflicted.

Cam then described how he saw Sir Jean de la Mere try to blindside the Earl but before he could strike, Cam had sent a grey-goose into the mercenary. And then another far crueler bolt which shattered Sir Jean's will to fight along with his knee. He told of how his final arrow ripped into the knight's back even as he fled the battlefield.

"So ye did not actually see Sir Jean die?"

"Oh yes, Sir Robert sent riders after Sir Jean and they found him lying along the roadside in great pain. They brought him back to the castle and laid him in a cell in the prisoner's tower. His cries went on for half the night. Many a man came and saluted my shooting, so at length I grew curious to see his wounds. I waited for his lordship to be done with the prisoner and only after he left the tower and all was quiet, I slipped up the winding stairs and entered Sir Jean's cell.

Here Cam paused in the narrative to partake of the wine. After a long drink he continued, "Long I marveled at his wounds. He lay stretched out across a wooden table set high for the greater ease of the doctors.

His blood lay in pools below the table. Naked he was, his wounds raw and oozing. With each laboured breath, Sir Jean produced a white bloody froth and I knew that he would soon meet death. Silently I gloated that I was the author of such misfortune. I stood by while the knight slipped ever lower. He opened his eyes once and he knew me not. I smiled as with his questioning eyes he begged to know my name *"I am death"* I told him in a deep voice."

"Does that shock thee m'lady?"

Katoryna allowed herself a moment to digest his delicious tale. Oh how she envied him, to have that power, to slay a man and watch him die.

"Yea, truly, I am shocked, Fontennell, shocked but not offended. Ye did your duty and Sir Jean de la Mere failed to do his. Now come, let us partake in the last of the Flemish wine."

When they had drunk Katoryna opened an oaken chest and from within drew forth a square wooden board decorated with sixty-four squares in equal rows of eight. Next she withdrew a box which contained thirty-two curiously carved figures. Half were of white and half of black, "Have ye ever played chess, Fontennell?"

He answered in the negative but this did not deter her and she proceeded to place the pieces on the playing board. "These are the pawns and there are eight. They can do little save open the way for their greater brethren." She almost added that pawns were just like her brother's serfs but she checked her speech. She need not have worried as it turned out; Cam Fontennell was a free man since his father, like his father before him, owned his own land. Poverty stricken they were, but free.

She continued, "This next piece is a castle of which there are two. Side to side and up and down does the castle move. Rather boring, I'm afraid."

"Next the knight, again two and they move in a hook, two up and once to the side. An odd moving piece but I can tell thee many a great plan I have seen ruined by an errant knight!"

"No doubt m'lady," Cam agreed innocently.

She smiled and picked up the next piece, "Now these pieces are well named - the bishop and they, just like their name sakes, never travel straight ahead, but are ever on an angle. Ye must be ever watchful of the bishops."

Katoryna picked up the largest piece. "Ahh, Cam, here is the point of the game, the king. He moves freely but ever so slowly. Aye he must rely on his lessers to win him the game. At last, my young archer, we come to my favourite, the queen. She is the most powerful piece, going every which way as far as she pleases."

"I see why ye like this game," noticed Cam.

"Indeed, now come let us play!"

Now Cam was not so ignorant of the game as he allowed, many an evening he had passed watching Robert and the Belgian. Katoryna and Cam played – her sly experience against his quick mind. The afternoon waxed late and they noticed it not, the supper hour came with them poorer by a dozen pieces and yet nothing could secure the check. Finally hunger won the day and they agreed to declare the contest a draw.

"My word, Fontennell, but ye play a shrewd game. Surely ye have played before?"

"Nay, m'lady, never on my pledge, but yet I sense that ye are but toying with me."

"Well, we must commit to another game tomorrow?"

"Indeed m'lady, ye honour me."

They quit their battle and together made their way to the now crowded hall.

The diners were well into their supper when Cam and Katoryna slipped into the Great Hall and for a moment the happy clatter of spoon upon bowl ceased as they each went to their respective chairs, Katoryna beside her mother, and Cam with a handful of archers along the wall. If his fellow bowmen thought anything odd of his entering the hall with the Earl's sister, they spoke of it not and greeted him in the usual way. Like Cam, these archers were young single men who lived right in the castle at the Earl's pleasure. They looked upon Cam Fontennell as their natural leader not only because he was the best archer among them save for Garfield, but Cam had the favour of his lordship and his lady. And now it seemed he had the favour of the Earl's prodigal sister, as well.

Maken made sure to greet Katoryna with a warmth she did not feel and the Norman in turn did likewise. For a time the business of eating kept conversation to a bare minimum. The harvest season was in full and this was reflected in the richness of the table with roasted pig, beef and fresh trout. Pheasant and poultry were cooked in sweet pies, with a half-dozen different vegetables all newly picked. Ripe fruit and loaves of bread were spread with newly churned butter. Great rounds of cheese and kegs of ale kept the diners content. Although it took some doing, eventually even the heartiest of appetites were sated and at last the dishes could be carried away and banquet tables dismantled. The floor was cleared for the evening's entertainment. The first event of the night would be simple bouts of wrestling. Sir Guy inquired of Maken, the state of her health and what, pray tell, could she tell him of his liege lord Sir Robert?

Maken carefully related the sudden end of her and Robert's trip and of the attack, minimizing his wounds and stressing their expectation of a letter of demands for his ransom.

He asked for an exact account of Sir Robert's injuries and again Maken limited her description to his sword cuts. The crossbow bolt wound in his upper back was not mentioned.

As she listened, Katoryna became incensed. To hear Maken tell it, one would think Robert had been barely scratched and what of his crossbow wound through his shoulder? Katoryna wanted to call her a liar and tell them all the truth, that the Earl had been badly if not mortally wounded and what was more, he would likely bleed to death before morning had come. But of all this Katoryna could say naught. To do so would cast deep suspicion upon herself. She would have to hold her tongue. Luckily for her the nuns of St. Alban had taught her that lesson well.

In answer to Sir Guy's other question, Maken stood and smoothed her dress around her belly. "I am with child, Sir Guy," she said rubbing the roundness, "but otherwise I am quite well."

The knight raised his cup and called for a toast in honor of an heir to Hammerstone. And he added a hope that the child would be male. And there was the rub. If the baby were a girl, Maken's case for inheritance would weaken since in those hard times, boys were recognized more readily than girls.

Maken allowed that it was her wish also and told Sir Guy they would all have to be patient and wait until the springtime.

Katoryna spoke up, "Nay Maken, we need not wait even a day!" She turned to her servant girl standing nearby. "Go ye right away and fetch old Frida. Tell her we have need of her!"

Addressing herself to Maken again, Katoryna said, "Old Frida is well nigh unsurpassed at calling babies. I cans't hardly believe ye did not call Frida at once and find out what is the child's sex!"

Maken smiled weakly. She had heard of Frida and her ability to tell if a woman had conceived. She was loath to have her opinion. Frida had lived within the walls of Hammerstone for all but seven of her uncounted years, but Maken knew her not. And not knowing her, Maken would not trust her. In her heart, Maken was certain she carried a son but what if Frida told the world she would have a daughter? Or worse, suppose someone paid the old hag to declare Maken to be barren. So great was her reputation as a mid-wife that everyone would believe Frida. A risk Maken was truly afraid to take.

Katoryna sat back, smiling. Her idea had met with universal approval and now everyone, even the men who lined up to wrestle, eagerly awaited the arrival of the old mid-wife. Maken could only sit as a blanket of dread engulfed her. Katoryna had her trapped like a stag before the hounds.

Frida, after a short time, was found and she came straight way to the dais. She bowed and waited.

Katoryna spoke up, "Old woman, cans't ye still tell a girl the state of her womb and what grows therein or has old age robbed ye of your powers?"

"I can do whatever I have ever done m'lady," the small wizened figure answered.

"Good, now employ these same gifts. Maken here is curious to know what is growing in her belly," ordered Katoryna.

"Aye m'lady." Frida walked to where Maken sat and held out her hand. Maken did not know what she should do. She looked toward Camille, but her mother-in-law had turned away and was gazing thoughtfully at her daughter. Maken felt a hand at her elbow and with a start she spun around. Sir Guy Northands had stood and was offering to help Maken stand. He smiled.

With no way to resist she rose out of her chair and stood before the crowded hall, facing the old mid-wife. The two women, old and young, stared at each other. Frida pulled from the folds of her tattered dress a long wooden needle, sharpened to a point and hung on the end of a single thread. The wrinkled leathery hand seized the softer smoother hand and held it out so that Maken's palm faced upwards. For a moment she feared that the old hag meant to pierce her with the needle, but Frida merely held the thread up in the air so that the wooden point could just graze Maken's wrist. Now moving the line, Frida slipped the needle up and down against Maken's flesh. To Cam Fontennell, sitting with the other archers along the wall, it seemed an absurd way to treat Maken. "What in God's name does the old hag think she is doing?" he whispered to Tom Whitefoot, a bowman fifteen years Cam's senior. Tom had seen old Frida at work many a time and now he took it upon himself to educate his young companion on the ways of midwives.

"Now ye see lad, that bit 'o wood, she be dangling against m'lady? Well that is a piece of apple wood. Ye see only a tree that bears fruit will work. She makes sure it rubs the lady's skin and now here comes the magic!"

Cam stood and leaned forward. Frida had quit stroking and now the needle hung still a couple of inches above Maken's arm. In wonder, Cam watched as the needle began to swing back and forth, back and forth. The old woman stood all the while as still as a statue carved in stone. The needle stopped, and then began again, this time in a round circle. It stopped again.

By now the whole castle had eyes only for the sliver of wood dangling above Maken's arm. For the third time the needle moved. Back and forth. It stopped and moved not again.

The old mid-wife stared long at the inert needle and when she was satisfied that it was indeed finished, she returned the instrument to the folds of her dress. Maken looked first at her wrists and then to Frida. She did not understand.

The old woman looked past Maken and spoke aloud that the crowd would hear her, "Three children shall she bear in her life. 'Tis plain - one daughter, two sons!"

"Yes, yes, in her life! Fine!" hissed Katoryna, "But what of now, is she truly with child?"

Frida looked to Sir Guy Northands and he folded his arms across his chest and with a nod of his head urged her to examine the earl's wife. Maken, if she could have thought of a reason to refuse, surely would have.

Back along the wall Cam turned and stared at Tom Whitefoot. Tom smiling, "Aye, that's grand then isn't it. Three babes she be havin'."

"I don't understand."

"It's simple lad, if the needle travels back and forth, 'tis the sign of a boy, if the needle goes in a round circle, 'tis a girl!"

He might have explained things further, but Cam had already turned back towards the dais to see what devilry the old hag was up to now.

Frida undid a clasp and took her cape from her shoulders. She wrapped it around Maken's waist and Maken nearly gagged at the wrinkled mid-wife's onion-laced breathe.

"Fear not, m'lady, ye will not be hurt. Just hold onto my cape." With that Frida dropped down and ran her gnarled old hands up Maken's dress. Maken stiffened as one hand slipped around her waist and rested in the small of her back. The mid-wife rose up enough that her ear lay against Maken's abdomen. Her free hand she slid up Maken's body until it lay on her pubic bone and just above the hairline. She pressed. Harder than expected from one so frail looking. Maken began to tremble and the old woman whispered, "Be still child!"

The probing continued upwards and then her fingers touched upon the pouch that Maken had fastened about her waist. The mid-wife paused and then slipped her fingers gently around the pouch. Maken thought she heard a gentle chuckle but she could not be sure. She fought to not panic. She concentrated on breathing. The examination continued. Up almost to her ribs and back down again. Frida grunted and removed her hands. She stood slowly, her ancient joints creaking. She looked into Maken's eyes as if to devine her thoughts. She turned from the object of her study and looked out over the waiting crowd.

Maken wanted to scream, so badly did she feel the tension about her. In the eyes of everyone that mattered the word of this little gnome-like creature was unquestioned. Finally Frida spoke, "The lady is with child, a male child!"

Right joyously was this news received and in a daze, Maken found her chair and sat down amid the thunderous cheers of the hall. She smiled weakly.

Sir Guy called for a toast and wished for the unborn a mighty arm. Barclay toasted to the hope of an easy birth witnessed by the father. This was greeted with a chorus of heartfelt here-here's.

The evening took on a festive air. Maken's condition was now happily confirmed, and a son at that. And after her terror had left her, Maken began to fell giddy. She felt that she had won a victory over her doubters. Certainly the Earl's liege-men seemed glad that she carried a son. That was something.

There were bouts of wrestling first, avidly followed by Fulke, who for so long had made his living as a wrestler. He had trained most of the combatants since it was the Earl's wish that all of his men be taught the most basic holds and throws.

Next up were bouts of quarterstaff and these were popular indeed. Being inherently more violent than the wrestling the crowd became more animated when the quarterstaff bouts started. The northern men, too, took a special pride in their cudgel play and held themselves to be the best in England at this specie of combat.

When it became apparent that Neil Cleeves would not partake, a full score of men stepped up to try a bout. Even without the great Cleeves taking part, the spectators were given a rare show of skill and courage. Long and hard were the rounds and only after many a bloodied head and countless bruises, was a victor declared.

Happy was Neil Cleeves when one of his own guards carried the day.

Katoryna was in a better mood than could have been guessed. Calling on old Frida had been a spur of the moment gesture - a free throw of the dice so to speak. It had cost her nothing and had scared the Saxon interloper half out of her wits. And besides,

Katoryna had laid her hopes in other directions. At any rate, by the second bout of wrestling, the Norman mistress had forgotten everything except the sweating fighters before her. She found herself hoping that Fontennell would step into the fray but to her disappointment he made no move other than to drink ale with his mates.

The last contest of the night was, as was becoming the custom at Hammerstone, an archery match. A smaller round was hung at the farthest reaches of the hall. This was wearisome for Maken; as keen as Robert's bowmen were she had seen too much of them to be entertained. Before they had shot three times, Maken had nodded off.

Not so Sir Guy Northands. He had not seen a shooting match save one, and that had been in the early spring. For years the Saxon yeomen had honed their skills to a state rarely seen. Even the least of these men could strike the inner ring of a round at sixty paces. The Earl had legalized their weapons and only now were the Normans seeing true Saxon skill.

Sir Guy watched with a growing amazement as man after man clustered his arrows into the target. Finally, Thurgar, the one-time poacher, was deemed the victor. Sir Guy, in congratulating Thurgar, implied that Thurgar was obviously the best of the Earl's archers.

"Nay, Sir Knight", said Thurgar, "thou should know that I am but one of many. If our captain Garfield were here ye would see an archer. None, save Fontennell sitting along yonder wall, can bend the yew like him."

"Indeed, let him come therefore and show us this talent."

Cam had not taken part. He had come to the point in his own mind that he took no satisfaction in besting the other men unless Garfield be among them, and Garfield was away to York. Also the day's activities lay heavy in his mind.

Sir Guy's suggestion was taken up and amplified by the crowd for Cam was popular and his skill admired. Katoryna, with her usual lack of discretion, yelled loudly for him to shoot. Cam nodded respectfully toward the lady and a happy murmur rose up as he reached for his trusty bow.

The target, a round sack stuffed full of straw, was taken down and Cam ordered it replaced with a shiny crab apple. While his younger brother did his bidding, he ever so carefully examined his clutch of arrows, looking at each shaft until he had found three to his liking. Next he strung his bow and fingered the line with beeswax. Finally, he was satisfied with his gear and he stood to the target. Smoothly he notched his arrow and aimed, his bowstring kissing his cheek. True flew the shaft and the crab apple exploded.

Laughing aloud, his brother set another apple up against the wall and Cam gave it the same treatment. The crowd cheered as Cam notched his final arrow. Colin looked back at him, his eyes shining in anticipation. He held the apple out and Cam nodded. The youngster threw it as high as he could. Cam's bow followed the arc of the apple's flight and, at its apex, Cam shot his arrow clean through its core. Thunderstruck, the hall was awed into silence. Colin ran and picked up what was left of the apple. The arrow had lodged into one of the rafters sixty feet above them.

Thurgar could scarcely believe his own eyes. Many a shrewd shot he had seen over the years, but never one such as Cam Fontennell had just made. He doubted if ever Garfield could have matched it. Cam Fontennell nodded to Maken who had awakened at the roar from his first shot and smiled at Katoryna. Katoryna returned his gaze, unconscious of the curious glances from her brother's liege-knights.

#5

Hammerstone Castle was fully repaired on the feast of Michaelmass. Barclay, for the first time in many weeks, could allow himself a moment's respite. A score of newly hired knights had filled in the ranks of the castle's defenders nicely. Each man he had hand-picked. Whether or not they were well mounted, or even well armed, did not concern Barclay in the least. The stables and armory of the castle were full and he instead looked to the man, his physical state and how he carried himself. Was his arm tight and strong? Were his hands toughened and callused from riding and sword play? And was he lean? A fat sluggish rider was a curse, apt to tire easily and wear hard on the mounts. Too pretty a man was out also. Barclay was of the opinion that too handsome a man tended to womanize too much and wilt in battle. Not always of course. Lord Robert was handsome and yet loved all manner of combat. Fontennell, too, had the eye of every young lass for miles about, yet he was brave.

Barclay was on the parapet of the Keep, a place he found to be conducive to thinking. And as always, there was much to consider. He gazed down across the inner courtyard at the newly roofed stable. The gatehouse foundation had been rebuilt and the secret opening that so nearly was the end of them was now sealed tight. Also, the drawbridge had been sorely tested when the invaders had let go of the draw chains, letting the heavy oak timbers slam down across the moat. The timbers had loosened in the crash and had to be re-braced. All this was completed and all he had need of now was to throw up some small cottages and the Earldom would be as good as new, as if the Earl of Crewe had never attacked.

Something moved behind him and he spun around, pulling free his dagger as he did. Colin

Fontennell stood nearby smiling, "Are ye going a-hunting, Sir?"

"Nay, lad! What means this, ye creeping up like a thief?"

The boy shrugged innocently. "I did not creep sir, I just walked." His words rang true. It was a trait of the Fontennells. They were quiet on their feet.

Barclay ruffled the boy's hair. Against his own better judgment he was becoming fond of the young imp, letting him away with too much. Coming up here without leave, for example. Barclay knew he should box his ears and teach the boy some respect. Instead he told Colin to fetch his older brother. The youngster soon returned with Cam.

"Ah, Cam, I hope I did not take ye away from anything important?"

"Nay, nothing that can't wait."

"And is she waiting?"

"Aye," Cam said flatly, his face a blank mask.

"And how goes it with the lady? Does she ever speak of the Earl or of Sir Roger?"

"The lady says little of her family."

"Little - or nothing?"

"Well, she has spoken of Sir Roger and wondered where he might be."

As he listened, Barclay leaned against the crannells and watched the workmen cleaning up the courtyard, loading the excess wood and stone into carts pulled by mules. A constant snake-like line of men shouldered large sacks of grain into the newly re-roofed granary.

Cam stood nearby and looked upon the busy courtyard, each man content to let silence reign for a moment.

After a while Barclay eyed Cam, "Ye have slept with Katoryna?"

"I did as ye have asked and befriended the lady."

"Quite right, Fontennell, I should not have asked."

Cam laughed, "But aye, ye were quite right about her. She is rather ... uh... passionate."

"Falling in love are we?" asked Barclay. Cam deflected the question, "Never fear, I'll not be forgetting our purpose."

"Maybe not, but the kitchen maids are saying the lady has fallen for you."

Cam shrugged, "Who can know the mind of a woman?"

Barclay had known this particular woman all her life and he was fairly certain he knew her mind. He hoped he hadn't put too much faith in Cam Fontennell's judgment. He was young with the hot blood of youth. Easily could his loyalties be shifted and his head turned by a woman such as Katoryna de Courtelaine. More than one man she had wrapped around her little finger. He meant to warn his young confederate but their debate was terminated with the appearance of Maken. She came to them, followed four steps behind by a handmaiden.

"Cam Fontennell, thou hast been a stranger these last few weeks. Art thou well?"

"Very well, m'lady," answered Cam and even now he felt the lesser man in her presence. He would have loved to explain his new-found friendship with Katoryna but Barclay was dead set against anyone else knowing their plans. 'The less said the better' was his favourite old saw. It pained Cam to see the distrustful look in her eye.

"The repairs to Hammerstone are at last completed m'lady," said Barclay. "We need now only to replace a few cottages and we shall be squared away!"

Maken seemed unenthusiastic. She spoke not and Barclay, who was getting rather used to her agreeing with his every suggestion, was puzzled. "Something troubles ye, Maken?"

"Aye, Barclay."

"Speak m'lady, ye have my ears."

Maken knew not how to begin or indeed what exactly she wanted done.

"I know not what to tell ye Barclay, only that Robert has a mind to build some different kind of village but what I cannot recall. He has so many ideas. I can not keep track of them all."

Barclay noticed she did not refer to the Earl in the past tense, even though they had yet to hear any news or receive any sort of ransom note.

"May I speak freely, m'lady?" asked Cam Fontennell.

Maken nodded, "Indeed, Cam."

"Well, I'm sure, m'lady, that I too heard his lordship's plan for a new village."

"Pray tell us then, what can ye remember of Robert's thoughts?"

"Aye, m'lady 'tis a clever and yet simple plan. He thought to build the cottages in a line, one with the other so that they shared a common high wall to the world. The corners would be anchored by the tavern, a church and on the streamside, a small mill. The walls would be thick and able to let six men stand abreast. The tavern would get a second and third storey, as would the mill. These then would be the guard towers of the town. Inside would be granaries, the archers' hall or barracks, shops and a forge. A wharf would be built along the riverside and Father Hubert's church would be topped with a watchtower and bell. That is why his lordship was making all those bricks!"

Barclay was speechless. This was a huge undertaking, one that would empty the coffers of Hammerstone and then some. He looked to Maken and her eyes were shining.

"Aye! Aye! Cam, 'tis a great thing ye have such a memory. This is, then, what we shall do!" she said.

Cam Fontennell answered, "I know not what we can do, m'lady, or even what we should do, but at least I know that is what our master would do, were he here."

Barclay needed time to think. Loath he was to commit to such a large undertaking.

"Let us at least have all his lordship's brick brought to the common. Then shall a decision be needed."

The Earl's brick factory had been fully engaged since the spring plow. Even during the harvest a crew of men laboured in the clay pits below the castle. Row after squared row of hardened gray masonry sat waiting to be used.

It was early morning, cold and clear, with a hint of frost kissing the grass. Cam Fontennell, Barclay and Father Hubert stood at the roadside looking down into the ever-deepening hole in the clay riverbank. The brick-makers stood about nervously. Something was up, they had been ordered not to start until Barclay arrived.

The steward gestured to one of the serfs. The man removed his cap and pushed his thick hair away from his eyes. He shuffled forward, "Yes sir?"

"No need to be afraid. What 'tis the matter, ye all look worried. Have ye been thieving the Earl's building stores?"

The serf drew back as if fearing a blow "Oh, nay sir, never. What would we do with them?"

Cam leaned over and whispered something into Barclay's ear. The steward listened closely and when Cam stepped away he spoke, "Sir Robert had told ye to labour your three days a week here without fail?"

The brick-makers nodded to the affirmative.

"Well far be it from me to counter any of his lordships wishes. Ye shall continue but first can someone tell me how many brick are piled here?"

"Oh m'lord, many!" The brick-makers were all agreed. There were many.

"There are thirty thousand bricks here," stated the priest.

Cam added, "Assuming each stack holds five hundred."

The brick-makers, unlettered to the man, had just seen a miracle. They stood quietly staring at their priest too awed to speak.

Father Hubert tried to explain why he could easily arrive at the total number of bricks but he could see his explanation did little good.

Barclay told the serfs to return to their brick-making and when they had went back to work, he bid Cam to tell Father Hubert of the Earl's plan for a fortified village. The priest knew of what the Earl was thinking since he too had talked of this with Sir Robert, building a church within the new village. The priest had grown up near an enclosed town and he liked the idea. And Barclay, seeing the great amount of brick Robert had caused to be made, began to feel more certain that Cam was right about the Earl's plans. Now the real problem. How would one build such a thing? Barclay had lived his life between Hammerstone and York. The castle of York was nothing more than a wooden tower. Long had the Cliffords of York looked enviously at the great stone walls of Hammerstone. But Hammerstone's mighty towers were built long before Barclay's time.

It was Father Hubert who stated the obvious. "My friends, we are not building a castle, just a village with a wall. Let us therefore build first what has been promised, namely the new cottages. If we do as the Earl had been planning we could be at least to spring erecting one row of cottages with a common back wall. Surely we can hardly err in doing that?"

Barclay agreed and Cam Fontennell was sent to York to hire stone masons. Before the steward left the brickworks one of the older men approached him, cap in hand and begged to ask a question. Barclay paused to hear the man out. To be proper the serf should have asked Myles, his Reeve, to forward his query.

"When do ye reckon his lordship shall return, sir?"

"I know not. Once as I recall Sir Reginald was gone for three long years and we suffered not from his absence."

The serf nodded, "Aye thou art wise to remember that, I had forgotten how the old Earl did travel."

Barclay accepted his praise with a nod, "Aye now away to your labours and don't concern yourself with the affairs of the Earl!"

"Aye, Aye, Sir!" said the serf, bowing as he backed away.

#6

No servant of the Earl of Leicester had to wonder where their lord and master was. Sir Simon de Montfort had been bellowing orders steadily from his solar since first light. His lordship wished to travel to Londontown and seek an audience with the King. Sir Simon was fed and mounted before the morning was even half-gone. He wished to travel lightly, taking only twenty handpicked bodyguards. The Lady of the castle was not asked to accompany her husband. When she let it be known that she would greatly desire to visit Stephen's court, Sir Simon coldly told her he had no time to wait for her and her handmaidens to prepare themselves, nor did he wish to travel with a litter in his midst. Another point, and one that he failed to tell his wife, was that he was of the opinion the capital's many pleasures could be better enjoyed alone.

The lady would have to take solace in whatever way she could. Cards and gossip, sewing and more gossip. At least the Earl's younger brother, Sir Howard, was staying home. Odd of him to miss a trip to Londontown, but since his disastrous adventure with Sir Jean de la Mere, Sir Howard was not inclined to travel and thus would often be available for a game of chess, a game beyond the grasp of most of the family, save his daughter, Marie. Sir Simon, of course, had no time for such trivial pastimes. His chess games were played in the real world and he was a keen and fearsome participant.

#7

The new cottages and how they would be built were explained to the Reeve, and Myles in turn, explained the idea to the villagers. He bid one and all to apply themselves to the daunting task ahead.

The first five cottages were laid out and the footings of the great common wall finished by the first of November.

The stone masons, dour faced men with thick necks and hands like gnarled oak, oversaw the removal of all useable stone from the ruined cottages. Though blackened, the stones were still of use in the foundation of the new walls. Barclay, showing an uncharacteristic burst of enthusiasm, predicted that the first five cottages would be finished before the Christmas feast. He divided everyone into teams. One team worked under the direction of the stone masons, one team devoted themselves to moving bricks upriver to the site and still another team cut timber and made posts, beams and planking.

The greatest help turned out to be the captured horses. They dragged logs, moved bricks, and pulled the ropes to lift stones and beams into place.

The first of November came and went and still no word was heard on the fate of his lordship. One cold clear morning three horsemen came riding out of the south. Boldly the strangers came, not checking the strength of their mounts until they sat directly under the very roof of the gatehouse. There they were immediately challenged by the guard watch, "Who art thou?" he demanded, and even as he spoke several of his fellow guards barred the drawbridge by standing across the gateway.

"I am Sir Walter Black and these are my companions, men of good standing, I assure you. I come with a message from our most gracious Lord and Sovereign, King Stephen!"

Now the guard that stood before the King's men was a veteran and he kept his wits about him, bidding the horseman to linger while he made sure they were properly greeted. To ease their impatience, he had some beer of good October brewing sent out to them as they waited. The guard slipped into the inner courtyard and sent a youngster running to give Barclay the summons. While the three messengers cooled their heels at the gates, Barclay, Maken and Camille had a hurried meeting. It took no great thinker to realize the King would have little good news for his liege-man's bride. All their hopes lay in delaying any claims to Robert's title, which might be brought before the King.

Barclay hurried to greet the visitors with all the decorum he could muster. Maken made a hasty retreat to the solar and it was left to Camille to take a chair in the Great Hall and receive the King's men.

Barclay stood at the entrance of the Keep while the strangers were led in. He noticed Sir Walter stared long at the huge iron cage that had held Sir Howard de Montfort. Sir Walter bid his companions to remain in the courtyard while he ascended the stair.

Barclay greeted the visitor with a bow. Sir Walter was led straightaway to the Great Hall where the lady Camille sat warming herself by a crackling fire.

The knight bowed and addressed the lady, "I come from the Court of Stephen, bearing a message from His Majesty. My name, good lady, is Sir Walter Black."

"Pray, Sir Knight, what desires His Majesty of us?"

"Perhaps m'lady, I should first inquire as to whom I address."

"I am Camille de Courtelaine, wife of the late Earl."

"I see", said Black, but obviously he was somewhat confused. Camille smiled, but offered no further comment.

Sir Walter had been told the Earl's wife was quite young and the Lady before him was obviously past the bloom of youth, although she was still a comely woman. Finally with no other course of action occurring to him, he ventured, "I am told that the Earl's wife was not yet twenty." (Some had said she was barely a teenager and others even said she was a Saxon, born in a woodcutter's cottage, but then court was always full of lies and innuendo).

Camille allowed herself a chuckle, "As I said, Sir Knight, I am the wife of the last Earl, Sir Reginald. My son is the current Earl and he is indeed married to a young lady, not yet twenty."

"Forgive me m'lady".

"Not to worry, Sir Knight, we here in the north rarely are seen in the capital. One therefore should not be surprised at thy confusion."

"M'lady. Might I enquire therefore, the whereabouts of his lordship? And if not the Earl, I should like to interview the Earl's lady."

"It grieves me Sir Knight to give you unhappy news but the Earl has been travelling these last few weeks, and we are not sure when he shall honour us with his presence," said Camille.

"You sound very matter-of-factly, m'lady. Do you not find it odd that his lordship has been away so long?"

"Not at all, after all Sir Robert's father was away for years on end."

"But the court has heard the Earl has been cruelly wounded, and the wounds may be mortal."

"Nay Sir Knight, the lady Maken, who was with him at his wounding, left him in good hands, and good health, with the nuns of St. Hild's."

Sir Walter continued, "Left a wounded man at the mercy of the priests then?"

"Not quite Sir, not with priests, but with the nuns of St. Hild's, an order under the protective friendship of the Earls of Malton. The mother Superior would never harm a de Courtelaine."

"I see. Well I shall at least interview the lady."

"Alas, my daughter-in-law is taken to bed, she is with child and the morning heaves leave her weak."

Sir Walter Black bit his lower lip, his simple task suddenly complicated. He wished his master would have let him bring a priest along. A priest would soon get the answers the King wanted; they had the knack of making people do their will. Sir Walter was a simple soldier and interviewing ladies was not one of his strengths.

He started again, "The court has heard, and on good account, that the Earl of Malton has died of his wounds and it falls to me to ensure that His Majesty's principal vassals are accounted for. King Stephen would rest easier if Sir Robert de Courtelaine made an appearance."

"Indeed, Sir, so too would I, his mother, but he is an Earl of the realm, and he comes and goes as he sees fit. No doubt he shall return soon."

Sir Walter had not counted on this. Simon de Montfort had seemed so sure of himself that the King had not questioned his tale. His Majesty had given Sir Walter no instructions in the case of the Earl of Malton being alive. Well, thought the dutiful knight, there was nothing left to do but return to Londontown.

#8

An evening fire crackled in the hearth and though it warmed the solar it could not ease the chill that had settled on Maken's heart. The visitor had shaken her. Long had she hoped for Robert to return before any of his peers took too much of an interest in Hammerstone's wealth. Now it was much worse – the King himself had noticed. Seated around her protectively were Camille, Cam Fontennell, Fulke, Barclay, Garfield and Father Hubert.

All were there at Maken's request. These six were unofficially Maken's war consul. Camille, because of her long marriage to Sir Reginald, knew of the allies and enemies. Garfield knew all the highways and byways for many miles — all the folk that travelled them - and he was, by popular opinion, the cleverest among them. Fulke stayed near because he was Maken's physical security, unless Maken dismissed him. Barclay, as steward, would be in charge of any reaction to the King's messenger. His thinking, while not as creative as Garfield's, was strongly built on the twin pillars of success: practicality and common sense.

The diminutive priest was there not only as their spiritual leader, but as a man born to a high Norman family, he was well versed in the ways of the court and he had an uncanny knack of perceiving men's thoughts.

Cam Fontennell was part of this inner circle because Maken wished it so. If Maken had a special reason for Cam's presence, she never spoke of it. Each had Maken's trust.

The arrival of the King's page was heavy on their thoughts for they knew full well that if Stephen ruled that Robert was indeed dead, he could then pick a new husband for Maken and she would be powerless to stop him.

"Me 'n my thick head," said Barclay, "I should have known this would happen eventually."

"Aye good steward, we all knew the King would hear of Robert's troubles. Thou has't spoken to the heart of the matter. The King would seek and profit in Maken's troubles," said the priest.

"But how so Father? Does Maken not pay the taxes, and fulfill the castle's obligations? Why therefore should His Highness enforce his will on Maken?" asked Garfield, for he knew little of the ways of the nobility and their unending search for more power and wealth.

Father Hubert cast an eye toward the archer, and then the expectant youngster before answering. She must know sooner or later, he thought.

"There is so much more at stake here than just the tithes of these northern acres, Garfield. Stephen could use his royal right to find Maken a new husband, someone who would protect his interests in the north. And who wouldn't jump at the chance to seize the lands and castle so long admired and envied. Long has the name of de Courtelaine evoked the jealousies of lesser men! And look, too, at the more earthly part of the bargain, a young bride of obvious beauty and charm, just the right elixir to revive some old man with a title."

"But the lady is with child!" cried Cam Fontennell. He, more than the rest, seemed outraged at the possibility of Maken being forced into another union. His hand moved to the hilt of his sword as if it had a mind of its own.

"Nay, my young friend, think not for a minute that the lady's condition would give anyone much pause," said Father Hubert.

Camille found Maken's hand and took it in her own, hoping perhaps to ease the shock of the priest's words. Garfield said naught, but he gnawed on his lower lip. This was a bad turn and he was heartbroken for Maken. Many a time he had seen a local lass widowed young and invariably she would find someone else, someone local and often for the better. But this

Norman custom, to marry a widow off without regard to her wishes was cruel.

Barclay thought only of one thing — how to delay the inevitable and give Robert, if he was still alive, every chance to return home before it was lost forever.

Father Hubert continued, "Think of the King, what a great windfall the death of an Earl with no male heir would be. He might sell the Earldom to the highest bidder, use it to secure the loyalty of a powerful baron or reward a trusted soldier. He would no doubt gain in whatever course he took."

"Aye and no doubt Stephen has heard the rumours of Sir Robert's three thousand pounds," said Barclay, cursing himself for ever finding the hoard of coins so cleverly stolen by Giles the old steward. It was dangerous enough to have the money within the walls of Hammerstone with Sir Robert's mighty arm present; it was downright perilous with him gone.

Garfield spoke, "Right then, we know what the King might do but the question remains, what shall Maken do?"

"More of the same, anything to put off the King, I guess," said the priest. "It was well that the Lady Camille met with the King's messenger for right smartly did she send him back to Londontown. He never even met with Maken! I can well imagine what Stephen will think when he hears of it."

Barclay, agreeing with Father Hubert on the need to delay, added, "We too should set the countryside full of rumors of the costs of repairing the castle, of hiring new troops, of high living by the lady. Anything that would make men think the gold is spent and gone."

Maken spoke up, so unexpectedly even Fulke lifted one bush eyebrow, "And what of the castle repairs and our new 'walled village?' Robert told me once that one could only build a new castle with the express permission of the crown and if the castle was built without this permission the castle was called an adulterous fortress?"

"*Adulterine*," corrected Father Hubert.

"Thou knowest what I mean!" Maken was angry at being interrupted.

"Of course my child."

"The only child here is the boy growing in my womb!"

"Quite," the priest agreed.

"Well?" she asked, ignoring the priest, "What happens if the King orders us to remove the new village?"

For a time no one answered. Finally the priest said, "Fear not m'lady. That law only concerns completely new castles. Of this I am quite sure." He wasn't really sure, but he recognized the need to keep Maken calm. She was showing now, the swell of her belly more pronounced every day and he feared for the safety of the baby. If the babe did not survive, Hammerstone and all that went with it would go to Sir Roger de Courtelaine and if he were dead, then to the black-haired pit viper down the hall. '*Mary, Mother of God, help us all,*' Father Hubert thought.

#9

The full moon cast a pale light across the gray stone battlements, as the night sentries walked their endless rounds. Only the hooting of an owl disturbed the stillness. Even the Ouse flowed toward the sea with barely a murmur.

High in the third floor of the Keep, down the hall from the solar, Cam Fontennell relaxed in the middle of a huge bed. Snuggled up against him lay Katoryna, her hand resting on his chest, her smooth thigh draped over his hips. She slept deeply, her body exhausted and her passions spent. He lay awake and stared into the darkness.

Eventually he slipped from her warmth and walked naked to the side table. He groped about in the dark for his clothes. Katoryna awoke and sat up, "Come back to bed," she said.

"Nay m'lady, morn shall come soon and I must be away."

Katoryna got out of bed and lit a candle. She stood bathed in the soft glow, her bare skin lit golden, "The morn comes here at the same time as in thine own room. Stay."

"Nay, lass," he said gently, "You are too heady a wine to partake of in the morning light. Should I awake with you I might not find the will to leave and I am bound to be in York today."

The Norman had lain herself across the bed and resigned herself to his leaving. She might have ordered him to stay but she was too afraid to anger him and if he still refused, what then? He might not come back. He might take up with one of the village wenches that were so eager to warm his bed. Besides her disappointment at his leaving was muted, for he had just now called her a 'heady wine', the first hint that Fontennell enjoyed her presence. How she savored the sound of it... his 'heady wine'.

Katoryna drank in the naked sight of him as he found his clothes. She had seen many men unclothed and was ever amused by their common embarrassment. How they would crouch and try to hide their privates or curse her bold looks and leave offended. Not Fontennell. He carried himself so well, so natural. He cared not whether she stared but went about his business. Lying there in her father's castle in the middle of a moonlit night, Katoryna suddenly came to two great decisions. One, she was in love with the boy-man before her and two, she would find a way to marry him.

#10

Stephen of Blois, King of England, was miserable. He was fifty-seven and felt it. He was sure he had an ache for every year of his life. Once he had been young and strong, the best lance in all merry England. Life was simple in those days, his only needs were a horse and his sword.

Alas, Henry the First, bless his soul, had died. Prodded and nagged relentlessly by his wife, Stephen had taken the throne. To this very day he knew not why, other than to silence his headstrong bride. And for what? Twenty years of constant warfare, endless marches, winning battles but losing ground. There had been enemies to meet, debts to pay and now Stephen was old and weary.

The King called upon his butler to bring a fresh flask of wine and the minstrel to play another song while he considered the latest news from his northern barons. Sir Walter Black had returned only that afternoon and reported that contrary to the words of Sir Simon de Montfort, Sir Robert de Courtelaine was not dead at all, but thought to be very much alive. Sir Walter had spoken not to Sir Robert's bride, but his mother.

"Why his mother and not his wife?" the King had asked.

"The lady is bed-ridden, ill with child your Majesty," answered Sir Walter.

The King grunted, accepting his messenger's reason. Left to his own counsels, Stephen was not a man to nit-pick and quarrel. He had fought for over a dozen years to maintain his grasp on a crown that had long ago lost its luster. It seemed that whenever his wife, the formidable Matilda of Boulogne, was away, his ambitions went with her. If she had been present when Sir Walter had given his report, that poor man might have found himself sacked before nightfall for not returning with the Earl of Malton's widow.

Sometimes when his bones ached and his mind wearied of the endless problems of state, King Stephen allowed himself to blame his clever ambitious wife for all his troubles. She and of course the other Matilda, his cousin the Empress Matilda, Stephen's constant combatant for the English throne. Once, while camped with his army, Stephen endeavored to wile away the night in a drunken revelry and with his wine induced approval, a minstrel had written a song, "My miserable life with too many Mauds". The King enjoyed it immensely and gave the minstrel a handful of bright pennies. The next day when he had sobered up he had the minstrel whipped for his impertinence.

"Your Highness."

"Eh?"

"About the Earl of Malton? Your Highness?"

Slowly the King pulled his thoughts back to the present, to the tired messenger before him.

"Ah, well, Black, what would it hurt to give the Earl a little while to show himself. Perhaps he is squirreled away with some young wench and has lost account of the passing days. We shall stay our judgment in this matter."

King Stephen remembered Robert de Courtelaine from the year before and had liked the bold youth. When the Lord Chamberlain had spoken hard words against de Courtelaine's father, de Courtelaine had advised the Lord Chamberlain he was welcome to return with him to his father's castle and tell the elder de Courtelaine face to face of his faults.

Even now, remembering the Lord Chamberlain's terror-filled eyes made the old King chuckle.

#11

Cam Fontennell often was required by the steward to journey to York. Before the Earl's disappearance Barclay would usually go himself, dealing with the merchants directly. Now he was deemed too valuable to leave Hammerstone and because Fontennell was trustworthy and of a quick mind, it fell to him to make the twice monthly journeys. Usually Cam took a half-dozen mounted soldiers with him for as soon as Sir Robert had gone the Bandit King, the one they called the Forest Ghost, had returned to raid the great road between Hammerstone and York. It was a testament to Cam's ascension within the hierarchy of the castle that he could, even at his young age, lead veteran soldiers successfully. What he lacked in years, he more than made up in ability and courage. He was tactful with his men, only checking their happy bantering when he felt the need to be wary and only Garfield the weaver could speed a gray goose shaft as well as Cam. Besides, Cam Fontennell had discovered the sweet joys of the world and the men knew that with young Cam they could count on a bit of fun at one of York's taverns.

One of their favorite inns was the Red Dragon near Clifford's Tower. The ale was good and the serving girls were a happy, friendly lot and not adverse to the odd stolen kiss. About a fortnight after the King's messenger had visited Hammerstone Castle, Cam and his fellows sat in the Red Dragon on sturdy benches along the back wall with stout ale at their elbows and crab apples boiling over the fire. By now the men of Hammerstone were treated with the familiarity of regulars and since Cam always paid with bright coin, the landlord took it upon himself to befriend their young leader. He would always send for his best ale and sit a spell with Cam and gossip.

Cam let it be known it was a high living crowd that ruled Hammerstone. What, with the huge costs of repairing the castle and hiring many mounted knights and the lady's love of fine things... Cam looked and motioned the landlord to draw in close. A great secret he would share for the sake of the kind hospitality provided.

"Mine own younger brother, a quick lad with the numbers, is the stewards counting clerk! Aye it's true!" Fontennell said.

"'Tis my own flesh and blood that counts the earl's money and he has told me that already fully half of the great hoard of gold found at the burned cottage has been spent."

Right well impressed was the landlord for this was news indeed. He nodded like the wise sage he knew he was, "Aye, Sir, 'tis true I doubt it not. We have heard of the Earl's habits. Why it is said that he bought his archers all buckles of pure silver and each man a shirt for everyday of the week!"

Cam Fontennell suppressed a smile, he was not wearing his archer's garb and the landlord would never guess this leader of Norman soldiers would also be a Saxon long-bowman. Cam let the tale stand uncorrected and simply agreed that Sir Robert had been a baron very free with his money. In truth, each archer had received a buckle but these were made of brass not silver and only one uniform per man was issued.

To show that he too was a man of knowledge, and a keeper of secrets, the landlord told Cam a bit of news.

"Ye know of course that his lordship Sir Robert de Courtelaine had a terrible fight with his brother, Sir Roger de Courtelaine?"

"Aye."

"Well now, when his lordship sent Sir Roger packing the knight and his friends came and stayed with us."

The landlord paused and leaned close to Cam so that their heads nearly touched. Cam noticed the older man had long gray hairs growing out of his nostrils, the longest he had ever seen.

"Now these young men were fond of their drink I can tell thee and Sir Roger grew weary of their company. He came to me and bid me total the bill and paying it he said he was leaving at once and to tell his playfellows when they awoke that he was called away to Londontown. His friends greatly distressed, left straightway for the capital also." The landlord could see that his tale was of no small interest to his listener.

"Aye, Sir, but here is the rub! Sir Roger never went south at all!"

"No?"

"Oh no, he went away to the north-east, up the Wold Way. Not only that, he hired away my best stable boy, Beck. I was sad to find the lad gone, I can tell thee!"

Cam Fontennell questioned the direction, "To the north-east ye say?"

"Aye. To throw his friends off the scent. Thou knows the northern road bends slowly around until it runs right back to the sea."

"The sea?"

"Aye, where else would a champion go to seek his fortune, but to foreign parts!"

Cam Fontennell nodded, seeing the sense of the landlord's guess. The landlord continued, "Now my brother's son worked upon the wharf at Kingston-by-the Sea and I sent word to him to look for a young knight, strong and dark-haired, attended to by my young man, Beck. Sure enough this very pair boarded a ship bound for Antwerp!"

"And then what?"

"Never heard of them since. Likely never will."

Cam Fontennell thanked the landlord for his hospitality and his story. Cam believed it all save one point. He was sure that Sir Roger de Courtelaine would return.

#12

Barclay, his ledgers done and in agreement, locked them away and took a walk out of the castle to see for himself how the Earl's money was being spent. Watching the workmen swarm up and down the walls, Barclay concluded the money was being consumed quickly.

He was pleased though as the eastern wall was at height and the row houses nestled against it were already enclosed and roofed. Several families would be in their new quarters by the feast of St. Stephen just as planned.

He spied Cam Fontennell up on the main south wall. Cam was standing with one of the stone masons aping the tradesman's every move. Why, Barclay could only guess. Boredom, maybe. Other than archery practice and Katoryna's bed, Cam had little to do.

Barclay climbed the nearest ladder and walked along the newly topped parapet to where the mason was showing Fontennell how to lay a nice even bed of mortar along the brick and how to use the trowel point to cove it out in the middle. He waved his trowel as he spoke, his voice oddly high pitched for a man so thick armed and burly. "Ye see now how I keep the mud wet and easy to spread. And mark ye also how I pull the mud down the wall, stretching it out."

Fontennell was so engrossed in his lesson that Barclay was looking over his shoulder before Cam noticed him.

"Changing trades are we?"

"Could be, Barclay, and as thou knows, knowledge is easy to carry."

"True enough, Cam, but can I take ye away for a bit?"

"Of course."

Barclay looked down along the wall. He had not actually seen the finished work until now. He felt Robert would have been proud of their accomplishments. The steward stopped himself ... *'would have been?'* He was now thinking of the Earl in the past tense, accepting his death. It saddened him and he walked away from young Cam lest the archer think him unmanly to show a tear.

Fontennell perceived Barclay's train of thought for he, too, keenly felt the absence of their liege lord. Barclay's attachment to Sir Robert was based on the long years of watching the able youth. Because of Sir Robert's trust in him, Barclay was well on his way to being a wealthy man.

Cam Fontennell regarded the Earl, not as a beloved son like the steward did, but as a great hero. To Cam's way of thinking Sir Robert could do no wrong. Had he not saved Cam and his siblings, fed them, gave them a home and above all, hunted down the thieves that had attacked them? Cam Fontennell was not ready to admit that such a man was dead. Not ready by a long shot.

When the steward had collected himself he turned back to where Cam stood, patiently waiting.

"Tell me, Fontennell, how goes they wooing of the Lady Katoryna?"

"Who can tell what a woman hides in the deeps of her heart? Her thoughts I have yet to know."

"Aye but rumor has it ye have grown right close," answered Barclay, pretending to watch the workers below them.

"Well ye did ask me to win her trust," said Cam.

"Aye, and the rest is of no concern to me. Think not that I would judge what you do in the dark of night."

A sparkle appeared in Cam's hand. A ring of gold set with a precious stone. Just as quickly it disappeared and Cam glanced about, sure no prying eyes could have seen it.

"The lady asked me to deliver this to a certain Jew in York along with a letter."

"She thinks she can trust ye?"

"No, she thinks I cannot read."

"That was well done, Cam."

"I am only doing what Katoryna asks."

"Why does the ring go to York?"

"The lady has need of money."

"I wonder why."

"Probably because I told her I have found her brother, Sir Roger."

"Did you?"

"Tell her?"

"No? Find Sir Roger?"

"In a manner of speaking."

"Indeed, tell me."

"Sir Roger left England a fortnight after his brother ordered him away. He abandoned his companions in York and hired a stable boy to be his squire. A Knight of the Temple and Sir Roger boarded a ship bound for a foreign placed called Antwerp. I think Sir Roger has joined the Knights of the Temple of Jerusalem."

Barclay looked at Cam in a respectful new light, "You have done well. 'Tis a shame ye cannot likewise uncover the whereabouts of his lordship."

"Aye, I've tried, God knows I've tried but there is nary a whisper anywhere about Sir Robert."

A loud burst of laughter interrupted their thoughts. There were two pulley lifts on the new wall powered by harnessed horses attached to heavy ropes. One of the horses had bolted, jerking the lift skyward and sending the man and the brick he was loading flying upwards. By lucky chance, and a stout pair of legs, he landed upright atop the scaffold, a feat that caught the fancy of his neighbours. They cheered him and he played the part well, bowing from his perch above their heads.

Cam and Barclay hurried along the top of the wall until they stood almost on the scaffolding. When the din had subsided, Cam called out to the man.

"Barry! The steward says be ye not so lazy and use the ladder next time!" More laughter. The acrobatic worker climbed back down and Cam and Barclay walked back across the new height of the wall.

"They are a happy lot in their labours," said Cam.

"Aye they should be, getting nice new cottages and all!"

Cam Fontennell smiled, "Come now, I know ye are pleased with this grand undertaking. Deny it not!"

Barclay ignored this comment, "About the Lady Katoryna, what do ye intend to do?"

"Do? What can I do but continue to aid her and learn her plans?"

Barclay realized Cam was right and that he would have to trust him completely in this matter. Somehow this youngster had made himself important beyond his years and this troubled the steward, for no one knew what thoughts ran behind those gray-blue eyes.

#13

Sir Simon de Montfort, the Earl of Leicester, was a man of unusual intelligence. He was bold when boldness was called for and discreet the rest of the time. When Kenton, his steward, came to him with news of the King's slothful response to the Earl of Malton's death, Sir Simon said very little. He was of the belief that every wall in the capital had ears. He questioned Kenton closely and then called for his supper.

"Shall I request another audience with His Majesty, Sir Simon?" asked de Montfort's steward.

"Nay, forget about the King's troubles as I have, and get thee prepared to go forth. I have a mind to go to the bear-pits this evening. The Duke of Devonshire has brought along some new hounds that he claims fight as if possessed by Lucifer himself."

"Yes m'lord."

The steward was old and had the wisdom of his years. He knew better than to question the actions of his lord. Even though they made the hard journey to Londontown for only one reason, namely to see the King force the widow de Courtelaine to remarry, and even though the King had ruined Sir Simon's plans, the Earl had said nothing.

As de Montfort's guards pushed their way through the mud of Watling Street, the steward wondered about the Earl's lack of action and as they paid the toll man at the high fenced bear pit, it came to him. De Montfort, knowing how slothful the Sovereign was when not at war, would wait until the Queen returned to Court. Looking at his master, the steward had to smile. Pushing through the filthy narrow streets the Earl had kept his head and expensive clothes covered with a heavy cloak because the wives of Londontown were none too careful about where they flung their dirty house water. To many of the Saxon population it was a great way to get back at their betters, dumping their waste all over some well-dressed Norman in the street far below.

Once they were safely in the crowded arena, Sir Simon pulled off his heavy cloak and a pathway magically opened before him. He picked a place to sit and the inhabitants of the ringside bench scattered. His lordship sat and his entourage crowded in on either side of him. Sir Simon snapped his fingers and a servant brought forth a large wineskin and delivered it to his master's waiting hand.

A dozen feet below the seating in the centre of a square sand-covered pit, sat a shaggy brown bear affixed to a thick post by means of a massive iron chain, several feet long. The bear sat quietly, his great furry head bowed as if he were at vespers. Now and then the beast would raise his head and sniff the air. Upon hearing the desperate barking of the approaching dogs the bear began to stir. As the hounds were led into the sand covered pit the crowd roared as one and the bear pulled to the end of its chain and swayed back and forth, the brown hair along his thick neck standing straight up.

The dogs, four in all, were led around the perimeter of the pit, all the while pulling on their leather leashes and jumping about so that only by hard and constant use of the whip could their handlers keep them on their course.

Now the roar of the crowd altered in pitch as the bettors picked their favourites and laid their wagers. Sir Simon scanned the rows of spectators. He tapped his steward's arm. "Cast thy eye about Kenton, cans't thou see the Duke of Devonshire in the press?"

The steward looked about, "Nay m'lord he is not present," he said after a moment's search. The Duke was a man renowned for his bright jackets and rich robes. If he were present, he would stick out like a pope in a peat bog. The master of ceremony, his tattered skullcap clutched in his grimy hands, shouted above the din, the veins in his neck bulging with the effort.

"My masters! My masters! Thy wagers are cast, let us begin!"

The hounds were released of their leashes and they attacked as one, snarling and fangs bared. The bear fell back to the centre pole and as the dogs jumped at him, the bear rose onto his hind legs and swatted at his tormentors. A might paw found flesh and a gray mottled dog cried out as it was flung a dozen feet back, its shoulder laid bare to the bone. His blood splattered onto the cheering aficionados.

#14

It was late and the City was asleep. Folk living a life of endless labour could ill afford to go without rest. Behind the heavy oaken door of the Oxford Arms and past the ever present guard, a smattering of the ruling nobility of the land played the night away in games and bouts of drinking.

Rich idle men, famous champions of the joust-yards, mercenaries and the like gathered here like moths to a light. It was here that the one time steward of Hammerstone found employ with the Earl of Crewe. Even King Stephen, in his younger days, could often be found within the tavern's walls.

Sir Simon de Montfort sat with his back to the wall near the middle of a long trestle table. His steward stood near his lordship, squeezed between baron and brick. Later, if he was lucky, his lordship would fall asleep and then Kenton would slip away for a bite to eat and a chance to rest his weary bones.

The butler would not have rest tonight though for a while. Sir Simon had struck up a conversation with Sir John Fitz Osbern, cousin of the Earl of Hereford and a fixture at the royal court. Sir Simon sent the butler to fetch his wine.

"Come Sir John, what news of Londontown?"

"Not much, Sir Simon, more of the usual. The King tried to convince Archbishop Theobald to guarantee the crown to Eustace no matter what happens. Prince Henry, it is rumoured, will invade in the new year."

"How shall the boy pay for such a voyage? I'll wager he never repaid the cost of 1147."

"True, but the King's spies claim the youngster will be formally given the duchy of Normandy."

De Montfort let out a slow whistle. This was news indeed. Another blow to Stephen's grip on the throne. With the wealth of Normandy at his disposal, Henry could raise a proper army. Sir John Fitz Osbern continued on, "The Queen has not yet returned from Kent."

"Kent? I thought Her Majesty would travel to Devonshire and then to the Abbey at Furness."

"Nay, the King and Queen have founded another abbey. It is to be called, I believe, Faversham."

"Indeed! Not on the scale of Furness though, surely?"

Sir John shook his bald head, "Nay, Sir Simon, the King's purse is not as deep as it once was, although no doubt his need for divine intercession is greater than ever."

De Montfort took a long pull at the large wineskin that his steward kept close by.

"I was never a great adherent to the belief that the constant mumblings of a herd of monks would buy me favour with the Almighty. In fact, the argument could be made, I suppose, that the Deity might well find these constant supplications to be rather tiresome. Just imagine it, Sir John, the din of thousands of monks across Europe, all praying for the souls of a few black-hearted kings and barons. Why, he would scarcely appreciate still another hive droning on."

"I never thought of it like that," said Fitz Osbern.

And the two drank until the Earl's wineskin was wrinkled and empty.

#15

The Tower of London stood beside the river Thames, a fear-inspiring symbol of Norman might. Built of white stone in the familiar square Norman fashion, few fortresses had ever become more famous or been able to instill such dread as the Conqueror's Keep. Her soaring heights and deep dungeons had little effect on Sir Simon de Montfort. The Earl of Leicester feared very little and regarded any visit to Stephen's court as a chance for personal gain. With nary a second thought, de Montfort dismissed his guards at the Tower and entered the fortress alone.

Queen Matilda of Boulogne had returned to Londontown on the New Year and was not at all surprised to find that the King and most of his court had gone hunting. Stephen had left only lesser officials to await the Queen's return.

No sooner had the Queen settled into her apartments then she had called for an official record of the court while she was away.

When that had been duly read to her, she then gathered about her certain household staff and they all related the real news of the day to her. Who was bedding whom, and how the King had spent his days and what word from Normandy and what her sons were about.

The Queen took in the news without comment. Stephen had bought himself a new raptor, this time a small hawk, hardly fit to ride the arm of a knight, let alone the King's. Why on earth would he not stick to peregrines? They at least were the suitable tool of a sovereign.

Long ago Matilda had resigned herself to her husband's slothful rule. How a man so bold and accomplished on the battlefield could be so timid at all other times was the question that dogged her married life. He was truly a genius tactician, but a fool of a strategist. Now well past his prime, the King had long lost interest in the day to day business of the kingdom. It was lucky for Stephen that the Queen, a direct descendant of Alfred the Great through her great grandmother, St. Margaret of Scotland, was well suited to govern. Or so thought the Queen.

Now the Queen asked those that attended her to list what guests awaited a royal audience. The list was long and dotted with men of prominence and position. And here they waited while the King enjoyed the hunt. Matilda sighed, "Whom shall we see first?" she asked the Chancellor and the old man offered up the opinion that she might have time to greet one supplicant before the evening meal.

The Chancellor, as head of the royal clerks, was certain that, of the guests, the Earl of Leicester, Sir Simon de Montfort would surely take up the least of Her Highness's time. A sweet little speech that lightened Sir Simon's purse by ten shillings. The Chancellor only made five shillings a day officially, but accepted various gratitudes as a perk of the job. And who could blame him. Someone had to keep things moving.

"Show the Earl in," the Queen instructed with a nod of her head. A moment later Sir Simon de Montfort was ushered into the royal apartments. The Earl saw nothing he had not seen before. He needed barely a glance about the room to note the absence of anything new. Matilda was not a spendthrift he thought idly.

He came straightaway to the dais and offered the Queen a deep bow.

"Arise, Sir Simon, thou art most welcome here. Come now, and give us news of Leicester."

Sir Simon accepted a flagon of wine and, toasting the Queen, drank. To his eye Her Majesty was looking older, the crow's feet around her eyes more pronounced and there was weariness about her. Still, the sharp-edged beauty of days past was there even after twenty-four years of strife. Sir Simon well remembered how, when Stephen was captured at Lincoln and all seemed lost, it was this thin woman before him that had drawn on a backbone of iron and almost by her will alone, had rallied their supporters and turned the tide back to her husband's favour. De Montfort admired her fortitude, but shuddered to imagine what it would be like to be married to such a masculine-thinking woman. He pushed aside these ponderments and answered Her Highness.

"Leicester is a quiet land, the weather is fine and the serfs obedient!"

"How fortunate," said the Queen, not knowing what could have brought de Montfort to court. He was a known schemer and the Queen was wary of such men. "Your lady is well?"

"Indeed, Your Highness, never better."

And this, the Queen reckoned, was ample polite conversation. "Tell us Sir Simon, what brings you to court? How might we assist you?"

"Not at all Your Highness! I come with your interests at heart."

The Queen's blue eyes narrowed, "How so?"

"The Duke of Devonshire tells me that the King has graciously founded a monastery at Faversham in Kent."

"That is true."

"Of course, Your Highness, well I could only assume it is a heavy debt to incur what with the young Anjou pup once again raising an army against your throne."

The Queen sat up, "What have you heard exactly, Sir Simon?"

"Only what the rest of the Londontown knows. That Geoffrey of Anjou is giving young Henry his inheritance very soon if he hasn't already done so."

"And?"

"And perhaps the King has not yet exploited all the revenues owed to him."

"Ladies," said the Queen with an abrupt wave that sent her servants to the far end of the chamber. She turned to de Montfort.

"Now Sir Simon, pray tell me what is on your mind."

"Dids't thou know that the Earl of Malton has been missing for many weeks, nay, months even, and he had been cruelly wounded besides. He leaves a young bride, pregnant of course, and a treasury of three thousand pounds. All of this left to the mercies of her northern neighbours. With no husband to protect her, how long shall the King's ward be safe?"

"The Earl of Malton is dead? Are you sure Sir Simon?" The Queen cast a searching look at de Montfort. He seemed sure of himself as always. Of medium height and lean of frame, Sir Simon was not a physically imposing man. His countenance was likewise unremarkable. Neither handsome nor homely, his hair was thinning and turned early to gray.

It was only when one observed the Earl of Leicester in motion that he began to impress. There was fearlessness about him, self-confidence in his manner and speech that suggested abilities unguessed. His gray eyes missed nothing, not even the slight tremor in the Queen's hands, a sign surely that his seeds of thought had been sown into a fertile field.

Queen Matilda's mind quickly saw what a financial boon the death of de Courtelaine could be. And not at a better time. Death and inheritance taxes, scuttage rates to be reset and if the young widow was comely so much the better.

As if the Earl could read her mind, he said, "She is a fine young thing and my brother claims a bit of a beauty."

The Queen smiled, *'Ah, here was a quick-witted man,'* she thought.

"Tell me good Sir, what would ye have done, were ye the King?"

"Were I the King? Ha! Never have I heard such a novel thought. It is so completely foreign to me!" Sir Simon said in a tone of deep shock.

The Queen laughed, "Oh Sir, thou art a liar. No man of your kind has not thought of wearing a crown."

"Your Highness!" he said in protest.

"Nay, fear not for I like your speech, Sir Simon. You are one of the few who are actually capable of an original thought. So now kindly reply to my question."

"Of course, Your Highness. I would send for the dead Earl's wife. Bring her to court."

"But she says her husband lives."

"Fine, fine then bring her to court until his return or his death can be confirmed. Take a scuttage fee, a relief fee for her unborn child and then marry her off to a loyal and trusted vassal."

"Anyone in mind, Sir Simon?"

"Possibly."

"For a fee?"

"Of course."

"As always, Sir Simon, thou has`t given His Majesty some food for thought," said the Queen offering the Earl her gloved hand. He bowed down and kissed it, then slowly backed himself out of the royal apartment.

As soon as the Earl had departed, the Queen called for a report of the King's whereabouts and for a royal messenger to carry a note to His Highness. She inquired into the whereabouts of her sons. William, the younger, was with the King, and Eustace was away scouting the southern coast for signs of Henry's arrival and re-assuring the King's supporters. The same as always, the son had more sense than the father. Matilda sighed and made herself press on. It was foolish to dwell on things that could not be changed. She would talk with her brother-in-law, Henry of Blois, the bishop of Winchester. The bishop was the richest priest in England and the Queen was of a mind to canvass him for some gospel books and vestments for the new abbey at Faversham. More importantly Matilda wished to pick his marvelous mind on the subject of the passing on of tithed lands and the remarrying of widows.

Sir Simon was warmly greeted at the Gates of the Tower by Kenton, his steward. Together with six guards, the Earl walked along the north bank of the Thames, east toward the fishmongers' wharves, passing along the way the occasional cluster of revelers still dressed up from All Fools Day. In London the foolery was taken to extremes and the mayor had to hire a special troop to control the crowds during the holidays. Sir Simon de Montfort cared not a wit for such goings on and went straightaway to his lodgings. In the morning next, he would return to Leicester.

#16

The King returned at last from his hunting, the game was plentiful and Stephen was flushed with the warm glow of the chase. He called for his wine, but before he could sate his thirst and even as his lips touched the silver rim, the Queen stepped out of the shadows. She bowed slowly, welcoming her husband home through a tight smile and not for the first time did Stephen note how masculine his wife could make herself appear.

"Your duties await thee, Your Highness," she said.

"I would have thought you would have attended to such things."

"A Queen can only do so much, I know my place. I trust ye know yours."

Then a great weariness came upon the King, "Come away then," he said.

The royal hunting party dispersed and the Queen, as she turned to follow the King, hissed at Sir Walter Black, "Come." Matilda ordered Sir Walter to wait outside the King's solar until he was called for. She did not wait for her husband to get undressed, but instead paced up and down between his bed and the fireplace.

"Can't thou tell me why the Earl of Malton's death seems to be of such little import to Your Highness? I had no idea that the royal treasury was so full that ye had no need of de Courtelaine's death fees. And what of Sir Walter Black's journey to Hammerstone Castle? What did he do there?" On and on she went, but the King heard little. Long ago he had perfected the art of not listening. Only the Queen's summoning of Sir Walter drew in the King's attention.

In his mind's eye, Sir Walter Black thought the royal couple looked for all the world like an animal tamer with a pet bear. The Queen, tiny but loud, the trainer, and the King, his great limbs and shaggy hair, the quivering bear. Wisely he pushed these thoughts aside and awaited his Queen's pleasure.

Her Majesty motioned impatiently with her hand for the knight to approach the royal chair.

"Many a strange tale I've been told since my return Sir Walter."

"Indeed, Your Highness," answered the knight.

"One rumour is that ye have ridden almost to Scotland to seek out a ward of the crown, only to return empty-handed! Can this be true?"

The knight scarcely knew what to say.

"Can it, Sir Walter?"

"N...Not...entirely Your Highness."

"How so?"

"Well it seems that the young lady in question is not really a ward of the crown. Apparently the Lady of Hammerstone is not a widow."

The Queen stood up and paced around the knight, "And how did you come to this decision over I might add, the direct advice of this court?"

Sir Walter Black shifted uncomfortably. What could he possibly say? He could only take his chances and tell the Queen the truth.

"His family, Your Highness, they seemed sure that the Earl lives."

"And what proof do they have that he does live?"

"What proof does the court have that he does not?"

The Queen's sharp features grew ruddy, "You dare debate me?" she said, staring daggers at Sir Walter.

Sir Walter fell to one knee and bowed low, "Forgive me Your Highness."

King Stephen spoke, "I have met this young Earl. A brave man, I wot. Even now I can see him dressing down the Lord Chamberlain." The King chuckled to himself.

"Yes, yes, he was a brave man, but now most like, he is dead. We should bring his widow here where she would be safe and then when the King does declare him dead, she shall be handy by where no-one can steal her estate," stated the Queen.

The King cast a wary glance at his wife. He knew full well what his scheming Queen was about. She intended to separate young bride from her husband's wealth.

"Aye, Matilda, we can bring the young lady here but I shall give her a husband some time yet. After all, he is young and strong, perhaps he will appear."

An hour later Sir Walter Black was again on the great northern road bound for Hammerstone Castle.

#17

A squire walked quickly through a crowded market past the peddlers and merchants, ignoring their cries in his haste. He strode past the town gates and into a meadow laid fallow. Dozens of brightly painted tents stood clustered about a mock battlefield, the perimeters of which were defined by a temporary fence of rope hung on sharpened staves of beech, driven into the ground.

The squire crossed the field around the groups of serfs who were charged with smoothing the field for the next day's conflict. In the centre of the field where the lists had run, he carefully lifted his costly cloak lest he muddy the fringes or dirty his rich hose. He could feel eyes upon him, jealous glances of the other servants and his purse, heavy with gold coin. At last he came to a pavillion of plain brown. No gaily hung ribbons flew here, only a battered war shield emblazoned with a rearing black stallion.

Two armed slaves stood before the entrance and held the curtain aside for the young man. Through another curtained chamber, he entered a room of oriental splendor where rich tapestries hung and new carpets covered the ground. Centered within was a large couch occupied by a man and woman. They continued their coupling and only when the squire spoke did they give pause.

"A word with ye, m'lord?"

"Can it not wait?" said the man from atop the girl.

"I think not, I've a message from Sir Neville Farnham."

Sir Roger de Courtelaine rolled off and with a snap of his fingers ordered the girl to stand. As she stood, he patted the soft round of her bottom, "'Tis a shame we must stop my sweet, yours is as honeyed a saddle as I've ever ridden."

The girl smiled at Sir Roger and wiggled into her dress even as Beck eased her out of the tent. He slipped a few coins into her hand and she thanked him. He turned away, the wench already forgotten, and addressed his master.

"Sir Neville has just returned from England. He sent a message from the court of King Stephen. Sir Robert de Courtelaine, the Earl of Malton is dead and even now, his widow is being called to attend the King at court."

De Courtelaine was already pulling on his hose, "We shall leave within the hour. Go ye to the other knights and tell them so."

"Aye m'lord, but I doubt they will welcome the news. They are counting on you to lead them in tomorrow's melee."

"Tell them it cannot be helped. Grave matters are afoot! I want to be to the coast before the week is out."

De Courtelaine was soon besieged by a score of angry combatants. To a man they had staked their hopes of victory and prize money on Sir Roger's lance. Now he was leaving without so much as a by your leave. Sir Roger sat in the mist of these angry wasps unmoved by their begging while his servants hurried to pack away his camp.

After the last of the disappointed knights had left, Beck helped his master with his travelling cloak and held his stirrup.

"Shall we ride for Calais, m'lord?"

"Nay, Antwerp, I must speak with the Grandmaster of our Order."

#18

Sir Walter Black had returned to Hammerstone. Maken had held out hope that he would not, but in her heart she knew better. This time, at least, she was prepared. A great feast was readied and Sir Walter was seated next to Maken in the great hall. Not only were all of the castle's regular troops assembled, but all of the archers too. A grand sight was the hall with every guest wearing his or her best clothes, and each archer his new belt and shiny buckles.

Seated as he was, close to Maken, Sir Walter could not help but note the lady's advancing gestation. Maken made a humble apology to the royal messenger for not receiving him personally on his first visit. This, Sir Walter accepted with grace.

When Maken expressed happy surprise at being honoured with another royal visit the King's man repeated the Queen's desire to see Maken safely at Stephen's court. At this Maken looked at Sir Walter in wonder and laughed. "Can ye possibly believe my life could be in danger whilst I reside among a force of men such as what sits here before ye?"

Sir Walter conceded the point that yes, the castle seemed secure enough, that yes, the lady was rather far along and no Her Majesty had not in fact declared Lord Robert to be dead officially.

Sir Walter was given a letter composed by Father Hubert in the most respectful of wording, attesting to this same position. The royal messenger made no comment to Maken although he knew full well that when he returned, the Queen's most trusted servants, men who would carry out her wishes without question, would likely accompany him.

In the courtyard as his servants prepared to take their leave, the Earl's bride once again approached Sir Walter. Nodding to a large box that an old man held,

Maken said, "A gift for His most Royal Majesty from the Earl of Malton, Sir Robert de Courtelaine. I pray that you can find it convenient to carry this to the King.

"Indeed M'lady."

The storm that Sir Walter expected would greet him when he returned to Londontown fell with a fury that seemed to rattle the very roof of the White Tower. The messenger had hoped to find King Stephen alone, but the Queen, anticipating his return, was awaiting him in her usual place beside her husband. She demanded to know where the Lady of Hammerstone was. Her anger seemed to radiate from her body, from her fingers clenched about the arms of the chair to the scarlet of her cheeks.

The King seemed bored and it was to him that Sir Walter Black directed his answers.

"I saw the lady in question Your Highness."

"And?"

"She is indeed quite heavy with child."

"All the more reason to bring her here to court!" said the Queen impatiently, "At least she would be guarded here in the tower."

The Queen looked at Sir Walter, her contempt plain. Many a man would have cowered before the royal anger but not the old veteran. Too many times in the heat of battle he had stepped between Stephen and death. Too many hardships he had shared and survived at the King's side for him to fear the King's wrath. No one questioned his loyalty. When the Empress's men had taken Stephen prisoner and his fortunes were at their lowest, it was Sir Walter Black that fought beside and was taken with King Stephen. Bonds forged in war are rarely cast aside.

Now once more standing before his King, Sir Walter answered the royal couple as honestly as he could.

"Did she not know I...um... we wish her to come?" asked the Queen.

Before the knight could answer the King spoke, "There was a time when the Earl of Malton kept as fine a garrison as could be found in any castle in England. Is this Hammerstone guarded as in days former?"

"Aye Your Highness. My supper I ate along with at least one hundred and fifty men and each man it seemed was of fighting age. The King chuckled, "Ah.. there ye have it my good Queen. Your little lost waif sits in a strong fortress with a full complement of soldiery to maintain her."

"That is not the point my lord. The point...."

"The point! The point! I say to you m'lady take care that ye don't embroil me in still another coil. And if ye are so sure that Robert of Malton has indeed perished then kindly produce proof. I weary of thy tale!"

The Queen fumed but said nothing. For some reason the King had a liking for these de Courtelaines.

"There's one more thing, Your Highness."

"Well?"

Sir Walter motioned to servants waiting at the door. Two of them quickly carried a large box into the King's presence. As they sat it down, Sir Walter carefully untied the cloth that covered it. He drew the cloak away revealing a peregrine falcon in a wrought-iron cage. The King left his dais and approached the large raptor. His eyes shone.

"A gift for His Majesty from Robert de Courtelaine, the Earl of Malton," said Sir Walter.

"Now this is a gift fit for a King!" said Stephen. He circled the cage, "Is he trained, Sir Walter?"

"To the best of my knowledge this bird was trained by the late Sir Reginald de Courtelaine."

"Ha! Then I have heard of this creature. Right famous is she. We shall work her this very day."

Queen Matilda took her leave and as she did the King's triumphant voice carried across the chamber lashing the retreating royal.

85

"Surely we cannot but pray for this young Earl to have a long life, he that sends us such magnificent gifts!"

Later, after she had drank some Flemish wine and had her hair combed out, the Queen allowed herself to consider the young woman standing in her way, far north in a gray stone castle. Naturally Matilda had learned all she could about the Lady de Courtelaine. Rumors of the young bride abounded, that she was a Saxon, a woodcutter's daughter, that she rode into battle dressed as a man beside her husband, that he had saved her from being burned alive. Despite herself, the Queen felt a twinge of admiration for Maken. The girl had heart and boldness in her conduct — and this latest trick, giving his Majesty a new hunting bird. Brilliant. Stephen would undoubtedly leave the de Courtelaine alone for months because of it. The Queen would have to find a new avenue to Hammerstone Castle's counting room.

In the afternoon King Stephen called for his huntsmen and his falcons. He rode north into the rich hunting grounds of South Essex and there he gave his new peregrine a taste of open sky. The great bird lived up to its fame, taking a grouse in her first flight and later, a blackbird. King Stephen named her Arletta, after the Conqueror's mother.

#19

Sir Roger de Courtelaine stood silently before John March, his Master of the preceptory. His head was bowed, chin on his chest as he waited the decision of his superior.

Roger, upon hearing of his brother's demise, had ridden with all speed to his home chapter in Antwerp. Long had he cast his thoughts toward England, ever wishing revenge on his brother. Now it seemed fate had sent him his chance.

Just when Roger was ready to draw forth his blade and skewer the master for making him wait like some no account serf, the white-haired warrior spoke, "So brother Roger, ye wish to found a new chapter of the Temple back in your native lands."

"Yes master."

The older knight looked long at de Courtelaine. March was sixty years old and for thirty of those years he had been a Knight of the Temple, *'The Order of the Poor Knights of Christ and the Temple of Solomon'*, to be exact about the matter. He had been among the original warrior-monks who travelled to the Court of Baldwin I, King of Jerusalem. Their purpose was to keep the roads safe for Christian pilgrims travelling to the Holy Land. His face was etched with deep lines but his eyes were clear and his body still gave testament to great strength. He distrusted Roger de Courtelaine. In the young Norman, he saw none of those qualities which had originally marked their Order: poverty, chastity and obedience. For many of their younger members, the Templars were no longer quite the "militia of Christ" that marked the early years. Champions like Roger de Courtelaine had indeed swelled the Temple ranks with new recruits but they were there for the wrong reasons.

John March sighed. He would be glad to be rid of this arrogant upstart. "Ye knows, Brother Roger, that the Temple cannot finance the new chapters?

"Yes."

"And you can?"

"Yes."

"Your brother's death has left you his title?"

"Yes."

"And ye intend on founding a chapter at ye father's castle?"

"Yes."

"Well then who would discourage such a plan? I shall send ye to our Grandmaster at Gisors.

"Gisors? Gisors, France?"

"Of course, where else?"

"But I am in need of haste."

"Yes and ye are also in need of the Grand Master's permission!" Sir Roger held his tongue and forced himself to bow, "Of course master."

"Now ye may ready yourself for your journey. With any luck at all ye will be in England with the Grandmaster's blessing by spring."

"Yes master."

"Now go and call my clerk; ye shall need a letter of introduction."

That evening, while the other Templars were at vespers, Roger and his servant, Beck, were away, riding hard for France.

#20

January came and went and likewise February passed and yet the King's messenger did not reappear. It was as if he had never come at all and Maken, swollen and heavy with child, began to think that the King had indeed forgotten about her.

Now in the final weeks of her confinement, Maken was in constant pain. The mid-wife was called and she pronounced the baby unusually large. When she walked, the weight against her back stabbed Maken like needles, her legs would go numb and she would stumble.

Finally she was forced to retire to her bed, much to her discontent. Long and dreary became her days. With little to do but wait for her labour to come, Maken began to reflect and ponder her future and a black gloom fell over her. At long last she faced the death of Robert and bitter tears she wept. Her mother was called to stay with her and Mary, her childhood friend, but they could do little to lift her spirits. Father Hubert was subjected to anguished grilling. How could God be so cruel as to allow such sorrows to happen to his children? The priest let her go on; he knew that Maken needed to vent her rage more than she needed a lesson in theology.

Maken found sleeping to be next to impossible. She grew pale and listless and would order everyone out of the solar while she stayed alone. This distressed her mother who thought it odd that Maken did not wish for company. Old Frida was ordered to stay near her and by mid-March the midwife declared the arrival of the baby to be soon.

Barclay came into his own during these bleak days. He ran the castle alone and did it well. His great responsibilities never intimidated him again.

Father Hubert prayed every day for the birth of Maken's child and fervently hoped for a male heir. But 'hoped' only — he felt it was wrong to ask the Almighty for a boy. Rather he prayed for the safety of the mother and child. And safer by far, would be for the birth of a son, an instant Earl, someone far harder to disinherit. Still, a boy would not guarantee much; infant mortality among titled wards of the crown was very high.

The walls of the new village grew steadily, the north wall with its snug homes tucked under its inner side was finished in February, and the Lady Camille laid the last brick on a windy afternoon.

A great debate began on whether or not the west wall should be gated. If two gates, one would be at either end of the village. It would be logical and handy for movement and loading grain from the new gristmill. On the other hand, two gates would be more difficult to defend than one. Long did Barclay consider these things, bidding the master masons to work on the far end of the wall until at last he decided to have only one gate.

The steward felt the safety of Hammerstone and the strength of her walls was paramount. The second gate was rejected above the protests of the village tradesmen and Barclay hired even more workers, urging them to raise the walls with all haste. Anchoring the expanse of the west wall was a gristmill, a full three stories high. Its foundations pushed deep into the river.

April came and still Maken did not deliver. A woman of Sheffield, born of that race of unbelievers, so severely persecuted but yet famed for her knowledge of ancient eastern medicines, was sent for. And despite the deep affection most felt for Maken there were none eager to fetch the Jew, all the way back to Hammerstone. Only when Cam Fontennell returned from one of his patrols did Maken find her champion. Stopping barely long enough to change horses he procured a sum of gold and was gone.

How Cam secured the Jew's services he never told but two days after he left the castle gates, he returned, the woman exhausted beyond belief on a horse beside him. Her name was Lydia.

Cam led her into the Keep. The servants scurried away as if the woman carried the plague in her woven bag. Cam offered her food but this she declined until she could visit the patient.

Her prognosis mirrored the mid-wife's. Maken was in the last days of her time and the agonies she felt could be attributed to the unusual size of the baby. The contents of the Jew's bag made the trip worthwhile for the woman brought with her a strong narcotic that she said came from far away, in the land of the Turks. Such was the nature of this sorcery that even a minute amount of the drug would cast the user into a deep sleep. Thus drugged, Maken rested.

Seeing Maken quietly sleeping, Lydia could turn her thoughts toward finding a quick return to the house of her father in Sheffield. She knew once her task was completed the archer's promise to see her safely home would be held in very light regard. However, on this point, Lydia was mistaken.

Cam Fontennell, having learned that Maken now slept soundly, gave up his pallet to the Jewish maiden and informed her that he would take her home to Sheffield as soon as the baby was born.

Cam showed her the way to the kitchen and saw to it that she was given sup. Her appetite sated, he showed her to his quarters and gave her instructions on how to bar the door.

Lydia was much affected by this show of kindness, for never did she hope to find a friendly face in this infamous castle.

"I thank thee for thy kindness."

Cam brushed aside her thanks, "Nay lady, it is I who stands indebted to you for the peaceful slumber ye have brought our Lady."

"But the daughter of Zion...."

"Tut, tut, now, I hold little regard for who ye may or may not pray to. My own family was slain by a band of English bandits who to a man called themselves Christian even as Sir Robert hung them!"

And with that declaration Cam took his leave.

Cam Fontennell walked down the hall after leaving his chamber and went straight to Lady Katoryna's large apartment. He knocked on the door and was answered by one of Katoryna's serving maids. "'Tis Fontennell m'lady."

The door swung open and Cam entered. Katoryna sent her maids scurrying out with an impatient wave. Cam removed his clothing and fell into Katoryna's canopied bed. She might have spoken up at his presumption and indeed, if her maids had been present she would have been forced to, just to save face. Now alone with him, lying so close, she said nothing. She simply removed her gown and slipped in beside him. In her mind were a dozen grievances she meant to present to him, to upbraid him for ignoring her for days on end, for bringing a Jew into the castle. These things Katoryna considered as she lay beside Fontennell and when she finally began to speak she found to her great disappointment that her lover was asleep. Katoryna curled in tight to his warmth and cursed her own weakness.

#21

Katoryna woke before Cam, and quietly slipped out of bed. She padded across the floor and opened the door. Instantly two maids were before their mistress. "Go ye to the kitchen and fetch up a goodly meal. And mind ye, if he awakes before ye return, ye shall feel the whip!" The maids ran.

Katoryna's apartment had a seat built into the window recess and here she sat still as a mouse, gazing at Fontennell. The morning meal was delivered and Katoryna dismissed her maids and when he finally awoke, she brought the platter of food to the bed. He ate quickly his mind already wrestling with the problem of keeping the unbeliever safe until the Lady could deliver her child. All the while he spoke not but finally he finished and then he turned his attentions to his bed partner.

"Come now, why the long face?"

Katoryna had begun to pout, her lower lip protruding like a young child's might. "You avoid me", she said.

"Nay, m'lady."

"I've not seen ye in days."

"I have many duties; errands have left me saddle-sore and weary."

"Yes, I've seen somewhat of these errands. Tasks that no true Christian would stoop to!"

"What? The Jew? Does thou not know the unbeliever has the wisdom of Solomon in her pouches?"

"Then take the pouches and leave her where you found her, why bring her here to pollute these true walls?"

Cam laughed out loud. He had little time for religious argument and particularly when it came from such a libertine as Katoryna.

"These true walls! What makes these walls true, unless ye refer to quality of their construction?" he said.

Katoryna collected the dishes from the meal and placed the platter on a sideboard near the door. Until she met Cam Fontennell she never felt the urge to do anything in the least ways domestic but now she found herself attending to her quiet lover like a lowly handmaiden. Somehow she took comfort in seeing to his needs.

It made her feel closer to him and she grew jealous to think of another woman, even a servant making his bed or preparing his meals.

And she hated herself for it. When Fontennell was away she could work up her temper and she would promise herself that she would be strong and put Cam in his place. But then he would return, his self-confidence a granite cliff that stood unaffected by the crashing waves of her anger.

She, who could make a man morose with her silence or a servant tremble with a glare, could not move Cam Fontennell to any state of emotion save in the pleasures of her bed. And this she knew would eventually pass and unless she found a greater hold on his heart, he would cast her aside. Ever she was looking for clues to his plans, his hopes, but in this Katoryna was unsuccessful. And still she tried.

"How wonderful it must be to have Cam Fontennell at your beck and call as my sister-in-law has."

"I owe Lord Robert my life and the lives of my kin likewise. Far be it from me to deny the Lady in her hour of need."

"Noble thoughts, but how long the hour? Doest thou not know a time shall come, and soon, that Maken shall be married off to the highest bidder? And then what? Where shall ye find shelter?"

"You quote things beyond my keen. I cannot worry myself with these concerns. Her fate is her own. And mine is mine."

"Aha! But there is where ye are wrong. Ye can do much for her!"

"I listen but hear no case, only riddles."

Katoryna came to him and grasped his arms and looked into his eyes, "Find my brother Roger. If he returns and is restored to his inheritance the Saxon lass shall be free to live her own life, her child safe under an uncle's kindness. And as for Cam Fontennell, you shall be a friend of the powerful, your chair in the castle hall secure."

"And how shall it be secure? I know not Roger de Courtelaine. Why would he call me a friend?"

"Nay, Cam, not just friend, but brother. Ye need a wife and I need a champion."

#22

Eustace, the King's oldest son, returned from the southern shires with grave tidings. All the rumours that raced through the capital during the winter were proven true in the bloom of spring. Henry of Anjou, freckle faced and red-haired, had indeed been given duchy of Normandy as a gift from his father.

Now rich with the taxes of his vast new holdings the ambitious teenager could at long last engage King Stephen in any way he saw fit.

In the south of England Stephen could count on only a few nobles to maintain their loyalty to his throne. Stephen approached his brother, the Bishop of Winchester, in an attempt to have Eustace named heir but to his great dismay he was refused. Even his own brother seemed to be perched happily on the fence.

Stephen gathered his supporters about him, and braced himself once more for war. A war he knew could well be the end of him and his line. Faced with his greatest challenge in ten years, the old King roused himself to the task.

Collected about him, three hundred knights, Stephen rode east into the fen lands to drum up the support of the barons that ruled those unhappy estates. Next into the beech forests of the heartland, Oxfordshire, Hertfordshire and north to Warwickshire and up Fosse Way. And at each stop the King would bargain for a renewed support. Lands, easements, new hunting rights and tokens of friendships that could lay waste to the treasury, were dice rolled by a desperate ruler gambling the future of the realm against the needs of today.

Near the end of his journey, Stephen and his retinue rode up to the castle of Sir Simon de Montfort. The King was well received; the banquet hall lacked for nothing befitting an Earl's table.

Sir Simon's spies, well-placed and well-paid, made sure that, before the King had settled into his rooms, his host knew intimate details of every promise Stephen had uttered in this latest campaign. As the day fell into night and the feasting ebbed away Stephen told Sir Simon of his great need of troops.

In his time the conqueror would have held the discussion to one word, "Come!" and the lords of England would have marched. But Stephen was no William and Sir Simon de Montfort feared him not. When the King called upon the Earl to honour his pledge, Sir Simon begged off.

"Ah Your Majesty, thou knows that my own lands are under new threat. My neighbours, and especially the Earl of Warwickshire, have been enriched by Your Majesty's generosities. I know that they are ever looking for the advantage against me." Sir Simon allowed himself to become angry, "'Tis not right!"

The King shook his head, "Nay, Sir Simon, thou knows the lies that follow a crown. Little have I promised for little do I have. Rights of hunting, fishing grants, nothing more."

De Montfort said nothing.

The King and his Earl stared across the silence for many minutes until the last wisp of pretense disappeared.

The King, an impatient man in all things save the hunt, could wait no longer.

"Come now, de Montfort, what is it thou needs? Already ye know what thy King needs."

Sir Simon de Montfort suppressed a strong urge to laugh. The King would have been far wiser to bring his Queen, a born negotiator, along with him He could hunt and she would fool the barons. De Montfort came to the point.

"All reasonable men agree the Earl of Malton is dead, the widow needs a husband, and her lands need a firm Norman hand."

"And?"

"And my son needs a title of his own."

"Continue."

"Ye marry the widow to my son and in return ye take the money hidden away at Hammerstone. Rumour sets the amount at three thousand pounds. Plus, of course, my son would certainly wish to show his loyalty with a strong pledge of mounted knights. Say, twice the usual number?"

"Well, Sir Simon, ye seem to have this all thought out right cleverly."

"Nay, Your Highness, 'tis nothing but common sense."

The King slouched deeper into his chair.

De Montfort said, "Your Highness? Now is not the time to hesitate, now is the time to be swift and now is the time to be sure of your friends."

The old man hardly heard the Earl's final arguments; he knew what he had to do, so great were his needs that nothing else mattered.

He agreed to de Montfort's plan, donned his ermine lined cloak, and retired for the night. Tired that he was, the King called for a strong wine and drank deeply of it before sleep would come.

#23

Maken screamed. And again. Deep long primoral wails that started in her belly and burst forth in torrents of pain. Loud agonies that gave the kitchen maids cause to pause in their labours and listen to hers. The older maids crossed themselves, the younger ones trembled and stared at one another, doubting their own ears.

At last the blessed day she had long dreaded was come. In the dead of night it had started, with a flood of water and a thick shaft of pain. And now the sun stood highest in the spring sky. Frida, the old mid-wife was there as was Maken's mother, Sarah. Worry etched across Sarah's face for the labour was hard and with little to show even after so many long hours. Twice Frida had probed with her long withered hands and now she sat at the bedside. To her the outlook was bleak. In these cases, more often than not, the babe died, or the mother died, or both would not survive the terrible strains of birth. And with a babe that large, his head would tear the mother dreadfully, causing a great loss of blood. Worse news than that, the babe was sideways and had stopped its descent. The Lady was in agony and little could be done.

Sarah paced and implored Frida to do whatever she possibly could. Frida, feeling slighted, assured Sarah that anything she could do she had already done. 'Twas not her fault the babe was big and not her fault Maken was young and her hips narrow.

Maken cried out and curled up in a ball, her legs tight against the curve of her belly. Naked, she rocked back and forth, the bedsheets wet with her sweat. She was near panic, for looking down at her hugeness she would not believe that the baby could pass through without killing her. She screamed her mother's name and sat up. She vomited. Sarah took up a cloth and crawled on to the great expanse of bed. She wiped Maken clean as best she could and held her. Sarah looked over Maken's head at Frida, pleading with her eyes. The old woman crossed herself, looked away and resigned herself of all hope.

A deep guttural bellow erupted from the centre of the Earl's bed. Huddled in a corner the Lady's two youngest hand-maidens looked on in wonder, "She's possessed!" said the smaller of the two. "Aye," answered her partner for in their young minds, their lady's moans were not possibly of this world.

Throughout the long morning, Robert's mother had paced the length of the hall taking pause at every sound from the solar. Weeks earlier Maken had let it be known that when her time came she would prefer to face child birth in private with only the mid-wife and her own mother in attendance. This Camille could well understand, birthing was an intimate time and one where a lady could be seen at her greatest disadvantage. She stayed away for as long as she could stand, but eventually the tension and worry were too great. After all, the child was her grandchild too. At the solar door the guard stood away in deference to her and yet she held back for a moment. Then another scream echoed from the solar and she rushed into the room.

The haggard appearance of her daughter-in-law shocked Camille. She tossed her robe from her shoulders and unceremoniously climbed across the bed to Maken. The very bed she herself had delivered two of her three children. But she took no time to reflect. She opened Maken's legs and gasped. The wee one was not so wee and although it had dropped well into the birth canal, something was wrong. Maken was in agony and yet Camille could plainly see the babe was nowhere near crowning.

"You! Fetch Fontennell!" Camille yelled at the two maids.

"We do not know where he is, m'lady," they answered not bothering to rise.

"If ye have not returned with him in two turns of the minute glass I shall have you both whipped until ye bleed!" They ran.

Presently the two returned with Cam Fontennell in tow. Sarah dropped a robe over Maken as the young archer entered the solar.

"Cam", said Camille, "pray tell me that the Jewess is still among us?"

"Indeed m'lady, in the west tower, quite safe."

"We need her. Now!"

He turned on his heel and was away even before the lady could finish.

Two weeks earlier, Cam had squirrelled the Jewess in a safe cell high in the Prisoner's Tower in the same room where he watched Sir Jean de la Mere expire. Barclay himself had put the key to her cell, and indeed her safety, in the hands of Fontennell. And this was no small concern, there were many that would have slain the unbeliever or at least cast her out of the castle. Such were the times.

Cam Fontennell was a man ruled by logic. If the Jewess could help Maken then that was Christian enough. Lydia began to pray when she heard Cam's footsteps. Other than supplying Maken with a sleeping elixir she had not been asked to perform any other services. She feared greatly for her safety for she knew of the fierce de Courtelaines of Hammerstone and their bloody history. Falling to her knees, Lydia called upon the God of Abraham and Isaac to give her strength in this her hour of doom.

The oak door swung open.

"Come lady, 'tis time," said Cam.

"'Tis not much time for reflection if this be the hour of my death!" answered Lydia.

"Nay, the Lady is having the child and it goes badly."

Even in her shocked relief, Lydia thought to collect her possessions and hurry after the archer.

101

Out of the tower, across the cobbled courtyard and into the great keep. Everywhere were cold shoulders and hard quick glances. None save Cam Fontennell would talk or even be near the unbeliever lest they pollute themselves.

They hurried on through the kitchen past the massive cook pots being filled to make ready for the evening meal. The Jewess parted the crowded kitchen like Moses parted the Red Sea. Quickly Cam led her on and at last to the solar.

The huge Belgian swung open the oaken door. Cam's journey ended at the doorway but the Jewess went straight to Maken not even pausing to make homage to her rank. With one look Lydia knew the lady was near death. Too long had the old midwife dithered and waited, drawing away Maken's strength and now she would need all the strength she could muster.

Lydia ordered Camille to help Sarah change the soiled bed sheets. She somehow managed to get Maken to stand, and cleaned her.

Lydia's leather pouch was emptied of its contents and a vial of some unknown elixir was opened and an amount carefully measured out.

"Sorcery! Evil Sorcerer!" moaned Frida, now standing away from the bed, forgotten "She casts a spell!"

Sarah took Frida gently by the arm and led her away. In the hall she called to Cam to take the old woman away, preferably somewhere quiet.

Meanwhile with the bed remade Lydia eased her patient back down. She saw the fear in Camille's eyes and the way the Earl's widow stole glances at her leather pouch.

"Fear not, m'lady. I am no sorcerer, nor am I a witch. And this elixir that I prescribe is but a stronger draft of the medicine that has eased the lady's pain these last few days. It is made of the gum of the poppy, only prepared in a different manner."

"What does it do?" asked Sarah.

"Makes her insensible, m'lady."

"Insensible to what?"

"To reality m'lady. And the pain."

"How then can she push down when we need her to?"

Lydia looked at Camille, "I fear the Lady is too weak to be of any use anyway. And also I must turn the child for it rests sideways in the birth canal. It shall be very painful, m'lady."

The narcotic began to take effect. The terrible pain eased and Maken's breathing slowed. She lay back in a stupor, a blessed painless realm of half-sleep. Dimly she could make out the face of her mother. And another whom she knew not. The stranger was speaking but Maken could not follow her meaning, so quickly did she speak.

#24

Slowly and firmly, Lydia relayed her wishes. Now she stated they must act and act speedily while the elixir was at its strongest. She made it clear that she needed stout-hearts and strong hands to assist. The two young serving maids must go.

"May I fetch our priest?" asked Sarah. The Jewess paused for a moment.

"But of course," she said, her heart sinking.

An eternity ago when she found herself riding northward with the handsome young archer, she had taken comfort in the fact that the Earls of Malton were known to be a godless brood, the kind of Norman that looked upon Jews as handy sources of income - helpless moneybags to be picked, released and picked over again the next time they needed money.

Priests, however, were of a different caste and their debates with the chosen usually ended with the Jew burnt at the stake. A religion of cooks, said Lydia's father (in private, of course) each meeting ended with a fire.

Now she knew to her great dismay that Hammerstone Castle was, in spite of its godless reputation, inhabited by a priest. And now, just as Lydia was about to perform a surgery never seen, let alone attempted by these Gentiles, the lady brings in a priest! Now a miraculous delivery would well be as dangerous as failure.

Lydia could not afford the luxury of fear. It was time to bring forth the child. Ever so gently she laid Maken across some pillows on her back so that her hips were higher than her head. Next she forced her hand up along the baby's head and body. Using her other hand to guide the head, she turned the baby. But not enough. Lydia stopped until Sarah fetched the extra rags and sheets.

The Jewess called upon the two women to ease Maken up until she was half standing with her bottom pressed against the edge of the bed. So smoothly that none knew her purpose until after the fact, Lydia slipped a razor sharp Sheffield blade from her tunic and cut a two-inch gap in Maken's opening. Without pause she produced two silver tongs and ordered Sarah and Camille to hold Maken tightly. Lydia inserted the curiously shaped tools up on either side of the baby's head. When she was sure she had the tongs in place on either side of the baby's neck, she began to pull down on them. Maken moaned.

Sarah and Camille looked on in horror. Lydia yelled for them to prepare a needle and thread as Maken's blood ran and covered her hands. Lydia paid no mind but kept up the pressure on her tongs. The baby seemed to crown and then stop and retreat. Lydia bit her lip and debated enlarging the cut and which lady to trust with the tongs.

A great contraction shuddered through Maken and the baby came forth in a frothy bloody burst. Lydia released her grip on the tongs and grabbed the baby and eased the still form into the cold world. Laying the baby on the blanket on the floor Lydia wished they would have sent for her when the lady's water had fallen. More out of duty than hope Lydia cleared out the tiny windpipe and blew warm breath into its mouth. The babe laid still and sadly Lydia turned her attention back to Maken, bleeding freely at the edge of her huge bed. Using special needles saved for just such a time, Lydia began the delicate task of suturing Maken's open wound. The cut was clean and straight, far easier to heal, than a jagged tear.

The lady Camille cried at the sight of her grandson lying unattended on the hard floor and she took the infant in her arms, praying that he might at least once sense the touch of human kindness. As she held him, the tiny mouth opened and a bellow, a shockingly loud bellow not the whimper of a frail newborn, but the yell of an angry hungry child, came forth.

In shock, Camille almost dropped the child. Sarah screamed in joy and crossed herself, "Hail Mary full of Grace," she said.

They wept openly, having seen the hand of God in this birth. Maken lay forgotten as the two crowded about the babe, "Aye he's the very imagine of his father," said Sarah as he opened his mouth on an offered finger, "He's hungry," Camille said, "I hope Maken can given him breast."

"Nay m'lady," said Lydia, "the babe cannot take his mother's milk until she is finished with the medicines I have given her."

"Why?"

"The elixir she drinks is dangerous to children. Passed on through her milk, it could affect the infant's mind."

Sarah gave her daughter a fearful once over, "Is Maken safe?"

Lydia nodded, "Yes m'lady, I only gave her enough of the potion to make her sleep through the worst of her pains. As soon as she is strong enough, she must be weaned off of it."

Camille gave the infant over to Sarah and called for Fontennell. He ran to fetch the nursemaid, a villager in seemingly constant reproduction. She walked as fast as her hips would allow her – her hips had been wobbly since her fifth child - to Hammerstone. The whole village had spoke of nothing else for the last fortnight and glory be she, Beasley Dobbs, would be the first to see the new Earl. Of course the child was male. Old Frida had guaranteed it and who would ever doubt her, why Frida had brought all ten of Beasley's children into the world losing only four.

The gate house sentries knew of her coming and she was allowed into the Keep without so much as a pause in her step. The size of the baby shocked even her. None of her children were of such proportion. She cradled him in her left arm and freed a breast. The child cried and she felt her milk flow. He was strong and gripped her with a gusto that made her wince.

"His lordship is not shy," she said laughing, for newborns, especially health ones, filled her with joy. She knew it made little sense for they usually were nothing but heartache and worry and yet she still loved them.

"Can ye come regular to nurse?"

"Aye m'lady, my eldest daughter is all but grown and can keep them all save the wee one."

"Well ye certainly should bring him - or is it a her?"

"A boy, m'lady."

"How lovely!" said Camille, "Well, just bring him along next time."

The newborn Earl soon tired and slept, his mouth still latched to the nipple. Beasley gazed at the still form at the centre of the bed, tiny in the vast expanse of sheets. A tear ran down Beasley's cheek, "So sorry for your troubles m'lady and ye, Sarah," She said. Sarah shook her head, "Nay woman, Maken merely sleeps, thanks be to God and this lady," she said nodding toward Lydia. Beasley leaned forward as if looking over Maken's countenance, only half believing the lady's claim. Maken moaned in her sleep and rolled her head and Beasley crossed herself, "Aye m'lady 'tis a wondrous thing."

#25

Cam Fontennell and Fulke stood outside the solar entrance and grinned at one another.

The youngest of the banished serving maids ran down through the greystone halls shouting the happy news as soon as she heard the cries of the newborn. Scarcely had she ran off when the hall began to fill with the citizens of the castle. Fulke and Cam found themselves surrounded in a press of the curious, all jabbering away, all wishing to see the new lord.

Angry oaths rang out and the unruly mob went silent. Barclay came striding up, "Stand away! Away I say! Back to ye duties ye treasonous lot! Who gives ye leave to abandon ye labours?" The servants retreated falling over themselves in their eagerness to escape the glare of the steward. Yet even as they left many cast a hopeful eye past Fulke and Cam in the chance that they might see something of the solar.

"As soon as the Lady warrants it, the young one will be shown to everyone from the balcony of the Great Hall!" Barclay yelled, for he wasn't really angry but he disliked confusion, especially near the baby.

The Jewess examined her patient and repacked the towelling against her stitches, informing the newly minted grandmothers that Maken's wounds had already ceased to bleed. Now she would need only rest and patience. As for the pains, Lydia had enough of her marvelous elixir to ease them for at least a fortnight.

Sarah lay beside her daughter and listened to her breathing, long and steady, felt her forehead and found no fever. She lay still; relief flooded her like a warm fire in December. All her hopes had been fulfilled, her daughter had delivered a son, and lived to see him. Any doubts or fears Sarah had of their Jewish guest were gone, swept away in the tide of Lydia's abilities.

As Lydia washed herself at a basin, Camille called for food and drink to be brought. When it arrived she came to Lydia and bid her sit and partake of some supper with her and Sarah.

"Good lady," answered Lydia, "Thine offer is more kind than wise, for thou knows, our religions do not encourage open fellowship."

"Nevertheless Lydia, we are in your debt and welcome a chance to share a meal with such a worthy physician. I am not of Norman birth and I hold little stock in certain ideals held so dearly by my late husband's people," said Camille.

"And I, fair lady, am in your debt, for the great service ye have provided. I doubt not, that my daughter would have died this day, but for you," said Sarah, her eyes glistening with grateful tears.

And the three, united in their common fight to bring forth the heir, sat together and sated their hunger.

Camille drank some wine and grew merry. The years seemed to melt away at long last. She felt she could breathe easier, their fight was all but won, and her grandson was the Earl of Malton.

Father Hubert arrived and was ushered into the solar by Fulke. Camille rushed to them, "Come, come and Fontennell too! Come look at this wondrous boy!"

"Truly m'lady, he is his father's son," said Fulke, noting the baby's size. Fontennell nodded in agreement although he knew little of such things, one infant was much like another to him. Everyone took their turn with their new lord and master. Whether it was from being passed about or just being hungry the baby wakened and began to cry lustily. Camille said to Cam, "Fetch us back Beasley Dobbs, tell her the child is in need of her."

"Nay! Nay I say!" Maken had awakened at the sound of her son's protests. "Bring him here!" She waved her hand impatiently. "Come now mother, quickly."

Sarah climbed onto the bed, the baby in her left arm. With frail hands, Maken reached for her son, her pale arms impossibly thin and Sarah was unsure if her daughter could even lift the sturdy boy. Yet she did, pulling the wailing bundle to her face. Such joy, such utter contention welled up inside her in this, her first touch of her own child. She felt a deep-seated urge to feed her own, to nurse him and content him, but she was taken by a fit of modesty.

"Fontennell, go ye for my father and likewise my brothers that they might share this happy day with us. And then Fulke, get ye straightaway to the Boar's Tooth Inn and purchase in my name two casks of my husband's favourite ale for the enjoyment of the villagers, that they may drink to my son's health. Also, buy the same again that those within the castle might also make merry."

As for Father Hubert, Maken cared little whether he stayed or went, he was her priest after all. "Barclay, ye may tell the kitchen that Sir Robert had a son! A great strong son! And tell them that once I give him substance, Father Hubert will show him from the Great Hall balcony." The two grandmothers exchanged worried glances. Lydia came to the bedside as Maken pulled the covers off her breasts.

"Nay m'lady, ye should not nurse the child while ye partake of my medicines."

"Why?"

"These elixirs are powerful. They might affect the child. 'Tis too great a risk m'lady."

"Affect? Affect how? Do they cast a spell?" asked Maken, her voice rising.

"Nay, m'lady, no spells! Rather 'tis more of a sleepiness and I am sure that ye would want not the boy to sleep all the time."

"Aye," Maken answered. She was trying to get him to latch on and it wasn't working. The infant could not lay on his own and nurse, she being too weak to hold his head. Maken tried to lift up, but she had not the strength to raise herself. She angered, "Come now help me sit up. You, mother, find some pillows for my back! Where are my serving girls? Call for them! Now!"

As she was lifted into a sitting position, Maken addressed the Jewess.

"If thy medications are harmful I am done with them. My baby shall be ever with me."

"But, m'lady, thy wounds may yet bleed and your pains shall be great until ye heal," said Lydia.

"Ha! Ye forget I am of Saxon lineage and we are a race much like your own, born of pain and suppression. I fear it not, and as for bleeding I shall have Fontennell fetch me some yew. That blessed plant has staunched many a grievous wound." This then was a dismissal and considering the works that the Jewess had performed, a graceless one at that. Sarah reddened for it was not to her liking to see Maken speak thus. She glared at her daughter, but Maken was intent on getting her son to take the nipple.

Sarah smiled at Lydia and gave her a halfhearted shrug. Lydia answered in kind, a nod and a slight raise of her shoulder that said she took no offence. After all, reasoned the Jewess, she had been treated far worse in her career and one could never forget the moodiness many new mothers suffered.

The baby began to nurse and pillows were stacked up behind Maken's back. She held her son and drew strength from his contentment. For a time the only sound in the solar was the gentle pull of his suckling.

"I can scarcely believe mother that ye would bring the gossipy Beasley Dobbs into my solar! Dids't thou not think of how she could crow? *'Oh yes, 'twas I that fed the youngster, poor Maken has no milk.'* Someone can go and tell her to stay home. Father Hubert, a blessing - come near and meet Robert William Alfred de Courtelaine, and may he be half the man his father is!"

When baby Robert William was sated and asleep, the priest took him to the balcony and showed

111

the bundled form to the gathered crowd below. Voices floated up, anxious voices asking of the babe's health. Father Hubert assured them all that the child was male, large and vigorous. Maken heard the happy response of the servants and men-at-arms to the priest's words and she was glad. They had wanted an heir as badly as she did.

Father Hubert brought Robert William back to Maken and mother and child promptly fell into a deep sleep, the baby tucked happily under Maken's chin.

For a long while, the Saxon grandmother looked at her daughter, trying to absorb the changes that she now could see in her own flesh and blood, changes that she would have never dreamed possible a year ago. Like some other soul had stolen into Maken's innocent body, ordering folk about, demanding things. The change in Maken was less of a shock to her mother-in-law. Camille was always with her and had grown used to her moods. In about her sixth month she had noticed the greatest change in Maken; the pregnant widow had retreated to the solar for long hours on end, demanding to be left alone without so much as a serving maid to stay with her.

It was her way of dealing with her hard losses, guessed Camille. 'Twas an odd thing though, an expectant mother to wish for solitude. Most women, especially those carrying their first, would usually take comfort in the company of other women, to talk and reassure, to gossip and forget the approaching pains.

Camille turned her attention to the lonely stranger sitting patiently by the bed. Waiting most likely for a suitable time to enquire as to when she might be able to return to her own people.

"Good lady, be assured that ye shall be safely conducted home as soon as Cam Fontennell, a trusted servant of the Lady Maken, returns. Also, ye must accept my monetary gift for thy great help," said Camille. To this Sarah added, "Think ye not that we do not hold you in deepest regard. I am but a poor Saxon woman and yet if there be anything that I or my family can do for ye, name it and know that it shall be done."

Answered the Jewess, "Kind ladies, be certain that all I need or ask is the safe return to the house of my father. We need little but yet I thank thee for thine offers. Besides thou must know this man Fontennell has paid a fee to my father 'ere I left his house."

Camille noted the foreign flavour to Lydia's speech and enquired about her travels.

"I was born in Alexandria in Egypt. While still a young girl, we moved to Cyprus and later, my father's business - he became a trader in olive oil - took us to many cities about the Mediterranean Sea."

"Indeed I thought the cut of your cloak was of another climate," said Camille.

"Oh this?" said Lydia, fingering the light gauze-like materials of her wrap, "Yes m'lady, this I bought in Genoa, marvelous workmanship, don't you think?"

Camille caught her breath. Genoa! And such memories flooded out of the lost pages of her mind. She closed her eyes to better savour the moment.

"M'lady? M'lady? Art thou ill?"

Camille blinked, "What? No I am fine." She reached out and felt the hem of Lydia's garment. The Jewess wore a light perfume, the scent of Jasmine, and to Camille it was like sitting once again in her father's warehouse with the scents of a dozen ports and a hundred spices filling the salty air and in the distance the cry of a gull. She drew away and asked where Lydia found such a beautiful cloak.

"'Tis a curious tale m'lady. The shop in Genoa where I found this was run by an old widowed lady, her daughter and her daughter's husband. It seems the matriarch was married to a trader that was lost at sea and she took over his business to keep from starving. Many times I visited their warehouse for the old lady was a shrewd one with the traders and always she found the best cloth."

"Their names, Lydia! Tell me their names!"

"Ah...let me think...it has been many years since I last saw Genoa."

"If ever ye remembered a name, I pray that you remember that one."

"It will come to me, I'm sure."

Camille fought down the urge to grab Lydia by the shoulders and shake the names out of her. Instead she sat still and waited.

Lydia thought and thought but could not remember. "'Tis an odd thing. I am usually good at remembering names."

For Camille it was important that she not give any clue to Lydia, she wanted the name to be uncoached. She knew well that the Jewess might agree with her just to appease her. She had seen it before with her servants.

"Think child! Think!" Camille cried.

Barclay and Father Hubert held their breath while Lydia sorted through the cobwebs of her memory. Both men knew the Lady Camille was born and raised in Genoa and that her father was a trader who had been lost at sea. Was it her family the Jewess had bought her goods from? After more than twenty long years would Camille at last hear news of them?

Lydia stared into space for a long time and finally she smiled, "Ah ha. I remember their names for it was across the doorway of their shop on a sign carved of wood and painted a bright crimson."

Camille smiled through her tears.

#26

Bung cast his eyes over his brother in something akin to wonder. Two years away had transformed the youngster; gone were the thin arms and slight shoulders. Taller by a span and heavier by at least a stone, no long hugs or tearful remembrances marked their greeting. If an onlooker would have witnessed their meeting he would never have guessed the deep bond between the two, that each would readily die in defense of the other and if Bung asked it, Beck would happily slip a blade into Roger de Courtelaine's back.

"Ye have prospered in your travels, brother."

"Aye."

"And what is this?" said Bung, pulling on Beck's small pointed goatee. Beck pulled away embarrassed.

"The ladies like it, especially the French mademoiselles."

"Now what of thy master, Sir Roger? Has he grown weary of foreign adventures?"

"No brother, these last few months have been nothing but glorious for Sir Roger, and enriching."

"And no doubt, brother, he being a Templar and sworn to poverty, he gave all of his riches to the poor," said Bung.

Both men laughed at such an unlikely thing, "Nay brother, the Templars like to have a champion among their numbers. It encourages others to join their cause."

"And does it work?"

"The number of Templars is ever increasing. The vows they take seem to be forgotten when they leave their monasteries."

"Still ye have not told me why Sir Roger has returned. Is it because of his brother's disappearance?"

"No, it is because of his brother's death."

"Death? Who said the Earl was dead? Certainly not his wife. Not the King. And if the King still thinks he lives, then I guess he still lives."

"'Tis not my affair, Bung, and besides, officially Sir Roger is here to found a new chapter house of the Knights of the Temple. At least 'tis what the Grandmaster was led to believe."

Bung was puzzled, little he knew of these Templars and their curious customs. Beck tried to enlighten his older brother somewhat.

"The Knights of the Temple take a vow of chastity, poverty and a vow to free and defend the holy city of Jerusalem from the heathens, The Arabs, the Moors and such."

"And this Jerusalem, it lies nearby?"

"No, not nearby, not in England, not even in Europe, it lies in a far, far place, to the east."

"Why then, pray tell, are these Templars here so far from their chosen battlefield?"

"I asked Sir Roger that very thing once, and only once mind ye. He boxed my ears right soundly."

Bung laughed, "And what of this vow of chastity, surely ye will not have me believe de Courtelaine has abandoned the fairer sex?"

Now both men laughed for Sir Roger was quite the rake in his former life. Beck, when he regained his voice, explained further. "To a Templar, at least those whom I have met, their vow forbids marriage, not the act of love."

"Ha!" said Bung, "In this at least I am in agreement with the Templars. Most men take a vow of marriage and give up the enjoyment of the flesh! But now of this last foolishness, the vow of poverty? I saw with mine own eyes your caravan's entry into York. The King himself is not as well mounted as the least of your company."

"Ahh...brother your last arrow hits closest to the mark. The Templars have no fear of money as far as I can tell. And who would upbraid them. The Bishop of Winchester is the richest man in England and the Bishop of Hereford not far behind. And remember the Knights of the Temple are a mighty force when gathered as one. Has't thou never heard how two hundred Templars held the mighty armies of Suleyman off for six months in Sicily?"

"What's Sicily?"

"A place near Rome, I guess."

"And even more than their strength of arms, they have the Pope's blessing. Aye only fools would cross the Knights of the Temple."

Bung heard all of this and still it made little sense to him, for a freeborn knight to place himself in the thrall of others.

"'Tis ambition brother, ambition and love of warfare that draws the young to the Temple's ranks. A Templar need not beg for a horse or scramble about trying to find armour, these things are all provided and glory is ever as close as the next battle."

Bung nodded and called for a final cup of ale. Beck noted that they were lucky to find a private spot at the inn and Bung smiled. Few knew that he, through one of his oldest lieutenants, owned the Red Dragon. Beck's old master had fallen on hard times and Bung had pointed the man into another trade. Bung stood and put on his cloak, "Take care brother, I will see you soon," and he was gone.

#27

Roger de Courtelaine rode a ways ahead of his men and then stopped to watch them. Proud he was, for he had twenty of the Temple's best lances under his personal command. True they were under the Grandmaster's orders to found a new chapter house, but in this Sir Roger knew there was considerable leeway just how he fulfilled his quest. He smiled.

They looked as impressive as they were lethal. They wore the new uniform of the Temple, an all white tunic with a red cross over the heart, underneath their Spanish armour and each man was armed in proof, for Sir Roger knew not what he might have to overcome. He was on the road leading east along the River Ouse and Hammerstone Castle was only a few miles away. His men knew nothing of his plans and they felt no need to. Sir Roger had the approval of the Grandmaster and that was enough.

#28

Neil Cleeves, the Captain of the guards of Hammerstone Castle, rode a fine dappled mare south of the Ouse. He arrived at a deep thicket of new green, dismounted, and led his horse into the forest depths. Salty streams of sweat dampened his jerkin and stung his eyes. Yet he hurried on pausing only now and then to confirm his path. He came to the end of his journey abruptly, a clearing in the woods lit by the spring sun. Bung appeared, unsettling Neil with the suddenness. The bandit himself was calm, standing there across the clearing with a line of men behind him. Bung watched the tall soldier enter the open glade, without so much as a look about, and how Cleeves tramped! Did he wear shoes of iron? And why the fear? Bung counted the captain as a valuable addition to his ring of spies and would have no reason to wish him ill. And if the Earl ever discharged him, Neil Cleeves would have been welcomed for his fighting skills. Bung greeted his guest.

The captain nodded to Bung and, as was his habit, straightaway told his news. "The Lady of Hammerstone has given birth to a son."

"Joyful news, Cleeves."

"Indeed the heir is said to be unusually large and robust."

"The lady is quite young. Did she have troubles with birthing such a child?" asked Bung.

"Aye 'twas a long struggle but the steward had a mid-wife hired, a Jewess from the south and she helped."

Bung handed Neil Cleeves a few coins and said, "Now I have some news for you. Thou art in great peril. Sir Roger de Courtelaine has returned and is bound for Hammerstone Castle."

Neil turned around and looked back whence he came, "I must be off," he said, reaching for his reins,

"And yet stay ye a time" said the Bandit King. Not ordering Neil, but his voice compelled him to pause. He waited to hear what the Bandit King might say.

"Why should ye rush back to Hammerstone? Very soon Sir Roger shall ask leave to enter the castle. God help the man that must answer that request! Sir Robert forbid his brother from ever returning but the Earl is gone. He who refuses Roger, should the King make him the next Earl, will be cast aside."

"Then what should I do?"

"Neither."

"I don't understand..."

"Do neither, stay a while here in the greenwood. Return when someone else has made that decision. If Sir Roger has been refused and rode away, well then ye need not do anything and if he greets you in the Great Hall with a cup of wine in his hand. Let the steward be responsible. Surely no one would fault that?"

Neil Cleeves considered the bandit's reasoning but disagreed. He thanked Bung for his advice and then took his leave. As he led his horse away Bung said, "And be ye crafty, Mr. Cleeves. Sir Roger rides with twenty mounted Knights of the Temple, each man skilled in their bloody trade."

#29

Sir Roger saw the brickworks before anything else and he rode right past the burial hills without so much as a glance, so intent was he at getting a closer look at the gray stacks piled high. He spurred his horse on, splashing across the pebbly ford and riding up the opposite bank. Directing his horse into the brickyard, the unusual sight of the works silenced him. He stopped and looked all around. Finally, he noticed the huge burial mounds back across the river. Long he stared at the grassy graves. A great battle had happened here and a part of him bitterly regretted not being there to partake. He walked his charger up the road enough that he could see the heights of the Keep, peeking over the green treetops. Emotions the Knight had rarely felt welled up within him and his voice gave as he called his men forward. He ordered each man to loosen his sword hilts and be ready for armed defiance. Roger himself removed his helmet that the watchmen at the gate of the castle might know him and give him entrance. A doubtful chance but worth the trying. It was unlikely that he would be able to simply slip into Hammerstone, the brickworks had been hastily abandoned not long ago, the fire still burned bright beneath the kilns. Likely the Templars had been spotted and a general alarm sounded, recalling the men to defend the castle.

Roger held his company at easy trot and came up around the final curve in the road and before him stood the castle now with her new walled village stretching out from the river. The Templar nearest de Courtelaine urged his horse up beside his leader and said, "Thou dids't not give your father's castle its just due, yonder fortress is of a size rarely seen!"

"Get back in line," barked Sir Roger. He was amazed that his weak brother would have such an urge to build. Coming toward the gates, the new walls looked huge.

De Courtelaine rode right up to the new gate. It was open, but still he stopped and dismounted. The gatehouse door opened and Alcroft, a guard of the castle for many years, walked out past the heavy iron gateposts.

"Alcroft! Alcroft! Is it really you?" said Roger, greeting the guard like a long lost brother.

"Lord Roger?"

"Aye, Alcroft, it's me."

"Ye are in a dress quite foreign to these eyes m'lord. If ye ride in the name of some southern Earl, or perhaps a Bishop..."

"Close, Alcroft," interrupted Roger. "I am a Knight of the Temple of Solomon and we are called to protect the Holy Land from the infidels."

Alcroft, not the quickest mind in the world, did not understand what that meant exactly. A hint of cheering could be heard from the courtyard.

"What news, Alcroft?"

"Oh great news m'lord, the Lady Maken has delivered a son, a strong healthy boy."

Roger ignored the stake pounded in his plans and smiled. "Ahh, what great luck that I, his legal ward, should be here just now to greet him." And with that the Templar led his men into Hammerstone Castle.

They walked their chargers across the moat and under the iron drop gate. Most of the villagers were crowded about the stairway leading into the Keep. At long last the sentries, most of whom had joined the crowd at the stairs, noticed Sir Roger and his men. Happy cries turned to silence as the exile walked slowly up the stairs, four of his men close behind. Roger ignored the villagers and at the top of the stairs, drew up to his full height - not the equal of his brother, but still enough to instill a sense of superiority - and marched into the Keep.

In the Great Hall it was more of the same. One would have thought it was May Day come early, such was the festive mood of the people. Roger did not wait.

He bid his men follow with a turn of his head and was through the kitchen before anyone reacted to his sudden appearance.

He took the stairs two at a time like a soldier running into the enemy's line.

#30

The long hours of Maken's labour, the fevered cries of pain ringing through the Keep had silenced the inhabitants of Hammerstone and filled Katoryna with a morbid curiosity. Over the years she had found secret ways to move about the lower reaches of the castle and would slip out of her rooms and watch her father administer punishments in his dungeon, a sport she had long been denied. And what an experience this birthing had been, a revelation really. Katoryna sat by her bedroom door, all the while, hearing each desperate minute.

Now it was over and sounds of joy replaced the pain. Katoryna didn't stir. For a long while she sat very still and let her mind linger. After a time she stood and sighed and resolved to view the result of all the morning ruckus. She opened her door and stepped into the hall, almost running into her long lost brother. She screamed his name and threw her arms about Roger. He pulled away from his sister's embrace, chastising her sternly. "Touch not the person of a Knight of the Temple of Solomon. We do not communicate in this manner!"

She stepped back surprised.

Roger moved forward and noting the lack of sentries, said to his fellow Knights, "See ye this, my brothers, such disarray in my father's once-proud house?" Not waiting for a reply, Roger entered the solar.

In her eagerness to hear news of her family, Camille had grasped Lydia with both hands imploring the woman to do her utmost to recall her time in Genoa. Seeing the Templar, Lydia freed herself from Camille's grip and stood away from the others. Roger glared at her, recognizing by her dress that she was one of *that* race that lived outside the Holy Church and believed not. Lydia's knees shook as four more of his brethren joined the Templar, each with the blood red cross on their white tunics.

Camille, still on her knees, could scarcely believe her eyes. Her youngest son had aged, there were lines about his dark eyes, but when he spoke, all doubts could be cast aside. He was his father's son in deed and in voice.

"What means this mother? Kneeling before the unbeliever like some pagan whore! And thou, ye mad priest, always have I guessed your true colors. Protector of fools! Lover of the Saxon scum."

Roger moved to the edge of the Earl's bed. He gazed at the mother and child quietly asleep. He cast a sideways look at Barclay. "And thou, the butler, at least you can claim ignorance of what is proper behavior in a lord's solar."

He stared at the newborn as he continued. "The King himself and the Bishop of Hereford wish me to interrupt my holy calling to come here and ensure that my ward, for surely that is just what he is, will be properly raised and I can see I've not wasted a trip. What scandal is this, my own mother kneeling before an unbelieving Jew? And with her priest looking on?"

Camille ignored her son and begged Lydia to tell her any names she could remember from Genoa.

"Silence, Jew!" yelled Roger de Courtelaine and Lydia stood muted as if struck dumb.

"Brother Toller, cans't though believe what ye see before you? Truly the Bishop of Hereford will have much to say on this little gathering."

Sir Roger picked up the sleeping infant and said, "Aye, as the King's surety in the Crown's interest in this child, I am assuming control of Hammerstone Castle. Kindly remove yourselves from the solar. It shall have to be purified with holy water after the unbeliever is gone."

He ordered his companions to gather the rest of their company and expel all visitors from the castle. He himself would present the child to the people. The two remaining Templars, large strong men, armed in proof, quickly forced Camille, Barclay, Sarah and Lydia out of the solar and into the hall. Lydia, they sent to the prisoners tower but the rest they locked away in Roger's old quarters, barring the door from without. Later the prisoners were joined by Maken, carried in by one of the men. Katoryna watched her brother carry the baby down the stairs and she followed. Sir Roger de Courtelaine was a man born to lead men. Never was this more apparent than in the first few minutes of his return to his ancestral home. Quickly he took control of the Earl's solar and next he met the general population. He entered the great hall and jumped up onto a table. He held the heir above his head and slowly showed him all around. "A boy! A fine boy!" he called out and when the people roared in approval he laughed and roared happily with them. "Yes, yes!" he cried. Roger lowered the baby down and called for someone to find a mid-wife.

Someone in the press called out wondering if the Lady Maken was recovering of her long labour or why did they need a mid-wife?

Roger nodded to the questioner and held up his arms that all would know he meant to answer the question. He waited for the crowd to quiet. Then he spoke.

"An unbeliever, a Jewess trained in the black arts of sorcery, hads't laid a spell on my brother's widow. Even as your priest stood by. But fear not! I have with me Knights of the Temple that have journeyed in the East, even to the holy city of Jerusalem and these holy warriors know somewhat of eastern customs and even now are reciting special verses to dispel the Jew's magic." The lies came easily and the listeners, oblivious to the outside world and fearful of foreigners, believed everything the knight said. As he knew they would.

Roger let his words sink in for a few moments before changing the subject.

"Now all ye here consider this. You have a new Earl and each of you must continue to do your duty. We must all watch over him and protect him. Everything else is immaterial. That is all."

Roger left the hall and returned the newborn Earl to the solar. He called upon Katoryna to join him. It was time for a family chat. She sat by the window and watched her brother. He walked slowly about the large room, brushing his hand across the top of Robert's armour breast-plate, standing in its frame with the rest of the late Earl's battledress, all polished and shining. And massive. Roger had forgotten just how big his brother really had been. Even as large as he was, Roger would not fill the armour by at least a span through the shoulders and he lacked at least four inches to match Robert's height. Ah, well, thought Roger, no matter, he would have the armour suit cut down to fit. The shining suit, with the rearing black stallion embossed on the breastplate was beautiful and he could hardly wait to wear it. Katoryna knew what he was thinking, "Large boots to fill, my brother."

"Hardly," Roger answered, "Any fool could do as well."

"Well ye had a busy day, the castle yours, the enemies cowed, and locked away. Ye must be proud."

"What victory is that to out-wit half-wits. I can only shake my head at the rabble my brother surrounded himself with. Is there no man within these walls that might be called competent?"

"Aye, Roger, there is! There are several men of good account. Neil Cleeves is Captain of the Guard and does well...and..."

"Does he? Does he indeed! Is he captain of these same guards that let me and all my host in without so much as a raised fist?"

"He's away on business and no doubt had he been here you would have slept under the stars tonight."

The baby began to cry and Roger ignored him. "Anyone else?" he said.

"There is one, Cam Fontennell is his name and he is a man born for the battlefield."

"Indeed, some young rake, you're bedding no doubt."

She reddened. "Well take ye heed of this, he put Sir Jean de la Mere in his grave and others besides!"

"Well then, that's something, we shall consider this *what's-his-name?*"

"Fontennell, Cam Fontennell."

All this Roger said in a half-interested voice as he paced about the richly decorated room. It had been a while since he had been inside his father's solar and the room held a great fascination for him. Katoryna grew impatient. "Roger! Be so kind as to at least pay me some mind! His name is Cam Fontennell."

He turned towards his sister and smiled at her. Amusing how transparent the female sex was, he thought.

"Yes I hear you – 'Fontennell'. Very well, we shall see what he's about."

Katoryna smiled in relief, "All's well then for he's very dear to me. I must say!" It was more than she had planned to say knowing how cruelly Roger could tease. She spoke anyway; she wanted her brother to know how important Fontennell was to her plans.

The baby cried louder now, his hunger growing more acute. Katoryna found his wailing to be annoying. "Don't you think he should be fed?"

Roger looked down at his nephew.

"What?"

"The baby! He needs to be fed! Here, let me take him to his mother. You can't just let him starve you know! He is an Earl and a ward of The King."

"Actually," said Roger, "I certainly could starve the brat. Half-Norman, half-Saxon bastard that he is."

He knew she was likely right, it would cause a bit of a scandal, the infant dying so fast in his care and after all he had years to effect an accident on the heir.

"Hand him over, Roger, I will take him straightaway to his mother."

"Nay, sister, I trust the Saxon not! Go ye and find a wet-nurse while I await ye here."

Katoryna eyed her brother suspiciously. "Ye'll not harm the child?"

Roger laughed, "Me? Nay never." He walked over to a large platter of food and drink from the kitchen. He dipped his finger into a flask of goat's milk and put it to the baby's mouth. The infant sucked hungrily on his finger.

"Quickly now, go!"

When she was gone, the Templar quit feeding the boy and walked out into the hallway. He stood by his old quarters close to the door. The infant, still famished, began to renew his protests. His cries were answered from within. Hearing him, Maken cried out for her son to be surrendered to her.

Roger laughed, "Is that fool of a butler awake? If so, bring him forth."

"I'm here, Sir Roger," said Barclay.

"Of course you are, thou fool."

"What do ye want?"

"Tut, tut, not so proud. Ye wish to see the child. Turn over the keys to the storeroom."

Roger quieted the baby with his finger and leaned close to the door. Maken was sobbing, "Barclay, give him the keys!"

Roger smiled. His sport was going well.

Barclay's voice came through strained and tight. "Give over the child first!"

"Nay"

"The child!"

"No, I say, and thou should know, he seems to grow weaker with need for substance."

Once again he heard Maken's desperate voice.

"Roger! Roger!" called Camille to her son. "Stop this cruelty and give over the child to his mother!"

"Silence, thou Jew worshipper. Speak not to a soldier of the Temple. Better ye pray to cleanse thy soul."

Maken cried out and a set of heavy keys set on a ring of iron slid out from under the door. Roger snatched them up.

"Now the child!" yelled Barclay.

Roger laughed and walked away.

"Oath breaker! Faithless cur! Hind coward!" ranted Barclay, but to no avail. The knight and child were gone.

Beasley Dobbs was summoned once again to nurse the new baby. She had told all her neighbours of the new Earl's size and strength, unheard of in a newborn. Robert William had not yet soiled his first swaddling cloth and already he was a legend.

#31

Maken's father and brothers were hunting far up the Ouse River and Cam Fontennell had to take to horseback to find them. Even so he was well into the afternoon before he managed to lay eyes on them. Actually they found him, suddenly surrounding him along the gravel road where it hung draped tight to the banks of the river.

"What news, Cam?" asked Myles.

"Great news, Myles. Maken has delivered a baby - a large strong boy."

His two sons shouted and even dour Myles smiled. "And Maken, how is she?"

"She suffered greatly in her labour, but God be praised, she is well!"

The hunt forgotten the four men turned for home. Cam offered the horse to Myles that he might see his grandson all the quicker. Myles, after giving the huge charger a careful look, declined the offer and walked on.

Silence ensued for a time, each man lost in his own thoughts and content to walk on. Owen, the younger brother, was less like his father and more apt to gossip. He broke the peace with a question for Cam.

"What, pray tell, is the Jew like. Are they odd in their habits?"

Cam shook his head, "Nay, Owen, they are, or at least she is, just like you and I. I cannot tell anything different about her at all other than she refuses pork."

Owen was disappointed. He had hoped to hear something truly strange and worth the great amount of gossip that the Jew's presence has caused. He tried again. "They say she knows magic and sorcery! They..."

"They! They! Who is 'they'? Tell "They" to consult with me. I brought the Jew to the castle. She is a good mid-wife, wise in the birthing of babies. If not for her I can say that Maken would have died and the heir along with her. Old Frida had long given up on the two when we fetched in Lydia."

"Lydia?"

"The Jew - her name is Lydia."

Myles gave his son a hard stare and the interview was over. The towers of the castle came into view and then the four were within the new village walls. Myles was soon surrounded by his neighbours all worried and shouting and pointing toward the gate house. Their cause for alarm was soon apparent. The drawbridge was raised and strangely attired knights held the guard-posts. Garfield joined his friends. "What castle's livery is that?" he said to Fulke, who was standing on the very edge of the moat's outer lip, obviously in deep distress. "I let the wet nurse go over first and damn them, they pulled the plank across 'ere I could step over."

"Ye have been in many towns and castles, Fulke. Whose livery do these soldiers wear? I recognize it not," said Garfield.

"Nor do I," said Fulke.

A villager, just evicted with the rest, spoke. "They be Templars and they are led by Sir Roger de Courtelaine, come home to reclaim the Earldom."

Oaths of disbelief greeted this news but the bearer was adamant, stoically holding fast to his story above their protests.

"We must gather the archers about us, and smartly too. Maken and the child must be freed lest Sir Roger bring them to harm," said Myles. The call went out for the bowmen to assemble at the Boar's Tooth Inn. Meanwhile Fulke and Myles agreed to stay by the gatehouse to keep watch on the strange troops now crawling like vines about the ramparts of Hammerstone.

Not long had they waited until they spied a group of soldiers pushing an unarmed man unto the very edge of the bloody wall.

"Holy Mother Mary!" said Fulke, "'Tis Barclay they've driven to the precipice."

"Aye and wounded him besides," noted Cam whose eyes were better than most. "He bleeds from the head and staggers."

Another figure appeared, his black hair a dead giveaway. All save Cam Fontennell knew it was the younger brother of Sir Robert that stood high above them.

Little time did the onlookers have to ponder his intent for after a quick exchange of words, Sir Roger pushed Barclay off the wall. The steward fell silently, hitting the river with a loud splash. A dozen men ran to a small punt laid up on the near shore and launched a rescue. Lucky it was, too, for Barclay, only half conscious and weakened, had not even the strength to grasp the gunnels of the punt, let alone swim to shore, only a few yards away.

A crowd gathered about the unconscious steward and Myles, seeing that he was still alive, ordered Barclay to be carried to the Boar's Tooth Inn and kept warm. The great common room was rapidly filling with the archers, each man armed with his yew wood bow and a quiver of long arrows. Every man seemed anxious to have his say and the noise grew with every new arrival.

Barclay came to and Garfield, who stood nearby, knelt down near his head. Barclay tried to speak but his voice was weak and faint. Garfield stood and called for silence. The din ceased and Garfield crouched down and listened to the steward's efforts. It was no use; Barclay, try as he might, was too weak to speak. His eyes, wide with fear, held Garfield's gaze but told the archer nothing.

"Damnation," said Garfield as Barclay lost consciousness again, "Stay ye by him and heed well if he speaks. Perhaps he has news from our friends inside the castle," said Garfield. He called for each man to ready himself for whatever may come and yet at the same time, do nothing until they knew what should be done. Garfield was well aware their chances of getting Maken and her child out of the castle were slim at best. If Sir Roger was half the soldier Garfield feared him to be, there was really no chance at all. And he knew that these men would die trying if only he gave the word. The responsibility weighed heavily with him and a deep tightening pain gripped his innards. Fear, pure and full, swept over him as the full impact of Roger de Courtelaine's return sunk in. If the errant knight could take and keep control of the castle, it spelled the end of the archers' troop, with its pay and unheard of rights. Short work would Sir Roger make of all that.

And Maken. What evil would befall her? She stood now between Roger and all the wealth of the de Courtelaines. God help her! Garfield resolved to kill the Norman, not in anger or as an idle boast, but in a moment of lucid clear sightedness. The weaver realized that the only sane course of action was to place one of his gray goose shafts through Sir Roger's black heart. If it cost Garfield his life then it was a price he would pay. He was never going back to the old life.

Garfield stood on one of the hard oaken benches, one that was next to a wall and in the attentive silence told his men what they must do.

"My friends, we must wait!" Loud mutterings of disapproval greeted Garfield's advice and many of the younger men, less controlled, with their hot blood, with their hot blood, brandished their weapons and called for Myles to speak his mind. But the majority overruled these younger men and such was their faith in Garfield's judgment that they agreed to abide by his word.

"Aye, lads, that's right," said Garfield relieved. Go attend to your usual labours, trust me in this affair and mark ye this, Sir Roger de Courtelaine shall never rule us. I take my vow on this!"

Thurgar looked long at the weaver, seeing now what was in Garfield's mind.

#32

Neil Cleeves, Captain of the Guard, arrived before sundown just as supper was being cooked. The planking was quickly extended across the moat and Neil entered Hammerstone without delay.

He knew Sir Roger and Sir Roger knew him. Neil did not fear the returning de Courtelaine and he was amazed to find the Templar and all his men comfortably sharing the lower keep with Barclay's hired lances. But the mercenaries were not his command, only the men-at-arms.

He went into the barracks first and all of his men, save those on guard on the wall, were clustered around in groups trying to decide what the day's events meant. Neil, like a cool northern wind, soon blew away the foggy opinions of the undecided. He stood to the centre of the barracks, hands on hips looking all about the lower room; his eyes burned holes in his men's consciences.

"Sir Roger has been banned from these lands and especially these walls. Who therefore gave him entrance?" Old Alcroft spoke up, "'Twas me sure enough, but Sir Roger is, after all, the babe's uncle and, well, I thought it proper."

"You thought? You thought? — you should have thought of this. The King has not declared Sir Robert to be dead so as far as we are concerned he is still alive. As is his commands. And bad enough ye permitted Sir Roger within the castle walls despite his banishment but ye also allowed all of his company to cross the drawbridge —and still armed at that!"

Alcroft wilted beneath his captain's stare. "But it's the baby's uncle and they are Knights of the Temple of Jerusalem, almost like priests!"

"Fool! What matter is it to us what they call themselves? If they are sworn to retake the holy city then they should do so and not bother honest folk in England."

"Well what could I do?" cried Alcroft.

"Ye could have told Sir Roger to encamp downriver a ways until the King ruled on this matter. Now we cannot retake or ever remove the Templars without risking many lives, the heir's included."

Neil Cleeves walked to the door and grabbed the handle in his huge hand.

"Alcroft, you are released, leave the castle before nightfall and never return. As for the rest of you, prepare for a show of arms. Any man on duty when the Templars entered here will forfeit one month's salary. Now all of you follow me once you are armed for battle."

Neil left the barracks. He went up into the prisoner's tower and saw the Jewess. He asked her how she had come to be imprisoned. He heard her tale, offered neither comfort nor opinion, and took his leave of Lydia.

In the courtyard his men-at-arms were streaming out of the barracks, two score and more stout soldiers, each man armed, with pike and sword. Some with crossbows notched with bolts and wound tight. Cleeves had heard much about Templars from the Bandit Chief.

Bung, of course, received news of this new order of Knights and what they did as soon as Beck left his tavern. As soon as they came near his lands, Neil Cleeves met the two Templars stationed on the Keep's doorstep. He was unarmed save for his authority as the Captain of the Guard of a castle protected by liege-oath to the Crown.

Neil walked up the staircase making as if to go straightaway within. The Templars stood in front of the door, barring his way. "What madness is this?" asked Neil Cleeves, "Who art thou that ye would overrun a castle under the King's protection? This is treason!"

"We are ordered to stand guard here by our master, Sir Roger de Courtelaine, who has laid claim to the right to govern this fortress, he is the infant Earl's uncle."

Neil nodded, "If that is the case than I should tell thee of two things. Firstly the King has yet to declare Sir Robert de Courtelaine dead, and thus the Earl's steward and wife are the legal rulers of this castle by law. And secondly, I can tell thee that the Grandmaster of thine Order is right now in York, not a day's ride away!"

The Templars paled. "In York, ye say?"

"Indeed, he is the guest of the King and they sup at the Great Hall at Clifford's Tower." The other Templar scoffed, "Thou should know this. Our Grandmaster has given his blessing to this endeavour and we ride with the Holy authority of the Pope. Besides it is very unlikely that the Grandmaster would cross the channel."

Neil was non-plussed and proceeded to describe their leader. "An old man, thin, with a scar down his right cheek? Aye, lads, ye best let me past and the others also."

The Templars gave way. Neil had hit very close to the heart of their fears, namely, that their captain, Sir Roger, was acting outside the perimeters of his mandate and outside the laws of their Order. If the Grandmaster was indeed not only in England but also as close by as York, Sir Roger had best proceed with extreme caution.

As Neil Cleeves swung open the door he called for several of his men to follow him. He had the Templars at bay now and he knew enough to push his advantage while he could.

Marching into the great hall as one, the men-at-arms lined up behind their captain standing ready to protect his person should the need arise.

"Good evening, Sir Roger. I am Captain-of-the Guard. I must ask you to dismiss your men although they may camp beyond the village walls."

His words, so boldly spoken, the Templars gathered about Sir Roger quit their feasting and stared at this stranger before them.

"Must you?" Roger de Courtelaine rose to his feet, "Must you indeed!" He came around the table so that he was eye to eye with Neil or at least eye to chin with the taller man.

"Use not that tone with a soldier of the Temple of Jerusalem. I warn thee!"

Neil never wavered. "Well I can tell thee, ye are a long way from Jerusalem. Have you told your brothers here that ye are banished from this hall and that Sir Robert's liege Lord, the King, is pledged to hold that ban?"

"Should he choose to."

"And he would not?"

"I am the heir's uncle and with Robert dead, the best man to guard his son."

"The King does not declare Sir Robert to be dead."

"Perhaps His Majesty has been pre-occupied with affairs of state and does not realize how long Hammerstone has been at risk."

"Perhaps we should send to York for a Royal decision," said Neil

"Aye, that would suit me. Send one of the Earl's liege-men; a Knight of good standing should present our need before the King."

"And by the way, ye might like to know thy Grandmaster is with King Stephen in York even as we speak." Neil took pleasure in the Templar's vain attempt to hide his shock at news of his master's presence nearby.

Roger de Courtelaine had not counted on Hugh de Payne ever crossing the channel. He had thought that if anything the Grandmaster would return to the Holy Land. Roger had hardly paid attention to de Payne's warning against raising the ire of the English nobility. The Grandmaster had spoken about the necessity of discreet dealings and cautious use of force. Oh, how the old man had droned on, his spotted ancient hands fluttering about like claws as he described their new chapters in London, in Garway, Herefordshire and in Scotland.

Roger didn't care. He just wanted permission to go back to England. Why, why had the Grandmaster followed him to England? Never once during their interview did the old fool even hint that he himself was coming across the channel.

All of these thoughts tumbled through Roger's startled mind and he knew not how long he stared at the Captain of the Guard. He became aware of many eyes on him and he stole a quick glance about the table. His men were nervous and clearly as surprised as he was that the Grandmaster had come. One of the younger knights pushed a serving girl off his lap and ordered her away.

Neil Cleeves pressed his advantage, asking for the Lady Camille and the Lady Maken and that he had great need to speak with the steward, Barclay. Also, he was eager to do his homage to the Earl's son, especially.

Roger answered with a smile, "The young lord is with my own good sister, Katoryna and he is the image of his father. Katoryna shall bring him down to you directly. As for the ladies they are not seeing visitors, so great a strain was the birthing, so large was the child, that neither the lady, nor her mothers, will be seeing visitors for a day or two." Roger nudged the captain and said, "Wait until ye see the wee one and ye shall understand why."

Neil ignored the Templar's friendly overture. "And I have need to speak with the steward," he said again.

"Barclay, if he is the steward, is not in the castle," answered the Templar.

To this the captain of the guard said nothing and as he considered Barclay's whereabouts his eyes happened upon Sir Roger's squire. A ripple of recognition washed through his mind and yet he could not place the young servant, "Your squire, Sir Roger? Whence came he? Is he local?"

"Nay," said Sir Roger, this lie not as smooth as the others, for he did not expect the question.

"Have we ever met, boy?" Neil asked, for it nagged at him to remember and yet not know the youngster's face."

"No sir, I do not recall, "answered Beck.

#33

Men were sent to call in the Earl's primary vassals, the five landowners, knights and each manor-lord in their own right. Sir Guy Northands arrived first. His was the nearest estate and servants had run to alert him of Sir Roger's return as soon as the Templar appeared in the village. He joined Neil Cleeves and Sir Roger at the high table of the Great Hall. He was the richest of the five. He said little while Neil Cleeves explained the situation before them, of how Sir Roger, being told of his brother's passing and being on Temple business in England had come home to Hammerstone Castle to assume his brother's place. Upon arriving home Sir Roger had learned that his brother was not dead officially. Now they must send someone to the King and get a judgment on the state of the Earl's health.

The question now remained, who should be sent? Sir Guy was obviously the man of highest rank after the Earl, but he was not eager to travel even though it was only to York.

Sir John Thornton was younger but lacked the tact to address the court. God only knew what rustic thought might he lay before the King. When he arrived and settled into his chair, little was said to him of the King at York. He too wished to see Robert's son.

Sir Alec Dupont, burst into the assembly flushed from a hard ride and was royally greeted by Sir Roger. Of all the Earl's vassals, Roger was closest in age and temperament to Dupont. Many a day they had spent at the hunt, many a night in riotous revelling and wenching. Sir Alec was happy indeed to greet the younger de Courtelaine home. A dead Earl meant little to him and having his old playfellow ruling Hammerstone would be fine by him. He spoke not of the heir, but called loudly for a pitcher of Flemish wine.

Sir William Baldric would not be coming; he was hunting with his cousins, the Howards, up north near the Roman wall.

Neil Cleeves pushed back his chair but before he could stand, Sir Roger jumped to his feet and took it upon himself to inform the rest of the company of his reasons for being there and what must be done next. This, of course, should have fallen to an officer of the castle and not to a visitor.

Sir Roger went on to explain that he wished to debate their course of action first and sup after. This, he said, because time was of the essence. He sat down; Cleeves stood and reminded the Hall that only the Lord of the castle could sit in the Earl's chair and no other. Several soldiers nodded their heads in agreement including Sir Guy, who liked things done properly.

Sir Roger's black eyes flashed and his face reddened but he vacated the Earl's ornate chair.

"Quelque chose," he said, forcing a smile.

His Templars answered him, "Oui, Oui", standing at attention while their captain moved to another chair. One Templar, seeing the Hammerstone men did not understand French said, "Revenons a nos moutons," producing a scowl from one of Neil's men. "Did ye say we are sheep?" he asked, putting his hand to his sword hilt, for he did not understand the loose translation *let us return to our sheep* often meant, 'let us get back on the subject.'

"Nay, he did not!" said Sir Guy, getting angry with the haughty Templars. "Let us all stick with a common tongue and common manners! Now are we agreed one of us should ride to the King to tell His Majesty of our troubles and return here with a Judgment? Well then, who shall volunteer to perform this service?"

No one spoke. In the silence, Sir Guy looked about the Hall. As Robert's oldest liege man, it was Sir Guy's right to go to court, but he did not wish to go on such a journey.

Roger loathed the thought of Sir Guy presenting his case to the King too. He wanted his old friend Sir Alec to go for he was sly and would know what to say. "If not the oldest, then it might as well be the youngest," he said. There were no objections and Sir Alec sent his squire running to make ready horses and gear. As an afterthought, Sir Roger decided that one of the Templars should go also that they might pay tribute to the Grandmaster. The knight he chose to send was one of his closest allies and a man well versed in his letters. He was not long in composing a letter telling of the terrible shape they found the castle in and the wicked ways of the young bride, not the least of which was her involvement with the unbelieving Jews. But before all of this Roger himself went to his sister's apartment and commanded her to bring the child to the Great Hall.

Katoryna agreed to bring forth the child as soon as he was done nursing. Her brother gave a sharp laugh, "Nay sister, bring the brat now for why should the Earl's vassals, knights all, and my own honourable holy soldiers wait on a child to be done with the teat of that old sow." He nodded dismissively in Beasley's direction.

Oh, he won't be long Roger, stay your haste but a moment," she said lightly. Roger, wearied from holding his natural arrogance in check, lost his patience with his sister. He moved, quickly, grabbing the infant up and pulling him away from his supper. The babe had been firmly latched on and poor Beasley Dobbs was forced to come to her feet with him, or risk losing a nipple. Finally young Robert William let go with a protesting wail.

Beasley, deeply offended, stuffed herself back into her gown and under Roger's glowering eye left the apartment.

"I don't see why ye cannot just leave the child with its mother."

"Be quiet fool, thou has't spent a year within the walls of St. Hild's and yet ye have not learned to be silent? Did ye leave of your own free will or did the holy sisters tire of your endless chatter?"

"I'm sure I was better suited to a nunnery than ye are fitted to thine Order, thou false Templar."

Roger handed the crying infant to Katoryna, "Well that may be true, my dear sister. Perhaps we shall see that you are returned to St. Hild's since ye are so well suited to the life behind the wall."

Young Robert William cried all the harder as they left Katoryna's apartment and descended the stairs. In the hall the infant's cries were answered in full. From behind the locked door of Roger's old room Maken screamed for her child to be returned to her. Katoryna paused for a moment, and had Roger not scowled at her, she would have taken the child to its mother. But they moved on. For Fontennell's sake she would appease her brother for she wanted Cam to be part of the new order in the castle. Any fool could see that both Camille and Maken would soon be pushed aside. For better or worse, Roger would prevail, a situation that Katoryna was beginning to fear.

Hearing her child crying, Maken found the strength to pull herself out of bed somehow. Pushing aside her mother, she staggered across the room to the door. She screamed over and over for her son and she pounded on the oaken door until Father Hubert and Sarah overcame her desperate grip on the door handle and were able to guide her back to the bed. A line of blood drops marked her journey. The Jewess had left a measure of her wondrous elixir and Camille deemed it prudent to give Maken some, enough to let her sleep that her body might have a chance to heal. With Sarah's urging, Maken drank of the medicine, grew silent and at last, slept. For a long while the two mothers and their priest sat in gloomy silence, the shock of Roger's return setting heavy upon their hearts. Sarah said, "That the child cries is a good sign. It proves that at least he still lives."

#34

The feasting started in earnest when Roger and Katoryna returned to the Great Hall with the heir. Roger left Katoryna to show the child to his future vassals and servants while he had some last words with Sir Alec Dupont and the Templar that was to accompany Sir Alec to the Court at York. Carefully he interviewed both men until he was perfectly convinced they were able to say exactly what he wanted them to say. When they were fairly away he returned to the hall.

The sight of his sister walking about the long tables with her nephew in her arms seemed odd to the hard-hearted Templar champion. Of children he thought little and yet here was his like-minded sister, fawning over the infant. How odd. Katoryna took her time with the heir and walked along each of the tables, letting each man take stock of the new Earl, testing the grip of the tiny fingers and lifting his arms. She would not, however, suffer the child to be taken out of her grasp. She chided the men saying their heavy limbs and thick hands were ill suited to holding young Robert William.

Sir Roger said nothing, rather he attended to the tasks at hand, namely satisfying his hunger and reacquainting himself with his father's vassals. Painfully he put away his natural arrogance and pride and assumed the cloak of long-lost brother and friend. Now, humbled by life's lessons and tempered by his newfound devotion, Roger de Courtelaine drew himself to be the perfect guardian of his newborn nephew, a benevolent teacher, holy, yet skilled in the arts of war. The knights sitting about the tables of the great hall could see there was no other man so qualified to train young Robert William.

Katoryna, having satisfied the men's curiosity, sat quietly along the wall nearest the kitchen. She wanted some quiet for the child while she listened to her brother's debates. The fate of Lydia, the Jewess came up, and the Templar's thought that she should be tried as a sorcerer. All the tokens of the black arts seemed present, eastern potions, supernatural healings and odd behavior. Of course, any behaviour they did not like was deemed odd and devilish by the people around her. Much would be made of the Lady Camille's supposed kneeling before the Jewess.

Neil Cleeves soon ended this talk, and reminded the visitors that the Jewess was a guest of the Lady and as such the honour of the castle guaranteed Lydia's safety. In the face of Sir Guy Northand's backing of the captain, Sir Roger could do little but cede the point.

Still, it was agreed to compel the unbeliever to leave Hammerstone without delay. A woman alone at night along these northern roads had little hope of reaching the relative safety of York unmolested and all those present knew it. Of course, this bothered no one just so long as the honour of the castle remained intact.

"What cruelty," thought Katoryna. The Jewess, through no action on her own, and here only because of her genius in the healing arts, was to be left defenseless in the night. Easily they could hold Lydia in isolated peace until the morn and even then it would not hurt Sir Roger to have the Jewess safely escorted back to her father's house. Katoryna, tired of her brother's hypocrisy, took her leave, stopped in the kitchen only long enough to call back Beasley, and returned with the child to her apartment.

#35

Two score of the Earl's archers sat about the second floor hall above the Boar's Tooth Inn. This was their meeting hall and rare was the night where at least a dozen of the bowmen were not to be found hanging about, enjoying the company of his fellows. It was a bittersweet day for in the midst of the horrible turn of events in the castle, Garfield's wife had delivered her child. A strong boy and Garfield's great joy was tempered by the cruel choices suddenly laid before him. He quietly drank his ale and accepted the congratulations of his friends.

All knew his vow to never live under the thumb of Roger de Courtelaine and none doubted his willingness to fulfill that vow. It would be hard to turn outlaw just when life was becoming so sweet, what with the archers and marriage and bright coins in his pockets, a future for him and for the babe in Edwina's arms. The future of full bellies and warm beds was now gone like dust in the wind. Bitter thoughts clouded Garfield's mind and he drank into the darkening night.

Cam Fontennell sat beside their captain and cleared his throat. The men sitting with him looked at him curiously. The mystery of Cam Fontennell only seemed to deepen with time. He lived in the castle yet was not Norman. He was an archer, yet not a villager, too young to be wise and yet self-possessed far beyond his years. Rumor had it that he bedded the Earl's sister and also that he bedded the Earl's widow. None could say. He lived not aloof but rather alone. Cam was liked by the other archers for, despite his great skill and high favour within the castle, he never gloated over the others and would sit and while away the evenings with the rest. But he never spoke of times he spent in the Earl's company even though many ears would love to hear any gossip about his lordship. Nor did he offer his opinion on anyone else. He deflected personal queries with a smile and a shrug of his shoulders.

Cam was a strict adherent to the old saying, *'The less said the better'*. So when he addressed his fellow archers the room above the tavern quickly went silent.

"Thou knows, each one of ye, what our good captain here intends to do. I do not doubt for a moment that he would be as good as his word concerning Sir Roger de Courtelaine, he is a brave heart and the best bow among us!"

Men shifted in their chairs and wondered to what purpose Cam was leading. Was he going to try to protect the Templar? The de Courtelaines? At whose expense?

Cam continued, "Aye, we know Garfield. But this deed is one he should not try!"

Thurgar, sitting along the wall whispered quietly to his neighbor, "Ahh, now at last, young Fontennell reveals himself at the expense of his fellow bowmen. Sleep with dogs, wake up with fleas, I always say."

Garfield interrupted, "Wouldn't thou have him over us? Ye know him not!"

"Nay Garfield, ye do not take my meaning. I never said he shouldn't die. I meant ye should not do the killing. Too many folk rely on you, your wife, your new son, the villagers, and the archers in this room. Nay, sir, if ye were made out-law many would suffer needlessly." For Fontennell this was a long speech. He went back to drinking his ale.

Garfield eyed his young friend carefully, even now seeing his intent. Meanwhile the few around the table within earshot nodded in agreement with Fontennell. Where would they be without the sly weaver to advise and guide them?

"Then who?" said Garfield.

Cam Fontennell smiled.

Garfield felt a flood of guilty relief, instantly followed by self-loathing. It was not in his nature to leave the hard tasks to another; he led by example.

But Cam's stand was based on a common sense. He was unattached. He was right and only Garfield's pride kept him from admitting it. Cam had no ties to hold him back. Fontennell drained his mug and stood. "I've always wanted to travel," he said and he left the hall.

Thurgar spoke, "Why not wait and kill the Templar some dark night and let no man take the blame."

"If no man is blamed then the Normans, and especially these Templars, would blame us all and kill many."

Thurgar felt foolish. Of course that was true.

"Nay, Thurgar," said Garfield gently, "it would not do at all but your idea was sound."

#36

Cam Fontennell believed Neil Cleeves to be a spy working in league with the Bandit King. The steward had warned him to keep his thoughts on this matter to himself. This Cam did but to satisfy his own curiosity he made a study of the new Captain. He knew that often Cleeves would travel alone and at all hours, never taking a force of men with him, preferring to chance the lonely roads on his own. And never was he bothered. Cam noted also that Cleeves seemed to take these solitary journeys when unusual events occurred in the castle.

Cam slipped out of the village and walked south along the rolling Ouse. At the battleford he hid himself near the crossing in a stand of beach. He reasoned that after a day such as this, Neil Cleeves would have much to tell the Bandit King. Cam resolved to follow the soldier and see for himself the object of Neil's many lonely wanderings.

The moon rose in the night sky and Fontennell stayed in his hiding place, his mind alert to any sound that he might hear above the river, still running fast and cold from the spring rains.

He liked the night, the calmness of the air and the quiet. He never was one to need the company of others and that was what made him a successful hunter; patience was his power to sit still and observe for long periods of time. Men, he thought, were as a rule far too hasty, in their speech, their judgments, and their plans. Take Garfield's actions today. He vowed to kill Sir Roger de Courtelaine. He should have known better. Even if he was planning to kill the Templar, why say it? And this from the villager that Cam considered the wisest. Of course the Saxons were, as a rule, a hot-tempered race. Ready at the drop of a hat to join in a quarrel and when their passions had cooled, equally as likely to walk away before the cause was settled.

It was not lost on Cam that when Sir Robert had taken it upon himself to hunt down the vagabonds that killed Cam's family, it was the Norman soldiers who never wavered but followed Lord Robert through all manner of weather while some of the archers wearied of the task.

Time eased on and Cam's thoughts turned to Katoryna asleep in her soft feather bed. How warm her skin would feel and how soft her hair. She said she loved him and wanted to marry him. How like her to say such a thing. She was bold and her boldness offended many people, but not Cam Fontennell. He liked it. He like her and enjoyed her company, enjoyed her bed. As for love and marriage, he didn't know. For one thing she would no doubt be married off to a wealthy Norman like herself. It was the usual way. But he would enjoy her while he could.

There were horses, several in a tight ride and they were almost upon him before he heard them coming. They reined up at the water's edge close enough that Cam could smell the horses and yet the riders were attired in such a manner that Cam could not make out their identity. Long flowing dark robes and full hoods. Cam moved out of the bushes enough to render the horsemen visible. There were five and one. The one being Lydia, the Jewess. The cloaked riders dismounted and ordered Lydia to do likewise.

She was ordered into the river. "But sirs, good men ye cannot abandon me to the darkened road surely!"

"Aye we can and do."

"Please sirs, I beg thee. Leave not a woman undefended in this wild place!"

"Go!"

Lydia began to weep silent tears. Two of her tormentors produced from the folds of their robes, bright swords with which they induced the terrified woman down the embankment. "Sirs, please I appeal to your oath of chivalry."

"Go!"

Now Lydia's feet were in the river, "Has't thou never read that holy book ye are bound to live by? Cans't thou not be as the Good Samaritan and show charity to one of another race?"

"Speak not of these things, unbeliever!"

"I believe in the God of Abraham, the same as you. Call me not an unbeliever," she answered.

The leader of the five or at least the one most given to speak, warned his fellow riders to beware of the Jew's voice lest she bewitch them with a word-spell. To Cam, the only thing Lydia cast was common sense. He did not know who this Samaritan fellow was but he did think it was a mean cowardly trick to force a stranger, and a woman at that, to take to the open road in the deep of night. Using the point of his sword the nearest rider forced Lydia farther from shore and into the deepening current.

"I am a guest of the Earl of Malton at the pleasure of the steward of Hammerstone Castle. Return me there at once!" she said remembering at last this consideration that these heathens granted one another.

"Liar! Liar!" hissed one of her tormentors.

"She speaks the truth!" said Cam, bursting out of his hiding place. "What means you this? Are you so cowardly that you would cast the lady into the night without even a guard?"

Caught in the midst of a very inglorious deed the riders turned on Cam.

"Who speaks thus against a Knight of ....."

"Enough!" interrupted their leader, "On your way, stranger!"

"Stranger?" said Cam, "It is you who are the stranger here. I am Fontennell. Who are you?"

"Well, Fontennell, if that be thine true name, what mischief brings a vagabond like you out, has't

151

thou never heard of curfew bell? Or art thou some thief out to no good?"

"Mark ye this, a curfew would not apply to me for I am the Earl's own squire and go at mine own free will. Now release the lady, she is a guest of the castle."

"I think not," said the Templar.

Now Fontennell drew forth his sword, "Come, let the least cowardly of thee step forth and we shall debate the lady's innocence."

Oaths of disbelief met Cam's open defiance. These men were professional soldiers, the most feared killers in Europe and they had grown used to their unquestioned superiority. The leader stared at Cam in the dim moonlight, appraising him best he could. He judged the Jew's champion and found him lacking, turned to one of his lesser companions and bid him to take up his sword and support their side of the quarrel.

The two men fell at one another and struck back and forth without pause. The Templar's companions stood away so that the sport could be better played out. And well they did for each combatant wielded his steel with abandon and many a wide sweeping stroke. The knights expected their man to make short work of the stranger and at first they thought he only allowed Cam to live, to use this chance to practice his swordplay. Since crossing the channel Sir Roger had kept the men from fighting for any reason. This did not endear Roger to his men. "Blades rust quick, and men quicker," they said.

Fontennell had no rust and twice his sword cut flesh while his opponent had yet to touch him. The two staggered about in the darkness on the uneven riverbank, each man fighting to keep his balance. The young Templar was becoming worried. He never guessed some local buffoon would be able to hold his own against a holy warrior, but he was out of practice and the heavy mock cassocks they wore slowed his sword arm.

Of all the men around Sir Robert in those short but happy days he was Earl, none had learned so much under his tutelage as Cam Fontennell. Whether it was because of his youth or his lack of friends before he met the Earl, young Cam had embraced the Earl's every word. And Sir Robert was an expert in hand to hand combat. The martial arts Cam Fontennell learned from the Earl, combined with his natural abilities, made him a far more deadly swordsman than his age and station would have warranted.

So now, standing on the clay banks of the Ouse, the young archer was wearing the Templar down countering each thrust deftly, parrying the blows away from his body with sidesteps and then striking back.

The leader of the Templars saw it first, even in the dim moonlight his practiced eye perceived his man would lose, possibly die and this he would not allow. He took his sword in hand and as Fontennell turned away dealt the archer a sharp blow to the case of his skull.

Cam collapsed in a heap at the feet of his surprised and relieved opponent.

"These islanders are a tenacious lot," said the leader. He ordered Cam's opponent to take Cam back to the castle and see that the archer was locked away. The knight swore under his breath, his night was over before it had started.

Lydia was gone. Caught up in the swordplay the Templars had failed to notice as she slipped away.

"Come now!" said the leader, "It seems the Jew has slipped away!" As their hoof beats faded away the Templar turned jailer stared down at the author of his ruined night. He took his sword and cut Cam several times about the arms and shoulders. It would not do to let the others know a local had bettered him. Carefully though, not too much, least his companions guess at his deception. He would have rather slipped the Spanish shaft between Cam's ribs and tossed him into the water. Savagely, he kicked the helpless archer a few times before tying him across his horse.

An hour later the angry Templar was back in the Great Hall drinking away his sorrows and Cam Fontennell was laid out in the very cell that so recently had held the unfortunate Jewess.

Katoryna sat quietly along the wall, content to listen to the dozens of different conversations going on about the room. Perhaps it was her having grown used to the almost constant silence of St. Hild's but Katoryna found her father's hall to be too loud and over burdened with fools. She was just about to retire to her quarters for the night when her heart jumped. She heard the name Fontennell. She sat up and scanned the tables. Yes, there it was again, and at the dais, Roger was talking with one of his fellow knights. A young man, tall and lean with freshly wrapped dressing on his right arm.

Katoryna got up and approached her brother's table.

"And he is in the prisoner's tower, ye say? Good!" said Roger to the knight.

"Did ye say something of Fontennell, brother?" asked Katoryna.

Sir Roger laughed, "Aye, sister, could this Fontennell be of a lean build and average height? Grey eyes?"

"Yes! That's Cam!"

"Well, I've news for ye. He is a trouble maker and on the morrow we show him the road!"

"What? 'Tis the one I told ye of! He is of great interest to me."

"Fear not, sister," said Roger, "I've no doubt you can soon find another young fool to rut with!"

Katoryna fought to control her temper. She knew that Roger was toying with her, enjoying her distress. She wanted to slap his leering face but did not, instead she shrugged, "Yea, thou are right, I suppose, but tell me, how is Fontennell now? Or have ye cut off his head?"

Sir Roger said, "Nay, Katoryna, we of the Temple waste not our blades on just anyone, only the blood of the infidels do we seek! Your young friend has been spared."

Roger smiled at her obvious relief at this news. She took her leave and as she walked away Roger called out, "If ye have a notion to say good-night to your champion, just come and ask me," and he held up a ring of keys. Katoryna recognized them for they were of a different make than the others, used only to unlock the doors of the prisoner's tower. He laughed as she stalked out of the Great Hall.

Of all the castle's servants none was happier to see Sir Roger return than Alicia, Katoryna's longest serving maid. Since Katoryna was but a babe, Alicia had been her daily companion. Only eight years older that her mistress, she was the nearest thing to a sister that Katoryna ever had. And Alicia was of an evil nature.

Lady Camille regretted ever letting the girl near her daughter, but Alicia was sly and sweet and for the longest time the servant girl kept her true nature hidden away. Also, Katoryna and Alicia were in many ways of the same mind and the two kept many secrets.

Katoryna grew into her teens and rumors of her misconduct became common. By that time Camille had lost any influence with the Earl and she was powerless to remove the servant-girl from her daughter's life. And worse still, Alicia had found special favour with Sir Reginald in ways that Lady Camille did not wish to contemplate.

But the Earl died and Katoryna went to the monastery at St. Hild's and Alicia found herself demoted to the kitchen as a scullery maid. Hard was her fall for she had always held herself above the other servants of the castle, lording over them and causing grief when she could. And the castle remembered. Gone was her fine cot in Katoryna's apartment, with her own water basin; gone were the sweet meats and wine from her mistress' plate. Now she slept with the rest of the maids in the loft on a straw pallet.

Katoryna's return improved Alicia's station but Katoryna had changed, fallen in love and now she had little time for Alicia's scheming. Sir Roger's return was Alicia's great opportunity. She was ready to do whatever she could to aid him in his claim for Hammerstone. There were many tales she could whisper in his ear and many secret things she could reveal. And when the outsiders were banished then things would return to the way they were when Sir Reginald was Earl.

Katoryna stopped on the stairs between the kitchen and the private hall. Alicia stood by waiting for her mistress to speak. Katoryna had a sly grin on her face like Alicia had not seen in many a moon.

"Alicia, Sir Roger's old rooms are guarded by a Templar. I would have him away for a time. Can ye bribe him to abandon his post?"

This was more like the old Katoryna, thought Alicia untying the top of her gown. Smiling, she promised to take care of the Templar, using a currency sweeter than wine and older than money.

Katoryna watched her maid go on up the stairs and when she was well away, Katoryna returned to the kitchen and called for the cook.

#37

Sir Roger's apartment was furnished with only the most basic of things, a bed, a table with three chairs and a large chest lay up along the wall. The walls themselves were covered in the usual array of smoke-dulled tapestries. Maken slept on the bed with a single blanket cast over her for warmth. It galled Camille to think of the thick luxurious quilts piled high in the solar a few short steps away. She removed her cloak and laid it over her daughter-in-law. Father Hubert stood by the door, listening perhaps for some clue as to what the Templars were up to. The door was thick and he heard little.

Sarah sat close by Maken, checking her often for signs of fever and marvelling that there was none. "The Jewess hast done a miraculous thing this day, has she not?" said Sarah.

"Indeed, hers is a race known for their doctoring of the sick. My father used to say all the wisdom of the world was in the east," answered Camille.

Camille paled and looked toward the priest sitting quietly by, "No offence to the Pope in Rome of course," she added quickly.

Father Hubert said, "I doubt that even His Holiness could have saved Maken and the babe."

"Shall the Bishop be very angry with you, Father?" asked Sarah.

"What? For tending my flock? I doubt it. I fear far more for the Jewess. I pray she finds sanctuary in this evil land."

The priest said no more but sat down with his back against the door. The two women fell silent also, their thoughts on the many troubles swirling around them.

The rattle of a key in the door-lock snapped Father Hubert to his feet. Without realizing it, the two mothers came together protectively in front of Maken's bed. They stared at the door, wondering what new devilry Sir Roger had in mind. Father Hubert doubted that Maken would be long in this world if the Templar captain was allowed to have his way. And after his mother, the infant earl would go likewise. Men had died for far less than what was at stake here.

The door swung open and Katoryna stepped into the room. In her arms she held a large basket. She came to the bedside and set the basket down. She pulled back a blanket and lifted the sleeping Robert William out of its depths. Ever so gently she laid the sleeping son with his mother. Katoryna held up her hand to quiet the surprised prisoners. She listened for footsteps. Hearing none, Katoryna implored the priest to come with all speed and assist her.

This he did and soon the two returned bearing baskets of food. Loaves of bread and cold meats as well as several flasks of wine. Three times did Katoryna and Father Hubert come and go, bringing warm blankets after the food and lastly sleeping pallets. Only when everything was safely in the apartment did she speak.

"There is much news and much to be done. The King is in York and Sir Alec Dupont has gone to plead Roger's case before him. Also the Grandmaster of the Temple is in York. And let me tell ye all, that piece of news took the wind out of Roger's sails! Now he must behave himself and all we have to do is wait him out. He would not dare harm us while we remain within these walls. But one of us must go to the village lest some of your hotheaded friends try to anger my brother. She looked at the priest.

"How?" he said.

Katoryna motioned Father Hubert to follow and let him out into the hall and down to the end of the passage. Through a door and into a smaller room usually reserved for guests too important to have slept just anywhere. Now this particular room faced to the south where the Keep was part of the outer parapet walls so that from the window case Katoryna and

Father Hubert could gaze straight down into the black depths of the Ouse.

Katoryna produced from the folds of her dress a coil rope, which, after she tied one end off proved to be just long enough to reach the water below. To the priest's wondering stare she answered, "In days past I sometimes needed to leave the castle without my father's permission."

"But how did ye...? ... I mean, did ye swim to the riverbank?"

Katoryna put a long finger to her lips and in the silence she and Father Hubert listened to the gentle lapping of the Ouse against the great stonework far below them. And soon, a faint new sound. Now louder, and the priest could make out the sound of a boat being rowed. In wonder he watched as a small punt stopped directly below the window.

Katoryna smiled at his surprise. "Everyone has their secrets. Father, I pray ye don't ask me of mine."

Father Hubert, for his part, was more worried about the descent down to the water than anything else. Once he had jumped off the tower and for a long time the shock of that fall kept him off the parapet. Even now, just looking down from the windows made his belly roll into knots.

"You are suggesting that I descend this great height to that boat by means of a rope?"

"It is heavy enough and look, it's knotted at every foot."

Father Hubert leaned so carefully out of the window, "But still, how would I climb down to where I could seize the rope?"

Katoryna stifled an oath and shaking her head brushed the small priest aside and showing the nerves of a burglar, slipped out the window and in one smooth motion had turned and lowered herself so that only her head and shoulders were above the sill. She offered the priest a tight smile and without taking her eyes off his, found the rope by touch and disappeared down the

159

wall. In a moment she was up again, rolling into the room as quickly as she had left it.

Father Hubert had seen how it was done, but stood rooted to the floor. She couldn't believe him. At this point she was ready to throw him out the window. Instead she endeavored to make his descent easier. She untied the rope and held it tightly, then strung it through the top of the window casement. Next, she rescued the rope again, and tied it to an iron door holder.

"There now, ye can easily grasp the rope but please go quickly. I would not for the world be letting my brother be party to my plans!"

Father Hubert crossed himself and climbed into the window opening. He banged his knee on the sill and grimaced. Now he paused yet again. A breeze had come up and he swayed with it.

"Think of your friends, the risk they run if they try to assault the castle. It would be all the excuse Roger would need to slay half of them. Think, too, of the heir, let not his head be put to risk!"

The priest nodded. Not for the first time he pushed his fears aside and left the safety of the high stone walls for the watery depths below.

When he was finally seated in the punt, Katoryna hurriedly retrieved the rope and closed the shutters. Far below the boatman, seeing the shutters close, took up his oars and ferried Father Hubert to the village side of the river.

Katoryna ran back to Roger's old apartments and locked the door behind her. Having done whatever she felt she could do, she sat down.

The Lady Camille looked at her daughter scarcely knowing what to make of this unheard act of kindness. Katoryna was not known for her compassion and yet here she was helping out, getting blankets, beds, bringing in food and wine. And what mercy it was, to defy Roger and bring Maken her child. It made no sense at all. Could it possibly be that at long last her willful daughter was developing a conscience?

"'Tis a fine thing to do, Katoryna, returning the child. I can tell thee the poor girl was going mad without him."

"Oh yes," chimed in Sarah. "I thank thee for bringing in the wee one. 'Twas a brave act no doubt!" Sarah might well have said more and added a grateful hug to boot but she knew how her Myles despised the Norman maiden. In Reginald's daughter the Saxon saw the worst traits of their foreign overlords - cruelty, remorselessness and pride - still, Sarah was deeply moved by this unexpected mercy.

Katoryna seemed shocked at the comments. It really hadn't occurred to her that she was doing something noble. No, in her mind, she was thwarting her brother's plans. Praise was a sweet fruit she had rarely tasted and she found herself blushing.

Not too long later the young Robert William awoke and straightaway told the world he was hungry. Maken's eyes opened and she half-raised herself before realizing that her child was nestled in beside her. She wept. Through her tears she kissed her son and offered him her breast. This he took, and Maken gasped at his eager strength. Then she laughed and stroked his cheek and called his name.

"The Lady Katoryna has defied Sir Roger and brought Robert William to you, Maken," said Sarah.

Maken tore her eyes away from her son long enough to say thank you to her sister-in-law. Not a very gracious response to a truly kind gesture, but the young earl was all she could focus on. Katoryna, if she felt snubbed, did not show it and as she stood and stared moodily out the window the two grandmothers watched her. For the longest time the only sound in the apartment was Robert William's suckling.

Katoryna abruptly turned away from the window and looked at the others. "He has thrown Fontennell in the tower," she said.

#38

It was well that Father Hubert had braved the climb down the sheer stones of the castle for the men gathered at the Boar's Tooth Inn were in an ugly mood. Barclay was awake and he had not ventured to say all but even the little he did say had enflamed many of the archers. Many a loud oath was spoken and many deeds vowed to secure Maken from the clutches of her well-despised brother-in-law, Sir Roger de Courtelaine.

Worse still, Garfield, the most sensible man among them, and their leader, was at home with his wife and new-born son. He had tarried for a time at the inn, fearing the tempers would boil over but his concerns at home proved the greater and he had left the men on their own, praying that cooler heads would prevail.

"Sirs, sirs! Hear me out!" the priest shouted, upon entering the archer's meeting room. He was breathless and wet to the knees from jumping out of the boat too soon and missing the foothold on the steep lip of the riverbank.

"Sirs! Please!" He yelled and the din died down as the archers noticed their short priest standing in his own puddle in the doorway.

"Thank you!" he said in great gasps, much relieved that they would listen. "I've come directly from the Lady Maken and I have much news."

"Aye, Father, 'tis good, speak on and we will listen," said one in the crowd.

"Aye! Speak!" shouted the rest.

Father Hubert was guided onto a chair.

"I have held the Earl's son and I can attest to his great size and health. Maken is naturally proud of her baby and has named him Robert William!"

Cries of 'well done' and the like rang out and the priest had to raise his voice to make himself heard, again.

"But that is not why I have come to you, no my news is of a graver nature! Ye harken to my words now. The King himself, Stephen of Blois, is even now as we speak, in York with a goodly company of soldiers and we await a royal ruling on the claims of Sir Roger!"

Father Hubert had no need to raise his voice now. "Also my friends, ye all have heard that Sir Roger de Courtelaine is a soldier of the Temple of Solomon and as such is sworn to conduct himself in the most Christian of ways. Well, now he must truly adhere to these precepts, for the leader of his Order, the Grandmaster himself, is in attendance with the King at York! Aye, all ye archers, our Earl's brother, it seems, has ran himself into a tight spot and it behooves us to lay in wait to see what the morrow brings. Some have even said that King Stephen himself shall journey to Hammerstone Castle and settle Maken's troubles!"

Having said what he intended to say, the priest slipped out of the gathering room and left the tavern. He walked to Garfield's home, one of the new cottages within the new village just three doors down from the Boar's Tooth Inn. He rapped on the door, a nice new snug-fitting door, and identified himself.

"Enter!" came the reply.

Inside was a domestic picture to warm the spirit. A comforting flame played on the hearth. The fireplace was well placed in the centre of the structure, in what was the kitchen. A sturdy brick chimney ran straight and true up through the sleeping loft and neatly out the roof. A large spinning wheel stood in the corner. Beside the chimney, a wide ladder with a railing ran down beside.

A head appeared at the top of the ladder. Garfield grinned and urged the priest to come up. Edwina and her new son lay in a large low bed deep under a canopy of blankets. Edwina smiled at Father

Hubert. He had a way with children and he picked up the infant and blessed him without the babe waking.

"A beautiful child!" he said politely. Actually, Father Hubert found all newborns to be rather ugly, red and blotchy with wrinkled twisted mouths and eternally wet bottoms.

They talked of Maken's baby and Edwina's baby and children in general until Edwina tired and drifted into sleep. Father Hubert motioned toward the stair and the two went down to the lower room.

Over a cup of ale, Garfield heard all that the rest had heard and more, for Father Hubert knew he could trust Garfield to keep his temper and his tongue in check. He had been deliberately vague with the archers, not wanting to enflame their hot Saxon blood.

He told of Roger's cruelty in keeping the child away from Maken, how she cried and threw herself at the door, heedless of her wounds. He told of how Roger forced Maken and the ladies out of the solar, even at the risk of hurting Maken in her weakened state and how they were locked up without so much as a wafer of bread or a sip of water to sustain them. At this point Garfield asked the obvious, "How, then Father, art thou free to walk among us, if Sir Roger had locked you away?"

"Ahh, well now, now ye come to the odd part of my tale. There we were trapped as tightly as ever a Christian could be. Oh how the ladies did weep at our station. I can tell ye right earnestly I prayed for deliverance and just when it seemed we had been abandoned, the door lock rattled and the door opened. It was the Lady Katoryna and glory to sweet Mother Mary, she brought the new Earl Robert William with her and gave him into Maken's arms. Oh, yes, Garfield, it was she that was our answered prayer. And then she called me to assist her and soon we had fetched beds and blankets and drink and food enough to last a while. And after the ladies were well provided for, Katoryna drew me into the hall and bid me to come to the village and warn ye of the royal interest in our Lady. We must be of a cautious nature, Garfield."

"Aye, Father, 'tis one thing to put up armed resistance against Sir Roger, but the Crown is another matter! Little can we do now," said Garfield.

"But," continued the priest, "we must even yet do what we can to help the cause. Show His Majesty a united front. The archers at their best. Perhaps he will help keep the troop together if he sees for himself their value. Plus, Maken's enemies will no doubt try to say the earldom has fallen into lawlessness since Lord Robert's death. This we can disprove with orderly behaviour."

"So ye think the Earl is dead?"

"Yes, and I think we all should begin to accept that fact. Most of all, Maken."

"It will go hard with her. She did love him."

"And he her."

"It was an affaire d'amour," said the priest after a while. He realized that the young Lord who had given them so much was gone and that with luck they might one day learn the manner and time of Robert's terrible misfortune. But now, they must think for the future and how best to protect Maken and her son. The infant was the new Earl and the anchor of all their hopes. And yet, Father Hubert could not keep his thoughts from tumbling back to before Sir Robert's disappearance. The fun it was to be part of the Earl's household, the hope he held in the future, hope that they all felt and the Earl's endless ideas. How strange it was and how like a dream it seemed now. Garfield interrupted the priest's chain of thought.

"His fearlessness, Father. It was his fearlessness that kilt him."

"Yea, I suppose ye art right, if he would have fled with Maken, perhaps they both might have gotten away."

"It's not fair, it's not right Father. Why, of all people should he have had to die? Can it be that God does not care? Why, if he is so powerful, why does he let such evil times befall us? If I pass by a drowning child and do not stop to save him, few would call me Christian! And yet are we not like a child drowning in one misery after another and does not God walk on by and leave us in our own wallowing pain? Does a streak of evil run in the Almighty?"

"Blaspheme not! Thou poor fool!" whispered Father Hubert, for he was choked at such heresy and could not find his voice. "Do you know nothing of what is written? Of why we mortals live on faith and faith alone? How we are called greater than angels in heaven?"

Garfield raised his eyes, "Now who blasphemes?"

"Nay, Garfield, an angel believes in God because an angel sees God, but we mere mortals, we believe only through faith and we that can hold true to that faith even in times of hardship and sorrow, are the truly fortunate ones and the truly chosen ones."

"Ye make it sound as if our troubles are really blessings!"

"Well on a higher count, on a spiritual level, the troubles that test us are indeed blessings for it gives us a chance to show our faith. Why? If following Christ meant a life of ease, what would be the point? That is why the ghost of Pentecost is called the comforter, to help us through our trials and tribulations. 'Tis God's plan to find worthy men."

Garfield had no answer but while the priest's words seemed to make sense he also could see how a Norman priest would find it handy to tell his Saxon flock to be happy in their poverty.

"Ye give me much to think about, Father."

"Well, yes, but now I must seek out Fontennell. He must have gone out into the countryside for I did not see him at the tavern."

The two parted company and Garfield climbed back into the loft. Even in the midst of all the excitement of the day the weaver soon fell into a deep sleep.

Father Hubert waited a good spell for Fontennell, but the archer did not appear and the priest retired to a corner and fell asleep. An uneasy peace lay over the village and men waited to see what the morrow might bring.

#39

Sir Roger de Courtelaine had known the maid, Alicia, for as long as he could remember. Well suited she was to the two younger de Courtelaines, for even as children the rapacious nature of the two was made manifest in their endless scheming and tricks. Alicia, older than they, but just as conniving, was a welcome addition to their adventures. It was she who first got them wine from the cellarer, she who taught them how to gamble with dice and it was she who slipped them into the servants loft and let them see for themselves how adults amuse themselves in the dark of night.

When Alicia was done with the guard he returned to watch over the Earl's widow and Alicia went back to the Great Hall. She found a quiet spot along the wall across from the dais and there she waited for the crowd to thin and for Roger to notice her. He had seen her as she had entered the hall and several times she had thought he was watching her.

Later, when the candles were burning low and most of the guests lay sleeping among the remains of dinner and the empty wine flasks, Alicia carefully untied the top strings of her gown and loosened it until the sweet round of her breasts shone golden in the candle light. Scullery maids slipped in about the inert diners carefully retrieving the kitchen cutlery and Alicia ignored them. She was, after all, the Lady Katoryna's personal maid once again and had no need of common friendship. The kitchen girls hated her even more now than before. Alicia savoured their anger, loving their jealousies.

She came to the dais and seeing Sir Roger was alone for the moment, approached his chair.

"Good evening, m'lord," she said, bowing enough that Roger could better appreciate her charms, "Shall I prepare thy bed?"

"I have no bed now; I am a Knight of the Temple and must do without worldly comforts."

"Well then m'lord, ye can find repose in mine." He said nothing for a while and she wondered if she had miscalculated. Perhaps she had offended him, but eventually he nodded and bid her to be away and prepare a bed. Giving him her sweetest smile, she took her leave.

At last the feasting was done and Sir Roger slipped through the kitchen and up the stairs to the family's private apartments. In Katoryna's room he found Alicia, sitting naked on the bed. Katoryna was not present and Roger guessed that his sister had found some soldier to spend the night with.

"Welcome home, m'lord," purred Alicia as Roger untied his belt.

#40

Katoryna was awakened by the cries of her nephew and she watched Maken roll onto her side and hold Robert William to her breast. His small arms stopped waving and his feet lay still as he turned his whole attention to his meal. Shafts of pain shot up Maken's back and her stitches burned raw, but she ignored the discomfort. How beautiful her child was; she marvelled at his perfect nose and his eyes, so much like his father's.

"Ye should drink of the Jew's elixir again, Maken, least the pain return," said Katoryna.

"Nay, m'lady. I cannot. Lydia said that her medicine can hurt the child."

"But still your wounds are raw and what matter if the child is cast into slumbers a little more, he's young."

Maken shook her head. How could she explain her fierce need to protect her child from everything? Now in her life, the well being of Robert William was paramount. She would rather endure the rack than see a hair of his precious head touched. This deep primitive fear for the welfare of her child was overwhelming. Her cuts would heal and she gladly met the pain of them. Katoryna could not know. How could she understand? She was never a mother.

Robert William had emptied her breast and in a truculent mood began tapping the offending gland with a tiny fist.

"Truly, Maken," Katoryna laughed, "he is a de Courtelaine!" Maken's eyes met hers, "Aye, that he is," she said.

Maken rolled onto her back and slid Robert William across her belly and carefully laid him on her other side. She winced as she rolled onto her right side and gave a fresh nipple to the child. He settled down and eyed his mother, as if to say, "Don't do that again, I was busy!"

Katoryna began pacing the apartment, walking from door to window and back, over and over. Her arms folded in front of her, tension radiating from her like sparks from a cedar flame.

Watching her sister-in-law, Maken finally realized, and she felt foolish. So obvious it seemed now - Katoryna was in love with Fontennell! Everyone, Maken especially, thought for the longest time that the willful young Norman woman was using Cam in the most base way. Only the suspicion that Cam Fontennell was using Katoryna as well kept his friends from warning him of her.

Now Maken saw Katoryna in a new light. Sir Roger had, for whatever reason, tossed Cam into the tower and in anger Katoryna had defied the Templar and brought the infant to its mother. Caught between brother and lover she chose the latter.

"Ye worry for Fontennell," ventured Maken.

Katoryna stopped her pacing. She was a proud soul and being in love did not change that.

"Why would ye say that?" she asked.

"I heard you tell the others of his imprisonment and I know you have a certain friendship with him."

Katoryna's fingers drummed on her arm. She reddened a little. "And what of it? Can I not have friends?" Maken smiled and cooed into Robert William's ear.

Without looking up she said, "Fontennell is a brave man and great archer. Why would you not like him? I know you value a fighting spirit in a man."

"It is said that you value him also."

"Aye, as a good soldier and help to my husband."

"And some say more."

"They lie!"

Katoryna searched Maken's face and said, "I know." She came and sat at the end of Maken's bed, "You loved my brother greatly, didn't you?"

"I shall always! None can compare to Robert."

"What shall you do now?"

"Whatever I have to. Whatever it takes to protect my son and see him come into his inheritance. This, at least, I owe to his father who fell to save us."

"Tell me what happened from the beginning."

"Beginning of what? That last day?"

"No, the whole adventure when you and Robert went travelling, just the two of you. Did you really not have any men-at-arms at all? Where did ye sleep at night?"

Katoryna had not meant to sound so enthusiastic but the rumours of this unusual journey had caught her fancy. She could well imagine herself and Fontennell one day riding off all alone over the distant mountains with nothing but their wits to sustain them...and a full bag of gold to ease the travelling, of course. She poured Maken some wine and waited for her sister-in-law to tell her tale.

Maken had never spoken of her last days with her husband. Maybe it was too painful to speak of or perhaps she just preferred to hold her memories in private, not sharing them lest they lose their luster in the telling. Until now she was jealous of those last moments. But she spoke now. For the first time she spoke of her love for the dead Earl. Not of his fine clothes or great castle. Not of his hundreds of acres or his villages, but of him, his laughter and happy teasing way. His great forearms and wide shoulders and how he would ride up in a thundering charge and sweep her up like a hawk plucks a field mouse. And those last glorious days, riding free and sleeping in those funny sacks that Robert had ordered. The joy of oneness and the joy of telling Robert that he was to be a father. His terrible battle with the mad troop of bandits led by their old steward Giles. The very memory of which stirred Maken's blood and deepened her resolve to fight to the end to protect Robert William.

As for Katoryna she was glad of the telling for it did her good to hear of her brother's courage and fight as he faced death. And if he had to die what could be more fitting for a de Courtelaine than to face his enemies alone with sword in hand and their blood on its blade. The salty wet ran down her proud face and there on this the darkest of nights, a bond formed between these two unlikely confederates. Katoryna vowed that she too would do whatever she could to further the cause of the sleeping child.

#41

Their passions sated, Roger and Alicia lay in the darkness and while Roger listened, the disgruntled new maid told him of all the things that had happened since he had left England. Of course, she told her tale with an eye toward her listener and to hear her tell it things had gone downhill indeed.

"The Saxon temptress had so besotted the Earl that now Saxons practically run the castle. Her father was the new forester, the first since the conquest. And a weaver, and mark ye that, a *weaver* was the captain of the Earl's special pet, namely that rag-tag band of ruffians that likened themselves to soldiers. It's almost funny really."

To these points, Roger had little interest. These appointments could easily be cancelled and the Saxon rabble cast aside. They concerned him not in the least. No, what he wanted was things of a more personal nature. Of what he just wasn't sure, but he knew the few things Alicia mentioned would hardly matter to the King or the Bishop. Roger knew that his brother's oft and foolish ways would be laughed at by the ruling class and nothing more. Zealously the great Earls protected their right to rule as they saw fit and for Roger to cast Maken out of the castle he would have to find a better reason than what he had heard so far. Of course, the Jew's presence in the solar might do the trick with the Bishop of Hereford (he hated non-believers) but Roger wanted to be sure. He needed a damning story - a scandal and so far only Alicia seemed willing to testify against Maken. Robert's Saxon wench had become remarkably popular with the servants, probably had bribed the lot of them - ruined them for good, no doubt.

Alicia nattered on and Roger only half-listened. He was tired from their lovemaking and her voice grated on his nerves. He was just debating kicking her out of bed when she said the most extraordinary thing. Roger for a few moments stopped breathing. Then he rolled out of bed and stared down at Alicia. She paused in her story telling and looked up at the Templar.

"Tell me again of what ye found while ye cleaned the solar!" he ordered.

"Oh well, yes, but mind ye I was there to clean and not to snoop even though you understand I am not by right a cleaning girl, but when m'lady left for the convent the others conspired to reduce me and belittle me. Why I can ..."

"Silence!" said Roger. "Now, thou foolish woman, tell me not of all your terrible trials on this cruel earth, but of what ye found in the solar!"

His interruption hardly fazed her.

"In the solar, in a wooden chest, his Lordship kept a great book bound in leather and once by chance Sir Robert happened to leave it out on the bed. Well I had heard rumours from some of the other maids of his Lordship's great book and so when I saw it lying there on the pillow I could not help but take a look." Roger slapped her hard across her bare backside. "That's for looking without leave," he said. Her thighs tightened as she flinched, fearing another blow, but Roger only urged her to continue.

"Aye, m'lord, but please strike me not!"

"Just speak!" he said. There was an edge to his voice and, warned, she continued her tale.

"Anyway, m'lord this book, you can't miss it, it's big and red and heavy and well... it was there and I had to move it to make the bed and so I opened it and read a few pages. Did ye know that your brother knew all the kings and queens of England?"

"So what of that? There have only been a few since the conqueror and of those before him, no one cares."

"But m'lord the Earl's book lists not only the kings gone before, but oh Sir Roger, the kings yet to come! For hundreds of years m'lord!"

Roger grabbed Alicia by the hair, savagely pulled her out of bed and across the apartment. The naked maid tried to straighten up but the Templar had twisted his hand around her hair so she was forced to run bent at the waist, her head banging against his hairy thighs. At the window he slammed the shutter latch up and kicked the shutters open. He pushed her head out and grabbed her leg. He forced her over the sill until she completely lay out of the window save for her knees and lower legs. Her back scrapped against the greystone walls of the Keep. Roger leaned out of the window, pinning her under him. "What means this that you would come to bed and lie to me?" he said angrily.

"I...do....not.....lie.... my.... lord...." Alicia twisted her head around until she could see the cobblestones shining dimly in the faint light of the moon seventy feet below. "Please....m'lord.... I .... don't.....lie." She couldn't lift her head enough to see much of Roger, only his eyes, hard and bright. "Are you a priest now that ye can read?"

"No, m'lord but I learned how with m'lady." Roger yanked Alicia back inside. Her hair fell down, hiding her face, blood dripping off a shoulder. She felt weak and in need of wine.

Roger wasted little time. "You learned to read? How?"

"I sat with m'lady through her lessons. I could not help but learn."

Roger went to the fireplace and knelt by the hearth. He picked a charred piece of wood out of the gratings and walked to the tapestry that covered the end of the apartment. He pulled back a corner of the cloth, exposing the gray wall behind it.

"**WHO AM I**" he wrote.

"Read this," he commanded.

"*Who am I,*" said Alicia.

"**THE LORD OF THE CASTLE,**" he wrote next.

"*The Lord of the Castle,*" she read.

Sir Roger stared at Alicia not quite sure of what to make of the maiden. This time he wrote:

ACJFM AA LOMM

Alicia paled.

"Well?"

"It means nothing, m'lord. I know not these words. Perhaps it is some foreign words if indeed foreigners can read."

"Alright," he said "I see that you can read. What else did it say?"

"Oh, m'lord, I could not look but for a wee time and I did not see a lot. It had funny little maps of things."

"Things, surely not things, maps are usually of places, and journeys, not of things!"

"But these were, m'lord, round balls and stars and the sun."

Roger thought that he would dearly like to read this "book".

Alicia smiled and said, "Shall we go to the solar and get the red book? Then m'lord ye can judge this 'thing' for yourself."

Roger's brow tightened and Alicia knew she had said something wrong.

"Nay, woman, we cannot for we have all agreed to keep the Earl's solar locked until the King can settle my claim. But tell me more of this strange book." Roger said this with a smile and he led her back to the bed. Happily she began to recite everything she knew or had heard of rumoured about the Earl's great red book.

Roger de Courtelaine at last felt he was getting somewhere. He would find and use this book and let its contents bury his brother forever. He let his mind leap ahead to a time when he would sit, unchallenged, in the Earl's chair and all this damn Saxon riff-raff were driven back to their troughs and sties. And Sir Robert's armour? Right quickly he would have it fitted to his own shoulders. He fell asleep with these sweet thoughts. Alicia lay awake for a time and wondered why Roger ever agreed to not go in the solar. Of course, she was wise enough to never ask.

#42

It was the witching hour and sober men prayed that no evil spirits came their way. In the great Borough of York, in the Clifford family castle few prayers were being said and sober men had long since retired to their sleeping quarters. But in the Great Hall, Sir John Clifford attended the King and many more besides, for King Stephen had come in force with every intent on building up his army in response to Henry of Anjou's return.

Besides Sir John Clifford and the King, many of the great northern magnets sat with them. Sir Hugh de Pruset, the future Bishop of Durham, the King's brother, the Bishop of Winchester, and Sir Simon de Montfort, the Earl of Leicester. While their lessers slept around them, these powerful men discussed the latest Anjou moves. Young Henry had come to King David of Scotland at Carlisle where he was to be knighted. Now King David had not come empty-handed but with an army of his Scottish clansmen. Ranulf de Blundeville, the Earl of Chester, too had played his hand and had come to the young prince with many men. United, these lords were determined to seek out Stephen, defeat him and cast him down in favor of Henry. All these things the King knew. His oldest son, Eustace, was sitting off by himself, and it was he who had ridden north with this latest news.

Eustace was in many ways very much like his father. He was strong, brave and a born soldier. And indeed his whole life had been, it seemed, one long campaign. Though equal to his father in the saddle, his was the broader thinking mind. Time and time again he had watched his father win great battles only to flitter away the gains. Politically he knew his father to be blind, unable to perceive a grand strategy which was a bloody shame since as a tactical general Stephen was unequalled in his time.

His squire pushed through the crowded hall, found Eustace and set before him a tray of food and a flask of wine. Eustace ate in silence, watching the men of Stephen's court as they tried to induce the King to follow the course of action that best suited their particular cause. Eustace felt pity for his father for he knew that Stephen was weary of the endless demands of office and yet to wear the crown was akin to riding a mad horse. The true danger was in getting free of the beast, not the ride. He likened his father to a bear surrounded by the hounds, too tired to run and wounded from the fight. Worse, they needed these men and the hundreds of swords each represented. And the man talking now, Sir Simon de Montfort, was especially important - his troops were well trained and many. However, Sir Simon was sly. He was a man in need of watching.

Eustace finished his meal, grabbed his flask of wine, and made way to his father's table. A spot along the board opened at his approach and he sat and listened to Sir Simon's words. The Earl was a persuasive man and the King nodded along as he spoke.

"Now we know, thanks to thine own brave son, that the Prince tarried at Bristol, instead of seeking out a quick battle. And why, Your Highness, 'tis plain to see, I'll wager young Henry is having a time trying to get all his Scottish friends to commit to war. Long have they sat on the fence and now he must beg and plead. And when they do move, it will be with very little heavy horse, for the Scots walk to battle. Meanwhile we are well provided for here in York and Your Majesty's forces are well assembled. Why therefore should we not march out to meet this latest challenge? I have heard some here tonight say we must go south and protect London. But why? Surely Henry knows better than to disrupt the capital. At the worst he will tax the fine burghers of the City and when he finally gets here we will relieve him of any such gains!"

Eustace smiled. Right cleverly had Sir Simon de Montfort brought the King to his line of thought. Everyone in court knew how Stephen loathed the shopkeepers of the City and their newly made up guilds and associations. Gathering their power and promoting their own interests before the crown's.

Eustace waited. He knew there would be a reason for Sir Simon's actions. There always was with his type. It was not long in coming.

"And Your Highness, a day's ride from here is Hammerstone Castle and the business there we must conclude. Besides, the hunting thereabouts is said to be unusually good. Why it's said even the serfs eat venison with the Earl's leave."

"What says you, brother?" said King Stephen to the Bishop of Winchester.

"'Tis well with me Stephen. Thou knows I am but a simple priest who takes what comes."

Stephen laughed, "Aye brother that is how ye will no doubt be remembered, as a simple priest!" Many chuckled at the thought for the Bishop was reckoned to be the richest man in England and the lavishness of his tables was legendary.

The King turned to the older man on his left. His simple dress and lack of jewellery set him apart from his fellow guests. For all the old man's poverty the King treated him with respect, for Hugh de Payne was the Grandmaster of the Knights of The Temple of Jerusalem. Stephen would have gladly given the Grandmaster an earldom and any title the Frenchman desired if he could have use of the Templars for just one campaign. The cream of chivalry, many of Europe's greatest knights had joined the warrior monks. Unfortunately for the King, the Grandmaster held to a policy of non-intervention in all matters political. And it was a wise policy for the Templars. By staying above the constant ebbs and flows of Europe's rulers, they would gradually become the middlemen of all dealings between nations. Mediators, envoys, dealmakers and money holders they were, and with all this would come wealth and power.

On this night the King of England sat in fellowship with the Grandmaster, each man an accomplished soldier, each justly as famous in the saddle, and each a leader of men. But this is where their similarities ended. While Stephen rode through life wearily and disillusioned, Hugh de Payne rode firmly, saddled in his own sense of righteous accomplishment.

The King's best years had been spent in tiresome and endless negotiations, often with men whom the King considered unworthy and cowardly. The Grandmaster needed only concern himself with the demands of his Order and his life was spent in the company of warriors much like himself. From these men he enjoyed total obedience. Such were the lives of these two now sharing a supper table in York.

"Sir Hugh," said the King, "on the morrow we have a certain matter to attend to at the castle of the late Earl of Malton, Sir Robert de Courtelaine. I can well assure you the game is plentiful on the way and the huntsmen have guaranteed the best stags in all England! Shall ye come?"

"De Courtelaine did you say, Your Majesty? I have a young knight in our order that hails to that name. Can it be the same family?"

The King assured the Templar that it was indeed Sir Roger's ancestral home that they were bound for and hearing this, the Grandmaster vowed to join the King in his journey. To the great relief of Clifford's steward, Stephen decided to retire for the night and with him went the hall. Still the steward had seen twenty pounds of wine and ale consumed since the King sat down to the supper feast. He could not bring himself to look at the butcher's tally.

Sir Simon de Montfort did not stay in Sir John Clifford's castle with the other visitors. He liked to have some privacy, and had ordered his steward to rent the whole upper floor of the Red Dragon. Sir John, hopelessly overwhelmed with honored guests, was too grateful to be insulted by Sir Simon's departure.

His steward had done his best to render the Inn's upper story fit for an Earl to live in. Sir Simon's own linen was on the bed and his favorite feather pillows lay across, his own chest was at the foot and silver candlesticks held tallow candles. The wine and wench, however, would be locally supplied.

For now, the Earl had other things on his mind and he waited impatiently for his son, Lionel, to heed his summons. After a short time the young man entered the room.

Lionel de Montfort went to the sideboard and poured himself a cup of mead. "Not a very fine table you are setting father," he said after sipping the liquid.

"Yea, the steward should have known better than to trust these northern yokels with our needs. I haven't enjoyed a meal since we got here," agreed Sir Simon. If they had been in public, young Lionel would have answered his father with the more proper, "*m'lord*", but when they were among their own, the de Montforts cast aside such formal titles. To his great credit, Sir Simon was close to his sons (his daughter he hardly knew) and in his later years these relationships would prove to be a great boon to the Earl. His sons learned the ways of court by closely watching their father's career. They could emulate him, and to great effect.

"Are we just partaking of this rather average draught or have ye called me to break my fast also?" asked Lionel.

"I've some news for you, my son. I've found you a wife. A nice young widow with a sweetly turned ankle and a counting room full of shiny coin."

"The Earl of Malton's widow? My, my, father, you have really outdone yourself. She has already whelped, I take it?"

The Earl sounded apologetic. "Aye, Lionel, 'tis true and not but days ago, I hear. At least that's the rumor, but no matter, the girl is young, she'll heal quick and ye can likely make something of her."

"Aye, what does the old gaffer say, *'young horse and good whip equals a fine rider'.*"

Sir Simon was blunt. "The main thing is that rumor puts her late husband's fortune in the amount of three thousand pounds."

"But the child?"

"The child gets the title, but the money, well the money goes to whoever has the keys."

"And to what do we owe the King for this great gift?"

"Two score mounted knights and three hundred foot."

"For how long?"

"The duration of the campaign or until Michealmass."

"'Tis a bargain, father, the Queen will want your head when she hears of it!"

Sir Simon laughed. It was true that the Queen was a far better bargainer than her husband. Out here, without his Queen, pressed for time and driven by need, Stephen did the best he could with these tough earls. And none were tougher than Sir Simon de Montfort.

For the use of his men the Earl would be given, through his son, the keys to the richest storehouse in the north.

Young Lionel wondered, and as he wondered he stroked the peach fuzz growing in a sparse clump on his chin. The earl thought the attempt at a goatee to be ill advised, but it was foolish to argue with his son over a point of fashion. There were so many other matters that he would have to force his son to see his way, that he was loathe to push unless he had no other choice. Like this de Courtelaine deal. It did Sir Simon's heart good to see how easily his son accepted the marriage. His was a mind very much like Sir Simon's but the wispy beard - it looked pathetic.

"This widow I am about to bless with my hand, what of her parents, what shall they say of me?"

"The parents? Ha! They are common Saxon stock and will know their place. No, you will have a free reign in your affairs. But even so, keep your wits about you and show a firm hand. This dead Earl, by all accounts, had some dangerous ideas."

"Like the Saxon archers?"

"Exactly. I would disband the lot at the first opportunity and the steward too. I wouldn't keep him. Get your own people running things."

"Aye, father."

With that bit of advice the Earl bid his son a good night, and called on his butler to bring him a last sip of wine. Sir Simon was well pleased with his day's work. Now he only had one more day of this uncertainty and then Hammerstone Castle would belong to his son, which of course, really meant that it would belong to him.

#43

Sir Simon de Montfort declined to stay within the confines of Clifford's Tower because he found the fortress to be too spartan for his tastes. Sir Hugh de Payne, the Grandmaster of the Knight's Templars declined to rest at Clifford's Tower for exactly the opposite reason, he felt that staying in a large warm tower would soften his men. They camped outside the west gates of the city. While he was in the east, the Grandmaster had read the writings of Setonius, the famous Roman historian. The historian's depictions of a Roman military camp caught the Grandmaster's fancy and he adopted the Roman practice of building a square camp every night, even down to digging a defensive ditch all around the camp perimeter and posting sentries on the corners and entrances. If nothing else, it kept the men busy and the local riff-raff away.

Few of his followers shared the Grandmaster's zeal for camp life but none would ever dare question the old man's sovereignty over them. The camp was built and trenched and a watch set even though an arrow's flight away, the town of York offered many a warm bed under sturdy dry roofs. And the chance of such a troop of hardened knights being attacked was nil.

The Grandmaster left Clifford's Tower and returned to his tented domain in the deepest of the night, wary and eager to find his couch. As he walked past his sentries, he sighed. There were two new horses at his tent and he knew he had guests to attend to. For a moment he was tempted to order the visitors away, but he forced that notion aside, driving it off as he would an infidel's sword thrust. Long years of endless duty had utterly burned away any frivolous notions his mind might have once held, if indeed Sir Hugh had ever had a frivolous notion. Men who knew him the longest said he was born with a scowl.

And a scowl he wore when he entered the outer room of his tent. A Templar knelt to his left in deep supplication, his uncovered head touching his bent knee. The knight remained thus, waiting for the Grandmaster to give him leave to rise.

Sir Hugh regarded the form before him; his tunic was soiled but well cut, made in Antwerp by the appearance of it.

"Stand, brother!" he commanded.

The Templar stood.

"What news of our brother, Sir Roger de Courtelaine?"

The Templar blinked, taken off guard by the old man's piercing stare and shrewd guess.

"Brother Roger is well m'lord."

"He is at his brother's castle, is that correct?"

"Indeed, m'lord, he is."

"Why?"

"Why, m'lord?"

"Yes, do you mock me? Why are ye here and not with Sir Roger. I was led to believe ye were in England to make Hammerstone our newest preceptory, not lounge about in York?"

"Quite, quite m'lord," said the young Templar. He knew better than to fool with the Grandmaster. He must be sure of his words; the old man was wary as a fox. He carefully explained how they journeyed to Hammerstone Castle, ready to assume care and control of the fortress only to discover that the Earl's family would not admit that Sir Robert was dead. They said he was only missing. The castle guard would not stand aside without word of the King. Worse, the once proud castle had fallen under the spell of a Jewess. Naturally Sir Roger had seized control of the solar, but is loathe to spill English blood.

At first the Grandmaster listened without interest, but the news of the unbeliever struck a nerve with the old Templar. His demeanor changed, he leaned

186

toward his disciple, his eyes took on a hard cast and he clasped his bony hands together.

"Where is this Jewess now?" he asked.

"She was under the grace of the steward, m'lord. An invited guest so Sir Roger sent her on her way rather than break the peace of the castle."

"A mistake! Christian charity does not apply to unbelievers!" the Grandmaster said in a burst of passion. Then he seemed to soften and the passion ebbed away, "Still, it was well to separate the child from the unbeliever."

"Thank you, m'lord."

"And now, who do you travel with, for I saw two mounts."

"Sir Alec Dupont, m'lord, liege-man and vassal of the Lords of Hammerstone and a true knight. He journeys to York to petition the King. As vassal he must know to whom he owes allegiance."

"You confuse me, did ye not say he is liege-man of the Earl of Malton? The Earl's bride has borne a son, and only the King can declare his son, the new Earl. This he has not done. Does it not seem logical that His Majesty should do this and make the child's nearest male relative his guardian?"

The Grandmaster grunted, "Kings are not always logical. Who knows His Majesty's mind? And guessing royal intentions is fraught with danger." For a while the old Templar said nothing and his young follower waited with bowed head.

"On the morrow we shall accompany Stephen to this troubled fortress and then we shall see. You may go," said the Grandmaster.

Long into the night after everyone except the sentries had gone to their beds, the Grandmaster sat in his chair. Thinking. He found that in his old age, he needed little sleep. Some men he knew needed more as they grew older even to the point of resting in the afternoon. Not him. Perhaps it was his hard life of soldiering or his restless mind, but whatever the reason he rarely slept more than three hours at a time. Nighttime, he found, was the perfect time to plan and consider and think, with no one to bother him with endless questions and duties, just blessed peaceful quiet.

Sir Hugh de Payne knew of Hammerstone Castle and he knew of Sir Roger de Courtelaine, who he was and how the young knight came to become a Templar. The blind eye the Grandmaster gave to his champions was not really blind. It was selective. De Payne believed in his Order and the strengthening of his Order was his only concern. The Templars needed a base in the north and Hammerstone obviously could use some Christian guidance. It was well that the King had invited him to Hammerstone Castle. He would not waste the visit.

#44

Sir Alec Dupont passed through the gates of York at the first lifting of curfew and he rode straightaway to Clifford's Tower. Citing urgent business, Sir Alec implored the King's guard to give him leave to enter the Keep. To this the guard politely replied that if the good knight would but wait a short time, His Majesty and all his retinue would be coming out these very gates.

"Bound for where?" asked Sir Alec. The guard shrugged. It was a foolish question. Kings rarely felt the need to consult with common soldiers about their travel plans.

"Right then, I'll just wait," said Sir Alec. The guard gave a quick nod and nothing more. He stared out past the visitor; evidently he had said all he was going to say. Sir Alec reddened. Damned impertinent guard. He had a good mind to box his ears. Sir Alec was working himself into a fine lather when the sounding of horn, high and clear interrupted his inner rages. On the other side of the gate soldiers were pulling free the heavy cross posts. Chains rattled and the hooves of many horses could be heard.

Sir Alec wheeled his charger around and stopped about twenty yards away from the gates. The guards brandished their pikes at the many beggars and bystanders urging them to get back. Sir Alec held his ground, his hand on the hilt of his sword. He glared at the guard nearest him. The guard ignored him.

'By Saint Peter! Are all these royal guards so ill mannered?' said Sir Alec to himself.

Now the gates were opened and King Stephen rode forth and with him a force of a size rarely seen in the north. And yet the King, seeing Sir Alec Dupont, halted beside the knight. "And who might you be?" the King demanded.

"Sir Alec Dupont, Your Highness. I've come from Hammerstone Castle."

"Ha!! Well young man we could have saved you the journey if you have come all this way to see us. We are bound for that very fortress right now."

Polite laughter from the host.

"Indeed, Your Majesty, you honor Hammerstone." The King spurred his horse away and Sir Alec joined the parade of riders following the King.

Sir Alec fell into a black mood. He had ridden hard all night on a dangerous road only to find he need not have left home at all. Worse, he had not even presented Roger's case to the King. Wasted trip indeed. And he had not eaten.

#45

The Grandmaster and his Templars were already waiting at the agreed upon rendezvous. The sight of the Templars caused a hush to fall along the King's column of men. Never was a medieval knight trained to the extent that these Templars were. In perfect unison the entire troop slowly turned out of their double file and into a straight single line facing the King's party. They unsheathed their swords and rapped their shields as a drummer strikes his drum and this they did so with such precision that the noise they produced sounded as one note.

Even the King, who had in his travels seen the Templar's skill before, marvelled anew at their horsemanship.

"Good morning, Your Majesty," said Sir Hugh de Payne, as he stepped his charger forward, "I trust His Highness slept well?" Almost a hint of a smile crossed the old Templar's weathered countenance.

The King wondered if the Grandmaster was mocking him for Stephen was known for his easy-going nature when it came to his troops and his men rode with little discipline. They fought well and that's all that concerned Stephen.

"Greetings, Sir Hugh. 'Tis a fine morning for a ride," the King smiled. The two leaders rode to the west and their respective forces fell in behind them, snaking out in a double line a half a mile long.

From a rocky crag high over the River Ouse, Bung lay hidden, as he watched the knights ride below. A few of his trusted followers lay hidden with him and like Bung they were curious to see such a rare thing as the King of England in the flesh if even from a distance. The Templars they found odd and the Grandmaster's fame had not reached their ears. Bung's men wondered what mischief their master had up his sleeve and each man tried to guess the amount of golden coins the capture of the King would warrant. The truth of the matter was that the Bandit King had nothing planned. Bung was just like the rest, curious, and so he had come. Now looking down on the procession he too mentally calculated the wealth before him. The King obviously could be ransomed off for hundreds of pounds or sold to the Prince of Anjou. Hard to do and dangerous but life was hard and dangerous. That never stopped Bung. It just made him plan more. And there was Sir Simon de Montfort, again a fortune in ransom just sitting there like a ripe plum. The Bishop of Hereford and the Bishop of Winchester, Holy Mary Mother of God, if one wasn't the richest priest in England, then surely the other one was. Each likely travelled with two hundred pounds in his strong box along with the material goods rendered unto them at every stop.

Bung cast an opinion of worth over all the notable citizens in the line and when he was done, he concluded that a successful raid upon the King's train could find him thousands of pounds richer. Bung savored the thought for a moment and then cast it aside. If he would have known of the King's trip a month ago, he might have tried it, maybe.

Bung stood up as the last of the royal party rode out of sight. The splendour of the knights, the beautiful clothes and the quality of their mounts left Bung's men at a loss for words.

"Seeing all this wealth makes a man hungry," said Bung. "Who has brought our victuals?"

"Right here master," answered one of his men, bringing forth a large leather pouch tied at the top with a length of cat gut. In a moment the sack was opened and the contents revealed three fresh loaves of bread, three potpies and a great round of white cheese fresh from the churn. Added to this was ale drawn from the best of the Red Dragon cellar, quite a tasty feast for six men. Bung made sure his men were well provided for and not just in the feeding of them, they were also well armed and he paid a surety in gold coin to Nathan of York to ensure a ready supply of healing herbs for his wounded. If the fates should turn bad and a man lose his life, he died knowing his loyalty would be repaid and his family looked after. For all this, Bung's men trusted him with their very lives. There was no enterprise that they would not eagerly attempt if their sly master but gave the word.

Of course, this largess did not cost Bung as much as one might think, because he rarely put his men at undo risk, so well planned were his raids. And he had decided on his latest venture. As the others ate their fill, Bung outlined what he wanted. They would follow the King's entourage, and after the Bishop of Hereford left the main party to return home, he would capture His Worship and pluck him as clean as a Christmas goose. And just to lull the Bishop into a false sense of security, they wouldn't strike until they were far off to the south - further than before. That way they could catch the Bishop's party unawares.

Bung's most trusted man, a Norman named de Roche, asked him, "Why do we wait for the Bishop? Why not depart now and wait in Herefordshire at our leisure? Surely the Bishop will come straight away home!" Now de Roche could speak up freely because when planning a raid, Bung welcomed debate and the odd time he had even been convinced to change a plan when a better way was shown to him. Bung only insisted on unquestioned obedience once the decisions were made. De Roche waited for his master to answer.

"We are not perfectly sure of anything, much less the thoughts of a rich priest. He could just as easily go to London as go home. There might be others who will try to rob His Worship. Then what would be left for us? And remember too, we are strangers in the south and the longer we are there the greater the chances of us being discovered. We shall find no easy refuge in the mid country, I can tell thee."

De Roche felt foolish. What his master said was all true.

Bung smiled, "And another thing, if His Worship is collecting tithes and rents as he goes, he will be all the better for plucking on his own doorstep - eh?"

Bung jumped up and dusted the crumbs off his jerkin, his sudden burst of activity startling the others.

"Come now my friends, let us be away."

#46

Henry of Anjou, the claimant to Stephen's throne, was likely on English soil, possibly at the head of an army. The Scots were on the move against him and yet the King seemed to be in no mood to rush to counter these latest developments. Today he was on the hunt and there was nothing that could deter Stephen from enjoying it. The falconer, again and again, was called to set Stephen's favorite peregrines to wing while the more serious-minded men about the King fretted about the lost time. None worried more than Sir Simon de Montfort. He wanted this business with the de Courtelaines done with. The sooner the better. As for the rest of the King's concerns, Sir Simon cared not a wit. Long ago he had realized Stephen of Blois had seized a throne he had little use for. Only his pride and his formidable wife kept Stephen going. And, of course, there was promise shown by Stephen's oldest son, Eustace. Brave and resourceful, the Crown Prince had already proven himself to be a good campaigner and more than that, he seemed to be a man of industry and common sense. Sir Simon looked across the backs of several horses and observed Eustace. The prince said little but his eyes missed nothing as he watched his father play with his falcons. Sir Simon guessed that behind his impassive countenance Eustace must have been steaming at his father's lackadaisical leadership.

The King's voice severed Sir Simon's train of thought, "Look, de Montfort, look at the size of this magpie!" The King gave the falcon a sweet piece of meat and plucked the smaller bird from the talons of the raptor.

"Impressive, Your Majesty," said the Earl politely. "'Tis a wondrous hunter ye have. Wherever did ye find her?"

The King handed the falcon back to his falconer, along with the still bleeding magpie.

"Actually Sir Simon, he comes from very near here. He was a gift from the Earl of Malton."

"A fair gift, Your Highness."

The King laughed and hinted that any time an Earl wished to be so generous, the gift would be welcomed.

Sir Simon used the comment as an opportunity to remind the King that it would be good to arrive sooner rather than later at Hammerstone Castle, but he reminded Stephen, like one would spank a hedgehog — very carefully.

"Your Majesty, if you do not intend on reaching Hammerstone by the curfew, would it not be wise therefore to send a herald on ahead to order the castle to keep the gates open until you arrive?"

"What's that, de Montfort?" said the King a little surprised. "Not make the castle by curfew? Good lord, how much farther is it anyway?"

"At a steady trot, Your Majesty, the better part of a day," answered one of the King's knights.

"Indeed, bring forward that man from Hammerstone - what is his name?"

"Sir Alec Dupont, Your Majesty," said Eustace. And the knight quickly found himself riding with the King. When Sir Alec confirmed that it was indeed still a long ride to Hammerstone, Stephen ordered Sir Alec to stay by his side.

"Now tell me, Dupont, how goes it in Sir Robert's earldom? Many are the tales we hear at court!"

#47

The King's party made good time once His Majesty decided to travel hard. They were, to a man, the best mounted knights in all of England and King Stephen, although an old man by the standards of the day, led at a fast clip that made many a younger man weary and saddle sore. At last around a curved hillside, and before them, lay the battleford and in the distance upriver the very tops of Hammerstone's stone towers. The King pulled up and waited for his men to arrange themselves in the proper order, the heralds leading.

As the parade formed the King gazed about the riverside, "Tell me Dupont, what are these great mounds over there?"

"Those, Your Highness," answered Sir Alec, pointing to the nearest mound, "are the burial mounds of those bold knights that tried to attack Sir Robert and the next mound holds the remains of the desperados that tried to storm Hammerstone at the time of Sir Robert's death."

The King raised an eye to Sir Alec. "Ye seem sure of thy Lord's death?"

"Yes, Your Majesty, regrettable but true, I am afraid. It is good that Sir Roger has returned to set things right!"

The King stared across the river at Robert's brick kiln. Sir Alec, who had followed his glance, said, "More of the late Earl's oddness, Your Majesty. His Lordship was ever adding to his pile of building stones. A dozen men work every day, day in, day out, even now doing nothing but cooking the Earl's gray clay loaves."

As if the dozen brick makers could hear Sir Alec, they stopped working and stared across the river at the mounted column. One of the dozen turned and ran hard up and over the rise toward the castle. Sir Simon de Montfort had quietly ridden out of place and was looking at the burial mound. How many good soldiers had his brother's foolishness caused to die right here on the very riverbank, thought de Montfort.

Everyone, it seemed to Sir Simon, had been given by God a cross to bear and his was his younger brother, Howard. One foolish venture after another and age had not lessened Howard's rashness. Sir Simon had reason to worry. In a move more hopeful than prudent, he had sent his wayward brother to Prince Henry's camp. His instructions were to ease into young Henry's circle of admirers and develop ties with him, giving Sir Simon a way to forge a bond with Henry when Stephen's end came. And that time was coming. Of that, the Earl was certain. He was becoming certain, too, that somehow his brother had not followed his carefully laid plans. Sir Howard had not sent word of his progress as promised nor had any of their friends in the south been in contact with him. Sir Simon knew it meant that either his brother had gone out on his own instead of doing what he was supposed to or he had met with violence of some sort. Sir Simon doubted the latter, not only was his brother a fierce warrior, he had left de Montfort's castle fully attended by six stout knights. No, Sir Simon concluded sadly, once again, his brother had proven to be too porous a vessel to hold much hope in. Bitterly he vowed never again to let that fool interfere with his plans. Someone coughed beside him. Sir Simon looked up. It was Kenton, his Steward. "The King crossed the river, m'lord."

"Right," said the Earl. He had not been paying attention, but luckily his son was holding his place in the column. He spurred his charger and splashed across the river with the rest.

#48

At long last the hard night surrendered to the bright glow of morning but the sun proved to be a false herald. Maken's troubles grew with the rising light. Alicia, now enlisted into Sir Roger's service, came to the apartment where Maken and the others were held. She did not enter but instead stood by the door and proceeded to tell Maken the latest news, namely that the King was this very day going to declare Sir Robert to be officially dead and young Robert William to be the new Earl of Malton. As Alicia's footsteps faded away, Katoryna said, "This is not the whole tale by a long shot. I'm sure my brother has't sent Alicia here for a reason. And ye all know he won't easily be pushed aside, royal decree or not."

To this the others said nothing. The Lady Camille agreed with her daughter but saw no point in commenting, least she cause Maken even more worry. Sarah understood nothing of kings and royal decrees and nothing of what a king could do to the Earl's widow, or why for that matter would a king wish to bother with Maken at all. If Maken had an opinion about Alicia's news, she did not voice it nor give any sign that she had even heard the maid's words.

She and Robert William were in a world of their own. He slept soundly, his head tucked under his mother's chin and Maken lay perfectly still, her eyes closed and her nostrils filled with the scent of her child. Each inhalement was another link of iron in the bond between mother and son. He smelled sweet, faintly of milk unsoured and something else - something Maken had never breathed in before - the smell of her baby and her mind could entertain no other function except to savour this precious essence.

Katoryna looked upon Maken with pity; the young widow seemed oblivious to her fate.

My brother is up to something, but what? wondered Katoryna. She found herself wishing Barclay was here for he was at least of a quick enough wit to debate Roger's motives and plans.

#49

In the village, life went on. After long talks with Father Hubert and Garfield, Myles told his neighbours to go about their business in the regular fashion. The woodcutters with their heavy axes over their toughened shoulders went out into the forest to the south of the castle. The brick makers fired up their kilns atop the clay banks of the Ouse while the stone masons and carpenters took up their tools and mounted the scaffolding that encased the walls of a steadily rising grist mill.

The archers dispersed to their regular tasks, each man keeping his weaponry an arm's length away in case Garfield should sound his battle horn, calling them to gather.

Barclay was awake and lay on a low cot in the Boar's Tooth Inn. He said little and the folk around him let him be, although the villagers were anxious to hear more of Maken and the baby, of Sir Roger and of the King. The landlord brought the steward a steaming broth and a pitcher of cold water and waited quietly by while Barclay ate.

A few doors down, Garfield heard a gentle tapping on his door. He answered and was greeted by the landlord's daughter, all of five years old. Gazing up at the archer she said, "Pappa says the castle man is out of his swoon."

Garfield bowed to the wee girl in solemn thanks, but she was already turned on her heels and gone. Garfield gave Edwina a kiss, took a last look at his new son and followed the girl back to the Boar's Tooth Inn. Barclay was sitting in the common room, the landlord hovering right behind his chair and seated around him a dozen idlers with nothing better to do this fine May morning. Even Quance, the horse healer, had come down out of the hills to offer up some restorative herbs to Barclay.

Garfield paused for a moment in the doorway to take in the sight. The steward, a Norman castle born and bred, was attended by a clutch of Saxon serfs, men who would have laughed at Barclays troubles a short two years ago. And Barclay who, as a lowly butler, would never stoop to giving any of these people the time of day, now as steward, had found in dealing with them that these rough unlettered Saxons were good people, deserving of his trust and loyal when given reason to be.

As for the landlord, he was like all true shopkeepers, a man with no feelings towards any race, the golden glow of commerce bathing everyone in the same light. Barclay noticed Garfield in the doorway and motioned for the archer to come and break his fast.

Garfield had already eaten. He shooed the onlookers away and when they were quite alone, Garfield told Barclay of all the rumors racing about the castle.

"This talk of the King coming himself, who started this tale?" asked the steward. Garfield could only shrug his shoulders.

"Some say the tale was started by Cleeves after he returned near the supper hour."

"Cleeves again," thought Barclay. It seemed the Captain of the Guard was away a lot, too much for a man holding such an important position in the castle. The man's wanderings would have to be curtailed. And Barclay's thoughts came back to Cam Fontennell and the youngster's warning about Cleeves.

"Where is Fontennell? Can someone fetch him?" he asked.

Garfield shook his head, "Nay Barclay, we have been looking for him everywhere and we cannot find hide nor hair of him. It worries me for he was of a peculiar mind when he last left us."

"How so?"

"Oh, he just seemed unsettled, nervous", answered Garfield vaguely. He saw no need to tell

Barclay exactly what Cam was thinking. He changed the subject, "Shall ye try to return to the castle?"

Barclay shrugged his shoulders. "Aye, I must, what would my master think if he were here, to see his steward sitting idly in a tavern whilst strangers stole his wealth?"

"I doubt that Sir Roger will let ye across the moat at any rate."

"Still, I will try. Lord Robert is owed that much."

With nothing better to do Garfield followed Barclay out of the Boar's Tooth Inn. Outside the pounding of hammers assailed the two. Workmen were laying the second floor of the new gristmill. Long planks of oak lay upon joints of thick mid-country timbers hammered into place by a score of carpenters. On the gristmill outer walls the stone masons stood bent in a line over their brick wall. Below their feet a steady trickle of mortar pattered down on the ground.

Fulke, whom they had not seen since nightfall, suddenly was beside them.

"Fulke!" said the weaver, "where have you been?"

"Keeping an eye on Myles, along with Father Hubert. Thou knows that Myles is a man about ready to burst. Pray that this terrible cloud passes soon for I fear that Myles cannot stand idly by much longer."

For the Belgian this was a huge speech, a month of words at the rate he dispensed them. And now they could see Myles, standing under the eaves of the outer tower and the priest nearby. A small crowd of onlookers hovered a few discreet paces away.

Myles two sons, their thick arms folded across their chests, stood beside their father, assuming his baleful glance.

The castle was unusually quiet this morning, the drawbridge was still pinned neatly against the Gate Tower and the parapets were unmanned. Barclay hailed the gatehouse guard, but the cry was answered not.

The crowd of men around Barclay grew angry, muttering under their breath and fingering their weapons. Myles in particular seemed to be losing his patience. Father Hubert was worried - any move on the archers' part would end in bloody disaster.

"Perhaps I should try," the priest said, but his suggestion was ignored.

"Barclay hailed the guards again and after a time he was answered. A Templar high above them standing atop the gate tower ordered Barclay to state his business.

Loud oaths answered the Templar's prideful speech, but Barclay prevailed, his voice carrying over his neighbours strenuous complaints.

"I am the steward of the castle - let me enter!" yelled Barclay angrily.

"Speak not so boldly to a Knight of the Holy Temple. Many an unbeliever I have slain for less!" said the Templar.

"Unbeliever, be damned! Look ye beside me. Here is my own priest, as holy a man as ever donned the cossack. 'Tis he who can attest that I am a true son of the church! Now let me enter or the King himself will call ye to account!" The warrior stepped away and out of view.

"Well spoken, Barclay. Well done indeed!" said Father Hubert and the men around them echoed his sentiments. Meanwhile, high atop the parapet the Templar was surprised at the sudden appearance of his leader. Sir Roger was clearly ill at ease. He feared he might have a hard time explaining to his Grandmaster his assault on Barclay. And he would not let the steward back into the castle until the King had come and gone. Desperately he racked his brain for a reason not to admit Barclay. And his time as a Templar had not been without learning. He was slowly becoming political. The solution was simple - Roger lied. He stepped up to the outer edge of the stonework and called down to the men gathered below him.

"No one may enter the castle now, the King himself bids us remain in excommunico until he comes or a knight of his house comes in his stead."

Barclay answered, "You then have broken the King's word when ye cast me off of the tower!"

Roger was caught in his own lie. He could think of nothing in reply so he left the tower and stalked back to the Keep.

#50

It was well into the afternoon and hot, the working men on the rope and plank scaffolding wiped away steady rivers of sweat and splashed themselves from water barrels nearby. The village was quiet in the heat.

Normally spring was a joyful time with much happy gossip and matchmaking. But now, the villagers sensed that changes were upon them, and they might all have a new Lord come nightfall. Not a living soul among them was glad for Robert had been fair to them and made sure they had food through the lean months of winter and wood for their cook fires. He had formed the archers' troop and filled its ranks with stout Saxon men, paid them in shiny coin and now they could walk with their heads held high, proud of themselves and their place in life. When the tinker's cart rattled into the village the womenfolk could look over the trader's goods with their purses fat with money while the tinker fawned over them. Gone were the days when he would not let them touch his tin pots least they foul the metal with their dirty empty hands.

None of the archers would confess to it but for many of them the best part of being one of the Earl's archers was watching the tinker grovel over their wives, hoping for a sale. The womenfolk too held their dead master in the highest regard for not only had he married one of their own, but he had obviously loved her and treated her well. Many a maiden had been imprisoned by their own beauty, locked into marriage without affection, without companionship, without hope. Maken had been blessed in this regard for she and the Earl enjoyed each other's company and were often seen riding together. Maken even hunted with the Earl's falcons, surely the ultimate sign of her exalted place in her husband's affections. And besides, Lord Robert had been a handsome man.

Father Hubert spent the greater part of the afternoon convincing the village men not to attempt a rescue of Maken and her baby until they knew what the King would do. He likened the effort to putting out a grass fire on a windy day, get one flame out and two more start. Luckily Myles held his temper and as Myles went so went the rest. An uneasy peace prevailed.

#51

Neil Cleeves proved himself to be a leader of men on this the last day that Hammerstone Castle would be without a master. At first light the captain of the guards had taken advantage of his Templar guests' state of intoxication and placed thirty men armed in proof at the solar doors, across the hallway to guard Maken's room. When the castle soldiers were placed to Neil's satisfaction he rapped on Maken's door and advised the ladies within that they were free to leave their cell. On the other side of the door Katoryna stared at her mother. Sarah went to Maken's bedside and placed herself protectively in front of her daughter and grandson

"Say again, Cleeves," said Camille loudly.

"We've got our own men guarding ye now m'lady, ye can come and go as ye wish," called Cleeves.

"That is well done captain," Camille said. Katoryna was shaking her head no. Camille nodded to show she understood. She cleared he throat and said, "Thank you, indeed, Cleeves, but the baby sleeps and we wish not to wake him. We shall stay here for now."

"Yes, m'lady," came the muffled reply through the heavy door. There was a pause and then Cleeves spoke again. "Lady Camille, I must be about my business and cannot stay, but worry not, for a full score of our own trusted men shall remain outside this door and likewise his Lordship's solar. None shall enter either apartment without my leave."

"Very good, Cleeves."

While Maken lay with Robert William blissfully ignoring all else, the other three women huddled by the window as far from the door as possible. In whispers they tried to guess the true meaning of Cleeves' bold statements. Had he really defied the fearsome Roger and taken control of the upper hall of the Keep? Was that really Neil Cleeves talking? The door was thick and they heard his voice imperfectly. Katoryna could well imagine her brother playing such a trick to bring out the heir without a struggle. She said as much to the others. Her mother agreed, but Sarah, uneasy within the Norman walls, urged them instead to flee and hide in the moors until the King's will was known. If only Maken and Robert William could exit the castle, the rest, she knew, would be easy. There were dozens of secret places between here and the Roman wall. This information Sarah did not share, old habits die hard and she reminded herself that these ladies were, in the end, still Norman. Myles would never forgive her if she let it be known that the locals kept hiding places ready.

Katoryna said, "What? Just run off into the wilderness and live on the moors? Surely not, and besides, Maken is still not fit to travel!"

"She could if need be!" answered Sarah.

Maken spoke. And there was wisdom in her words. "We stay put, my son and I. He is the lawful Lord of this castle and lord of all who live within its walls. He is the Earl and as such is protected by all who are claimed as liege-men. If we run, if we go to any other shire then no one is obligated to help us. No! The Earl stays and so does his mother." These words Maken spoke with such a force of conviction that no one could debate them.

#52

The wind turned and blew from the sea and clouds covered the noon day sun. When the rain came, it came in a good hard North Sea squall, blowing the wet into every nook and cranny and forcing the villagers to quit the fields and run for shelter. The villagers were free to crowd around the castle gate and join in the gossip and speculation. Their curiosity was soon rewarded. At the height of the downpour a single horseman came riding hard, the mud flying up from the hooves in a brown mist. The beast was a large powerful animal and riding him was a knight dressed in a finery rarely seen in the northern dales. And yet some recognized the fantastic armor that graced his person. The man was Sir Walter Black of the King's household and he came up to the gates of Hammerstone to herald the approach of His Majesty, Stephen of Blois. Even if Sir Walter Black had been a complete stranger to the guards of the castle, they might have well granted him entrance on the strength of his appearance alone. His coat was of silk and his breast plate and gauntlets were of the brightest Spanish steel. A heavy silver chain proclaimed his office and his shield bore the cross of St. George, the saint of England and symbol of the state.

Sir Walter, of course, had been a guest at the castle more than once and now he paused to admire the new village walls that had risen so dramatically since his last visit. Having looked to his heart's content at the growing village, Sir Walter stared at the large crowd of onlookers milling about the closed drawbridge. He spied Fulke in the press, recognized the huge Belgian and asked him why the castle was still at curfew.

"Templars, Sir Knight."

"Templars?"

"Aye, sir, a band of Templars led by Sir Roger de Courtelaine, brother to Sir Robert de Courtelaine, Earl of Malton and lord of this fortress."

"Yes, His Highness is aware of the Templars' presence. They have asked for the King's ruling on the future of the castle."

This piece of news started the crowd talking but the knight silenced them with his next statement. He said, "His Royal Highness, King Stephen shall be here 'ere the supper bell tolls. Make ye selves ready!"

He urged his horse through the crowd and called on the sentry to admit him, citing the news he carried and his need to find shelter from the inclement weather, it being a royal offence to deny aid to a King's messenger.

The sentries must have consulted their superiors for it took some time before the walkway was offered across the moat. While Sir Walter Black waited he said to Fulke, "How is it that ye are not with the lady Maken? Art thou in her service yet?"

"Aye," said Fulke sadly. "Aye, Sir Knight, I serve the lady till death itself finds me, but alas, I was sent on an errand by m'lady and while I was away, Sir Roger ordered the castle sealed."

"On whose authority?"

"Only the authority of his sword."

The villagers proclaimed Fulke's tale to be true and their anger manifested itself in their loud oaths and curses. Sir Walter held up his hand and when it grew quiet again he reminded them that the King himself would be in this very spot and Sir Roger would have no choice but to bow to Stephen's authority. And he told them that the Grandmaster of the Knight's Templars, Sir Roger's liege lord, was in the King's party and would also be here soon. This bit of news seemed to matter little to the villagers, the Templars being an unknown tribe to them, but Sir Walter Black knew differently.

He knew Sir Hugh de Payne, and he knew Sir Roger de Courtelaine had put himself in a tight spot with his master.

The drawbridge door opened and the plank was slid out. Sir Walter entered Hammerstone.

#53

If Sir Walter thought he would find the Templar captain in a contrite state of mind, he was mistaken. He had no sooner entered the castle when Sir Roger de Courtelaine met him in the Great Hall.

"Welcome, Sir Walter, you do us honor to visit. And at a perilous time at that!"

"Indeed, Sir Roger, the castle seems secure."

"Yes, to the laity who only see the secular world, the castle appears unmolested but thou knows, we of the Temple must confront evil in its more dangerous form, the spiritual, and believe me, there had been heretics at work within these once holy walls."

"You astonish me, Sir Roger!" Sir Walter was more astonished at Sir Roger's description of Hammerstone as holy, more than anything else, but he let that thought pass by, unspoken.

The Templar guided Sir Walter to the dais and they shared some of the best of Alfric's cellar. Sir Roger built his case against the unbelieving Jewess, claiming that by use of the spells and potions of unknown eastern origins she had induced the Lady Camille and the Lady Maken into bowing before her and granting her favours as yet unknown. And all this while the local parish priest stood idly by. What greater proof of her dark powers need be seen than that? To even control a priest of the Holy Church. Shocking! Sir Walter Black asked the Templar where the Jewess was and what he was going to do. Sir Roger said that against his better judgment he allowed the unbeliever to leave the castle unharmed since the steward had foolishly invited her into the castle. God curse his soul. Sir Walter asked why the steward would invite a Jewess into the castle. The Templar showed a flash of the infamous de Courtelaine temper.

"I cannot say, but I threw the fool out of the castle."

"Yes, I suppose that was the thing to do," answered Sir Walter. He saw little profit in arguing with Sir Roger when the King would be here soon. He changed the subject. "I must see the Lady Maken."

"She is unwell, her labours have exhausted her."

"It will not be a long interview."

"Still it would not be wise."

"His Majesty has ordered me to see the Lady. I must therefore do my duty wise or unwise."

"The Lady may not let you into her apartment. She is fearful of everyone, no doubt the result of the strong elixirs the Jewess caused her to take."

"These points are well taken and I thank thee, but nevertheless I must see the Lady. I shall go now, Sir Roger. Perhaps ye could have a servant show me the way?" He stood up and as he was leaving he turned back and asked Sir Roger to call Fulke in from across the moat. This the Templar could hardly refuse and soon Fulke and Sir Walter found themselves before the men-at-arms outside the solar.

Fulke, the men greeted warmly, for the Belgian was well liked and they nodded respectfully to Sir Walter. When Fulke made to enter the solar, the guard captain said, "The Lady is not in the solar but rests across the hall in Sir Roger's old room."

"'Tis odd," said Fulke. Fulke rapped on the opposite door and hearing his familiar voice, Maken ordered the door opened.

"Fulke, ye have returned," Maken said sounding happy to see her body guard. The Belgian giant knelt before Maken and begged her forgiveness for allowing himself to be locked out of the castle and leaving her and the child unguarded. Terrible guilt he felt, having let her down and he fully expected to be cast out of her service.

But Maken patted the prostrate man on the shoulder and bid him to forget the Templar's trickery as she had and stand firm with her against their new troubles. Fulke, the unflappable, wept and vowed to

214

never leave her or Robert William's side again. Someone else would have to run errands.

Sir Walter Black stepped forward, "M'lady."

Maken looked up. "Sir Knight! Welcome!" Somehow she kept her voice level hiding the terror that engulfed her.

The knight bowed, "M'lady. I come in the King's name. It grieves me m'lady to speak but it is my duty to tell thee, it is with great sadness that His Majesty, with great regret, must confirm the death of Sir Robert."

A single tear ran down her cheek, but Maken did not swoon.

"His Majesty himself shall follow this very day." He took a deep breath before continuing.

"And with him rides your new husband." The words, heavy and hard drew the breath out of the apartment. Sarah gasped at the suddenness of it all. It staggered her and God only knew what this news would do to Myles.

"And to whom am I betrothed?" asked Maken.

"Thou will be happy to know he is young, nearly an age to you - a bit older - not much - and he is said to be of an even temper."

"Has he a name?"

"Of yes, of course, you might well have heard of him. Lionel de Montfort, son of the Earl of Leicester, Sir Simon de Montfort."

"Surely you jest. Sir Knight, thou knows the Earl has had reason to distrust these de Montforts! Sir Simon's younger brother hates us."

"Nay, nay, fear them not! They think highly of you!"

"They think highly of my son's estate."

Sir Walter Black reddened a little. Though this was perfectly true he would not admit it, and having it said so bluntly by the aggrieved party made him feel uncomfortable - dirty almost. This was all part of being one of the King's most trusted aids. Many a time he had wished that his master and himself had remained simple soldiers far from the maddening intrigues of court.

He returned to the task at hand, getting the reluctant Saxon widow ready to greet her new husband.

"Come now, m'lady, ye must have known this day would come. The King must have strong leaders lest unrest and civil wars return."

"Ha!" said Maken. "I'm sure the King has learned that lesson at least."

"The King would not appreciate your tone, m'lady."

"And I don't appreciate being sold off to the highest bidder, much less into a family that has so recently quarreled with my own!"

Sir Walter might have raised his voice and said more but the Belgian quietly stood and placed his great bulk between himself and Maken. The visitor withdrew.

#54

The King and a hundred more crossed the battleford and Stephen, flanked by the Bishop of Hereford and the Bishop of Winchester, led the way up the gray clay banks of the Ouse. The King checked his horse at the sight of the thousands of squared, stacked bricks, but as his men surged around him, he spurred his charger on. The Grandmaster, surrounded by his Templars, came next and then came the Earl of Leicester and all of his retinue.

In the village, Garfield heard the rumbling first, and he slipped into a shadow under the wall to better see that which was approaching. And well was he rewarded, for never had Hammerstone Castle ever welcomed such a dazzling show of wealth and martial splendor as rode up that day. The King wore full armour. His hair, although gray, was long and thick and flew behind him with each step of his charger.

An ermine trimmed cape hung open from the royal shoulders, and across Stephen's chest the best Spanish steel shone brightly.

The flower of Norman chivalry held tight behind their King, shield after gleaming shield.

Barclay, not a man given to desire of material things, stood silenced, in awe of the wealth pounding past. Little could they know that as rich as he seemed, Stephen was poor compared to the glorious wealth of Henry Plantagenet, his young rival. In stark contrast to his fellow travellers, Hugh de Payne's simple monk's garb set him apart and the villagers were as curious about the old Templar as they were awed by the King. All too quickly the King and his company were across the moat and through Hammerstone's greystone gateways. Their audience with their King was over.

Myles watched too, with Father Hubert, who explained who was who to the woodsman. Myles motioned to Father Hubert to follow him away from the press around the drawbridge where they could talk privately.

"What thinks ye of the churchmen being with the King?" asked Myles as soon as they were alone.

"The Bishop of Winchester is the King's brother - he may be here unofficially. The Bishop of Hereford is here, no doubt, to oversee the marriage of Maken or at least the official pronouncement of Lord Robert's death. We are after all, in his realm, religiously speaking."

"'Tis what I feared. The King is not going to waste any more time and my daughter will be thrown to the dogs!" His voice hardened. "'Tis an evil day, Father, an evil day!"

Looking at Myles, the priest felt much the same for he was fond of Maken and was sorry to see her in such a fix. Myles held no hope for Maken, but the priest held true to his belief, that good could come of any trouble. Man just never seemed to get it, the endless twists and turns that one's life could take. His own life was a perfect example, his coming to Hammerstone Castle the best thing ever to happen to him and yet he was here purely by chance. Or, as he liked to think, by Divine Intervention.

And now what the priest prayed for was a way back into the castle for he was certain that young Maken would need all the support he could give her in these next hours. He returned with Myles to the gatehouse and joined Maken's friends in their vigil.

#55

Whatever he had been told about the state of Hammerstone Castle was utterly wrong, thought the King as he dismounted and looked around. Stephen was in the inner courtyard and before him on the great steps stood the Lady Camille and all around her, arrayed in neat military rows, and in a double line facing one another from the lady all the way out to where His Majesty now stood were the men-at-arms. The disarray and lawlessness that had been rumoured about at court was nowhere to be seen and the castle seemed ready and perfectly defended.

The Lady Camille descended the steep staircase regally, her head held high. At the bottom she bowed gracefully before the King and bid him welcome to the home of true and loyal subjects.

Stephen was ever courteous to the fairer sex and his eye found much to like in Sir Reginald's widow, for the years had not lessened the natural beauty of Camille.

"Good Lady," he said gallantly, "This simple soldier has rarely been more pleasantly greeted than here today, and I can see that the martial readiness of Sir Reginald's house has not lessened with his most unfortunate passing."

Camille bowed at the compliment and then acknowledged the great men drawing up now beside the King. The Bishop of Winchester, the King's richer brother, nodded formally, the Bishop of Hereford, not to be seen in a dimmer light against his fellow churchman, offered his ring to Camille to which she kissed in homage. The old Templar bowed slightly. The Earl of Leicester bowed low to her and, kissing her hand, expressed his joy at meeting his old friend's widow and allowed that her beauty had not waned.

"A kind thought, Sir Simon," said Camille, and with that she led them into the Keep under the famous boast etched in stone and into the great Hall, *'Enter in Fear For This Is the House of the Mighty'*. The hall was brightly lit and the welcome aroma of venison on the spit filled the King's nose. Camille nodded to a servant waiting at the kitchen door and a moment later a long procession of maids carrying platters of food streamed into the hall. Camille had guessed correctly that the King would be hungry after a day in the saddle and would gladly let courtly etiquette suffer to the benefit of his stomach. The rest could only scramble to find a place at the tables.

The dais table had to be lengthened to accommodate the honoured guests and there was much scuffling to determine just whose lineage superceded whose, and who would sit closest to the King. In the end it was the King and Lady Camille, each flanked by a bishop and the Grandmaster of the Temple at one end, and this only because the Templar felt it beneath him to debate where to sit. Sir Simon, needing the help of at least one of the Bishops, felt it ill advised to quarrel with either of them so he, too, anchored the dais on the opposite end to the Templar. Not long into the feasting Sir Roger de Courtelaine burst into the hall, his eyes black and glaring at his mother. He came straightaway, bowing to the King and his Grandmaster. He was acutely conscious of how odd he must have looked, running to the feast table late. Camille was asking the King if the hunting was good, when her son, rather rudely, interrupted. The King did not enjoy his conversation being ended and he said so, adding that he would not suffer the Lady to be checked in her speech. Hugh de Payne, the Grandmaster, watched all of this and, even before his young champion could answer the King, took things into his own hands. He begged to be excused, pleading that pressing affairs of his Order awaited and saying that he needed to speak with Roger.

The Grandmaster had been given a room in the Prisoner's Tower at his own request. His high station gave him the right to demand an apartment near the King's, but the Grandmaster disliked the thought of the noisy Keep. Also, the scarce furnishings of the average prisoner cell was more in keeping with the astute life he lived. And, of course, it offered Sir Hugh a greater degree of privacy.

Silently the Grandmaster, his two pages and Roger de Courtelaine made their way to a quiet cell. To the servants they passed, the four looked like ghosts from St. Nicholas come to ferry the sinners below. Sir Roger, the prodigal reformed, kept his head well covered and acknowledged no one.

In his cell, the old Templar held out his ring for his disciple to kiss. This Roger did, remaining on bended knee, while the master appraised his brash, young adherent.

"Is it a northern custom to insult your King and your Grandmaster at the same time or have ye taken full leave of your senses?"

Sir Roger answered not, not even so much as to raise an eyebrow. He knew of the old man's temper and he knew that he had erred terribly; stupidly he had let his temper get the better of him. But he had forced his anger back. He would learn from this, take his master's chastisement and be wiser for it. The old man said, "Speak!"

"'Tis not a custom, Father, I have found myself lodged in a coven of unbelievers, lovers of sorcery and dark arts and I find I could do little to arrest their evil. It wears a man."

Sir Hugh de Payne motioned to his pages for a drink. "Tell me more of this heresy that ye have found."

This Sir Roger did, carefully reciting the case he had devised against his sister-in-law. How she was wanton, how she let her hair hang freely regardless of the company she was in, how she wore men's clothing and often would go hawking with a young squire named

Fontennell. Of these two much was suspected and rumoured. Only the rack would reveal their tale. Roger, with his own eyes, had seen the ladies of the castle partaking in an elixir that a Jewess had fashioned. Why, his own mother bowed before the unbeliever, caught in her daughter-in-law's evil ways.

"You have witnesses?"

"Of course... and I have something more. Much more."

"Indeed?"

Sir Roger, in his excitement, had disregarded protocol and came face to face with Sir Hugh. "I have proof, incontrovertible proof, that my brother was either insane or in league with sorcerers or those who practiced blacks arts."

"How so?"

"Before he died, my brother made a book. In this book he had written down all the sovereigns of England in a great long list."

The Grandmaster shrugged. "So the Kings of this land are well known, anyone could remember them if they wished to."

"That's just it, m'lord, 'tis a list that goes not only back in time, but forward! Aye m'lord, forward hundreds of years."

"Show me!" ordered the Grandmaster.

"I cannot, as of yet, m'lord, the book rests in the solar and we have by mutual consent agreed to keep the Earl's chamber locked until the King decides the fate of the castle."

"And who has the keys?"

"Ah... I am not sure... the steward likely and he has run off. Right now the castle men-at-arms are charged with guarding the door."

The Grandmaster looked at Sir Roger for a long while, trying to decide whether or not he should believe his young Templar. He wanted to. The Grandmaster as a rule tended to see evil in most everything not associated with the Order of the Temple, rich earls included. One had to be careful, it was vital to the growth of the Order that the Templars be welcomed in the highest circles and no doubt these de Courtelaines had friends among the powerful. If charges were to be laid, it would have to be by the Church itself, by one of the Bishops in attendance here now. He would speak with whichever holy magistrate was not chosen to officiate in the wedding. This Bishop would no doubt be receptive to what the Grandmaster would have to say. As for this book of the Earl's, this work of the devil, who better to be entrusted with its destruction than the Knights of the Temple? Naturally a copy of the "List of Kings" would be made and hidden in the Temple's Fortress at Gisors.

"Who has seen this book?" he asked now very interested.

"One of my sister's maids."

"Bring her here, now, and anyone else that might assist our cause."

Sir Roger bowed low and left to do the Grandmaster's bidding. Next, the old man beckoned to one of his pages, "Come, Malcolm." When the youngster drew near the Grandmaster said, "Now, thou art a witty lad with a quick mind and tonight I need you to use it. Go ye to the feast hall and mark ye do so with discretion so that none at the dais should note your coming. Find a seat far enough away to be unnoticed and yet near enough that ye can follow the King's conversation. Note all that is said!"

The young Templar nodded that he understood. The Grandmaster continued, "Ye know why His Majesty is here in this outlandish wilderness? He is about to oversee the marriage of the Earl's widow to Sir Simon de Montfort's son. I've forgotten his name."

"Lionel is his name, m'lord."

"Yes, quite right, Malcolm. Well done. Anyway this de Montfort has no doubt convinced the King to join these two great Earldoms and somehow he has brought along one Bishop to marry and each man has laid claim to the right to perform the marriage and naturally accept the many church tithes and fees that go hand in hand when such a service is rendered. Do you see the King's problem?"

"Clearly," The young Templar said. "His Majesty needs the support of both holy officers of the Church and yet he must pick one over the other, or else delay the wedding and not get the succession taxes he needs to meet the new threat from Prince Henry of Anjou."

"Exactly!" said the Grandmaster, well pleased with his young apprentice. Brave knights he had by the score, but to find a man of tact, and intelligence, and still young enough to train now that was a different matter. And it was so delicate a thing to discover someone who was sly, yet trustworthy, able to scheme and conspire to a hidden end, and yet be true to the Order and most of all, true to the Grandmaster. Malcolm was a lucky find. The second son of a minor noble in Saxony, he had a martial upbringing, and with no title to inherit, he joined the Templars, realizing even at his young age that the Order was one of the few ways he could ever hope to better his lot and make use of his abilities.

Tonight the Grandmaster would expect him to use that intelligence. "Now Malcolm," he said, "Watch the King and mark ye who he picks to conduct the marriage. When ye know His Majesty's choice ye must be wise and clever and find a way to bring the other Bishop to me. I shall do the rest. Now go!"

Malcolm, the young Templar, covered his white robe with a plain brown cossack and walked back into the Keep. The sentries gave him scant regard - a squire needed little salutation - a nod was sufficient. Like a fox sliding into a hen house, young Malcolm slipped into the Great Hall and wormed his way forward until he sat not a dozen feet from the royal seat.

The King, well into his cups, was talking with the Lady Camille. "Tell me, good Lady. Tell me of these marvelous archers ye have hidden away in your northern fortress. Rumours of their abilities have even reached our ears. What of this band of archers and what became of them when your heroic son passed away?"

"They are still with us Your Highness. Far be it for me or anyone else to break the bond betwixt the Earl and his archers. Thou should know that the Earl's archers are a loyal troop and stoutly led. Would you like to see their skill, Sire?"

The King brightened. "Indeed!"

The Lady Camille beckoned her hand-maiden to come. The maiden, who was watching her mistress closely from her place along the wall behind the dais came instantly and knelt at Camille's feet.

"Bring me the Captain of the Guards," whispered Camille.

Neil Cleeves, having been given his orders, bowed, and left the dais to see out the archers in the village. He tossed a cloak around his shoulders and walked out of the Hall, the noise receding with each step he took. An uneasy peace blanketed the gate tower and both a clutch of Templars and a score of men-at-arms stood stiffly before the closed drawbridge, each faction manning a side while keeping eyes trained on one another. Neil Cleeves glanced upwards confirming what the shadows already told. It was too far into dusk to be lowering the gates, but he had his orders. He hailed the sentries atop the tower and asked for the size of the crowd across the moat.

"Large sir, I expect the whole village awaits word of Lady Maken."

The guard looked again and added, "They be quiet and peaceful like, saints be praised."

The captain considered the sentries words and ordered every available man posted to the gate while he went out. He waited for his reinforcements before ordering the drawbridge lowered. The opened gateway revealed the captain of the castle guard standing in front of a resolute wall of guards all armed in proof.

High above were many more of the same with bows at the ready. Neil walked across the chasm from Norman stronghold into Saxon village. If he felt any unease he did not show it, but walked easily into the mass of villagers. The crowd parted when Myles stood forth.

Myles came before Neil and, looking past him at the heavily armed men-at-arms, said, "A wee bit nervous tonight, Captain?"

Neil laughed easily, "Nay, good Myles, not I, but how does that old saying go? *'Uneasy is the head that wears the crown'.*"

Those standing nearby nodded to themselves, for what Cleeves said made perfect sense to them. The guards were there because the King was there.

"What of my daughter and my wife?" demanded Myles, in no way afraid of the larger man despite the guard captain's martial abilities.

"Aye, and what of the wee one?" piped up a voice in the crowd. These queries stirred the villagers and their murmuring grew louder and fanned out until Cleeves had to shout against the din. Finally he held up his arms and bellowed, "Silence.......silence, I say!"

When this brought the desired effect, Neil Cleeves spoke again. "The Lady Maken, along with the heir rests in the Keep. With them is her mother and the Lady Camille. All are fine and the baby eats well. They are guarded but not under guard. They can come and go as they please."

"Then why has my daughter not come?"

"Has't thee not heard? Her labours were long and hard. The child is large and well made. The lady needs rest and quiet. If ye wish, Myles, return with me and see her yourself." The Saxon did not expect this and he stood silently.

Neil Cleeves spoke, "The King wishes to see the Earl's archers show their skills. Who shall come?"

No one spoke.

"Come now, will no one come forth? Where is Garfield?"

Someone said the archers captain was gone to look for Cam Fontennell and no one knew where. Myles was thinking that a few good archers with him would not be such a bad thing and he called out the names of six good men, bid them to dress in their full gear and follow Neil Cleeves.

Six archers returned in short order. Their remaining friends urged them to do the Earl proud, and show Stephen what a northern man could do. With the Captain of the Guards leading the way, the group entered the castle.

#56

Myles, as gruff and reserved as he was, could not but be greatly moved at the sight of his first grandchild. The boy was large with thick fingers and a square strong look about him. Myles could easily imagine Robert William as a young man with a quarterstaff tightly held in a sure grip. He even picked the infant up and talked to him, something Sarah noted he had never done with his own children. To his daughter he gave a quick kiss and asked how she was faring, deliberately vague, hoping no doubt for an equally vague report on her physical state. Like many men, Myles knew birthing involved a lot of blood and little modesty, and he wished to know no more.

Katoryna, unnoticed until now, stood and asked Myles what news there was to be had. Myles, who had no love for the proud Norman, stared at her coldly.

"And what interest might ye have in my news?" he asked.

"We might well have a common interest, bold Myles," she answered.

"'Twas Katoryna that saved me from the wrath of the Templar, father," said Maken.

"Aye, Myles, if not for the Lady Katoryna, Sir Roger would have stolen the child and put us away in the tower." added Sarah.

To be indebted to the long despised de Courtelaine was a bitter wine to drink, but Myles knew he should be thankful for the Norman lady's efforts. He should say something or make some gesture of grateful acknowledgement, but he seemed unable to find the words or even give Katoryna a friendly nod. The icy awkwardness was melted when Katoryna smiled at Myles and asked again for news of the Hall, with a sweet *"please"* added no less.

Myles cleared his throat and stared at his feet, at the door and finally at the lady. He seemed to nod to himself as if to say, *'Tis alright to speak.'*

"The King feasts in the Hall. With him sits your mother, the Earl of Leicester, Simon de Montfort and two rich men."

"Ahh yes, the Bishops," said Katoryna.

"I know not which they are but by the richness of their cloaks and the rings on their fingers I would guess them to be officials of the church."

"Yes, Myles, those two men are the Bishop of Hereford, the greatest landlord in the north east and the other is the Bishop of Winchester, the King's younger brother and by all accounts the richest man in all England. Surely you noticed the family resemblance?"

"Yea, truly, they are all rich and fat," observed Myles.

Katoryna laughed and when the mirth had passed she said, "Speaking of holy brothers, I wonder what mine is up to. Did you by chance see him in the Hall? He would have been very near the King, I think."

"Nay, m'lady, the Templar was called away from the feasting by the leader of his Order."

Katoryna moved for the door "Called away you say? In that case I believe it is high time I took in the feasting and visitations myself. Farewell for now." She said as she disappeared out the door.

Scarcely had she gone when Father Hubert came in. He was tired and to Sarah it seemed there were new lines across his youthful brow.

"Good to see you, Father Hubert," said Sarah.

The priest bent over and tickled Robert William under his chin, "I cannot tarry long I'm afraid, but I wanted to see Maken and the heir, before I paid my respects to my most worshipful Bishop."

Maken asked the priest if he would do her a great favour. She asked that he would observe and note all he could about the young de Montfort and bring this intelligence back to her as soon as he possibly could. To this he readily agreed. When Father Hubert's footsteps had died away, Myles asked his daughter who this de Montfort was and why did she wish to hear news of him.

This was the moment Maken had been dreading. "Have ye not heard, father? His Majesty King Stephen has been so kind as to bring me a husband. His given name I can't recall but he is a de Montfort, rich and powerful enough to buy anything, even earldoms complete with a wife!"

"This is impossible! How can ye be so calm?" He looked to his wife, "And thou - dids't thou know?"

Seeing his mood, Sarah shook her head, "No," she lied.

"We shall flee!" he said, even now looking anxiously at the door.

"Nay, father, dids't you not hear me. The King himself has chosen my new mate. Where would we go? We would have to leave England and then as nameless beggars and outlaws and my son would likely lose his birthright. No father, 'tis no time to run!"

Myles thought for a moment, "Take up the cloth and get thee to a monastery."

"Nay father, to do so that would mean giving up Robert William to the church and God knows his life would be worth little then. His guardianship would be sold and the church would find a way to seize Hammerstone."

"Get Father Hubert back here and have him marry ye to one of the local lads. Thurgar's boy - he always was sweet on ye!"

Maken shook her head slowly. "Nay! Nay! Nay! Only the crown can give permission for an Earl's wife to remarry. To this castle, for better or worse, my future and my son's future is here. And here we will stay, strengthened by Robert William's birthright, protected by our friends and family, where young Robert William will be ever watched and guarded. Where my new husband, whoever he may be, will be the outsider, the one alone. All that matters to me is my son's safety. For that reason I must do as the King wishes."

Myles sat down. In his heart he knew Maken to be right. Given an excuse, their bloodthirsty Norman neighbours would siege Hammerstone for themselves and the boy's life wouldn't be worth living. Maken saw Myles shoulders sag and his eyes redden.

"Come now father, has there ever been a Norman stouter than us? We shall not fear this one. He shall come to fear us! Remember this is my son's castle and I make this vow: he shall live to rule it!"

Her bravado, however false, moved Myles and he too vowed to see the infant into his inheritance.

"Fulke," she said softly, asking the Belgian with her glance.

"Never fear m'lady, I'll not be tricked into leaving the wee one ever again," he said.

"Right then let us move on and not scare ourselves into failure," said Maken. As if to agree with his mother, Robert William began to wail. "Bring him here," she commanded Fulke as she untied her gown.

#57

Bung, a curious man by nature and an opportunist by trade, sent a half-score of men to follow the King's progress for as long as he remained in Bung's domain. The Jewess survived the Templar's debaucheries and the Ouse's cold waters and when Bung's men pulled her from its dark banks they took off their cloaks and covered her.

Now their captain on this trip was Coor Ashby, and he recognized the battered woman. Wise was their master to forbid the misuse of the prisoners before they were brought before him. This one, the daughter of the richest Jew in the north, often had healed Bung's people, and she would no doubt receive kind treatment at their hands. Coor made a fire and sat guard over her while the rest of the band returned to patrol the river road.

When the men were long gone, the fire had warmed Lydia, and she could sit without shivering, Coor gave her some wine. "Tell me m'lady how comes thee to be found in such estate? Who submitted ye to thy trials?"

Lydia answered not for she knew better to accuse a Templar of such a shameful act. They would burn her as a heretic and maybe her father besides. But the woodsman who looked across the fire at her deserved an answer.

"Their countenance was not revealed to me, good sir, I knew them not."

Coor changed tack. "How dids't thou come to be on the river? Come the eve, it is not wise to be out alone, m'lady."

"Not by choice, good sir. I found myself needing to get to York, but alas was waylaid."

"Did no one come to thy aid?"

"Yes but in some halls to help a ...um ... a woman of my station would not be called a proud deed so for now kind sir, let his name be hidden until I know of his wishes."

"Ye mean because he helped a Jew?"

Lydia's fear was clear, she wished to remain anonymous.

"Fear not, m'lady, my master holds no ill will towards thy race as you shall see. I am sure you will be delivered safely to your father's house."

"My father may not be able to deliver any gold to thy master. Our wealth is not as great as many think."

"Perhaps not by your measure, but great by ours. At any rate, sleep now and as soon as you feel you can travel, I shall take you to my master. Ye are among friends."

#58

The King could hold his wine to an extent that amazed the Lady Camille. Her husband, Reginald, was known for his cups, but even he could not hold a candle to the King's consumption. Flagon after flagon he emptied and all without any signs of inebriation. The very size of the King, like his thirst, was greater than those around him. Here in the Great Hall in the midst of a hundred of his subjects and surrounded by two of the most powerful pillars of the church, not to mention an Earl, the King displayed none of the regal qualities one would expect in a reigning sovereign. Stephen jested and swore oaths and laughed at the commonest thing, a serving girl stumbling or a knight overcome with ale, sliding off his chair and crashing ensemble to the flagstones. The music he called for was the music of the camp, simple and loud tales of fighting and wenching and of dying well.

Long the royal party feasted and drank and traded jests and tales of the hunt. Camille played the part of the host perfectly, ever smiling at the inane things men find amusing. The call for a show of archery was at last a welcome change for even Camille, a lady with no interest in things warlike.

Not long after the King asked of the archers, a half-dozen strong looking men all dressed alike in their green tunics and thick leather belts entered the hall. Each man carried a quiver full of arrows across his back and each, in his hand, carried a great bow of Spanish yew. The bows were long, easily the height of all but the tallest of men.

A round of hay, covered with a dark sack, magically appeared on the side wall and the six bowmen came before the King and bowed low. Camille bit her lip in disappointment when she saw that Garfield was not among the shooters. To Thurgar Booth she asked, "Good Thurgar, where is thy captain? I did fully expect to see his marvelous skill displayed here this evening."

"Greatly sorry, m'lady but our captain is out looking for Fontennell, who has gone missing."

Camille had hoped for just such a turn in the conversation. She wanted to release Cam out of the tower but as yet she didn't feel it wise to cross Roger until she knew how the struggle for the castle would turn out. But this gave her a lovely reason to gainsay her son's order.

"Guards! Quickly now, go fetch Cam Fontennell and bid him gather his weapons and come straightaway to the Hall!"

A guard ran to do her bidding and right happily too for not only was Cam popular with the men, but all were anxious to see him shoot before the King. It was the opinion of the castle garrison that Fontennell was the best archer in the Earl's troops. The villagers of course maintained that Garfield had yet to be bettered.

Thurgar and his fellow bowmen made ready to shoot when the Bishop of Winchester, bored with the foolishness of the feast and impatient to know who would officiate in the morning wedding ceremony, stood up and demanded the King reveal his intentions before the hall was subject to a long boring display of Saxon buffoonery.

The royal table went icy. The King, for all his faults, was a man with a soldier's sense of courtesy. Never would he insult the host in such a manner and besides he really looked forward to seeing these bowmen of whom fame spoke so highly.

"Ye must excuse the good Bishop m'lady, spending so much of his time with his nose stuck in scriptures, he knows little of the manners of the Hall and nothing of the manly sports!" said the King to the Lady Camille. He felt obligated to say something. He expected his brother to apologize at once to the Lady. The good Bishop, for his part, felt it far below his station to retract his own words and the long feasting had shortened His Worship's temper. He folded his arms across his velvet robes, set his jaw and stared straight ahead. There would be no apology.

Anger and frustration blackened the King's humour and his face flushed red. "Ye demand an answer brother? Ye shall have it. The Bishop of Hereford shall marry de Montfort here. He at least..." Here the King stopped. He could not upbraid a Bishop further, especially here in public. Words spoken in the Hall lived forever.

The Bishop of Winchester stood, and with him all his entourage in the Hall. He nodded to the Lady Camille and to the King. "The day waxes late and, as my brother has said, I am unused to the feasting hall." He left in a moment, only the dignity of his high office slowing him down.

Well did the young Malcolm heed his Grandmaster's words and the Bishop of Winchester was out of the Hall only a few steps when the Templar met him with a great show of deference.

"Most reverent sir, I come with a message from my master, Sir Hugh de Payne, Grandmaster of the Knights of the Temple of Jerusalem."

"What?" asked the Bishop for his mind was on his brother's insult.

"My apologies, your Grace, my master begs a moment of your time. One church man to another."

The Bishop considered the young Templar who, making his request, had bowed low and remained so. His vanity soothed by Malcolm's show of respectful piety, he agreed to speak with the Grandmaster.

What Sir Hugh de Payne spoke of soon improved the Bishop's mood.

#59

Katoryna entered the hall and found her way to the dais just as the Bishop of Winchester was leaving. She quietly took his spot near the King. True to form she had managed to upstage a dozen important men with a smile and good timing. The archers again were made to wait while the newcomer was formally introduced to the King. And, because the King liked the look of her, this took some time.

Thurgar and his fellow archers could only stand nervously by, checking and re-checking their bows, sliding more beeswax along their bowstrings and eyeing their arrows for straightness. Finally the King and Katoryna were well enough acquainted to allow the shooting to commence.

Prompted by Neil Cleeves, Thurgar Booth bowed to the King and then the lords and ladies sitting on his either side. He turned toward the target hanging at the far end of the hall, a hazy round through the dim smokiness of the room. Stare as he might, the Saxon could not see the target.

"Have ye not a bulls-eye to hang on the target?" he asked. While a white cloth was found, Thurgar suggested to Neil Cleeves that the King might better see the results if more torches were set out and Cleeves, agreeing, ordered more.

Now the stage was set and the Lady Camille urged the archers to do their very best for a new golden sovereign would go to the man that shot the best of the six.

All six bowmen bowed to the Lady and vowed to do their utmost. Thurgar held his nerve and lay each of his shafts well into the target with the third shot hitting just in the white of the center. Up next was one of the youngest archers and his arrows too all found their mark although none touched the white.

The rest shot with the same skill, displaying competence but no real genius. The King was politely unmoved and the Lady Camille looked more and more toward the doors. She now placed all her hopes on the young favourite. But where was he? Cam should have been already in the hall. She grew worried.

The King shifted in his chair, "Is this the lot of them, m'lady?" he asked. Camille looked over to the doorway one last time and glory be, Cam Fontennell walked into the hall. He was quite a sight, clothes torn and bloodied and his hair uncombed. If his recent adventures had shaken him, he gave no sign. He strode purposefully, his shoulders square, as he came through the boisterous crowd to kneel before the Lady Camille.

"You are wounded, Fontennell! I do not expect you to shoot," she said when she beheld his cuts.

"'Tis nothing m'lady."

"But can you take bow in hand? I fear for you."

"Fear not, m'lady, I stand ready to do whatever thou bids me to do."

Conflicting emotions raged within Camille. On one hand she truly was fearful of Fontennell's health. His skin was a sickly pale and the open wounds on his arms oozed. On the other hand, she dearly wanted to prove to the King the value of Robert's archers. Then, if by cruel chance, the troop were disbanded, the bowmen might readily find work in the King's service. If only Cam could show the King some of his wondrous talent.

Katoryna was of a surer mind and in no uncertain terms exhorted Cam to show the hall his skills. To Katoryna, a bit of blood was nothing compared to the chance at glory. And what better way for her lover to make a name for himself. She could barely restrain herself from going down to him and physically forcing him to shoot.

She need not have worried. Cam Fontennell knew his own abilities and was not afraid to show them. And besides, the first thing he noted when he entered the hall was the other men's shooting, evident by the arrows jutting out of the target in a large unhappily loose circle. Only one shaft had been well placed. Cam wondered why Garfield had not come and represented the Earl's archers. It was not like Garfield to refuse.

"And who might this be?" asked Stephen.

"Cam Fontennell, Your Highness," answered the archer with a bow. The King wondered how Cam came by his wounds and why he was so disheveled. Cam apologized, saying that he came straightaway to do the Lady's bidding as it would be discourteous to leave the Lady waiting. As for his wounds, he told how he was attacked while he was out on a watch.

"Out on a watch," said Stephen. "If ye were on a watch would ye not be on the ramparts of the castle?"

"Nay, Your Highness, my Lord, Sir Robert de Courtelaine ordered that his lands be ever watched and to that end we patrol the earldom."

"Ye speak as if your master still lives," noted the King.

"He does, Your Highness. I have no doubt!"

This last statement caused a crackling of comments and oaths. Cam ignored the noise and stood before the King.

"Shall I shoot, Your Highness?" he said. The King nodded, waved his huge hand and bade Cam to begin.

The guests were unimpressed with what they had seen thus far. The shooting had been adequate, but hardly awe-inspiring. When Cam notched his first arrow, he could hear catcalls and laughter from the visitors' tables. Some noticed that the young archer did not check his shafts, but pulled them randomly from the quiver across his back. He lifted the bow, sighted the arrow and shot and again without pause, and yet again. As his quiver emptied the hall became as still as a winter forest. Shot after shot struck into the white cloth until the target looked like the tail of some strange bird. With one shaft left, Cam lowered his arms and looked about for his brother. He knew that the youngster was bound to be somewhere in the hall and sure enough Cam heard the happy squeals of his brother who, armed with an apple, had come running. He stopped a few yards from the dais and waited expectantly for Cam's signal. Cam nodded and Colin tossed the apple up high as he could. And here the bow of Cam Fontennell became famous for in one smooth motion, he lifted his bow and fired. The apple burst asunder as the arrow passed through it. The arrow struck one of the rafters high above the tables and there it would stay, a monument to the power of the English long bow and the skill of one man.

Like floodwater bursting the damn, the acclaim of the hall rained down on the archer. Those visitors that had jeered only moments before now clapped and stamped their feet. Coins rained down about Cam's feet and Colin ran to collect them. The other archers and the men-at-arms folded their arms across their proudly swelling chests and nodded to one another.

The King was astonished at Cam's skill. He motioned Cam to approach the royal chair. Cam did and knelt in front of the King.

Stephen twisted toward Camille who was still clapping joyfully at Cam's shooting.

"Er, Lady Camille, what is the young man's name again?" asked the King.

She stopped clapping and flashing her eyes brightly said, "Fontennell, Your Highness, Cam Fontennell".

Stephen looked down at Cam, still bent low. "Arise, Fontennell," he said. Cam stood. "Thou art an archer like none I have ever seen. There is always a place for men such as you in my own royal guard, if you are of a mind."

"You honour me beyond my worth, Your Highness"

"Well, what of it? Shall you come to London and be a royal guardsman?"

"I cannot Your Highness, not without the express leave of my liege Lord Sir Robert de Courtelaine."

The King clearly did not believe Sir Robert de Courtelaine was still alive or why else the Royal visit. Still, the King did not argue with the young archer. "Ye are a loyal man Fontennell."

"Aye, Your Highness. I have good reason. When evil men robbed and killed my parents, when the Sheriff of York would not stir past his gated walls for fear of attack, it was Lord Robert who came forth and raised a troop and hunted down those murdering bandits. Joyfully I saw Lord Robert hang them all. After, the Earl in his goodness, took us all in, me, my brother, my sister, and gave us a life."

For Katoryna this was the best possible turn of events - the answer to her prayers. Not only had Cam been given the chance to show his great skills to the King, the King had offered him a place among his own. What great fortune. Fontennell's fate need not be tied to Hammerstone. He could always find employ with the King's guard. All she need do was convince Cam to take up the King's offer, something she was sure he could do once the de Montforts ran the castle. Now her only real hurdle would be to get Cam to the altar.

The Bishop of Hereford was not happy with this talk of the Earl still being alive. The man was dead, everyone believed that, and why should he be forced to listen to some young lay-about say anything differently.

"Young man," he said, "dids't thou not hear of the King's decision? The Earl is dead and gone and ye would do well to heed the Royal judgment!"

Fontennell reddened, but held his tongue.

"Come now, His Majesty has offered you a place, as you say, more than you are worth. What is your answer?"

Cam Fontennell stared at the bishop. As he began to reply, the Lady Camille stood and interrupted. "Fontennell, my most worthy of friends, ye are tired and wounded, ye have my leave to retire for the night and perhaps in the morn, the good Bishop can speak with you when ye are rested and fed."

"As ye wish, m'lady," said Cam, knowing and seeing at once the wisdom of Camille's suggestion. It would do him no good to quarrel with such a powerful man.

Cam left the hall and Katoryna smiled gratefully at her mother. For a moment, there it looked like the damned Bishop would turn the King against her lover. Camille was quick to get Cam away and she was beginning to surprise Katoryna. The widowed lady was a greater wit than what Katoryna ever could have guessed. Right smartly had she prevented Cam from getting into a dangerous argument with the Bishop.

Sir Simon de Montfort had said little during the meal. He watched, he listened, he traded jests with the folk around him, but most of all, Sir Simon waited. Like a cat waits for the mouse to move or the robin waits for the rain to lift the worm, so did Sir Simon de Montfort wait for a perfect opening to implore the Bishop of Hereford to call forth the bride and seal the fates of Hammerstone with his own. Sir Simon de Montfort was a master of court intrigue and none could be slyer than he, nor more patient when the prize was near.

Proudly he beheld his son sitting among the locals, not at the head table, but near enough that he could come easily at his father's call. Not for a moment would anyone guess that the young man was but a night away from getting his hands on a great fortune. He was calm and smiling, speaking when spoken to and saying nothing. Sir Simon felt a great pride in this son, wise beyond his years, so unlike his foolish uncle, Howard. Sir Simon wondered for the hundredth time where his brother was and why had he not returned. Sir Simon shuddered to think he had almost given the Hammerstone woman and all this wealth to his headstrong brother.

A royal messenger entered the hall and was even now speaking with the King. Sir Simon waited, hoping the King was of a mind to share his news. As it happened the messenger's tidings were such that the King had little choice but to share it. The Scots were on the march and were on the English side of Hadrian's Wall. Prince Henry's bribes had long last born fruit. This intelligence King Stephen spit out through clenched teeth, for it was a fell stroke against him. He stood and ordered men to ride at once to York for reinforcements and likewise to all other towns still loyal to Stephen. The uneasy peace was over.

Camille sat quietly still, against the growing din. Men brushed by her in their eagerness to speak with the King, as each hoped to be given a worthy assignment. Some were rewarded with the orders to ride north and appraise the strength of the Scottish column.

There is and always has been a species of man that thrives on war. To the poor, war was a horror which must be endured. To the clergy, it was a foolishness which must be tolerated, and to the Kings of Europe, it was a gamble which must be ventured, but for the paid soldier - the mercenary - war was his life-blood and battle was the stage upon which he made his fortune. Long years of civil war and rebellion had made England a Mecca for men of the sword.

Sir Simon de Montfort had profited and grown richer in these times, as much as any man and yet he felt a great sadness as he watched the King surrounded by this armed rabble. Sir Simon could remember a time when good King Henry ruled and men such as these would not dare approach the King's table without his leave. He doubted greatly whether Henry would have allowed riff-raff such as this to even sup in his presence.

But Stephen was no Henry and times changed. De Montfort privately held Stephen in low regard, a man with little tact and no ability to think past the moment. Of course, Sir Simon was nothing if not pragmatic. He never let his personal feelings interfere with business. And this was business.

He stood and forced his way to the King's chair, his son right behind him pushing back the crowd to give him room. De Montfort said to the King, "'Tis a lucky turn indeed, Your Highness, that we find ourselves well placed."

"Indeed, Sir Simon," agreed the King. "Hammerstone would be a tough nut to crack, I'd wager."

"Shall ye not stay here then, Your Highness?" asked de Montfort.

"No, Sir Simon we must raise enough men to strike the Scots and strike soon, before our enemies can join forces. We will march to York, strengthen our numbers and turn north."

The King noticed the younger de Montfort standing behind his father. He felt bad for the man; after all this travelling he still would not have his marriage.

"Sorry, my boy, no time to consummate things. A greater duty calls," he said.

"If it pleases Your Highness," said Sir Simon, "we have no need to consummate anything and we would not wish to cause the Lady Maken any undue stress. But consider this. If we have the good Bishop here perform the marriage ceremony, as the protector of the mother and child and thus commander of the castle garrison, I could call the men into your ranks and we could strike north in the morning. Meanwhile the Lady Maken could rest and regain her health, secure in the knowledge that she was a widower no longer."

The King turned to the Bishop of Hereford, "What say'st thou my grace?"

"His plan has merit, Your Highness."

The King turned to the Lady Camille. She bowed her head toward Stephen. "We of Hammerstone are accustomed by our long service to the crown of doing whatever our King demands of us. But if it is just a matter of troops, why I am certain we can permit the King to employ ours in his hour of need."

"Nay, m'lady, 'tis not that way, not so simple," said Sir Simon quickly. The King looked past Camille, at the Earl. De Montfort was caught at a loss for words and in danger of drawing the ire of his King. Stephen thought little of men who overstepped their rights. The younger de Montfort stepped into the breach, "Forgive me, Your Highness and m'lady. What my father means of course is that men, fighting men, need to know who is their master, and men fight best under their own liege lord. Otherwise they be little better than hired mercenaries."

"Even so, my lords, my daughter-in-law is hardly able to attend the altar, let alone the marriage bed," said Camille.

Lionel de Montfort answered, "Think not of me so cruelly, m'lady. Never would I wish to see the Lady Maken in any way distressed or ill-used. I look to my father's example for guidance and the long years of happy marriage between he and my beloved mother."

"Well spoken young man," said the King and, without another moment lost, called for the Bishop of Hereford to make ready himself to join the Earl of Malton's widow and Lionel de Montfort in holy matrimony.

Camille stared long at the soon-to-be master of Hammerstone. Long would she remember the words of de Montfort and inwardly she died a little, for Sir Simon's callous treatment of the mother of his children was known everywhere. She stood and said, "I shall tell the Lady Maken of the King's wishes and hopefully she will be well enough to come down with little delay."

To this Sir Simon answered, "Nay good lady, it is perhaps not wise to use the hall, if the lady is ill. We could easily have the Bishop marry them in the solar. Surely there would be room enough."

Camille, surprised at the Earl's chivalrous gesture could only murmur thanks for his consideration before she left the hall. But there was more. The Earl took it upon himself to accompany her to Maken's side, to better, he said, welcome Maken into his clan and assist her in any way. He and Camille left together.

#60

When Fontennell left the scene of his triumph he went straightaway to see Maken and the new baby. He, like Myles, tried to get her to reconsider marrying into the hated de Montforts. But to no avail, she was resigned to her fate. Finally when she had heard enough and was weary of this debate she said, "Fontennell, the servants have told us you have been invited to join the royal household. No doubt great fame and honour await you. Therefore, since 'tis obvious ye have not the will to stand by me in my hour of need, I release you to go freely where thou will. Ye are not the first to be cowed by these de Montforts. So be not ashamed. Ye go with my blessings."

Cam Fontennell could not believe his ears. Not for one moment had he entertained thoughts of joining the King's company. And as for the de Montforts they were nothing to him. He feared no one and the de Montforts had already felt the sting of the de Courtelaine's archers. They died when you shot them, just like any other.

Cam spoke in barely a whisper, so distraught was he at the thought of leaving with the knowledge that Maken had found reason to doubt him. "Take this blade, m'lady. Better ye slay me then cast me out so dishonorably." And he waited with head bowed, come what may.

Maken bid him rise and when he had stood she put her thin arms around him. "Do not hold the future to be so grim, Cam, for who knows what may come?"

"'Tis true, m'lady," he answered, "but I feel thou should not join with this man."

"I have no choice," she said and of this they never spoke again.

There was a knock on her door, and then the sound of Camille's voice.

"Enter," said Maken

Fulke stood and drew closer to Maken, his hand automatically resting on the hilt of his dagger.

Cam Fontennell barely had time to separate from Maken's embrace before the Lady Camille, and close behind her Sir Simon de Montfort, walked into the room. The Earl's eyes went straight to Fontennell standing close, far too close, to his future daughter-in-law. Simon did not wait for Camille to speak. He was a man used to being in charge and so he took it upon himself to inform Maken that her time of mourning was over and the hour of her remarriage had at last come. He was sly enough to greet Maken's parents and remind them of their daughter's great fortune to not only be married into one great baronial family, but two. His words were met with an uneasy silence. He was a dangerous man. He was not overly large, nor physically imposing in any way, and yet his was a presence impossible to ignore. When he smiled his eyes remained flat and to Maken they were like those of a snake, soulless and full of malice. He spoke again, "It is sad that you are unwell and weakened. If you wish, the Bishop has most graciously offered to conduct the marriage right in the solar. You may even stay in bed if you wish."

Camille gave the Earl a nervous smile. "That is most kind of his Worship, most kind indeed. I am sure this would suit the Lady well and......"

"No," interrupted Maken, rising from her couch. "No my Lord, these rumors thou has't heard are but lies, as ye can see, I am rapidly regaining my strength. Right shortly I shall join you in the Great Hall." She walked to the door and said, "If you kind sirs will excuse me, I shall don a costume more suited to the festivities that await."

"As you wish," said Sir Simon with a tight smile. He took his leave but before he did, the Earl whispered to Father Hubert, "His Worship, the Bishop of Hereford has't given me a message for you. To wit: It is on your head if the Lady does not appear in the hall ready to take her vows."

Father Hubert said nothing, but stared on at the door after the Earl left. Camille, trying to make the best of things now that Maken had accepted the inevitable said, "That was a kind offer, to come to us, was it not?"

"No, m'lady, it was a sly offer," said Maken. "De Montfort's taking of this castle outright would be so much easier if I were to die and that death would be a lot less suspicious if I was already too ill to be married in public." She laughed bitterly. "Nay, m'lady, I shall trust my new relatives not. Not now, not ever!"

The priest, Fontennell and Myles filed out. Fulke waited, not willing to go except on Maken's express command. Maken, in her one concession to her growing unease, asked Fulke to find Alfric, the cellarer, and bring her back some Flemish wine. As he left, she also bid him to send up her handmaidens that they might help her prepare for the wedding. He found the old cellarer, gloomily watching his collection disappear with a speed unparalleled in his career. He moaned when he heard Fulke's request. "My Flemish, Fulke, why my Flemish? 'Tis hardly a dozen left and that from a gross a day ago!" Fulke was unmoved. "I care not even if it be your last, just bring it forth!"

Alfric reluctantly rose from his stool and slipped into the wine cellar. He handed Fulke a single bottle and patted Fulke on the shoulder. "In good health my friend," he said before taking up his station on his stool in front of the cellar door.

Fulke waited a time outside Maken's door until he deemed her to be dressed before he announced his return. He was taken aback at the sight of the lady. She stood in the centre of the room. She was wearing the same green gown that had so dazzled the castle on her first meeting with members of the de Montfort family. A maid was standing beside Maken combing out her auburn tresses. One side was already combed and swept up displaying her graceful neck to sweet advantage. To Fulke, his mistress seemed to have grown even more beautiful in her trials. Her hard birthing had rendered her white complexion even whiter, making her eyes seem larger and greener than before. Now with the emerald hued dress against her skin she looked radiant. And Fulke, servant or not, could appreciate how Maken's new womanly curves were shown to good advantage in the cut of the gown.

"The wine, please! Fulke! The wine!"

Fulke snapped to attention. Maken was holding her hand out for her Flemish wine.

"Oh yes, m'lady, here ye go," he said hurriedly. Maken took the bottle and before Fulke could find a goblet to fill Maken had uncorked the wine and taken a long swig of the fiery liquid. The maiden doing her hair forgot herself and dropped her comb. Never had she seen the Lady drink in such a manner, like a common wench. She dropped down to retrieve the comb and Maken grabbed it from her. "Just put my hair up!"

A gentle knock at the door. Father Hubert was waiting to accompany Maken to the hall.

"Just a moment," called out the Lady Camille. Maken sent the comb dropper out and bid the other named Tess to stay and attend to her. She ordered Fulke to carry Robert William and stand nearby throughout the ceremony. It was time and Maken almost faltered, but she gathered her will and squared her shoulders. She took two steps toward the door and stopped. Without turning to the two grandmothers she said, "Forgive me. I take part in this hateful travesty only for the sake of my son. He is all I have of Robert now. If not for him I could call my brothers to help me flee into the hills. No matter what may come in the days ahead, never forget that."

With these words, Maken left the room.

#61

Sir Simon de Montfort did not wait with Father Hubert in the upper hall near the solar. Instead he returned to the great hall and informed the King that the Lady Maken wished to be married here in the hall so that all could see her happiness.

Returning to his chair beside his son, Sir Simon found the groom to be in a very good mood, even giddy. The young de Montfort moved his chair near to his father's that they might better speak without being over-heard.

"This dead Earl, father, he was an odd fellow!"

"How so?"

"I've been speaking with some of the men-at-arms. They claim he never has called for his right to first night privileges. Not once, and many men have taken wives hereabouts. They say, too, he was ever out and about with his favourite archers, he never went wenching in York, and only once took his wife along and on that occasion he make her travel dressed as a man!"

"Well each to his own, I suppose," said Sir Simon, clearly less fascinated with the dead Earl's life than what his son was.

The younger de Montfort was unfazed by his father's lack of interest.

"And isn't it said that the widow is a small thing, boy-like almost?"

Sir Simon de Montfort turned and starred long at his son, "You have been into your cups over much, my son and this line of conversation is ill-timed and utterly useless."

Sir Simon leaned toward his son until their heads were touching. In a harsh whisper he gave his son an earful of advice. "Speak not ill of the Earl, my young fool! Look ye about his hall. 'Tis filled with men who held Sir Robert de Courtelaine in high regard.

Make no enemies needlessly. Put away thy cup and thy excessive speech and prepare to greet your bride. She shall join us directly."

Lionel de Montfort reddened at being chastised but held his tongue. His time was coming and in a few short hours, he would rule a great castle and then he would say what he wished. And if his wife turned out to be as homely as he was beginning to fear, well there would be ample gold to fill his bed with more suitable flesh.

Sir Simon de Montfort was weary and beginning to feel nervous. The prize was close - oh so close. Now all he needed was for the widow de Courtelaine to make her entrance and they could get the marriage out of the way before anything could foul his beautifully laid plans.

He was angry that his son, normally so reliable, had started drinking Flemish wine. The potent drink hit the young knight hard and Sir Simon prayed that the lad could at least complete the vows without incident.

Just when he was resolved to go and fetch the girl himself a herald called.

"The Lady Maken enters!"

Maken came through the door and whispered to the herald, "Announce my son." The herald paused, "M'lady?"

"The Earl of Malton! Announce him!"

The herald waited for Fulke to carry Robert William into the hall.

"The Earl of Malton," he cried.

A loud cheer rolled out over the tables and to the rafters. The de Montforts looked on in stony silence.

Maken walked to the dais, and with a bow, presented herself to the King. When Lionel de Montfort beheld his bride for the first time, all thoughts of the wenches of York were driven from his mind. So much for all the rumors of a skinny boyish waif. To his young eye, Maken was the very picture of womanly beauty. He could think of nothing except his need to possess this woman, in every way and as soon as possible. He stood.

"Well! It seems the groom is willing," said King Stephen. The people laughed at the King's jest and the Bishop of Hereford motioned for the two principles to gather before him.

As they moved toward the King, Sir Simon, seeing the effect Maken had on his son said, "She is pretty to your eye?"

"Indeed father, you gave her but short review. She is beautiful. I can hardly wait to seal this marriage."

"Patience my son, not a false step now," Sir Simon whispered but the young groom paid no mind to his father's warning. Maken was close now and looking down from the dais, Lionel enjoyed a clear and tantalizing view of the sweet curve of Maken's full breasts. She lifted her head and looked at her soon-to-be husband for the first time. Seeing him staring, she smiled, nodded and quickly looked away. She felt a sudden wave of panic rise up and she fought to hold it back.

Until she saw Lionel de Montfort standing beside his father and staring down her dress, Maken had been able to put her impending betrothal out of her mind, treating it as something remote and impersonal. But now, the hall was filled with strangers and de Montfort was undressing her with his eyes. She knew that in a short while she would have no choice but to submit to this unknown man; she felt violated and but a pawn in the hands of evil men. She wavered, unable to continue the charade.

Just then, as if he could sense her despair, Robert William cried out and she looked to her son, her resolve hardened. She stood up straight and met her fate with all the courage of a Christian walking to meet the lions. The Bishop of Hereford asked the King if there was any reason to delay. The King said no and that if anything, they should proceed with all due speed, as great events were unfolding even as they spoke.

The de Montforts stood across from Maken and Fulke who had contrived to slip in behind his mistress. He, alone in the group now standing before the Bishop, knew of the terror Maken was enduring. He had seen it in her eyes when she looked over to Robert William as he cried in Fulke's arms. Events were now firmly out of Maken's hands and Fulke knew that the least he could do would be to stay with her. It would be a comfort to her, he knew, to have his massive presence close by.

The Bishop of Hereford was making quite a show of conducting the marriage. He loved being the center of attention and so he filled the air with long colorful phrases all spoken, of course, in his native French, the language of the court. Maken never heard a word of it. As the Bishop droned on she took the time to consider the young de Montfort as he stood across from her. He starred at her when he wasn't watching his father.

Maken found herself unable to create any feeling toward her groom, good or bad. He was bland, neither ugly nor handsome. Not overly tall, nor could she see in him any claim to strength. The large hands, the broad shoulders of Sir Robert de Courtelaine were now to be replaced with this slightly built, forgettable man. It was, she knew, of little importance how he looked, she could never love him nor did she care. The only thing that mattered now would be Robert William.

#62

There was a bustling noise outside the great hall and the sound of argument. The Bishop of Hereford ceased his foreign droning and turned towards the interrupting sound. For a moment, a great burning flash of hope flared in Maken de Courtelaine's heart. Standing at the very edge of a great black abyss - a shaft of light. And yet only for a moment, for it was not her long-lost husband coming through the high-arched door, but the Bishop of Winchester and his minions and behind them, Sir Roger de Courtelaine. As soon as he entered the hall, Sir Roger looked straight at her and the smirk that cut across his face chilled her heart. Even before the King's brother spoke a word, Maken knew her life was in peril.

Gilbert Foloit, the Bishop of Hereford scowled at his fellow pillar of the church, interrupting his work. It was bad form to intrude upon another churchman's domain.

His anger turned to shock when the good Bishop of Winchester called for the King to stay the proceedings.

Stephen answered his brother in a weary voice, "What now brother? What, pray tell, can ye possibly wish to say that can't but wait until this happy celebration is concluded?"

"Only the most pressing of news Your Highness. Only news of which the de Montforts must be allowed to hear least that later they claim they were tricked into a dishonourable union."

"Speak not in riddles your Worship", said the King angrily, for it was well known Stephen disliked intrigue of any type and had no patience for it.

"What news do you speak of? Is the Earl not dead? Has he been found?" demanded Gilbert Foloit, the Bishop of Hereford. "I must be informed of such things at once!" he said. Maken suddenly came alive, "Is this true, your grace, is my husband alive?" She forgot all else and ran to the somber churchman. He drew away from the woman, "Pollute me not!" he cried. "There are serious charges laid against you. Be warned!"

Shocked silence.

The Bishop of Hereford was the first to recover his wits and he demanded to be told of the charges laid against Maken.

The Bishop of Winchester's clerk stepped forth. He was an older man, rail thin and bony. His voice however was strong. He faced Maken and loudly called out the charges against her.

"We hereby give notice and due order the woman, Maken de Courtelaine has been called forth to answer the following charges: To wit: She has been known to act in an unseeming and wanton manner even wearing her hair loose and unbound in public, dressed as a man, masqueraded as such, and committed on several occasions adultery with one Cam Fontennell, a man in her employ. Lastly she engaged in the black arts, namely had the curse of second sight and of foretelling the future. Of these charges the evidence shall be shown, as required."

"Bloody liars!" yelled Cam Fontennell, having come into the hall just in time to hear the charges read. He jumped toward the dais at the same time, drawing his sword.

Instantly he was grabbed by the King's body guards. They disarmed him and held him before the King. Stephen, unperturbed at the commotion said rather dryly, "I take it the young man is willing to step forth if the Lady requires a champion."

Fontennell, hearing the King said, "Indeed your Highness, I am willing!"

"He cannot! He is co-accused," said the Bishop of Hereford.

"All the more reason he should," said the Bishop's royal brother. Their aides looked on uneasily.

255

Quarrels of this nature, especially in such a public forum, could only come to no good. Before the riff could deepen, however, Maken spoke. "I need no champion. These charges, laid in such an abrupt and cavalier fashion are utterly false and groundless, save for the first and I know of no law which lay claim to my wardrobe."

The King who, as already noted, disliked intrigues of this nature, implored his brother to drop the charges, citing his need to be away in the morning. The good Bishop said this would be impossible.

In a space of but a few moments, Maken found herself behind a wall of men-at-arms. The dais, a marriage alter no longer, was now a prisoner's docket.

The Lady Camille could only look on in horror as Maken stood to face this, her greatest threat yet. Not only was she fighting for the birthright of Robert William, but if the Bishop of Winchester's charges could be proven, then Maken's very life was in grave danger. The penalty for second sight, or witchcraft as many deemed it, was death by fire - burned at the stake.

Camille could only reflect on the utter madness of it all. She looked at Katoryna but her daughter was looking elsewhere at Cam Fontennell, caught between two huge guardsmen. Katoryna's face was a mask of despair and with good reason. Camille knew full well of the bond between Katoryna and Fontennell and she could guess what this could do to all her hopes and dreams.

The King urged Maken to call for a champion, but Maken would not.

"Come now m'lady, 'tis for the best that ye let the arm of a true knight defend ye."

"Nay Your Highness, but what I do ask and I think rightly so, I ask this assembly for time to consider my defense and time to respond to these ridiculous charges."

The King looked on the lady, his strong features twisted into a grimace. He hated this nature of dispute.

Vague charges, long-winded churchmen chasing ghosts, no honor, no test of strength man to man. Why would the lady not agree to a quick end to this foolishness? He had not the time, nor the patience to take days to settle Maken's case. And even now he wished he could just ignore the charges and throw them out as pure foolishness. But he could not. The Bishop of Winchester, his own brother, had been instrumental in helping him win the throne. The King could not afford to alienate his brother anymore than he already had. Stephen had planned all along to let his brother conduct the wedding and take all the marriage fees but once again the King's temper had ruined his careful planning. If the Bishop wanted a trial, a trial he would have! It was ever thus with Stephen of Blois. He would work hard and long at some great strategy only to undo its gains in some rash act.

Years before, Stephen was well stationed in the loyal town of Lincoln, a city defended and amply stocked. This well-placed position the King ceded and instead rode out to meet a superior army ably led by Robert of Gloucester and Earl of Ranulf of Chester. He was defeated and although he fought with great valour, Stephen was captured and it was only through the Herculean efforts of the Queen that he was ever released.

Now the two Bishops argued over who should judge the Lady Maken. Gilbert Foloit, although young and only recently into his station, argued hard that the honour was his as he was the ranking clergy of the region.

The Bishop of Winchester was equally sure that since it was he that first discovered the den of iniquity, it should fall to him to preside over the proceedings. Back and forth the two churchmen argued while the King and his court looked on. Standing nearby, hidden in the press was the Grandmaster's young clerk, Malcolm. He was waiting for a break in the debate and when the two reverend prelates finally paused, the young Templar slipped into the space between the Bishops and the King and quickly knelt before Stephen begging His Majesty's indulgence.

"Speak then Sir Knight," allowed the King.

The Templar suggested that a simple way to solve this argument would be to ask his master, Sir Hugh de Payne, Grandmaster of the Temple of Jerusalem and a man well-acquainted with the struggle against the dark forces and a man commissioned by the Pope to judge this case. "Sir Hugh has, in his time," said the Templar, "presided over dozens of trials of this nature."

The two Bishops thought it better to cede the game to the third party than to be bettered by his opposite. They agreed. With the King's leave the Templar went to notify his master.

Sir Hugh de Payne, the Grandmaster of the Temple, wasted little time setting in motion the wheels of justice, misarranged as they were. He set up his court of judgment with a few quick instructions. The clerks were placed, his seat of judgment put behind and above the clerks, and the first witness was called, all in no more time than it takes to tell the tale.

At first, Maken only stood by while the Grandmaster's minions filled the court, but when the old man motioned for the first witness to come forth, Maken turned to the King, who was now drinking wine with his son, Eustace. Stephen seemed to have lost all interest in the proceedings. Maken called out, "What justice is this Your Highness? How is it that a loyal subject must answer the unfounded and baseless charges of a stranger to our lands? Art thou not our law-giver yet?"

It was bold speech, but Maken was like a fox cornered by the hounds, finding courage in her desperation. The King answered her. Softly, almost gently, he told her the dispute was of a spiritual nature and best left in the hands of the sanctified and pious members of Heaven's earthly army. She was sorely tempted to ask for proof of Heaven's approval of those who would judge her but she knew they would only hold her words as proof of heretic thinking. She turned from the King and concentrated on the first witness who was even now threading his way to the dais.

The man who had brought forth the charges against Maken, the Bishop of Winchester, now donned the robe of Prosecutor.

To the first witness, a Knight's Templar, tall and grim looking in his simple rough spun tunic, the Bishop addressed his first questions:

"Your name Sir Knight?"

"Sir Neville Farnham, Your Grace."

"Your liege lord?"

"Sir Hugh de Payne, Grandmaster of the Knight's of the Temple Your Grace."

"And what light can you shed on these proceedings?"

"I was with my fellow Templars when we first came to this castle, among the very first to enter this Keep. With us was our good captain, Sir Roger de Courtelaine, and as we entered into our captain's ancestral home I came to see that Sir Roger was quiet and worried, not at all himself. I asked him what was amiss and he said he could feel an evil in the air - that something was ungodly in Hammerstone Castle!"

The Grandmaster nodded his grey head as if to say, *'Ah yes, I've often noted evil in the air myself.'*

"And then what happened?" asked the Bishop.

"Sir Roger said that he was worried for his mother and straightaway left and went to the solar."

"That is well said, Sir Knight. You may step away," said the Bishop.

"Now I call upon Sir Roger de Courtelaine to speak."

There would be no cross-examination of the witnesses.

The clerks bent low over their writing tablets, furiously working to keep their accounts abreast of the testimony.

259

"Your name, Sir Knight?"

"Sir Roger de Courtelaine, Knight of the Temple of Jerusalem."

"And who is your liege lord?"

"The Grandmaster of Our Most Holy Temple, Sir Hugh de Payne."

"Now Sir Knight tell this assembly what ye perceived when ye entered into your father's ancient solar?"

Like any good dramatist, Sir Roger paused for a moment as if to steel himself against the sad memories he was being forced to recall. When he had his audience's full attention and every voice in the hall was still, he spoke, "I entered the hall that leads to my beloved father's private rooms and as I approached the solar door I could perceive a strange and unclear odor coming from beyond the door. Entrusting my safety to The Almighty I boldly forced open the solar door and came thereby into at long last my dear mother's presence. And what accursed sight should I see but my mother, my own flesh and blood on her knees, prostrating herself at the feet of the unbeliever who, even as I watched, was burning an evil potion nearby."

As for my wayward sister-in-law, she sat upright in the bed laughing and pointing at the monstrous size of the infant child. And when I beheld the mighty length and girth of the child I marvelled that the lady survived the birthing. As I drew nearer to the women I could sense a great evil at work. I could feel it in the air, and yet, I moved forward!"

Whenever the Templar mentioned a sense or feeling of evil all the other Templars nodded in agreement, trusting in Sir Roger's ability to sense things in the realm of the sixth dimension. Maken saw this and noted to herself that second sight apparently was a common affliction among the Knights of the Temple. She forced herself to look back at Sir Roger. She knew she would have to pay close attention to his words seeking out flaws and provable lies in his testimony.

The Bishop urged Sir Roger to tell the court what he did next. He said, "I sent the unbeliever away and out of the castle, lest she cast her spells over more of the innocents within!"

This part of Sir Roger's tale caused an indignant wave to crash against the dais. The bulk of the guests and especially the Templars grumbled to one another and shook their judgmental heads. The good Bishop finally had to stand and cry out, "Silence!" which was against his dignity. He turned a kind eye to Sir Roger.

Acknowledging the opinions expressed so firmly in the crowded hall, the Bishop said, "My good and worthy Knight, ye say ye just *'sent the unbeliever away?'* If that is true then I would say that right lightly has the Jewess paid for her sorcery!"

"That is only too true," agreed Sir Roger.

"Then why dids't thou let her go? Is it wise to offer good Christian charity to one who would not acknowledge the source of such mercy?"

"No, Your Worship, it is not wise, but I had little choice. She was an invited guest of the steward and as such could claim the protection of the castle."

The Bishop nodded, satisfied with the Templar's reason.

"*Amende honorable,*" said the Bishop with a shrug. "And what occurred next?"

Sir Roger related how he put the ladies in a different room and under guard until he could speak with someone in higher authority for he was loathe to sit in judgment of his kin. Later he found servants that attended the lady Maken and he confirmed what his own eyes had seen.

"Can ye bring such a witness forward?" asked the Bishop.

"Yeah, truly, if the word of a Knight of the Temple is not enough, I have such a witness," said Sir Roger, rather surly.

The Bishop attempted to smooth Roger's ruffled feathers.

"Thou knows, Sir Knight, your word is fully enough for me and for any true knight of the cross! But we here today shall give the world every possible shred of evidence so that none shall ever doubt our sense of justice and fair trial. After all, His Majesty must attend to all creeds of man that might inhabit this kingdom."

The Bishop smiled at Sir Roger and clapped his hands together. "Now where is this new witness? Verily I should like to illuminate her testimony."

Now every neck cranked about to see who the unnamed witness might be. There was a slight shuffling of bodies at the kitchen door and Katoryna's handmaiden, Alicia, entered the hall, pushed as it was by unseen hands from without. Alicia meant nothing to the guests, but the people of the castle, especially the upper halls servants, stared at the sight of their fellow maid coming into the hall to answer to the Bishop of Winchester himself.

Alicia was nervous but not so nervous that she could not savor the sharp jealous stares of the others, all those spiteful swine now having to watch while the greatest men in the whole of England listened to her every word! Alicia fought to keep a suitably mournful expression on her face. It would not do to gloat at a time like this. She would have years afterwards to enjoy her victory. Sir Roger had all but told her that when he became the Lord of Hammerstone, she would be given a higher place than the common servants would and she would share Sir Roger's bed.

But now Alicia knew she had to quit her daydreaming and attend to the game at hand, for there before her sat the King in all his splendor, and at his side, many knights. To her left, in robes ever finer than the King's, stood the Bishop of Winchester ready even now to put her to the test.

Luckily for Alicia, she kept her wits about her and remembered to kneel before her betters. She dropped to her knees and bowed her head almost to the flagstones. There she stayed until the Bishop of Winchester ordered her to arise.

Maken was not very much surprised at Alicia's treachery. She had never trusted the maiden who sulked about the upper halls. That was one of the reasons Maken had seen to it that Alicia worked in the kitchen after Katoryna entered the convent.

Katoryna on the other hand was shocked at her own handmaiden daring to speak without her leave. She would have decapitated Alicia on the spot if she could have laid her hands on a sword. Katoryna glanced at Sir Roger and then she knew. Her brother was behind Alicia's appearance before the court. As angry as she was with her wayward servant, Katoryna was even more angry with herself. Why had she not kept a closer watch on Alicia, she knew better than anyone how underhanded and devious the woman could be. Katoryna felt sick. The Bishop was starting on Alicia, and Katoryna could only watch helplessly as the maiden played out Roger's hand.

The Bishop of Winchester focused on Alicia.

"Your name, child?"

"Alicia, Your Worship."

"Your employ?"

"Pardon, Your Worship?"

"What do ye do here? How do you earn your keep?"

Nervously Alicia tried to speak but being the center of attention before the King and these bishops and a host of other highborn lords filled her with a dread unknown. Sir Roger stared hard at her, willing her to calm down. The Bishop said, "Be at ease my child. You are not on trial here. Just answer my questions and ye can do no wrong."

"Yes, Your Worship," Alicia answered with a weak smile.

The Bishop turned to the young priest who was holding the office of clerk. "Where were we?" asked his worship and the young man glanced down at the parchment spread across the table. He read back a little, his lips moving with the words. He looked up.

"You were inquiring into the nature of the witness's employment, Your Worship," said the clerk.

"Oh yes," and the Bishop turned back to Alicia. "Now for whom are you a handmaiden?"

"The Lady Katoryna," answered Alicia, too nervous now to say anything but the truth.

"For how long have ye served the lady?"

"All my life, Your Worship."

The Bishop began to pace to and fro in front of Alicia, as he directed his questions somewhere out into the space above the assembled heads. Alicia found this unsettling. She glanced at Sir Roger and the look on his face - the scowl, the hard set of his jaw told her in no uncertain terms that she had best answer the rest of the Bishop's questions with a greater degree of fidelity to his plans than she had shown thus far.

"Are you listening to me, my child?" asked the Bishop. He had caught Alicia unawares.

"I'm sorry, Your Worship, I heard not what you asked!"

"I said, tell us whether or no ye have ever seen the accused act as if she were a man."

"Oh yes, your Worship, many times. Maken even went so far as to have an archer's uniform made to fit her and this she wore when she went riding with the Lord Robert."

"Indeed."

"Oh yes, Your Worship and of course after the death of his Lordship it is said that she wore archer's garb whenever she wished to be with a certain archer incognito."

Now this bit of news sent the crowded hall into a spasm of tittering whispers over which Maken's shocked denial burst forth.

"Be silent, m'lady!" hissed the Bishop to Maken, "It is not fitting that the accused speak out before her time. Be silent!"

He turned back to Alicia.

"Speak more of the Lady's nocturnal ramblings."

"Yes, Your Worship. Many times, archers would be seen out and about the village and from a distance none could be identified. Often these supposed men would be seen after curfew outside the castle and even the village!"

The Bishop nodded understanding at once the implication.

Encouraged, Alicia went on. "And of course everyone knows how Maken would act quite wantonly. You have heard she would always wear her hair unloosened and she rode astride her nag not side saddle as a proper lady would."

"Yes," said the Bishop. "Now tell of the Fontennell fellow."

"He has the Lady's ear and is ever nearby and he spends his nights in the upper hall where only the Earl's family sleeps."

"And?"

"And? And is it seemingly odd that this young unmarried man should spend his nights in the private quarters of the Lady?"

The Bishop seemed to expect more and finding no more forthcoming he moved on.

"Now, my child, tell of the Jewess. How did she come to be attending the Lady and what did she do?"

"I know not how the unbeliever came to pollute the walls of Hammerstone Castle. Perhaps it is true that the Jewess came of her own accord."

"And why did the Jewess come to attend the Earl's widow?"

"The lady being heavy with child had ordered that old Frida, the village mid-wife stay nearby."

"This Frida, is she skilled in her trade?" interrupted the Bishop.

"Aye, Your Worship, she is known from here to York. Aye, and maybe further, for her wondrous ability to bring forth wee wains."

"Then why did this Frida not bring forth the Lady's child?"

Over to one side Roger de Courtelaine smiled for here, he knew, he would be shot that would bring down his quarry.

"Frida came to the solar and she at once noted the size of her ladyship's belly and when she felt the baby's head with her own hands, she wept and, trembling, she came to her feet. "The child is too big to come forth, only a <u>sorcerer</u> could possibly bring it out alive. And at any rate, the birthing would kill Maken!"

"Speak on my child. What did the Lady do then?"

"They sent Frida away."

"Who's they?"

"The Lady Maken and the Lady Camille."

Alicia paused for a moment and then added, "And Father Hubert."

"Speak not lies of the Holy Church, my child, recant thy words!"

Alicia hurriedly did so. "I'm ... I'm not sure what the priest said, Your Worship."

The Bishop of Winchester was beside himself. "Do you mean to tell me that a priest, a Holy Friar of the Catholic Church, stood by in this same solar while the Jewess was sent for?!"

Alicia looked at the Bishop, then at Roger and then back to the Bishop.

"Yes," she said.

The Bishop of Winchester listened to the loud responses of the packed hall, enjoying the Bishop of Hereford's deep embarrassment. The high officers of the Holy Church looked across the dais at each other, the Bishop of Hereford red-faced and angry because a priest under his domain had apparently erred so terribly and the Bishop of Winchester smug and proud, smiling in a condescending smirk at his younger brethren.

The Bishop of Hereford was sure this whole trial was only to embarrass him in front of the King, and he was not sure how to get out of this coil with his dignity intact.

The crowd rumbled and roared and the Bishop of Winchester stood there smiling. It was the Lady Camille that came to Gilbert Foloit's rescue. She stood forth and addressed the court.

"Good Sirs, Most Worshipful churchmen. Think not for a moment that our priest was involved in this visit. Loudly and firmly he chastised me for bringing in the Jewess for indeed it was none other than I that caused her to be brought to Hammerstone and it was I whom overruled Father Hubert and bid me hold his peace while Lydia of Sheffield saved Maken and my grandson with her heavenly skill. Father Hubert would have not suffered to stay even in the same castle as the unbeliever as you call her, even though she does believe in God. He only stayed so that if mother or child should die he could at least grant them absolution."

The Bishop of Winchester nodded and turned again to address his witness. Camille interrupted again. "There is no need to ask anything more of this most untrustworthy of servants. Ye can ask me anything of the Jewess and I shall speak the truth. God be my judge!"

There was little the Bishop could do in this matter for what could he say about Camille? She was not on trial. Maken was and the word of an Earl's widow would surely stand higher than a serving girl's.

The Bishop excused Alicia but told her to stay within the hall lest someone needed to ask her anything more.

The Lady Camille stepped forward so she faced the Grandmaster and the Bishop of Winchester. The Bishop ordered her to relate all that she could about the Jewess, her visit to Maken and what she did while in the solar.

These questions Camille answered, "The Jewess, Lydia of Sheffield was asked, no begged, to come and aid Maken, whose very life hung in the balance. Lydia's use of certain herbs and plants lessened Maken's pain. The Jewess, skilled in the art of healing, brought forth the child alive and strong. Then the Templar had come and thrown her out of the castle - a woman alone on the northern road."

"My son Roger forgot his place, insulting the good name of this castle and me in particular. The Jewess saved my grandson and my daughter-in-law and if that is not an act of Christian charity, then nothing is!"

"Thank you, m'lady, you may be finished now. I am done with ye," said the Bishop of Winchester. He did not like witnesses to speak unbidden, but Camille had to be given a certain courtesy. It was her home and her grandson's vassals stood not a dozen paces away and he knew that the oldest of these, Sir Mortimer, would unsheathe his sword for the sake of the Lady's good name. Many more things he should have asked, like how was it that a Knight of the Temple happened to find her prostate before the unbeliever. But he would let her go, these northern damsels were a noisy lot, noisy and disrespectful.

Maken was growing weak. She felt light-headed and an uncomfortable line of heat was beginning to slowly march down the inside of her thighs. She had been standing too long and her wound had reopened. She fought to remain focused in the face of her tormentors. Her mother, sitting close by, could sense how weak Maken was. Sarah bit her lip and prayed for God to give Maken strength.

"We are a just court and we permit the accused to speak if she chooses. Or, even now, we will accept a call for a champion to defend her name if the Lady requests," said the Grandmaster, speaking for the first time. He looked at Maken, "Do you make this request child?"

"No thank you, Sir Knight," said Maken.

She stepped back to the dais table and taking up a flask of Flemish wine, took a long deep pull of the fiery liquid. She waited while the wine took effect, warming her and clearing her head. She considered everything that she had heard and put her thoughts into order.

Finally she looked up and focused on the ancient Templar. "As I said, Sir Knight, I cannot but try to guess your purpose in coming here. Right royally have ye been welcomed here and yet ye have answered my hospitality with charges and threats of death. If this, then, is how ye answer kindness given to strangers, then I will be glad when ye return to the holy city you swore to protect."

Now Maken addressed the Bishop of Winchester. "And how is it Your Grace, that my own Bishop, who stands here among us, had not seen any deviltry in Hammerstone Castle? Surely if there were charges to be made, the good Bishop of Hereford would have made them?"

"My child," said the Bishop of Hereford, "thou has't nothing to fear if thou be free of sin."

"If this then is my lot, to be tried by strangers and foreigners and with the blessings of His Highness, then I have no choice but to answer the charges brought against me. Charges I might add that are so ridiculous and without merit that I would not sully a good Knight's name by calling on a fellow Christian to answer them. I will answer them myself!"

"Firstly...."

"Stop," said the Grandmaster and the old man whispered to his clerk who in turn motioned to Sir Roger to approach the Judge's chair. Roger instantly came to his master. "Wherefore is this magical book ye had told me of. Tell thee truly, without something more, thy case is weak."

Sir Roger, turning to the King, said, "There is important evidence in the solar, Your Majesty. Shall I call on the men-at-arms to break down the door and retrieve it?"

269

Neil Cleeves, when he saw the King nod in approval, stepped forward, "If it pleases Your Majesty, the keys can be had. There is no need to ruin the door."

To this Stephen waved his arm. "Whatever, but be quick! Great matters await!"

Eustace, standing near, smiled to himself. He knew his father's words were for the sake of form. The old adventurer was far more curious to see what was hidden in the solar, than what his enemies were doing.

Neil Cleeves left the hall and when he returned he promptly gave the key to Maken, who complained of the infringement on the castle's rights, before turning the keys over to Sir Roger. He in turn sent Alicia and Cleeves to collect the evidence.

A large book of red leather was delivered. Alicia stood nearby and crossed herself. Sir Roger stared long at Maken, confident that the contents would be the final nail in her coffin. Maken showed no emotion, but stood wearily waiting for the Bishop to give her permission to say what she would next. Roger wondered if the fool even knew what was written inside the covers.

"You may speak now, child," said the Bishop of Winchester, nodding to Maken.

"Your indulgence, Your Grace." Said Maken and she looked to Neil Cleeves. She addressed him in a hard voice, a tone no one here had heard yet before, and a tongue that gave proof that although her body was weak, her resolution was strong.

"Good Neil, my faithful captain, as soon as our esteemed guests are finished with the wench, Alicia, escort her out of the castle. She is forever banned from Hammerstone, from the village, and from the manor houses, from all lands under the rules of the Earls of Malton. Never shall she return."

Alicia paled and looked to Sir Roger de Courtelaine for reassurance, but Roger ignored her and in one awful moment of certainty she knew the Templar had deceived and used her for his own gain. She had nowhere to go and was without a place in the household. She would have to try to get as far as York and hope she could find employment, likely by selling her body on the filthy streets of York. Alicia could hear the murmurs of agreement now coursing through the hall. No one would weep at her leaving. Maken was beginning to speak and Alicia was forgotten.

"Honored sirs, Your Majesty, I shall address these charges in the order that they were brought before me. To answer them in order of their own merit would be pointless since they are all uniformly baseless and unsustainable."

"To your questions of my deportment and dress since my marriage to Sir Robert: While he lived, my husband was Lord of the castle and I wore my hair freely because he desired it so and likewise my dress. And yes, he and I had matching uniforms that he himself ordered to be made. You would know that if you only ask anyone here. Now if this court is saying one should not obey their liege-lord, I should like His Majesty to tell us this!"

The King stood, "Thou speaks rightly, m'lady and no court would convict ye of any wrongdoing in this regard!"

Now a man of tact and subtlety would have not spoken so, overruling the Grandmaster's prerogative. He would have remembered that he was but a spectator here. But the King was a simple man and acted as his emotions led him, not for one moment worrying about the ramifications of insulting the Bishop or the Grandmaster of the Temple. The old Templar could only concur with the King. This he did and Maken knelt before Stephen in thanks for his judgment.

Maken tried to stand slowly, rising, and as she straightened she wavered on her feet.

"Come, lady, take a chair. Ye need not stand any longer," said the King, his chivalrous nature responding to Maken's courage in the face of her deadly charges. But Maken had, she knew, the sympathy of the crowded hall and she meant to exploit it to the fullest.

"Nay, Your Majesty, I shall stand. Never let it be said that Maken de Courtelaine refused to stand before any court no matter how foreign its members be!"

Sir Roger was losing his patience. He slid over to the Bishop of Winchester and reminded him that another more credible witness, Sir Alec Dupont, was available to testify in their behalf. The Bishop nodded and resolved to call the Earl's liege-man to the stand.

Maken addressed again the charges against her. "On the subject of Cam Fontennell, he is a good and loyal servant, brave and trustworthy in the eyes of my absent husband. He has indeed often lived in the upper hall, but always at the order of the de Courtelaine family. He has never shared the solar, or any other room, with me." Camille noted privately that Maken had carefully stepped around Cam's liaison with Katoryna. Even in her desperate hour, she kept loyal to the two lovers.

Maken seemed to stand straighter and her voice could be heard clearly even at the farthest reaches of the Great Hall.

"This last accusation, that I engage in the dark arts, that I can somehow tell the future, and that the Jewess practiced these same arts with me, these charges are utterly unprovable and groundless. Sir Roger claimed to have been able to sense evil here but why could his fellow Templars not sense this? Or, indeed, why did no one at all sense this 'evil feeling'? Perhaps the evil Sir Roger feels is that which he brought with him, the deep hatred he has for his brother and his brother's family. We know he has come to England to found a new chapter of his sect. These charges are nothing more than cruel attempts to seize this castle."

"I have always been taught that all goodness comes from God. How then can the ability to heal be called evil? At the Abbey of the Fountain, thousands of folk, common laborers, knights and nobles, churchmen, all come to drink of the blessed fountain and enjoy its healing power. The Son of God himself was a healer, or so says my parish priest."

272

"'Tis true my child," said Father Hubert, in a loud voice for he was proud of Maken. Stoutly and with no small wit had she defended her name. He had enjoyed watching her verbally spar with the Bishop and at the same time she had managed to get the crowd behind her cause. His career within the church was very likely over and at the very least, he would be severely censored for not speaking out more against having the Jew administer potions to Maken. At least so he thought. Maken, however, was not yet done and she compared her innocence to that of the Templars themselves. A desperate throw of the dice, but a shrewd one.

"Many tales I have heard, my lords, of the mighty feats of arms the Knights of the Temple have performed. The whole of Europe is in awe of these brave and holy warriors. Many tales are told how the Templars wounds would be cured, while in the Holy Land, wounds that would have rendered them lame had they occurred anywhere else but Jerusalem." Maken looked into the eyes of Sir Hugh de Payne. She had guessed that the Templars had also made good use of the Jewish genius in the healing arts. A wild shot that struck gold. Maken could tell by the dismay in the Grandmaster's expression.

"Even so, my child, thou must account for the other things, namely thy conduct with your servant Cam Fontennell. Call forth Sir Alec Dupont," said the Bishop clearly.

With a quick look toward his friend Sir Roger de Courtelaine, the young manor lord took his place before the court. Without even a glance toward his liege-lord to be, Sir Alec told the Bishop of Maken's supposed affair with Cam. He implied that everyone knew of the affair but were afraid to speak of it. That Fontennell slept every night in the Earl's apartments. As he spoke, loud oaths and angry dissentions came from throughout the hall. Fontennell had to be restrained or he surely would have attacked the knight.

Katoryna stood. "My lords, holy officers of the church, ye can cease in your persecution of the Lady. Cam Fontennell spends all of his nights with me; he and I are lovers. All these months since my brother's death. Fontennell and Maken are not what you imply and an evil day it is when a knight swore to the service of the House of de Courtelaine will tell such lies about his betters!"

When Katoryna finished speaking a shock of silence struck the assembly. None more shocked than the Lady Camille, who never expected her daughter to have the moral fortitude to blacken her own reputation to save Maken's. Maken, having resisted the urge to expose Fontennell and Katoryna's affair felt a great release. The sudden dismayed look on the Bishop's face made her feel like laughing, so transparent was his disappointment. His case was crumbling.

Maken found old Sir Mortimer sitting nearby and said in a loud voice. "Mark ye Sir Mortimer! Mark ye how Sir Alec Dupont, my husband's sworn liege-man has't misused and broken his holy vows against my family. 'Tis treachery!"

And the old man nodded grimly.

The Bishop of Winchester now played his final hand - his ace-in-the-hole, as it were. He called to one of his lesser brothers to place on the table the Earl's red book. This was done and when it was laid before the good Bishop he beheld the bright red leather book as one might gaze upon a rotting corpse or a serpent coiled and ready to strike. The Bishop nodded to the young priest that had carried the book to him, "Come brother and reveal to the court what words we might find within these pages."

This the young priest clearly did not want to do, but as kings can rarely be second-guessed and bishops never, he reached out with shaking hands and swung open Sir Robert's book. Reading the inner cover he stepped away and crossed himself. The curiosity of the hall rose to a fevered pitch. Men pushed against the ones in front of them to gain precious feet towards the dais.

"Come now! What ails thee brother?" said the Bishop impatiently. "Read to the court the text before you!"

The young priest spoke not. He merely pointed toward the book's inner cover and the writings on its parchment. The Bishop, forgetting his own distaste for the volume, stepped forward and read the following:

"This book is only for the Earl of Malton's eyes. Let a curse of early death fall on anyone else who opens these pages!"

The Bishop stepped back again greatly confounded. He, like the great majority of men in these ignorant times, was superstitious and truly feared a curse. Here he stood, a pillar of the Holy Church, a man of immense power and wealth and yet stymied before his own brother the King, his own servants and worse of all, before the Bishop of Hereford. And the young Bishop, Gilbert Foloit, was smiling.

Still the Bishop of Winchester dare not touch the cursed pages. Like a statue he stood unmoving, for what to him must have been an eternity. The Grandmaster looked at the book with less fear than these native islanders did. He had been across the seas and fought campaigns in deserts so barren that he drank goat's blood to stay his thirst. He had crawled through the caves of the dead deep below the walls of Jerusalem in search of the Tomb of Christ. A dead Earl's rambling over a dusty book held little sway on his mind.

"'Tis but a trick to keep the righteous from reading his blasphemy. Fear it not!" said the old Templar.

"Is this true, woman? Is this but a trick?" whispered the Bishop, a note of desperation in his voice.

"How should I know, Your Worship? The book was my husband's private journal and I would never dream of breaking his trust. My bond to him was forged in the Holy Church, blessed by God." Maken paused and looked all about the hall, glancing at the many faces staring at her. Here and there, now and then, she would pause and stare into someone's eyes.

"I can see my lords that to leave the book unopened would only serve to condemn my husband's memory with slanderous gossip. I shall therefore endeavor to open the volume." The assembled guests, although curious about the nature of the book, seemed to view her intentions with a sense of dread. Many crossed themselves and others begged Maken to not open the cursed book. Maken arched her eyes, "Shall I, m'lord Grandmaster?" she asked. All eyes turned to the old Templar. If the young widow's aim was to put the responsibility for the book on the Grandmaster then, thought he, she had succeeded. Many a disapproving eye looked his way. What this rabble thought of him mattered not a whit to Sir Hugh de Payne, but he admired the tenacious nature of de Courtelaine's widow. Although the odds were clearly against her and as obviously ill as she was, she had acquitted herself bravely. Not that it would matter in the end.

"Open the book, by all means, my child," he said. He tucked in his long robe about himself and sat down.

Again, many of the onlookers implored Maken not test the book's oath. She paused for a moment until the room seemed ready to snap.

And then she did a very odd thing. Foolish it seemed at first. Maken took her son from Fulke's great arms of oak and bending over the Earl's book, she used Robert William's tiny hand to turn the cover page. The book now open, she stepped back and stared at the Grandmaster. He in turn nodded to the Bishop who did the same to the young priest and since the nervous clerk had no one junior to nod to, he again approached the red book.

Like he was peering down a snake hole, the priest let his eyes venture across the written page. In utter silence he read the first page and finishing he stepped away.

He gave a short laugh, relieved that no further words of doom were forthcoming.

"Well?" demanded the Bishop of Winchester, voicing the thoughts of the multitude.

"Well, yes...er......yes...... Your Worship. 'Tis quite innocent, just a list of the Kings of England."

"*We* shall decide what is innocence and what is not!" warned the Bishop.

"Of course, Your Worship!" agreed the priest.

"Now that you have given us your esteemed opinion, brother, kindly read the text. Lest I am forced to find ye a job in the fields with all the others!"

The priest began to read the text:

Greetings to the Lord of Hammerstone. Read these words of wisdom, they shall help ye rule. Firstly a list of our kings, not all and not from the beginning for the mists of time have hidden much. Learn this that when ye are among your peers, ye can speak with some wit, as becomes an Earl. These names, these kings, are our common history.

Alfred (The Great), son of Aethelwulf
Edward (The Elder), son of Alfred;
Athelstan, son of Edward;
Edmund (half-brother to Athelstan);
Eadred, son of Edward;
Eadwig, son of Edmund;
Edgar, son of Edmund;
Edward (The Martyr), eldest son of Edgar;
Aethelred II (The Unready);
Edmund II (Ironside);
Canute (Cnut The Great);
Harold I (son of Cnut);
Harthacanut (son of Cnut);
Edward (The Confessor);
Harold II (cousin of Edward), and this ends the line of Saxon Kings.

William of Normandy (called the Conqueror), the first Norman King Cousin of Edward)

Remember to your Saxon serfs, these are sainted names. The names of Alfred and Aethelstan in particular should be treated with respect as they ruled with the greatest power. Give them their due honor as kings of men and ye shall gain the respect of the native islanders. Remember this.

William, Duke of Normandy, called the Conqueror William II (son of the Conqueror)

Henry I (4th and youngest son of the Conqueror)

Stephen of Blois (son of Adela, nephew of Henry)

These then are the Kings of England. Be wise and note that the name de Courtelaine is not here listed. We are a great family with much honor but we are not royal nor wish to be. We know our place and shall defend the King just as we shall defend our own birthright against all that bring us quarrels.

Roger de Courtelaine yelled at the reader. "Quit mumbling foolish words of advice, continue with the list!"

"Hold thy tongue brother Roger, thou knows it is the good Bishop's place to direct the court."

"Thank you, Grandmaster," said the Bishop of Winchester. The Bishop echoed the Templar's demand and with a wave of his hand urged the reader to read the rest of the Earl's list.

"But Your Worship, 'tis the end of the page. Cans't thee have the lady turn the page?" asked the priest nervously, even now after reading one whole page.

All throughout the evening the King's oldest son Eustace had been coming and going, ever consulting with the King's outriders, knights whose job it was to scout the countryside for any sign of threat. And now, with the Prince of Anjou in England and his Scottish confederates on the march, Eustace was wary and ever eager to hear the latest news. He re-entered the hall just in time to see the priest balk at touching the red book.

"What foolishness is this?" the bold Prince asked one who stood near.

"The priest wishes not to touch the book, it is cursed by the author. Doomed is the mortal man that touches it, if he not be the Earl of Malton!"

"Then why must he bother with the book at all?"

"The Templar de Courtelaine claims it to be full of heretical writing and black magic," whispered the onlooker, never taking his eyes off the dais.

"'Tis a warning in the front, m'lord that promises an early death to those who open the book out of turn."

Meanwhile the priest at the centre of the drama turned again to Maken, but alas for him, the rigors of the trial had finally caught up to the young widow. Maken had collapsed in an unconscious heap.

Camille rushed to her prostrate form. "She is bleeding my lords. She needs rest!"

While Maken was attended to, Eustace hurried onto the dais, roughly pushing through the press.

"Give way, give way!" he barked.

Eustace was in many ways an improved version of his father, the King. He had Stephen's great courage and mighty arm but where the father was easily sidetracked and prone to pursue fruitless tasks, the heir was a superb strategist. Little time did he waste on unproductive ventures, never risking battle unless the possible gain outweighed the risks. Many a time he could only bite his tongue at his father's endless skirmishes and pyrrhic victories.

And now this. The Prince of Anjou, newly rich with the Duchy of Normandy, marching north and the Scots coming south, even now possibly only hours away and in the face of this what did his father the King do with what little time they had? He whiled away the night in a pointless quarrel in an obscure castle, on an out-of-the-way river. Why in God's name were they not in York? At least there they could block their two enemies from joining along the great northern road.

Eustace shoved the poor priest aside and flung open the next page. Looking about at the shocked faces staring at him, Eustace swore at the collective foolishness of men. He cast his eye on the opened page. Reading quickly, he addressed the Bishop of Winchester, "'Tis nothing of magic written here, just curious opinion on the running of the castle, scraps of wisdom a father might give a son."

Eustace looked to his father, the King. "Your Highness, the Scots are moving, this we know. Shall we not take sword in hand and seek out our foe? If we tarry here much longer, the Prince of Anjou will join with his Scottish allies and we shall be in the minority!"

Stephen knew the truth in his son's words.

"My good Bishop and brother, is there anything else in the character of this fine young lady that ye wish to show the Grandmaster? As for myself I see nothing here to condemn her and since the affairs of state must once against take centre stage, I must leave at first light. Cans't ye not, Sir Hugh, give us your judgment in this matter? Time waxes late."

The Grandmaster of the Knights Templar had not led the Templars from obscurity to international importance by acting rashly. The royal heads of Europe and the powers of Rome trusted the Templars, trusted them to respect the right of this ruling class and so when King Stephen gave his opinion that Maken de Courtelaine was innocent of the charges against her, Sir Hugh de Payne agreed with him.

She was declared free and now four things happened. The servant girl, Alicia, was seized upon and thrown out of the castle, banished from the Earldom and sentenced to death should she ever return. Secondly, young Alec Dupont was challenged to a duel by Sir Mortimer. The old warrior, showing that age had not yet eroded his sword play, slew the young turncoat, an act that endeared him to the castle and re-affirmed his place as the most important of the Earl's liege-men.

The third thing was, of course, that Maken was pronounced free to marry.

And lastly, the Grandmaster, deeply at odds with his errant champion, declared it was time for the Templars to depart. Roger begged to be granted two days leave to say goodbye to his mother and the old friends of his youth. Out of character, the old warrior granted Roger his leave.

#63

Sir Simon de Montfort said, "Lord Bishop, surely now we can complete the ceremony that we came here for? The Lady Maken is freed of these charges?"

"Quite true, Sir Simon." The Bishop of Hereford looked over at Maken who was now coming to. "The Lady is weak. How could she possibly take her vows?"

The young de Montfort spoke, "She need not rise. I shall kneel beside her if that is agreeable to His Worship."

The Bishop of Winchester smirked when young Foloit looked at the King for guidance. A Bishop need not consult the King in matters of the state, it was the other way around. The new Bishop of Hereford should have remembered that. It was bad for the church to be served by weak men.

The King, with a wave of his hand, showed his desire to see the marriage completed. Lionel de Montfort took elaborate pains to remove his sword and kneel beside Maken. He used his cloak as a pillow for her head and held her hand as the Bishop of Hereford led them through their vows.

Maken, through a foggy haze, consciously fought to follow the Bishop's words. She managed to say the required lines before lapsing back into unconsciousness.

De Montfort gently kissed her brow and as he stood, in a loud voice ordered his new bride to be taken straight to the solar that she might rest untroubled by anyone. As servants carried her away, the groom smiled at his father. Fulke, walking past with Robert William, thought the smile was that of a cat who just swallowed the canary.

In a remarkably short time, the King had retired for the night and the Great Hall had emptied. When Lionel de Montfort headed toward his father's room, Sir

Simon said, "Shall ye not take your rest with your new bride?"

"No", said his son. "The lady needs quiet and rest and I dare not intrude."

The Bishop of Hereford clapped de Montfort on the shoulder and complimented him on his kindness.

The Knights of the Temple left the castle and camped alone along the Ouse River.

#64

At first light the massive gates of Hammerstone Castle swung open and the drawbridge was lowered. At once the King's men began filing out of the fortress. Eustace was the first horsemen out of the castle and his bodyguards scrambled to keep up to him as he thundered toward York. The King was not far behind. Sir Simon de Montfort approached the royal horse and the King, dispensing of any formalities, called, "The hunt is up. The Scots are near and with any luck we can meet swords 'ere the morning is past!"

"'Tis well, Your Highness," said Sir Simon.

The courtyard filled rapidly as the King's men poured out of the Keep and mounted their waiting horses. Out of the barracks came Neil Cleeves, and with him, all armed in proof, was the bulk of Hammerstone's men-at-arms. Seeing the surprised look on the King's face, Sir Simon said, "My son has seen fit to send out the Earl's archers and likewise his men-at-arms."

The King looked at de Montfort, "I would hope he would not leave the castle at a disadvantage."

"Never, Your Highness. I've instructed several of my own men to oversee Hammerstone until we return."

The King gave the Earl of Leicester another hard glance. It took little imagination to see what de Montfort was doing. By switching the Earl's men for his own, Sir Simon was effectively taking control of the castle and insolating Maken from her supporters. 'The old fox de Montfort was wasting little time in plucking Hammerstone,' thought the King.

Stephen watched the soldiers of Hammerstone fall in behind Neil Cleeves. If the guard captain had any opinions on leading his men away from the castle, he did not speak of them. When Maken's new husband ordered him to muster the troops, he bowed and set out at once to do de Montfort's bidding.

Sir Simon de Montfort's men were taking up the stations vacated by the Hammerstone men. High over the King's head the de Montfort coat of arms was flashing against the sun shielded arms. Inside the Keep, Fulke watched nervously as familiar faces were replaced by strangers. He drew back into the solar and barred the doors, dropping the heavy locking bars onto their iron catches. He looked at Maken, only now beginning to wake up. Nearby Camille sat trance-like, perhaps thinking of the cruel turns that life always seemed to take. A serving girl stood near ready to assist her mistress should she arise.

Heavy footsteps approached and Fulke, showing a quickness of step that belied his vast bulk, moved about extinguishing the lamps until only a dim light shone on the great bed. Fulke slipped back into the shadows as the oaken door was knocked on from without. The servant girl ran to the door and said, "Who calls on m'lady?"

"'Tis I, Lionel de Montfort, her own true lord and master!" came back the reply.

The servant girl looked at the Lady Camille but Maken's voice came from the bed. "Open the door child and quickly!"

As the youngster strained to lift the oaken bar to free the door, Maken struggled to her feet.

Lionel de Montfort came into the solar; he was dressed for battle, armed in proof, a massive sword buckled to his waist.

Maken bowed stiffly. "Ye cut quite a figure, arrayed in such martial splendour, Sir Lionel."

"Indeed," agreed de Montfort, "'Tis good ye are up, our time is short for now but I tell thee truly, I shall be expecting a warm greeting when I return. Right patiently I've been with ye, but now, my sweet wife, 'tis time to pay the piper."

He slipped his hands under her nightdress and pulled it off her shoulders.

Camille stood. "Sir Knight, pray thee remember the Lady is still weak and in no state to accept your hospitality!"

"And I pray thee remember, old woman, 'tis I who rule here now!" He did not take his eyes off Maken's naked form, shivering in the half-light. "Leave old woman, and take your serving girl with you!"

Suddenly a huge hand gripped de Montfort's sword hand and twisted. De Montfort cried out as Fulke, unseen until now, led him away from Maken.

"Death is near Sir Lionel, so ye best go and attend the King, like your father told ye." said Fulke.

Maken came between them. "Fulke only looks to your well-being, m'lord. And I shall indeed be ready when ye return but I pray ye stay in the King's good graces and be quick to ride to his defence."

Mollified somewhat by Maken's friendliness he released his grip on Maken and Fulke released his hand on de Montfort. De Montfort rubbed his wrist and eyed the huge Belgian.

"Dids't thou not hear my orders, fool? I said that all of the Earl's archers are to be in the courtyard ready to accompany the King!"

"Fulke is not an archer, nor is he a member of the castle guard. He is my sworn guard and servant. That is why he tarries here!" said Maken.

"Well, in the future, keep this great ape away from me!" snarled de Montfort and with that, he was gone.

Camille pulled Maken's robe up around her shoulders and gently led her back to the bed. Fulke was red faced and Maken was shocked. Never had she seen the affable Belgian so angry. "Do not fret so, Fulke, I can handle him. It will just take time," said Maken to soothe him.

"We must leave, m'lady. De Montfort lies and he shall try to harm the child!"

"We cannot."

"But you must, m'lady. Look about you. All of your friends are sent away and gone."

"You are still here, Fulke."

"Aye, but not for long I'll warrant. And when I'm dead who shall guard ye then? Who shall guard wee Robert William?" Fulke spoke earnestly and yet Maken was swayed not. She had already decided what she must do and if that meant putting up with the unwanted advances of an unloved husband, then so be it. She warned Fulke to hold his peace and not give de Montfort a reason to dismiss him.

"I need you close by," she said to him.

#65

Lionel de Montfort barely had time to find his way out of the Keep and mount his charger when the royal party began to trot out of the courtyard. He jostled his way through the press and caught up to the King and his father.

"Ah, there ye are my son!" said Sir Simon. "I thought ye had lost your horse!"

"Nay father, I was just saying good day to my bride."

"Aye lad, can hardly blame ye for that!" said the King. "The lady is a sweet thing, eh Sir Simon?"

"Indeed Your Highness, Lionel is a lucky man."

"I'll be luckier still when I get rid of all these Saxon vermin hereabouts, and these damned archers especially!"

Sir Simon looked sharply at his son. He had warned him again and again to speak little of his plans and certainly not in front of the King. Marriage it seemed had made the young de Montfort bold and unmindful. The King cautioned him, "Do not be too hasty in this regard my young friend, these Saxons are marvels with the bow. I myself would consider their employ."

Now these were gracious words indeed from the King and young de Montfort would have been wise to humbly accept them but the newly married Lord of Hammerstone just shook his head, "Nay, Your Highness, in this I must disagree. They cannot be trusted and a Norman can die from an arrow's wound as easily as a Scot."

Perhaps if he had more sleep or had a better breakfast Lionel de Montfort would have been more discreet, but the truth was, he had discovered his new bride to be much to his liking and he was consumed with his desire for her. Loathe he was to follow his ambitious father into the field. He bitterly resented being expected to leave his newly gained castle. Besides, his father hardly needed his help. He had never distinguished himself on the field of battle, nor won any laurels at the jousting lists.

Sir Simon was quickly losing patience with his son. Always the boy had been reliable and now he was acting like an ungrateful fool. Sir Simon was glad he had at least the sense to behave around his new bride and that the marriage was completed.

The Bishop of Winchester was at loose ends. Little use did he have for a ride against the Scots but he had even less use for the Bishop of Hereford's company. He rode out with the King, much to the consternation of his clerks, holy cowards one and all. Visions of huge bloodthirsty Scots terrorized them as they rode, duty-bound, behind the bold Bishop.

The Bishop of Hereford lay sleeping high up in the Keep in one of the better rooms. He lay in a feather bed and on the floor around him, his servants lay in deep repose. The young bishop had been cruelly used, his dignity shredded by the Bishop of Winchester's interference. He would need a good long rest before resuming any official functions.

Maken ordered lookouts to be posted along the roads so that she could be made aware of de Montfort's return as soon as possible. She resolved to be ready to greet him properly as he wished.

Eustace did not sleep but took to the saddle in the witching hour. While his father slumbered the prince led scouts in a great arc across the northern reaches of The Earl of Malton's lands. The Scots were coming and Eustace vowed to know their exact position and their number and whether they were led by the King of Scotland himself or a lesser man. If David did not command them, it would likely mean that Prince Henry had not forces enough to overwhelm Stephen. David, being cautious, would not risk his crown in a direct battle.

All these questions drove Eustace. He thought not of the tables of Hammerstone's great hall, all laden down with the fat of the land and deep skins of wine. He thought not of the soft feathered beds, nor the sweet maidens that eagerly wanted to warm the royal favour. Eustace was royal by birth and by deed, and he rode on.

Now there were only so many roads that could allow the passing of troops and this especially was true in the wild lands between York and the Roman wall. Before the first light of day the English had found the fires of the Scottish camps. Eustace counted the fires and circled the host and when he was satisfied with his estimate of the Scottish forces, he slipped back whence he came. He met King Stephen and his liege-men only two miles northeast of Hammerstone Castle.

Hardly had Eustace reined in his charger then he was relaying the whereabouts of the enemy. "The Scots are more to the east then I would have guessed, just south of Fountains Abbey," he said.

"And?" asked the King.

Eustace smiled, "They shall pass through a deep ravine that runs down into the swale. We can meet them there to our great advantage. But we must be jogging, 'tis a good ride from here."

The King turned in the saddle and addressed his followers, bidding them to make haste. Eustace, although he had been riding hard since the deepest of the night, paused only long enough to change his horse for a fresh one before turning again toward the north.

#66

Viewed from the towers of distant York, the Pennines look like an endless ragged ribbon of smoke blue. But to the King, riding at the foot of the ancient range, the peaks hung heavy over him, watching and pushing down unseen on his weary shoulders.

Far ahead Eustace led the English horse and even at the great distance between them the King could easily tell his son from the rest. Tall in the saddle rode Eustace and a sweet wave of paternal pride added to the watery redness of Stephen's eyes. On sudden impulse he spurred his horse and joined up with the prince. "What thought my son?" said the King.

"What thinks ye of this m'lord? We do not let the Scots see you. We let them into our ambush and then I parley with them. They will ask of the King's whereabouts and I will say ye are in York with the full army. They will think we are a greater force than we are and then I doubt not that they will be dismayed. I will suggest that they return home peacefully with no men dead, no ill will between us."

"'Tis a sly policy, a plan worthy of your mother," said Stephen. In his son he could see the workings of his wife's mind. Eustace was a rare example of a child that had inherited the best of both parents. He had Stephen's great strength of arm, his warrior's rage in battle, the bold fight that men follow without a shadow of a doubt. And yet this was the marvel of Eustace, at least in Stephen's eyes. Eustace was a born politician, able to see the minds of men and guess their next move. Like the Queen, he could see a plan through and bend men to his will. His mind did not wander nor his purpose waiver. In his heart, Stephen knew Eustace could be something that he himself could never be. Eustace could be a great king. It was for this belief in his firstborn that Stephen of Blois continued the endless fight to hold the crown, so that one day, this magnificent son of his would have what he so justly deserved. It was not for himself, for he sometimes wished the crown had never come to him. He hated the politics of court and Stephen was tired of it all. What a relief it was to leave the planning to Eustace.

Sir Simon de Montfort's paternal thoughts were of a different view than his King's. Where the King's son was dutiful and trustworthy, Sir Simon's younger issue was suddenly becoming unmanageable and wayward.

The Earl sighed. Such was life. No matter what great plans he might devise or what pains he took to ensure their success, there was always the unforeseen. There was always something to throw a man off balance. De Montfort, a realist above all, knew there was little he could do right now with Lionel, at least not in front of the King.

De Montfort looked over at his son, the dead Earl's helm sitting heavy on his head. The hauberk, too long for his body. Lionel had left his own armor at Hammerstone and worn this, as if to proclaim his sovereignty over the de Courtelaine castle. Sir Simon thought the wearing of Sir Robert's armor to be childish and vain, and it angered him that his own son, so carefully trained, would so quickly disregard his advice.

The end of the march caused de Montfort to cast aside his musings and attend the King. They were in the beginning of a deep cleft in the hills and Eustace was urging the captains to quickly divide their men and scale the heights to either side of the road. Cam Fontennell and Garfield led their archers to the north side of the road. The Prince's plan was easy to execute. It was a simple ambush, each troop in the sight of one another and the action to run together. Eustace reasoned that since he was leading men unknown to him and unknown to each other, the simpler the plan the better.

On the north side, the archers, led by their captains and the castle troops, led by de Montfort, faced

292

the King's soldiers across the ravine. Sir Walter Black stood at their center and a line of men stretched out a hundred paces on either side of him.

Out of sight of the road but visible from the crown of the hill, Sir Simon de Montfort and Eustace sat at the head of the mounted knights, one hundred strong. The King, at Eustace's request, rode behind with a guard hidden from view. Along the line of archers, men were sitting in the morning sun, some re-waxing their bowstrings and many bringing forth pouches of fresh-baked bread loaves and rounds of cheese, to be washed down with the best of the northern ales. For what wife would let her man away without at least a good lunch?

The castle's soldiers, a few yards away could only look enviously at the village men happily munching away. There had been no food issued to the garrison as they formed up and marched out of the castle hours earlier. The odd man had contrived to secure some substance but for the most part the men went hungry. Most had assumed that the younger de Montfort would be leading his father's own troops and they would maintain the castle walls. Thus, few men had any food to bring. Lionel de Montfort rather enjoyed their discomfort. A few men grumbled along the line and he jumped on the opportunity to exercise his new-found power.

"Cleeves! Quiet those men!" he yelled. Down in the bottom of the ravine Eustace looked up, a pained look on his face. De Montfort's son struck him as being a first-rate fool and this proved it. The Scots might be moments away and yet there was de Montfort yelling at his men. So much for the element of surprise.

Eustace knew he had to do something lest the fool give their trap away. Eustace spurred his horse up the hill, crushing underfoot the sweet green grasses. The charger had to half-jump her way so steep was the slope. At the crest he dismounted and quietly went down through the English line. Meeting de Montfort he made the excuse of wanting half the archers across the road. And as they split up, half followed after Fontennell who in turn trailed back down the hill after the Prince, Eustace. As he went through the men, he urged silence, over and over, so that even the simplest of men would know to hold his tongue.

De Montfort, not realizing the command was actually directed at him, loudly seconded Eustace's words. When Eustace and the rest were away, de Montfort ordered the archers to put away their food, leaving no doubt about how he felt about the villagers bringing such things along. Of course, to all the veterans within earshot this was the words of a child, for any man that had campaigned at all knew that finding food and securing a dry place to sleep was the foot-soldiers first concern. The battles took care of themselves.

De Montfort, oblivious to the mood of the men, walked down the line of foot soldiers. He had unsheathed his sword and was admiring its fine Sheffield blade. "No fear, men! Take no notice of these Saxons. It's time they were disbanded anyway. 'Tis not to my liking to see the natives armed," he said to Neil Cleeves.

Neil thought differently but he was not so naive as to tell that to his new lord and master. He liked being the captain of the guards. But he had taken part in two violent battles where it was the archers who had carried the day. And he knew their loyalty to Sir Robert had been total. What a waste it would be if de Montfort were to just throw the archers aside. He looked past his preening commander where a few yards away Cam Fontennell was staring at them both. Their eyes met. Cleeves wondered how much Fontennell had heard. As always the young bowman gave nothing away, kept his thoughts to himself. Certainly the archers standing nearest had heard de Montfort clear enough. Even now they were whispering among themselves until

Fontennell waved his finger at them and they become as mute as the gray stones on the hillside.

De Montfort turned toward the archers and gave them a long baleful stare. Behind him Neil Cleeves looked at Cam and rolled his eyes. Cam's eyebrows rose ever so slightly and de Montfort was on him. "What 'tis it, serf, that ye wish to speak? Verily I can see it in your eye, ye doubt me!" he said, his voice high and nervous.

"I, sir, am no serf. I am freeborn, as was my father and his father before him," said Cam Fontennell calmly.

De Montfort was about to provide a retort when one of Eustace's scouts came scrambling across the hillside. "They are here," he said and ran on down over the embankment and out of sight.

All down the English side the muffled sounds of swords being unbuckled and bows being strung rose and dissipated in the gentle morning sunlight. A minute-long eternity passed and the Scottish brigade marched into the hollow. Right under the English noses and none the wiser. They went so far past that Neil Cleeves worried that something had happened to the mounted knights hidden behind the knoll.

Eustace was there now alone and easing his horse down the roadway. The Scottish column stopped and stood in their own dust.

Eustace rode to within twenty paces and turned his mount sideways, as if to stay their progress by himself alone.

"What news of our Scottish cousins?" called Eustace in a loud voice. The Scots answered by drawing their weapons. The English sprung their trap and as one the lines of soldiers appeared above the Scots.

Sir Simon de Montfort led the English knights out of their hiding place. They filled the roadway and spilled into the ditch and even up on either hill. When the horsemen were finally all grouped together again, they presented a fearsome sight. Worse for the Scots, they had no horse, save a half dozen mounted men including Ranulf, Earl of Chester. Even Ranulf's English rebels were only common foot soldiers. Eustace called out, "'Tis a shame, Your Grace, that ye all would die on such a *bonny* morning, and for no reason."

Ranulf, taller than Eustace, gray-haired and dressed in chain mail in the Norman fashion, eased his horse ahead. Eustace signalled and a hundred arrows were notched and two hundred swords held high. As these things went on around him, Eustace held a white flag of truce out, asking formally for a parley. Ranulf looked up either bank and did not like what he saw. He had heard of a band of northern archers, raised by the Earl of Malton and to a man, deadly accurate and pitiless, preferring slaughter to ransoms. They were said to be clothed in green tunics and armed with longbows. Looking at the English line, Ranulf knew it was these same archers that now confronted him. He accepted Eustace's offer of a parley. He sheathed his sword and rode to meet the Prince.

Both sides stood down and lowered their weapons.

The Scot asked to speak with the King to which Eustace answered, "The King is not among us and, ye should know, John of Anjou's plans are common knowledge. He meant to meet you in York and after the city had fallen you were to drive south and confront the King at Lincoln. Correct?"

The Earl's face gave him away and Eustace smiled. "Fear not m'lord. 'Tis no damage done. Go ye back whence ye came and send word to Henry that ye have been struck with a sudden fever and had to return home."

Ranulf said nothing at first. He stared at the Prince, then his saddle, then the archers and back to his saddle. He thought about how easily he had ridden into this ambush. It was vexing. Ranulf mentally added up the likely casualties if he tried to fight his way out of this accursed ravine. Which really meant, would he survive the fight? He reckoned not and if by some trick of fate he did, what then? He had no horse and no way to slip into York as was planned. Stephen, old as he was, was still a warrior to be feared, and if he were ready and waiting for his enemies then the battle would be hard indeed.

Eustace waited. Ranulf pondered the hard coil he now found himself in. He could well imagine what a grey goose shaft could do to his person. He had seen arrows shot from longbows sink three inches into solid oak. Ranulf decided to go home. He would leave one of his sons as a surety, that would be expected, and he would go home and wait for sweeter opportunities.

Eustace did not gloat. He simply acknowledged the wisdom of Ranulf's decision and with very little ceremony the Scots, led by the rebel Earl Ranulf, retraced their steps and returned to Scotland. Ranulf's son, John, found himself riding with the King. He didn't mind, he was in no danger, many of his cousins lived in York and the inns were known for sweet wenches and good ale.

#67

Noon-time found the English column four miles southeast of the ambush site. The King stopped by a gentle curve on the Ouse and while the soldiers took their ease along the low banks of the river, their leaders debated their next move. The King wanted to go west and rest at Hammerstone. It was close by and his men would be fed for free in the Great Hall.

Eustace could see his father's point but to his thinking it was more important to get themselves to York as quickly as possible and thus be ready for Henry's approach. There was even a chance that the Prince of Anjou might take the town if Stephen did not act quickly.

Standing nearby but staying silent was Sir Simon de Montfort. His son, the new master of Hammerstone Castle was not so quiet. Young Lionel had been in a state of near terror when the Scots had first appeared. He had never been in actual battle and the sight of the burly slab-armed Highlanders nearly made him soil himself. All he could think about was one of those huge Scottish claymores splitting him open like a ripe fruit. He nearly wept for joy when the Scots turned back.

But now that was behind him and he could say that he had led men against the Scots and lived to tell the tale. He felt wonderful, powerful, a leader of men, a warrior. His father would have to accept him as an equal.

Sir Simon watched his son strutting about like a rooster, telling the men of Hammerstone how wise the Scots were to retreat and expressing his dismay at not having the chance to engage them. Sir Simon wanted to box his ears. This morning's work had been a clever bit of gamesmanship on the part of Eustace and nothing more. Why was the boy acting like he had just won a great battle? The Prince of Anjou was still to be reckoned with and if he had taken York in the King's absence, then by Holy Mother Mary there would be long hard days ahead.

De Montfort walked over to the group of knights surrounding Sir Lionel. The younger de Montfort was telling them in a loud voice that with men such as themselves, he had no need of the Saxon bowmen and he was rather embarrassed to think that he was forced to lead such low-born creatures. Sir Mortimer House disagreed with his new overlord. He had taken part in the Battle of the Ford and helped defend Hammerstone Castle along with these same Saxon archers and he knew just how deadly a force they were. When supported by heavy horse, as Sir Robert had said, they could sway any battle. Now this young fool was apparently going to just throw this marvelous weapon aside. It was madness.

"Ye might think about the archers a wee bit more, my young Sir, before ye disband them. They are a ferocious troop in a fight, I can tell thee."

Lionel de Montfort smiled indulgently at the old warrior. "Ye are most kind to point that out to me, Sir Mortimer, and I will certainly consider your advice, asked or not."

The old veteran spit in the grass and stomped off.

Sitting out along the sweet green banks of the Ouse, the archers took their rest, but all among them there was unrest, for they heard de Montfort's loathing of them, that he might disband them forever. And Fontennell, the best or second-best bow among them, had been offered a place in the King's own guard. He had said no, that he preferred to serve Sir Robert's widow, but how long might that last with Sir Simon de Montfort's whelp ruling the roost? The possibility of Fontennell leaving them had made the men realize just how much they liked having him with them. He had much to boast of but never did, and he had never used his favour with the Earl to his own ends, nor did he ever gossip. They trusted him.

Lionel de Montfort was uncomfortable in the Earl's helmet and mail-coat. Unhappily he took off the headpiece and tossed it into the grass. Watching the finely crafted helmet roll, Thurgar Boldt said sadly, "Look, lads, are we not just as that iron pot, both wrought to perfection by Lord Robert, both proven in battle, but now to be cast aside?"

Sir Simon de Montfort kept one eye on the King while trying to see that his son did not get himself into any coils. Sir Simon had ridden with Stephen of Blois long enough to see that the old warrior was getting ready to remount. The King did not believe in long respites while in the field, it tended to make active men sleepy and slow. Stephen signaled to his master of horse, and his men checked their saddles. Lionel de Montfort, however, had just shrugged off his newly acquired coat of mail.

"Lionel!" yelled Sir Simon, his Norman temper finally getting the best of him.

The King lifted a boot to stirrup but before he swung up a guard posted ahead of the column called out a warning. A single rider, a knight well armed was riding toward them. The King pulled his foot free and stood clear of his horse to better see who approached. He had not long to wait. The strange rider thundered around the corner and into view. Tall he was and the foam dripping off his horse gave evidence of a hard ride. His mail was coated in dust and dark bloody stains marred the over-vest. His head was encased in a brightly coloured helm and, to the surprise of all, he rode not to the King, but rather rode straight to the de Montforts. Sir Simon at once recognized his brother's armour.

#68

Robert de Courtelaine felt pain. He had felt it since he awakened in a dark hole in a barn of stone. And the pain was killing him. It was not the intense pounding headache his forced inactivity had caused, and not the dizzy nausea his loss of blood induced. Nor was it the sharp bloody edge of his various woundings. No, these pains, these physical pains, were common to him and well within the scope of his resistance. Of these, he did not concern himself. It was the pain of knowing that by his own rash actions he had lost everything. He had ignored Barclay's good advice and now Maken might well be dead, the castle in God knows whose hands. Self-loathing and deep regret drowned him and for days uncounted Robert lay in a despairing haze unconscious of the dark filth that surrounded him.

For the first weeks he was tied to a low cot and once a day someone would feed him. He heard no other voices. Once Robert thought he could hear the faint lowing of cows, but yell as he might no human voice answered. Time passed and one day several men came, hooded and silent and they put a leg-iron on him and chained him to the wall of the building. Robert did not resist them. His spirit broken, he lay quietly by while the iron was pounded into place.

It took a great while but Robert's wounds closed and crusted and itched and finally they could be called healed. Even in this cold prison, he was young enough and strong enough that time alone healed him. (Robert would find however, that from that winter on, his shoulder that had been pierced with the crossbow bolt would always ache at the first sign of rain.) Robert de Courtelaine, lying in his self-loathing filth, may well have never regained his will to survive. He may have lain there hidden, unknown to the world, a shell of his former self had not fate once more intervened.

On Plough Monday, (not that Robert knew it was Plough Monday), he had a visitor. On this warm morning the jailer did not leave Robert his meal. He set lamps on shelves by either side of the door and having lit the room to a murky pale, the jailer stood back against the stone wall. The door opened wide and the tall form of Sir Howard de Montfort filled the doorway.

"I am truly glad to see ye are alive," said the visitor and he walked nearer to Robert, who was sitting on the floor with his back against the wall. De Montfort stared at Robert for a while, waiting for the young Earl to recognize him. Long had Howard de Montfort dreamed of this day; over and over playing out the little drama before him. The shame of the Earl's birdcage where he had hung for months, each moment of hell would be repaid. Slowly.

Robert was watching him. He remembered. Good, de Montfort smiled, "Greetings Sir Robert. Welcome to your new home. Not quite the view you afforded me, but perhaps we can find other ways to occupy your time."

Another servant entered the hut and proceeded to lay a fine meal out for the tall knight. A small table at de Montfort's elbow, a round of fresh bread still warm from the oven, a roasted chicken, dripping sweet rivers of grease. Lastly a large skin of ale, the very kind that lay cooling in the depths of Hammerstone, was placed alongside the food. Sir Howard smiled and began to eat. As he sated his hunger he told Robert the state of things. The smell of the chicken, still warm from the spit, awakened in Robert such feelings of hunger that he likened it to being stabbed in the stomach. For a while he tried to listen to what de Montfort was saying but his poor enfeebled brain would only acknowledge the scent of warm food. Sir Howard enjoyed the agony in Robert's eyes and he ended his sport by feeding his leftovers to a hound that had wandered in.

Sir Howard sat for a while, long enough to let the odors of the meal dissipate and when he felt that Robert could think straight again, he spoke.

"I would have thought you might have been curious to know what became of your little red-haired wife and that lovely castle of yours. I was wrong I see." De Montfort left and his man followed him out.

#69

No one came back for two days and Robert's stomach knotted from the savage hunger Sir Howard had awakened. Robert paced as much as his chain would allow and rubbed his belly but nothing helped. On the third day in the morning when the frost still had a hold on everything, Robert's jailer returned with a bowl of porridge and a pail of water. He set the bowl and pail just barely within Robert's reach, a spot he could determine from the flattened arc that marked the extent of Robert's chains.

Robert jumped for the food and snapped to a stop at the end of his chain. He fell and without rising he clawed the bowl to his lap and like a dog protecting a bone, wrapped his filthy arm around it and shoveled the pasty oats into his mouth.

The jailer stood watching Robert eat and said, "Eat slow least ye get the heaves." Having given his medical advice, the jailer left. Robert stopped his gorging and stared at the doorway. He took a handful of water and drank. He sat and waited for his stomach to settle. He ate sparingly of the rest and made it last the day. That night it rained and laying in the dampness Robert wished he had remembered what de Montfort had said about Maken.

The next day the jailer came and gave Robert his meal. This time Robert stared intently at the soldier, for the first time paying attention to his surroundings.

The following day the sun shone down through a hole in the roof and lit up the ancient stone barn. Below the gaping wound in the roof the rain had kicked up the sand on the floor so that it looked for all the world like a crater moonscape. Robert doubted that anyone else hereabouts would see the resemblance and the thought made him melancholy. For the first time in a long time, he missed the old life, he missed noisy streets and missed his family. Then he thought of Maken and wept guilt-laden tears. He had reflected on the foolishness of his conduct these last few months, the chances he took, and the chances he made Maken take with him. It would be a great miracle if she had ever made it back to the castle alive. And what about the baby? He might have been a father had fate been kinder and he less foolish.

But in his misery he remembered the old saying, "Your most important move is your next one." And this he knew was true. He resolved to try to escape to make amends to everyone that he had failed and to regain what he had lost.

De Montfort returned a few days later. He was defying Sir Simon by keeping the Earl of Malton alive but it was so sweet a vengeance to see the young de Courtelaine chained and miserable that he just couldn't resist prolonging the proceedings.

"Good morning, my young lord," Sir Howard said, smiling at the lump shivering under a sheepskin. He motioned for his servant to make more light and as they lit several lamps de Montfort settled in a stool brought along for his comfort.

"Are ye still uncaring for the fate of your Saxon bride? Are ye that uncaring, my young friend?"

Robert uncovered his head and stared at his tormentor.

"Ah, awake after all."

"What of my wife, de Montfort?"

"My! My! He speaks! Wonderful!"

"My wife!"

"Tut, tut, my friend, we have time for her later but first I think it best if we just start from the beginning, about the time you abandoned your wife to those invading soldiers. You know of course who led them? Your father's old steward, Giles. It's a faithless breed ye have raised up north is it not?"

Robert willed himself to remain calm.

"About your wife."

Robert's hands trembled and he clamped them together below the sheepskin.

"She lives. Somehow she found her way home. Hard to believe, is it not? At any rate she did indeed return and just in time to see Hammerstone attacked and a bloody attack it was. Many died on both sides before the invaders were repelled. They claim the outer walls ran red with blood and the burial mound was even bigger than the first.

Robert's mind reeled. Maken alive — the castle attacked — many dead. He should have been there. And missing all of it was a bitter pill to swallow. His face had paled a chalky white and Sir Howard de Montfort smiled, "It is good the castle did not fail, eh?"

"Yes it is good," answered Robert slowly, not sure why de Montfort would be glad Hammerstone was untaken.

"Yes, the widow de Courtelaine shall make a far better bargain for some lucky man if she has something more to offer than her body."

"What?"

"Oh, dids't I not tell thee? The King, being hard pressed for money, has seen fit to sell thy widow's hand to the highest bidder." Sir Howard got to his feet and dusted off his garment. "Even as we speak the King considers who should marry Maken de Courtelaine. He has pronounced you dead." At the door de Montfort turned back and said, "Foolish of me is it not, to be here talking with a dead man when the crown has young widows for sale?"

Robert did not hear any more. He sat stunned. De Montfort's words hit him like a hammer, pounded the air out of his lungs. Robert did not hear de Montfort leave nor did he see the sunset. For a time he could only breathe and that alone taxed his mind to its full capacity.

#70

It was many days before Sir Howard de Montfort returned and in those days between his visits, Robert died a thousand times, drowned by his own guilt. If he had some reason to go travelling unprotected, if he was forced to ride into danger, then he could have the comfort of knowing none of this was his fault. But it was his fault. Barclay has warned him again and again not to travel without guards. And Robert, in his naive vanity, would not listen.

Now someone else would sit in his hall, rule his castle, sleep with his wife, raise his child, do all the things he should be doing. His despair deepened.

Sir Howard, when he finally returned, noticed at once that his news had had an effect on his prisoner. He was glad. De Montfort walked around the building looking about the walls and noticing that gaping hole in the thatched roof. "Lucky for you the hole is not over your chain, eh?" He sniffed the air. "Still, it would be a good thing if you were washed down, your sty is filthy and I can scarce stand the stench of you."

De Monfort walked to the doorway and called to his servant. "Jorge, set not my table. I fear the prisoner is too foul for me to sup near."

"If I am foul smelling it is because you have made me so!" said Robert out of the darkness.

"Quite right, my young guest, I have, haven't I? And it is a sweet notion, that I have laid ye as low as you ever did me."

"Why don't you just kill me?"

"Kill you? Now what fun would there be in that? Doesn't sound very knightly to me, to just give up like this. I am ashamed for you, an Earl and Sir Reginald de Courtelaine's son, just giving up. Do you not wish to know who has won the bidding war for your young widow? Who shall share her bed?"

Robert's eyes flickered but he did not answer. De Montfort walked to the door, "Oh well, if ye do not care..."

"Tell me" Robert could not help himself. He had to know.

De Montfort smiled. This was his moment and, standing tall and free in the sweet sunlight, he could not help but laugh in pure delight. He let back his head and roared in glee. He peered into the gloom at those two unhappy eyes and he laughed all the more. "It is a small world isn't it?" he said. And after he had left, his laughter seemed to hang in the still air, mocking Robert's misery.

For a time Robert doubted de Montfort's words. The King was not a cruel man and the de Courtelaines had always been loyal. And even if the King wished Maken to remarry could she not refuse and join the church? He knew of others that had done that very thing. Why even queens had taken the vows just to be rid of unwanted suitors. Surely Maken could take the same road. She could run. Fontennell would help her, and her father, and Garfield too. She would have all the aid she needed. Robert suddenly had another notion. Maken could bribe the King, the Earldom was rich enough - or it was at least when he had left it. He tried not to think about it but in his mind's eye he could only see Maken and de Montfort in the huge bed in the solar at Hammerstone. It was a hateful, raging, jealous picture that refused to fade. That night he awoke from a nightmare and in it Maken was with a strange man, and the man was having her, not by force or fear, but with her happy and eager. Robert awoke with the horrible vision of Maken sitting up in their huge bed, naked and hot, smiling down at her new husband.

Robert lay in his own filth, too miserable to sleep. The rain came again and he watched the raindrops build their new moonscape under the open hole in the roof.

#71

Sir Howard de Montfort let his words fester with his prisoner for a fortnight before he again appeared. This time he was in even better spirits than his last visit. Robert had not seen anyone for three days and he was weak with relief to see de Montfort's servant enter the hut. As always the man waited for Robert to toss his feed bowl out toward the doorway. After the servant poured the food into the bowl came the tricky part. Obviously he couldn't just toss the bowl back, he would have to place it near enough that Robert could reach it but not so near that Robert could reach him. For the first few weeks he used a broken spear shaft to slide the food bowl into Robert's dank corner but as time went on and he judged Robert to be too weak to be a threat, he tossed aside the broken spear and simply placed the bowl at the end of Robert's chain.

Today Sir Howard followed the guard in. He liked to watch the once mighty Earl reduced to shovelling porridge into his filthy mouth like a common street beggar. Robert knew de Montfort was enjoying his debasement. Robert hated him for it and hated himself worse for not being able to control his terrible hunger. He knew a better man would ignore the food until his tormentors left. A better man would show no weakness. He would be strong. Robert tried, but the hunger - the mind consuming pain of near starvation - had easily smashed his resolve. He quickly poured the porridge into his mouth and cleaned out the bowl with a finger, not stopping until the bowl was as clean as a friar's bald pate.

"I see that you haven't lost everything after all. Your castle, your wife and your freedom, yes, but by God you can still find an appetite!"

"Untie me and I will show you I still have the ability to kill you, you coward!"

"No, I think not, ye had your chance when I was hanging in your cage for all the world to see. No, you shall die here but not the way you would hope. When your time comes, you shall embrace death and be glad of it."

"Go to hell," said Robert.

De Montfort laughed. "Some day perhaps, but not for a while. You should be congratulating me. My good brother, the Earl of Leicester, Sir Simon de Montfort, has just lately concluded a pact with His Majesty, a pact that unites the house of de Courtelaine with the greater house of de Montfort. I am to marry the widowed Earl's young bride, as you have already guessed."

Robert paled.

"Don't look so glum my young fool. So what if she is thirty years my younger and Saxon to boot. In my hands she will learn to be a quiet wife. And a welcoming one."

Robert lunged at the tall Norman only to be cruelly flung down as his chain snapped tight. "You piece of filth! Maken would never marry one such as you freely. If this travesty comes to pass it is only because it has been forced on her."

"Think what you will, but I know better. She could have taken up the vows and joined the Holy Sisters at St. Albans but what fun would that be. Giving up the ease of castle life and the joy of my bed? Not likely. She could have run, lived in the forest. After all, who would miss a Saxon wench enough to go find her? Isn't that where ye found her in the first place?"

De Montfort came nearer. "Face the truth, my young friend. Your wife loved your money far more than she ever loved you. Ye should have married a Norman. One of your own kind. What does a Saxon know of loyalty and obedience? Is it by luck that we rule these vermin so completely? No, it is because the Saxon is not capable of trust nor will they ever show a resolute front in the face of danger."

310

"You lie!" said Robert, his heart breaking despite his proud words.

De Montfort allowed himself to grow angry. "I've heard enough of that from you. Perhaps I shall bring you proof of what I say. I shall make a present of something besides your wife. Your armor, maybe, or Maken's hair. I'm sure you would recognize her red hair if I had her shaved bald?"

De Montfort began to collect his things, his sword and cloak and as he did, he said that this would be their last civil visit for when he returned he would begin the tortures that Robert so clearly deserved.

"I will be married by the time we meet again, de Courtelaine, and your widow will have already had the first of many, many beatings. I've no use for Saxon wenches, as you well know, and think of this also. They tell me the lady is at any time now ready to bring forth a child. Your child. Be assured he or she will share your fate. If the child lives, and that is uncertain, it will know the lash. Such is the fate of those who quarrel with a de Montfort!"

Sir Howard left and Robert was alone.

For a long time Robert knelt facing the door, not moving so much as a finger. Only his heart still worked of its own accord, or else he would have ceased to live at all, so numb had his mind gone.

A thought, or simple beam of reason, unwavering and persistent, shone into Robert's cloudy mind. And the thought was this: *If this was the end, why should he passively let it happen?* Better to go down fighting than to do as he had been doing for these last terrible months, waiting to die. Robert was ashamed when he thought about it. It was time to redeem himself.

He gave his chain a mighty pull and fell down. His hand hit something hard, buried in the dirt. He grabbed at the object and pulled it up into the light. It was the old discarded spear that his jailor had once fed him with. Surely this was a sign from God. Now to find a way to use it to his advantage.

311

Robert stared at the ground and pondered his situation. He watched as an army of black ants invaded and pillaged his supper bowl. Like tiny Visgoths sacking Rome, they marched across the brown floor dirt, each labouring under a morsel of booty. The long line of ants moved steadily away and into the cratered moonscape under the gaping hole in the roof. Robert looked up at the hole and back down to the floor. And he smiled. At long last, he felt his luck was changing.

The shaft of the spear he pushed against the roof above his head. It reached. Robert began poking holes into the straw thatching. It was old and ripped easily. In a short while he had opened a hole above his head.

Next he sharpened the end of the spear, honing it to a point on the rough stones in the wall above his chain anchor. When he was satisfied with the sharpening, Robert hid the spear down beside him. Ever so carefully, he slid his food bowl in closer to the wall. How he prayed for rain and waited. Nothing fell that night other than darkness and lying there in his sandy cell he could now enjoy the star filled heavens through the roof. High up, almost hidden behind the bare rafter, he saw the sailor's star, the constant northern, and the little dipper, pouring into her big brother, as she had through the ages.

To Robert they were things of great beauty, after the blackness of the thatch.

The next day neither his captors nor the hoped-for rain came and he spent the day praying for his freedom.

That night the stars were hidden in cloud and Robert was awakened by the kiss of raindrops on his face. 'Now,' prayed Robert, 'let de Montfort come forth once more before he goes to Hammerstone.'

#72

John Gaunt was a frustrated man. Twenty years he had been employed by the de Montfort's and he still was amazed at the differences between the Earl, Sir Simon and his younger brother, Sir Howard. Where Sir Simon was calculating and patient, Sir Howard was impulsive and reckless. Sir Simon was unwavering once he decided on a goal and bent his whole mind and body to reaching that goal. Sir Howard blew hot and cold, dancing from one whim to the next with little thought of tomorrow.

And today was no different. Sir Howard was due in York this very morning to meet his brother and the King. Finally, they were going to formally agree to the marriage of Sir Howard and the widowed wife of Sir Robert de Courtelaine. But Sir Howard had other plans. He was once again riding east, away from the great northern road that would take them to the gates of York.

John Gaunt knew where his master was heading, he was going to visit his prisoner, the very man whose wife he was about to marry. In his folly, Sir Howard had not done as his brother had ordered. He was to kill the Earl of Malton, bury the body and return to London town. But Sir Howard, not satisfied with taking de Courtelaine's wealth, castle, and wife, wished to toy with the unfortunate Earl, to make him suffer as he had suffered. Of course, he could not put de Courtelaine in a cage in his brother's courtyard. Sir Simon would not have allowed that chance, but Sir Howard would have his revenge and de Courtelaine would die a broken man.

He would die, but it was a risky way to kill and John Gaunt would rather see the deed over and done with.

Sir Howard reined up in the wet grass. Just ahead stood the round stone barn, a lonely reminder of the Scandinavian raiders that built her. Inside, chained to the wall was de Courtelaine.

"Go forth and feed thy charge!" commanded Sir Howard.

With a nod, John Gaunt rode up to the building and dismounted. He brought forth a pot of food from his saddle bags and entered into the gloomy cell. The guard paused at the doorway and let his eyes adjust to the gloom. It was a dangerous thing to walk into a darkened room without letting one's eyes adjust to the dark. Especially when that room was a jail cell holding a man famous for his martial prowess, and weakened or not, John Gaunt feared the man. Worse, Sir Howard feared de Courtelaine and left it to John to feed him.

Something was different. The roof had collapsed some more, in the latest storm. He could see the prisoner clearly for the first time; he was sitting against the stones, his skin soaked through the ragged remains of his clothes. The rain had obviously poured down on the earl, adding insult to injury. All around de Courtelaine were cratered puddles and in front of him his bowl overflowed with water, the worn ground that marked the earl's range of motion erased.

John stepped forward toward the bowl and somewhere in the back of his mind an alarm sounded. He slowed, but for so long had he done this distasteful task he did not stop. As he bent down to empty the bowl the alarm clarified. The bowl was farther from the door, the chain too short. Stones loosened from the wall. These things he noted, but too late. The Earl appeared suddenly above him, a stone in his hands and the stone came down, bringing darkness.

Robert grabbed his victim even as his back hit the floor. He dragged him in close to the wall, leaned across his stricken form and unsheathed his broadsword. Robert glanced at the doorway. Nothing. Good. He pulled his chain over the bloodied stone and

314

hammered at it with the broadsword, striking again and again until it broke and fell away. Robert stared at the scored stone. He was free!

It was the rain that saved him, that and the broken spear. Watching the ants had given Robert the idea of hiding the length of his chain by opening the roof and washing the floor markings away. The trick was to know how far back to place his dinner bowl. Too far back and de Montfort's man might notice something amiss. Not far enough back, and Robert would leave himself with too little room to jump the guard.

As it happened, he had worried for nothing, as de Montfort's man came into the hut with hardly a second glance and Robert made no mistake when he pounced.

Now he had not a moment to waste. He chanced a peek down the hill and sure enough Sir Howard de Montfort sat astride a fine Spanish mare down on the pathway. Robert eased his head back into the hut.

Thank goodness! De Montfort was alone. Robert pulled John Gaunt's tunic off his inert form and pulled it over his own head. He took a close look at his fallen guard. Damn! His hair was dark and cut in the Norman bowl, a style Robert could never bring himself to wear. Worse still, the Norman had no helm, nothing that might hide Robert's blonde locks grown long in his confinement. Nor his beard, matted and sparse, hanging down like drool.

Robert thought for a moment, grabbed his own dinner bowl and walked out into the sunshine. He held the bowl up, so it hid his face and pretended to clean it out. He slipped back into the dark hut. From the dirt, John Gaunt moaned. Robert pulled off the tunic and tried to make the fallen guard sit up, but it was no use, the man was still unconscious, despite his moaning. Robert pulled him up into a sitting position and braced him with his knee. Robert pushed the tunic back over Gaunt's head and shoulders, grabbed the broken spear and used it to brace Gaunt into a kneeling position, the butt end pressing against his chest and the sharpened end Robert wedged into the base of the wall. He stepped back into the shadows to the side of the doorway. From there it looked like John Gaunt was bent over, possibly to talk to the prisoner.

Sir Howard de Montfort looked up the hill. He was impatient. Waiting for Gaunt to signal all clear always tried his temper and today Gaunt was taking his time feeding the Earl. Sir Howard used to go right in while de Courtelaine ate, but he found the Earl paid him little mind with food in front of him, so now de Montfort waited. He liked to play to an attentive audience. Earlier on he enjoyed withholding meals from the Earl and then he would eat something in front of him. The Earl, he was sure, came within a hair of begging for food, more than once. But they were past simple torments now. Sir Howard spurred his mare up to the entrance of the hut. He would give John Gaunt a piece of his mind, wasting valuable time cleaning the Earl's bowl on today of all days. Today, when they had to be north to York and then on to Hammerstone Castle. Back to the stone fortress that once made a mockery of him, a de Montfort. He would not have stopped by at all, but he could not resist watching de Courtelaine's face as he told the Earl that today was the day he took everything that once was his, his castle, his horses, his gold and his woman. Sir Howard laughed and drew his sword. At the doorway he saw that his servant was bent down, talking with the prisoner. Sir Howard roared at John Gaunt for he had strictly forbidden anyone from speaking with the Earl. He charged through the doorway and dropped his sword. He bent to pick it up and screamed. His hand was still tightly gripping the sword handle but it was no longer attached to his arm. Robert, standing in the shadows, had timed his stroke perfectly as Sir Howard slipped by him.

Robert kicked de Montfort hard in the ribs and the tall Norman rolled into a ball beside his servant. De Montfort screamed in agony as his spurting stump was driven into the ground. Robert plucked the severed hand from the sword hilt and tossed the bleeding mess to de Montfort, "Pull yourself together," he said, and walked into the sunshine.

Moaning, Sir Howard staggered into the light, leaned against the doorframe and tried to stop the bleeding.

"Where are your men? A coward like you never travels with just one guard." Robert asked as he scanned the surrounding countryside.

"In the village," said de Montfort, now on his knees in the grass, the pain growing with every gush of blood.

"Which village?"

De Montfort nodded vaguely toward the northern road. "Briarsby," he said through clenched teeth. He watched Robert walk away holding both his sword and his servant John's sword. He waved them about, checking them for heft and balance. He eyed the edges of the blades and the condition of the grips.

At last Robert turned back toward the wounded Norman, "I say, de Montfort, your servant there has a better blade than you. How odd."

De Montfort, in agony, screamed at Robert, "Look what ye have done! How shall I live with just one hand?"

"You won't," said Robert.

Despite the pain, Sir Howard held his hand tightly against the stump of his severed arm, trying to stem the flow of blood that was now gathered in the grass between his knees.

He was not having much success and in a dazzling moment of clarity, Sir Howard de Montfort understood his situation. After twenty odd years of warfare, night-raids, over hard endless miles, eleven pitched battles and scars too numerous to count, he had suffered his last wound. As the red pool below him grew and blackened, Sir Howard de Montfort realized that his day of reckoning had come.

"Kill me," he said.

"I think I already have," said Robert still examining the two swords in his hands. He held them up into the sunlight. "Yes there's no doubt, de Montfort, your servant's blade is by far the better balanced."

Robert tossed Sir Howard his own sword. De Montfort picked it up. He held his bloody stump up and behind, taking the fighting stance. He swayed a little, but wavered not. A true Norman. Robert bowed, acknowledging his bravery. They came together and sword met sword. But not for long. De Montfort had lost too much blood, along with his sword hand, for the outcome to ever be in doubt. Robert, weakened and stiff from his wounds and confinement, nevertheless found flesh with every thrust. A hard slash to the elbow and de Montfort dropped his sword. "Kill me!" he pleaded.

"I will, de Montfort, and quickly too, but first tell me of your brother's agreement with the King concerning my wife. Speak or I will carry you into yonder forest and the wild boars can have live flesh for supper. Tell me what I wish to know and you die a quick and honourable death. That is my offer.

De Montfort talked.

#73

It was early afternoon and Robert sat beside a tumbling brook of sweet water. After he had fulfilled his bargain with Sir Howard de Montfort, Robert had gathered up the armour and weaponry. He took the dead knight's horse and rode until he had found this lovely brook. He bathed for the first time in months, trimmed away the worst of his beard and braided his long hair. He stood on the mossy bank, exulted in his freedom, glorified in a clean body. He had sorted through de Montfort's possessions and from these dressed himself in armour. A leather pouch enriched him by twenty pounds. Having left everything else in a pile beside his old rags, Robert mounted up and rode north.

He swung west of York, used the lesser paths to find the Ouse River and at last found himself on a bluff overlooking the river and the ancient road he had ridden so many times. Robert paused here in his journey and let his emotions run their course. So many dangers weathered, so many precious days lost forever. He had been foolish and reckless with his own safety, with Maken's safety, but now he was granted another chance. He had walked through the valley of death and returned in one piece. This, Robert knew, was no less than divine intervention. God himself had chosen to let him live. He vowed to make the most of this heavenly gift.

He fought down his giddiness as a great warm wave of relief washed over him. The dangers of the open road were behind him and Maken was alive and well and waiting within the safe walls of Hammerstone Castle. It never occurred to him that even if Maken had ridden to safety on the day they parted, the King would quickly marry her off to the highest bidder. And would she refuse? Would she give up the rich life of the castle for the sake of a dead love? And what of his child? Was the baby born yet? And with this last thought Robert felt a new and deeper need to be home. He rode off the bluff's grassy edge and trotted onto the road. He looked down and his stomach rolled. A jagged stab of fear shook him. The roadway had been pounded with the hammering of hundreds of hooves. A large force of mounted riders had ridden toward Hammerstone and not so long ago. Visions of his castle in flames, Maken being taken and his people slaughtered flashed through his mind. He spurred the big mare and hurried west. Robert held his horse to a gallop and not long after, perhaps a mile later, overtook a team of oxen pulling a blacksmith's wagon. He pulled his visor down and rode up beside the plodding beasts. Sitting, unperturbed in the crude wooden seat, was Bart, the giant blacksmith, Robert's personal ironmaster.

"What news, blacksmith?" Robert called out.

The giant Saxon regarded his accoster with a slow look. Finally he said, "There is much news. Too much almost for one man to tell."

"I wish to know of these things. Namely, what do ye know of the horsemen that made these tracks, the whereabouts of the King, and lastly, what can you tell me of the Lady of Hammerstone, Maken de Courtelaine."

"All of your queries are but eggs from the same nest, Sir Knight. These tracks are indeed those of the King and his retinue. Many notable lords ride with him to witness the joining of the houses of de Montfort and de Courtelaine. Sir Simon de Montfort, the Bishop of Winchester, the Bishop of Hereford, and of course, the King's heir, Eustace.

"So they are all at Hammerstone Castle awaiting the arrival of Sir Howard de Montfort, the intended groom of the widowed de Courtelaine?"

"Nay, Sir Knight, thou art truly behind the times. The wedding is done and Sir Simon de Montfort's son has married the widow in the uncle's place."

Robert was staggered and he had to put both hands to the pommel lest he fall.

"When did this happen?"

"Only last night after curfew."

"'Tis only a rumor perhaps?" asked Robert hopefully.

"Nay, Sir Knight, no less than four riders have come out of Hammerstone on errands and each man stopped and told me the same tale. At any rate the banquet was shortened with news that a Scottish column was within miles of York, heading south to join with the Prince of Anjou. The King and all with him left at first light this morning. Only a handful of soldiers, mainly Sir Simon's by the sounds of it, are left to maintain the walls of Hammerstone."

"And you, blacksmith? You follow the King's troops and make a trade repairing their weaponry?"

"Aye, or at least I did.

"So ye wish to serve de Montfort?"

Bart looked at the stranger and picked up the reins, "I've spoken too freely as it is, Sir Knight. I know not to what end ye ask these things of me, so I best say no more."

"Thou has spoken wisely but fear me not for I am like coins in a Bishop's purse with the words I hear. The coins go in easily but never come out."

Having the stranger speak so boldly at the expense of a Bishop made Bart feel at ease and he asked to see the stranger's face, but the Knight refused, citing a vow to not reveal his face until he had fulfilled a task unnamed.

Bart held up his hand apologetically. "I did not know, Sir Knight. Forgive me."

"No harm done blacksmith," said Robert, his voice muffled under his helm. Fear me not for I have no friends among the de Montforts. I care not for their kind."

"Nor do I, Sir Knight!" said Bart, "'Tis why I return to Hammerstone. The Lady Maken will need all the friends she can find now that she has her son to guard."

"A ..ss.. son, you say," Robert stammered, his voice tight.

"Aye, Sir Knight, why else would she willingly remarry? To protect the boy's birthright. Her true love was Sir Robert de Courtelaine and now all she has of him is the child. And she must forfeit what little remains of her own happiness to guarantee the son's."

"How old is the boy?"

"Only a few days, the marriage could not even be consummated."

Robert's head swam. Tears ran under his visor. He fought to hold them back.

"This de Courtelaine sounds like a rash young fool to me!" said Robert

"Aye, Sir Knight, he might have been that, but we of Hammerstone loved him well. He was bold of deed and true of heart."

Robert would hear no more and bidding the blacksmith farewell, he galloped west toward Hammerstone. Under a bright May sun, Robert sweated in the heavy armour, but he paid little mind. He glanced over the river and spied splashes of bright colours that waved through the trees. He reined back hard and as the big mare slammed to a stop, her big haunches quivered with exertion. Robert paused only for a moment and then rode to the river. With little regard for the current or depth of the water, he crossed the Ouse. The horse nearly floundered at midstream, but Robert would have none of it and with a series of hard spurs the horse and rider were across.

#74

Straight toward the King's retinue he rode and before the outriders and guards could check his progress, Robert was in the centre of the horsemen, beside the King and now past His Majesty, stopping at last before the de Montforts.

Sir Simon surveyed his wayward brother with ill-concealed disdain. The wet horse, the filthy clothes, bloodied no less. It was obvious that once again Sir Howard had not only disregarded Sir Simon's carefully laid plans, he had also managed to get himself into a quarrel. Well this time he would regret his foolish ways! He waited for the inevitable excuses but Sir Howard said nothing, did nothing, just sat there in arrogant silence, his visor still down as if he planned to do battle.

King Stephen walked over, curious to see what the Earl of Leicester would do with his errant brother. The assembled men took their lead from their King and gathered around like the crowd at a mid-summer fair.

Sir Simon's face reddened. As much as he relished the chance to vent his anger at his brother, he preferred to settle family quarrels behind closed doors. He did not mind having an audience to hear him give someone a dressing down but this one promised to be a little messier than that.

The crowd drew in closer and even the good Bishop of Winchester showed an interest. Still the visitor said not a word. The men of Hammerstone kept themselves apart from the others and took their rest on the grassy banks of the river. Many of them had seen the rider from afar but felt no need to share news of his coming. Now they remained apart and talked amongst themselves, waxing their bow strings and counting gray-goose shafts. Only Fontennell seemed to have taken any notice in the lone rider. He had watched this knight approach with ever increasing interest and when the rider stopped in front of de Montfort instead of the King the archer had gathered up all his gear and went straight to the centre of the gathering crowd.

Sir Simon de Montfort could hold back no longer. "What means this?" he demanded, "Coming now so late in your time? Were thou lost?"

Lionel de Montfort piped up, "'Tis obvious Father that Uncle has heard my happy news." The younger de Montfort ignored his father's icy stare and prattled on, "I really must thank you, Uncle, for the fine castle ye have given me with your tardiness. And a sweeter wench one could be hard pressed to find, I can tell thee. And eager, Uncle. Thou has't truly missed thy mark this time!"

Addressing the younger de Montfort, the rider said, "So it's done then, you've married her?" The rider addressed the younger de Montfort.

"Yes uncle, I fear you are too late."

"Have you consummated the vows?"

"My, but aren't we nosy!"

"Just tell me."

"No, I've not had the pleasure, but that will come." Lionel de Montfort smiled because he could well imagine how angry his uncle would be to lose such a young sweet prize.

Sir Simon de Montfort, Earl of Leicester, rose up in a lordly fury, "'Tis well ye have finally returned. I have much I wish to say to you."

The stranger undid his headgear and pulled it off. Two hundred eyes watched as a strong chin, covered in a short blond stubble showed, and then the straight nose and green eyes of Sir Robert de Courtelaine came into view. Like a dark specter coming back from the dead, like an avenging ghost, the rider was not Sir Howard de Montfort, but Sir Robert de Courtelaine, the long-lost lord of Hammerstone.

King Stephen in a great voice yelled, "'Tis the dead de Courtelaine!"

Lionel de Montfort shrank behind his father. Sir Simon stood thunderstruck, speechless and staring.

Cam Fontennell had already seized the Earl's mail coat and helm from de Montfort's page and with a simple "M'lord." presented Robert with his old armour.

The archers heard the King's cry and as one they ran to their lost master. They pushed the King's and Sir Simon's men out of the way in their eager joy. Robert leaned out and gave the men his hand. First to the left, then to the right, ending with he and Cam Fontennell shaking hands. He dismounted and Fontennell dressed him in his own armour. De Montfort's things, he began tossing aside.

"Where is my brother?" asked Sir Simon, as he gestured to his servant to retrieve his brother's possessions. Robert flung Howard's helmet at Sir Simon's feet. "If you want to speak with your brother, you will find him in hell, where I sent him!"

"You jest."

"Do you think he gave this armour of his own free will?" answered Robert.

He held his hand up and called for the archers to collect themselves and make ready to return to Hammerstone Castle. This was met with universal approval among his men. To the King, the wondrous re-appearance of the lost Earl was both a tale worthy of a song and an unfortunate hindrance. The warrior in Stephen glowed in the return of a brave man while the part that was the head of state lamented the loss of the archers.

"Your Highness," said Robert bowing low. "Please excuse my unfortunate state, one which I know is hardly fit for your Royal presence. I must beg your Highness's indulgence for I only now escaped from a harsh imprisonment." Robert backed away and remounted. He left the King without another word, surrounded by his archers and his castle guards. Cleeves, too relieved to speak, just followed along.

Lionel de Montfort, come out of his shocked surprise and turned to his father, "Shall we just let him leave? What of your brother? What of my castle?"

He went over to the Bishop of Winchester who was quietly watching Robert slowly disappear around the long bend in the river.

"Your Worship! M'Lord! We are married, are we not? You were there. Is a Bishop's bond not good?" This last question came out in a whine. The Earl of Leichester winced. Now was the time for silence, for thinking and carefully planning the next move. The Bishop of Winchester looked at the younger de Montfort. "Go to your father. De Courtelaine is in a foul mood and thou knows he has a blood-filled past." He smiled as he spoke and to soften his hard words, he said, "I shall go also to Hammerstone and see that your interests are not washed away when de Courtelaine confronts the young Bishop of Hereford."

The Bishop brushed aside the thanks of the now brideless groom and called for his servant to mount up.

King Stephen called Sir Walter Black aside and said under his breath, "Go ye also and make it known to de Courtelaine that anything we have done, we have done in the best interests of his young son, and the welfare of his earldom."

The King then called to his brother, the Bishop of Winchester, "Good brother. I shall send forth my own trusted servant, Sir Walter Black, as a surety of your safety in these northern wilds."

"Very kind of you indeed, Your Majesty," answered the Bishop with a smile for he was suddenly in a fine mood. The thought of watching that young fool Foloit wilt before the fury of de Courtelaine amused him greatly. Unravelling the legal status of the twice wedded woman would try the wisdom of Solomon. And what of any monies the de Montforts may have removed from the counting room of Hammerstone Castle? The good Bishop laughed and spurred his mare onward, sending gray dust high into the noon-time sky.

The King, to save face, had sent Sir Walter Black to deal with the Earl of Malton. He did not need to show any signs of stress with the Prince of Anjou somewhere between him and Londontown and many peers of the realm waiting for one side or the other to crack.

Now the King would have to show de Courtelaine every consideration lest his fellow barons take offence to one of their own being used unfairly by the crown. And make no mistake, Sir Robert was by no means helpless. His fearsome reputation on the field of battle, his great wealth, the obvious loyalty of his men and the mighty walls and well stocked cellars of Hammerstone Castle made the name de Courtelaine one to be reckoned with. There was always the danger, too, of de Courtelaine going over to Prince Henry. The King looked back toward the river. Now he wished he had gone himself or sent Eustace along with the trusty Sir Walter Black. Eustace was wise beyond his years and young enough that perhaps he might have struck up a friendship with de Courtelaine.

The King sighed and told his son to follow Sir Robert also. The Prince of Anjou was north of Londontown and York still a hard day's ride away. He called for his charger and mounted up. He never returned to Hammerstone again.

#75

If Cam Fontennell shared in the joy of seeing his master safely returned he never showed it. He perceived that Robert was in a dark mood and he hushed the happy men with a stern look. They marched upriver in silence, in a pack behind Robert's horse, military correctness tossed aside, as the archers strained to get a good look at the haggard face of Robert.

The road back was smooth and the castle's turrets were barely a mile distant. They had not gone far when Robert ordered Cam to maintain the men in an easy walk. He himself could not wait another moment, not even for his loyal archers to protect his back. Lionel de Montfort's mocking words, even though they were meant for Sir Howard de Montfort, burned a raw wound in Robert's mind. In vain he tried to dismiss the image of his Maken waiting happily for another, but he could not. Under his lash, his horse thundered around the last bend in the river and finally the great gray walls were before him. And more. The new village stood proudly in its brick cocoon. He pulled up and stared. He had forgotten his plans to wall in the village and now here it was.

Robert pulled his basque down; he did not yet wish to reveal himself. He rode into the castle. Men appeared at their posts and a squire came running. Robert did not recognize the youth. Obviously he was de Montfort's servant. Cam Fontennell's little brother was not present.

She was in the green dress. The one that had won the hall over and so entranced Robert.

"Welcome Sir Lionel." And she smiled.

Fulke appeared at her side and when her words met with no reply the Belgian offered her his huge arm to lean on.

She said, "Thou hast returned early m'lord."

Robert removed his helm. "Actually, I fear I've come too late."

Maken fainted.

The Hammerstone Series

Hammerstone 1147 A.D. - The Birthright
Hammerstone 1148 A.D. - To Have and to Hold
Hammerstone 1149 A.D. - Til Death Us Do Part
Hammerstone 1150 A.D. - Kings, Vows & Deceptions
(and in the works ....   Hammerstone – The Earl's Curse

I wish to thank my readers. Your feedback and support is greatly appreciated.

You can contact me directly by (new) email:
hammerstone.bobolink@gmail.com

I welcome your emails and answer each one personally.

Mark Anthony Parks

Printed in the United States
By Bookmasters